NO MARRIAGE IN HEAVEN

By Grace Nies Fletcher

IN MY FATHER'S HOUSE
PREACHER'S KIDS
NO MARRIAGE IN HEAVEN

NO MARRIAGE
IN HEAVEN

BY

GRACE NIES FLETCHER

1960

E. P. DUTTON & CO., INC.

NEW YORK

Library of Congress Catalog Card No.: 60-5992

TO

ADDIE AND HAROLD SEAVEY

KEEPERS OF THE LIGHT

FOR A QUARTER-CENTURY

To the Reader:

Anyone who has known and loved Maine or Boston will recognize the background of this story immediately. But the characters are sheer fiction, bits and pieces of people I have known, molded into forms of my own. Marcy and David never lived in the basement apartment on Mount Vernon Street, Beacon Hill, nor Serena and Rye in Gull Rock Lighthouse on the Kennebec River. But I have visited happily both places and hope I shall be invited again. This is a personal invitation to you to journey along with me to these beloved scenes and lonely people who were groping for a hand to hold onto in the dark, even as you and I.

GRACE NIES FLETCHER

Sudbury, Massachusetts

NO MARRIAGE IN HEAVEN

Chapter One

MARCY stood in front of the big mahogany-framed mirror on her dressing table, but the slender bride in her white satin gown, looking back with wide, dream-shadowed eyes, seemed to have nothing to do with her. Even her own familiar bedroom seemed unreal, the virginal white-painted bed with its crisp organdy valance, the frilled curtains at the windows looking out on the wide vine-shadowed veranda, and the blue-and-white matting on the floor, cool for the blazing Texas heat even now that it was September. She smiled, and light flowed over her face. Ever since she had awakened this morning, and had read David's letter, Marcy had been walking in a great lambent wheel of happiness that whirled faster and faster, shutting out everything outside. People spoke to her and she answered, but the words came from away off, the fine print at the bottom of the page that no one read; the only reality was this luminous cloud through which a great bell clamored . . . Or was it her heart thudding out the beloved name? . . . David . . . David.

"Marcy Minton, this hem's still crooked as a worm!" Momi wailed, sitting back on her heels to stare at the satin folds swirling about her daughter's slender ankles. Momi was as soft, as roundly comfortable as the red wool pincushion pinned to her ample bosom, but the wedding dress would never be finished to her satisfaction because in her heart she didn't want it to be. Momi sniffed, "I never thought I'd be prettyin' up my first-born to be marrying a dam' Yankee preacher!" There were real tears in Momi's eyes, blue as Marcy's own, yet tiny lines fretted the corners of her lids.

"But you *like* David! He can't help it if he was born in Boston!"

"That's just it. I wish I *could* hate him. It'd be easier."

Momi wiped her eyes with her scented white linen handkerchief whose sharp scent of verbena would always be protecting
arms about her whether Marcy wanted them or not. Momi
wailed: "Do you realize, Marcy, that Boston's almost two
thousand miles from here? You might as well be in your
grave for all I'll see of you! If you'd married Sam, now, he'd
have built you a house up on the Heights; I could see you
every day. Oh, Baby, are you *sure?*"

"Do we have to go all over that again?" Marcy murmured
wearily.

"Well, I reckon, after spoiling you for nineteen years, we
can't expect you to consider us!" Indignation dried Momi's
tears as she bent again resignedly to the hem of the white
satin gown.

Was she really spoiled? Would David think so? *Fair as the
moon, clear as the sun . . . terrible as an army with banners
. . .* Marcy drew a deep, ecstatic breath, remembering David's
letter this morning on her breakfast tray; sometimes the in-
tensity with which David loved her was almost frightening.
Was she truly beautiful? Marcy glanced anxiously in her mirror where her soft dark curls made a cap for her proud head;
her heart-shaped face was pale with the heat and excitement,
but her white neck and shoulders were gracefully erect under
the real-lace bertha of her dress. "All de Mintons mighty
stiff-necked," Aunt Riah used to grumble when her foster
child wouldn't do what she wanted. Family did mean something. Marcy turned her head slightly to admire Grandma
Minton's pearl earrings (small but real), approved her satin
waist so slender David's hands could meet around it, fingertip
to fingertip—David's strong hands with the little golden hairs
on their backs. . . . Color blazed in her cheeks. *Set me as a
seal upon thine heart . . . for love is strong as death. . . .*

David's envelope, thick, cream-colored, with her name on
it in his distinguished black scrawl, had been on her breakfast
tray this morning when Aunt Riah had brought it in so that

her "bride-baby" could rest in bed on her "Big Day." As Marcy ripped open the seal, her hands had trembled with eagerness:

"Good morning, my darling, on our wedding day! I have no words big enough to tell you how much I love you. But a king-poet said it for me centuries ago: 'Who is she that looketh forth as the morning, fair as the moon, clear as the sun . . . terrible as an army with banners? . . .

"'Set me as a seal upon thine heart . . . for love is strong as death; jealousy is cruel as the grave. . . . Many waters cannot quench love.'

"I am yours always.

"DAVID"

The lush, spicy-smelling words were, of course, from the Song of Solomon; but who but David would make them into a wedding bouquet? It was like his giving her the small gold cross, set with tiny pearls, to wear around her neck instead of an engagement ring. Marcy's hand stole up toward the fine golden chain hidden under the lace of her bertha, then dropped, for there was no use making Momi vocal again. What if all the other Minton brides had all worn engagement rings? But David's poet-king had been right about jealousy being cruel as the grave. Sam had been making a nuisance of himself all week; if he made a fuss at the wedding in that hush when the minister asked if anyone had just cause why she and David should not be married, what would she do? Marcy's hand jerked so suddenly that Momi scolded, "Just stand still a few more minutes, Sugar; I'm almost through."

Maybe Sam had a right to be jealous, Marcy admitted to herself, though she had never promised to marry him, not in so many words. But they had known each other all their lives, nearly, ever since that morning at the crick, when she'd known from the look in Sam's eyes that she was already a woman.

That summer at Paw's sheep ranch on the rolling prairies

beyond Fort Worth had been sheer magic. Marcy had been twelve and Li'l Emily, nine. Paw and Momi had slept in one tent and the sisters in another, all meeting outdoors for breakfast under the big cottonwood trees, getting so starving hungry they could hardly wait for the cornpone to brown in Aunt Riah's big black frying pan. The pan had been so big and heavy, Aunt Riah'd once killed a rattler with it just before it hit out at Li'l Emily's bare leg; but Emily had neither moved nor cried out, and when she saw the snake was dead, she'd laughed. Aunt Riah'd muttered, scandalized and shaken, "That chile ain't got no more nerves 'n a rattler her own se'f; what she wants, she'll git."

Hauling drinking water from the crick while the water was still cold enough to fill the canvas water bags that hung dripping all day from the cottonwood tree had been Marcy's job that summer. Early mornings she would tumble off her cot, fumble sleepily for her riding habit hung on a nail on the tent post, stumble, yawning, outdoors where her pony was already saddled, rarin' to go. With the bags hung over the saddle horn, her pony knew as well as she did where they were headed, was crazy-mad for water in this thirsty land.

"Bueñas dias, Señorita," Manuel had beamed. Paw wouldn't let Marcy ride alone for fear her pony'd stumble into a prairie-dog hole; besides, the filled water bags were heavy. She'd stretched like a sleepy kitten, had agreed, "Yes, it's going to be a pretty day, Manny."

She remembered dreamily even now how the friendly saddle had creaked under her light weight, how the mist had risen, light and fantastic ahead of her. It had been like riding into a fairy tale, more beloved because it was familiar. She watched the streak of light running along the horizon flush to pink, red. Many-colored banners, yellow, violet, rose, were flung across the sky, till the whole heavens were ablaze. For an instant, as the sun rose over the horizon, the prairie, mile on regal mile, was turned to cloth of gold. "Round as Cinderella's pumpkin." Marcy blinked at the orange sun, already hot. "I wonder . . . will my Prince be waiting for me, just over that next rise? Hey, whoa, you!" As her pony, scenting water, had started off at a dead run, she sawed frantically at the reins, but she had barely time to tumble out of the saddle before the water-crazed animal began to roll over and over in the cool crick.

"City slicker, hunh?" A tall gangling boy grinned as Marcy emerged on the bank, dripping and furious, her skirt clinging to her slender legs, her thin gingham blouse plastered to her body.

Marcy gasped angrily, "I . . . I was just thinking!"

The boy on the bank had red hair that blazed above his thin freckled face which flushed for no reason at all as he looked at her. "Howdy." He kicked at the ground with his scuffed high-heeled riding boot, asking: "You're Minton's gal, ain't you? I'm Sam Diffendorfer."

Young Sam from the Big D ranch! Marcy nodded, impressed, for he was a sort of prince at that, with his paw owning all those longhorns. But cattlemen had no use for sheep ranchers. Yet young Sam was staring at her as if some of the sunrise gold had caught in her curly brown hair; and suddenly she'd known that she was a woman, almost. "I got a teepee set up, below the bend of the crick," Sam told her, low so that Manuel, filling the water bags, couldn't hear. "You reckon you could sneak off, come swimmin'?"

"I reckon," she'd agreed.

Paw'd have skun her alive if he'd known how often Marcy had slipped off that summer to play Indian with Sam, who was thirteen, a year older than she was. He'd called her his squaw, "Big Mouth," and she, furious, had pulled his red hair till the tears came, knowing he wouldn't dare hit back at a girl. That fall when they both went back to town to school, she'd seen Sam often, and when he went away to college he'd invited her down for the fraternity dances, even if she was still only in high school. They'd taken for granted that they belonged together like bread and butter. If Sam hadn't rushed off so fast to the war in the spring of 1917, without even waiting to graduate from college, she might have married him. And then the same war that had taken Sam away from Marcy had brought her David.

Marcy put her hand up to feel that the little golden chain about her neck was safe under her dress. Momi snapped: "Why don't you pull it out where people can see it? Know he's given you something, anyway!" David had had the cross outlined with pearls set in one side; while on the other was engraved *October 18, 1917*. As if she could ever forget the date when she had met David! He was as different from Sam as moonlight was from high noon. She'd always known exactly what Sam was going to do or say. With him there was no mystery, no "army with banners." The scream of tortured car brakes came in through the open bedroom window, startling Marcy back to reality.

"My good land, who's that?" Momi worried, her mouth full of pins. "Who's coming here in such a tearing hurry?"

Marcy stiffened, listening. Did the brakes belong to the big red Mercedes Sam's father had given him as a coming-home present from France or to David's decrepit Model T, roaring in from Camp Bowie? No, David had already sold his car to a sergeant out at camp; but perhaps he'd borrowed it to run into town. . . . Momi rushed out into the back hall, called down the back stairs to the kitchen where Li'l Emily was superintending the excited servants getting ready for the wedding reception this afternoon. "Li'l Emily, honey? Don't let anyone come up here, you hear?"

"But I *want* to see David!" Marcy flared.

"See the bride in her wedding dress before the ceremony?"

Momi gasped, horrified. "Bad luck'd perch on your doorstep like a big black crow. . . . Why, Li'l Emily, what's wrong?"

"N-nothing, Momi." But Li'l Emily had run up the back stairs so fast, she was breathing hard. She hesitated there in the bedroom doorway, a thin tense, dark-haired girl in a red gingham dress; her black eyes meeting Marcy's blue ones in the mirror, the very immobility of her face warned that something was terribly wrong but that Momi mustn't know. Li'l Emily was still as plain as when she'd been a baby, with her pointed chin, her straight brown hair pulled back behind her ears, her skinny expressive hands, but she was a lot smarter than you were, Marcy knew. What could possibly be the matter?

Fortunately, just then the front doorbell jangled loudly and voices gushed up from the front hall. Li'l Emily said with relief: "It's Sally Lou and Molly with the wedding veil. I've been keeping the neighbors out of Marcy's hair all morning, but you'll have to handle bridesmaids, Momi."

It worked. "I'd better go down," Momi worried, hurrying for the front stairs. "I do hope Sally Lou could fix that lace so it doesn't show. Your Grandmother Minton wore it and then I did. . . ."

The instant her voice died away down the stairs, Li'l Emily gasped: "Marcy, Sam's down in the kitchen! He's at least two sheets to the wind and rarin' to see you. I told him he couldn't, you were trying on your wedding dress, but I can't hold him any longer. He said, 'They ain't gonna be any wedding! Not to that dam' Yankee psalm-slinger!' " Li'l Emily shivered. When Sam reverted to slang, kicked off his college like too tight shoes, it meant he'd gone back to his reckless childhood on the range. "Oh, Marcy, I'm scart he'll do something crazy!"

Marcy's eyes widened anxiously. "He's got his nerve, coming here this way!"

"You can't hardly blame him!" Surprisingly, Li'l Emily flared up in his defense. "He's loved you for donkey's years, and you've led him on, plenty. Till David came." Li'l Emily was twisting the belt of her red gingham dress in thin brown fingers, and there were actually tears in her black eyes as she spat out the words, "David was singing duets with you on the front veranda while Sam was fighting rats in the trenches in France!"

Why, Marcy realized, too surprised to be angry, Li'l Emily loves Sam! She's only sixteen but she isn't a child any more. Marcy made up her mind quickly. "Send Sam up here to me. I can manage him."

"In your bedroom?" Li'l Emily gasped, looking wildly around the high-ceiled room with its white-painted bed.

"Of course not, silly. Out on the veranda." Her voice died away in panic, for booted footsteps were already pounding up the back stairs. Marcy's satin skirts whispered anxiously across the floor as she ran out onto the wide vine-shaded veranda that kept the sun from the back bedrooms, and Li'l Emily flattened herself against the corridor wall, her eyes as big as black buckets, as Sam rushed by her.

His big bulk filled the veranda doorway, his red hair and blue eyes blazing at Marcy standing there, her wedding dress swirling about her frightened satin slippers.

"You're lookin' mighty pretty, Big Mouth," Sam drawled. "But you better git shed of that fancy rig. Our train leaves in half an hour." *Our train.* Marcy's eyes widened as he swayed slightly, drew two long tickets out of his pocket, waved them at her like flags. "Cost me a pretty penny. Uncle Sam paid my way to Europe, before. I drew out all I had in Paw's bank. You reckon three thousand'll git us to Paris, France?"

She forced her stiff lips into a smile to show this was all a joke. "Don't be foolish, Sam. I'm not going anywhere with you!"

"Oh, yes, you are, Big Mouth. You can't sweet-talk me out of this one." Was he aiming to kidnap her? Sam, the way he was now, was perfectly capable of it. When one great freckled hand grasped her arm so hard it hurt, Marcy knew better than to pull back; instead, she raised her great long-lashed violet eyes steadily to his, fought his hot blue gaze.

"Let go my arm, please, Sam!" She held her breath, let it out as, slowly, reluctantly, his hand fell away, and her dark lashes dropped, a delicate, triumphant fan against her white cheek.

Sam groaned, "You really aim to walk out on me, Big Mouth?"

"I'm sorry, Sam. I truly am."

"Sorry!" Sam snarled. "Marryin' a snifflin' parson when you know perfectly well that we—"

"Quit that! He isn't a snifflin' . . ." Oh, dear, you'd never get rid of Sam that way, quarreling. You'd simply have to make him understand how it was, that you had no choice. Marcy tried. "You and I, Sam . . . we were just boy and girl playing at being in love, like we played Indian. It was part of our growing up."

"So what's wrong with that?"

How could you make him see that your love for David was different? The very stuff of which life is made? The sun, the earth, and the stars? If Sam didn't know this sort of loving already, there were no words big enough to tell him.

"I have a right to be happy!" she flared. "David and I . . . Oh, you wouldn't understand!"

"Wouldn't I?" Couldn't she get it through her thick lovely little head that he felt the same way about her? Sweat broke out on Sam's forehead, as he retorted: "You think so now. But you like new things, then git tired of 'em." He knew her so well; but he didn't know David. "What you gonna do then? Pick up your doll rags 'n' come home?" When she didn't speak, he rushed on. "There's another thing: a preacher ain't got no home, not even a hole of his own, big as a prairie dog has! Most Methodist ministers move every three years. That ain't no way to live."

She jerked her hand away from his, proudly, "David will take care of me!"

"But who'll take care of *him*? Aunt Riah's done everything but breathe for you sense you were born. You ain't never even boiled an egg. Why, when we went campin', upriver"— his blue eyes crinkled into sudden laughter in spite of himself —"you couldn't even burn bacon good."

Marcy drew a deep breath of relief; now that Sam had begun to joke, he was licked even if he didn't know it yet. He begged: "Paw'll stake us. The beef market's strong. I'll take you any place in the world you want to go. There's a little park in Paris I want to show you, with a merry-go-round and kids singin'. . . ."

"I'm not for sale, thank you, Sam Diffendorfer!"

"I wouldn't give a bent nickel for you!" Sam yelled. "I'm just purely offerin' to marry you!" Molly and Sally Lou were right downstairs. If they heard him yelling, it'd be all over Fort Worth before the wedding, Marcy knew, desperately. "Stop it, Sam!" But his lips silenced hers so hard she could barely breathe.

"You want to ruin her?" Li'l Emily was pounding on Sam's arm with clenched small brown fists. She warned frantically: "Sam, listen! Momi and the bridesmaids are coming up the front stairs! You got to get out of here, quick! Hear?"

What Li'l Emily said was true; the twittering feminine voices were coming nearer by the second. Sam let Marcy go so abruptly she staggered. "If you ever need me, Big Mouth," Sam uttered thickly, "it ain't but two days and three nights to Boston." He tossed the long tickets, fluttering onto the floor, but Li'l Emily snatched them up, thrust them into the front of her red gingham dress. The clatter of his big boots was so loud going down the back stairs, how could the rest help hearing? The two sisters stared anxiously at each other, but the excited babble of voices did not falter as the bridesmaids came on down the corridor.

"I declare, you look sweet enough to eat, in yo' weddin' dress, Sugar!" Sally Lou cried from the bedroom doorway. Her sharp little beak of a nose pointed at the angry stain of red in Marcy's cheeks, the loosened curl fallen down on her sweat-damp forehead. Sally Lou was blond and thin; Molly beside her was plump and rosy, a sparrow and a robin, chittering. Molly's bird-bright eyes swept beyond Marcy to the veranda, but there was nothing there but hot sunlight patterned on the veranda floor.

Momi shrieked: "Marcy Minton, you've crushed your wedding dress! After all my hard work. . . . Aunt Riah! *Aunt Riah!*"

The roar of the engine of Sam's was like a shout of pain, Marcy thought dizzily, as the big red Mercedes tore out of the back yard. You were safe; he was gone; poor Sam. . . . But what else could you have done, loving David so badly it hurt?

"Marcy," Li'l Emily said too loudly, "look how nice Sally Lou's fixed your veil! Why don't you try it on?"

Sally Lou, diverted, announced proudly that she'd mended every little ole bit of that lace her own self, as Marcy sleep-walked toward her mirror, and let them drape the lace veil over her dark curls. If they didn't all go away, leave her alone, she'd scream. . . .

Aunt Riah, limping into the room, all two hundred pounds of her big, black, and comforting, threw Marcy a sharp glance, saw she was near to hysterics, took instant charge. "Chile, yo' plumb tuckered out." The old woman set down the silver tray she carried with a sandwich on it and a long frosted drink exuding delicious coolness; her white cap slipped sideways on her grizzled woolly head as she glared at the rest, her hands on her blue calico hips. "Miss Marcy ain't eat a flea's brekfus', so I brung her some lunch. I done set a table for you ladies down on the front veranda where hit's cool. Yas'm, Miss Susie," she promised Momi, "I'll press the dress tereckly. Hit ain't hurt none. Now git along outa here, y'all, whiles I puts my bride-baby to rest he'self."

They all went, laughing. So Aunt Riah knew about Sam; there wasn't much escaped her sharp eyes. Marcy gasped, her knees buckling so she had to grab for her dressing table, "Oh, Aunt Riah, I can't eat a thing!"

"Jest rest yo'se'f, honey."

Big loving hands pulled the heavy satin dress off, half-lifted Marcy onto the cool white organdy bedspread, tucked a pale-blue satin pillow under her whirling head. "Ain't nobuddy gwine pester my baby no mo'," Aunt Riah promised darkly, plunking her big bulk down into the protesting rush-bottomed rocker beside the bed. Just having her there, big, calm, a bulwark of love, was wonderful. She'd taken care of Marcy almost before she was born, because she'd been Momi's little maid since she was first married. "Aunt Riah's been with me since she was no bigger'n a pint of black coffee," Momi always said. The big woman urged Marcy, who was shivering in spite of the heat: "Go to sleep, heah? Need yo' rest fo' de Big Time this afternoon."

The Big Time that was her wedding to David. Her fingers pulled out the little gold cross, closed upon it, an anchor, holding her safe and firm. Marcy drew a deep relieved breath and closed her eyes obediently. Strange that it had been Momi herself who'd introduced David into the Minton household! She'd brought him back with her from Camp Bowie that bitter winter afternoon.

Camp Bowie, with its thousands of homesick boys from all over the nation, had been flung up so hastily outside Fort

Worth in the war emergency that at first there hadn't been enough of anything, not even of blankets to cover the hundreds who came down with the dreaded "flu," which developed too often into pneumonia. When the Texas northers had roared down upon the camp, the hospitable Fort Worth housewives had rushed out with all their spare quilts, but when they'd seen the rows of cots set up in the drafty corridors because there was no more room for them in the hospital wards, these horrified mothers had talked the harried camp commander into letting them take some of the sick boys back home with them, and send for the family doctor. It might not have been strictly military, but it had saved a lot of boys to die on the battlefield. Momi had brought home David, put him in the downstairs bedroom off the veranda to keep him away from the family, and had turned him over to Aunt Riah's care.

"He a mighty sick boy," Aunt Riah had worried, next morning, coming out to the kitchen with its great range, its shining copper pans where Marcy was sitting at the table, yawning, drinking a cup of black coffee after her late dance the night before. She'd sung with her ukulele at the Red Cross concert and afterward had almost danced her slippers through, since there weren't nearly enough girls to go round. Aunt Riah announced, filling her hot-water bottle: "But de Lord'll keer for his own. He got a golecross on de coat I hung up in de clo'se press."

"A *chaplain!*" Marcy was startled.

Aunt Riah asserted: "He be a mighty big, fine man when he git some meat on dem bones. Got gole hair stick to yo' finger when you bresh it." She chuckled, "Sho sign he good at lovin'."

"But he's a Yankee." Marcy yawned. "Momi said so." With the phone ringing for her all day and half the night so that Paw threatened to tear it out by the roots to get some sleep, why worry about a sick boy from Boston where they liked snow and codfish? As the busy days slid by, Marcy might have forgotten about the convalescent in the downstairs bedroom, except that Aunt Riah talked so much about him. "You're partial to him just because he's a preacher," Marcy had teased her.

"You stiff-necked 'n' jealous," Aunt Riah had declared. "I'll pray for you tonight at camp meetin'."

Paw and Momi would never have gone out to dinner that evening, left Marcy alone, if they'd known what was going to happen; not exactly alone, for Li'l Emily was upstairs in bed with a cold and a book, but Aunt Riah had gone for her happy hollering time to the camp-meeting tent on the edge of town. The light in the downstairs bedroom was out, so the Yankee was most likely asleep, Marcy figured, prowling around the living room, picking up a book, putting it down again. The quiet had made her restless, the way it does when moonlight lies thick as frosting on the magnolia leaves, so she took her ukulele out with her onto the front veranda, and sat down in the big swing. She strummed softly, humming the words,

" 'I dream of Jeanie with the light brown hair,
 Borne like a vapor on the summer air;
 I see her tripping where the bright streams play' "—

When a tenor voice joined hers, Marcy's startled hand twanged discordantly on the strings. How he could sing! A pure tone, natural as the mockingbird that shouted in the chinaberry tree in the front yard. When the song was finished, the Yankee, standing in the doorway to the veranda, had ventured: "You're Miss Marcy, aren't you? Lying there in bed, I couldn't help hearing you people talk, putting names to voices. I'm David Gallant, your grateful boarder. The doc says my germs are all gone. I hope you don't mind my coming out?"

"Oh, no. I mean, yes, of course, come out." The moonlight gleamed upon the cross on his uniform collar, the bars on his shoulders, as he crossed the veranda, and she added, "Captain." What a silly way to stammer, as if she'd never met a man before! "Won't you sit down?" There was no place to sit except the step or beside Marcy in the swing; she knew which a Texas boy would choose but not a Bostonian. . . .

As his shadowy figure settled gratefully down beside her, she could tell by his long legs how very tall he was.

Why should her blood race so at his nearness? Her heart pound so foolishly? Marcy was furious at herself for feeling such childish confusion before this stranger. And yet there was something about him, something hauntingly familiar, like a strain of music you can't quite remember. . . . "Gole hair," Aunt Riah'd warned, "stick to yo' finger. . . . Sho sign he good at lovin'."

"May I try your uke? I used to play in college."

When he reached for the instrument his fingers brushed hers, and fire leaped so frighteningly between them that Marcy jerked back her hand. This moonlight madness was incredible, but it was happening. Surely only a poet's Juliet blazed into love at first sight! It couldn't happen to her. "It's such . . . a . . . lovely night," Marcy managed haltingly, as in a dream. Or was it a nightmare, this wading through deep waters, finding it hard to breathe, struggling against this crazy shouting inside her, wishing he'd take her into his arms? Why did she feel as if some missing part of herself had just slid into place, making her whole? That she'd never be lonesome any more? This was ridiculous. Say something. "You feeling better, Mr.—Captain Gallant?"

She became conscious that his body so close to hers was trembling, too; she could feel his breath hot on her cheek, but she didn't dare turn her lips toward his. She hadn't yet even seen his face clearly but already she knew. . . . "Marcy Gallant," David murmured, his big hand covering her two small ones so hard it hurt, and the pain was joy. "It's a lovely name, a right name. Marcy Minton Gallant!"

Could he possibly mean—no, of course not. He was just sweet-talkin'. But did his breath catch in his throat too, did his whole body sing with your nearness? Marcy Gallant. How can a voice speak out of the darkness and you know at once that it speaks to you alone? That when he calls, you must always answer?

"We spoke our own private language before the beginning of time," David had told her later, gravely.

Was this true? Marcy wondered now as she lay there on her bed, clutching her tiny gold cross so hard the sharp edges creased her soft palm. Was there really only one man for one woman? As David was right for you? Was this yearning for David's lips, his strong arms, a thirst that would pass when quenched, as Momi had warned? Marcy wet her dry lips, remembering how she'd struggled to pretend that first evening, to hide how she felt, as a girl must, to keep from being hurt. She'd sung, she'd laughed, she'd chattered like crazy—until David's lips had silenced hers. The night had exploded into unbearable splendor, and the morning stars sang together. . . .

"This is a fine way for a preacher to act!" she'd managed to murmur against his mouth.

"A preacher is a man, too!" David had held her closer. "I'll court you later according to all the rules; but tonight let's just be honest. Do you believe in miracles? I do."

Loving as you and David did was a miracle that must go on and on to your children and your children's children—

Marcy Minton felt the tears prick under her closed eyelids as she lay there for the last time on her virginal white bed. Someday, if she was lucky, she'd hold in her arms a son with fine gold hair like David's. Yet she knew so little about babies. . . . What was that queer buzzing sound?

Aunt Riah looked so funny leaning back in her chair with her eyes shut, her mouth open, and her white cap to the side of her gray hair, that Marcy giggled, and Aunt Riah was awake instantly. She'd had twelve babies by assorted husbands, some not even husbands; and she wouldn't put her off like Momi when Marcy asked her questions. "You'll find out soon enough how selfish even the best of men are!" Momi had evaded, blushing. But Aunt Riah was honest as sunlight, and as natural.

"Aunt Riah, does it hurt bad to have a baby?" Marcy's violet eyes were enormous in the vine-shadowed room.

"Yas'm, it hurt. Nebber mind, honey. After de hurt, come de glory. Ain't nuthin' shine up yo' soul more'n lookin' down at a li'l cuddlin' baby got yo' man's eyes." The rush-bottomed chair protested wildly as Aunt Riah shifted her vast bulk, laid her warm loving black hand on Marcy's small white one and the two curled together, comfortingly. "Yo' raised on a ranch, chile. You know how come de li'l lambs, colts, all de li'l critturs?"

"But . . . but they're just *animals!*" Surely all this glory you and David felt wasn't just . . .

"Debble 'n' angel in ebery man." Aunt Riah chuckled richly, her bountiful breasts shaking. "Debble in you, too, honey, when de lightnin' strikes."

Devils and angels . . . Did Aunt Riah have to use double talk as Momi had? The old woman chuckled, "Yo' David think you de sugar in his coffee. You got nuthin' to worry about. But you brang dat fust baby right back home heah for yo' ole mammy to nuss, you hear?"

"But I can't, Aunt Riah!" Marcy swallowed the enormous lump in her throat, realizing for the first time that what Momi had warned was true; Boston really was two thousand miles away, a cold strange Yankee city where she'd know no one but David! Panic, homesickness poured over Marcy in a great frightening wave. Maybe she'd never see any of them again, not Momi nor Paw nor Li'l Emily nor Aunt Riah. She could be sick, hurt, and no one would know. She was, actually, marrying a stranger she'd known only a few months. "Davey, I'm not 'an army terrible with banners!' I'm afraid. . . ."

Chapter Two

THE wedding at St. Paul's that afternoon was elaborate, sumptuous, with a wedding party of six bridesmaids in yellow organdy and gay hats with no crown but a wide transparent brim, and a flower stuck over the right ear. Li'l Emily as maid of honor wore yards and yards of flowered yellow and white, from which froth her small determined dark face looked out as incongruous as a weed in a bed of chrysanthemums. The six white-clad ushers earned the gold tie clips David had given them, for the church, which seated four hundred, was full to the very last pew. Momi grumbled that if there was anyone Paw'd sold a life-insurance policy to he'd left out, she didn't know who it was; but with his being chairman of the Fort Worth board of education and of St. Paul's official board he couldn't afford to offend anyone. Momi had done her best to make the church look like the wedding picture she'd seen in one of the woman's magazines, with tall white candles tied to the end of each pew with a huge satin bow of ribbon, with masses of white flowers everywhere. The bishop was to marry Marcy and David, assisted by their own minister, but as she stood at the back of the church the altar was such a jungle of white flowers and candles that the gilt cross was almost hidden. Waves of heat, the scent of blossoms, the sudden stir of hundreds of eyes turned to look back at Marcy standing there, waiting interminably in her white gown, made her wonder, uneasily, where David was.

David had hated the idea of a big wedding; he'd wanted the two of them to be married quietly in the little chapel of St. Luke's in Boston, where he was to be the new assistant minister. He'd explained, rather shyly: "There's peace there, honey. Afternoons, when the sun shines through the rose window, there's a crown of red, yellow, and blue jeweled light

29

on the stone floor. Just you and me and Dr. Harrison, a couple of witnesses, and quiet words to remember. . . ." Momi had all but screamed at David: "You want her to sneak out of town? Ride three days on the train with you *without being married?* Of all the crazy notions . . ."

You'd think this was Momi's wedding, not hers. As she stood there, waiting nervously for the organ to trumpet as it had yesterday at rehearsal, Marcy's bouquet of white roses and stephanotis trembled in her white gloved hands. What had all these people to do with her and David? They were mostly Momi's and Paw's friends; some of them she hardly knew. She had to walk down that narrow strip of white the ushers were unrolling down the aisle; what if she stumbled?

"We're off, honey!" Paw, looking uncomfortable in his stiffly starched white suit with the high collar and tie, offered Marcy his arm, the organ pealed, and Marcy watched the bridesmaids start cautiously down the aisle, first on one foot and then the other. The little flower girl, Linnie, Cousin Hester's youngest, a small red-haired child in a yellow dress with a wreath of rosebuds on her head, tossed a handful of white rose petals onto the aisle, but when Marcy walked forward on Paw's arm, Linnie cried, "Oh, you're stepping on them!" and bent hastily to pick up the roses, then straightened as Paw shook his head.

A ripple of stifled laughter swept the wedding guests in the rear pews, but it broke the tension. Linnie was a darling.

Paw and Marcy followed her slowly, crushing rose petals step by endless step down the long aisle. Waves of heat, smiles at Linnie, murmurs of "Isn't she lovely?" swirled around Marcy's head under Grandma Minton's real lace cap and veil. She was dimly aware that the bishop and her own minister in their white surplices had moved in among the altar flowers.

At last she found David's tall broad back, white shoulders squared, bright soft hair, as he stood there beside his grooms-

man, Cousin Ben Hunter. *Davey, I'm here.* . . . As if he'd
heard her frantic, silent call to him, David turned, looked
back up the long white aisle, smiled at Marcy.

"*I have no words big enough to tell you how much I love
you.* . . ."

Suddenly, smiling at each other, she and David were alone,
making their private gift of themselves to each other. No one
else in the world mattered. The candlelight rimmed with glory
her lifted face, her floating veil, her slender white figure, as
she came to him, trusting, radiant, unearthly, a child of light.

The three nights and two days on the train from Fort
Worth to Boston that were to be their honeymoon passed all
too quickly. It was September, 1919; the war was over but the
"civilized" world was a volcano recently erupted, still ominous. The newspapers brought into their snug Pullman home
black, alarming headlines: Wilson demanding almost hysterically that the United States should join the League of
Nations; Senator Henry Cabot Lodge, against any entangle-
ment; while from the side lines Senator Beveridge shouted,
"Not only America first, but America only!" But while the
world seethed, Marcy and David went on living in an irides-
cent soap bubble of their own. Hand in hand, they wandered
into the diner when they were hungry, peered out dirty windows at passing scenery but saw only themselves, felt only the
nearness of each other.

Yet she had her moments of uncertainty. One morning
when he greeted her with, "Good morning, Mrs. Gallant!"
she burst out, "But, Davey, it isn't fair. I'm not *me* any more!
I'm not Marcy Minton, but you go right on being David
Gallant."

David faced her soberly, patiently, not as if she were a silly
child who didn't know her own mind as Momi and even Sam
often thought her. David said quietly, "When we have children, they will be part of us both."

She slid her hand into his, moved closer on the gritty red Pullman plush seat, murmuring dreamily, "Do you want a boy first or a girl, Davey?"

"Twin girls," David told her promptly. "Exactly like their mother."

"Boys. We'll call them Peter and Andrew."

"Maybe," David chuckled hopefully, "we could go right on through the twelve apostles?"

"*David Gallant!*"

It wasn't until the train was nearing Boston that David began to wonder uneasily if Marcy might possibly be disappointed in the apartment he'd picked out. He'd thought himself lucky to find a flat he could afford when he'd come on two months ago to meet Dr. James Harrison, to audition for the job of assistant pastor at St. Luke's Church; but now David suddenly wondered if he shouldn't have let Marcy see the apartment before he risked a down payment. He told her again, anxiously, that there were only two small rooms and a kind of kitchenette, but at least Mount Vernon Street was on the right side of Beacon Hill, the residential, not the cheap boardinghouse side. "It's a good address, darling, not a slum."

Marcy grinned delightedly. "I didn't know you were a snob, Davey! We got an awful lot of wedding presents. Momi'll never get them packed up to send to us. Good thing the apartment's furnished."

David explained: "The chief thing is, it's within walking distance of St. Luke's yet we don't have to pay all outdoors for rent. If we're going to live on an assistant minister's salary . . ."

"Of course we are," Marcy interrupted firmly. "If your mother could make out on a preacher's pay, I can." She slid her hand into his, for his mouth had tightened. Both his preacher-father and his mother had been drowned in a sailing accident in Maine, but this hadn't kept David from still loving the sea as much as Marcy did the Texas prairie. She asked gently, "What was your mother like, Davey?"

"Little and gay. She was a great help to my dad," David told her. How could you describe anyone when you'd looked at her only with the eyes of love? "'A minister's wife can make or break a man,' my dad used to say. 'If the parish like her, it's half the battle.' Mother sang soprano in the choir, ran a Sunday-school class, directed the Christmas pageant. . . ."

Marcy protested: "I expect to feed you, keep the house, of course, but . . . A banker's wife doesn't have to be assistant teller! Momi doesn't help Paw sell insurance; he'd hate her to. The church didn't hire *me!*"

"That's what you think." David grinned. "You'll learn, darling." How could Marcy possibly understand, without growing up in a parsonage as he had, how the preacher and his whole family were on duty twenty-four hours a day, seven days a week, if anyone was in trouble? Maybe it was asking too much of a girl only nineteen to take on a job that stretched one's patience until it broke or the preacher and his wife extended themselves to meet the unending pull of the parish need. Yet Marcy was more than a beautiful child; there was a strength in her, as there had been in her pioneer ancestors who'd traveled by Conestoga wagon from Ohio to Texas. Otherwise she wouldn't have defied her whole family to marry a penniless Yankee. David bent to kiss her, ignoring the fellow travelers beaming up and down the aisle. "No one could help loving my good wife!"

"I could teach horseback riding? Or tap dancing?"

David roared with relieved laughter. "The Sunday-school kids would love it, but I doubt if Soaks would consider that tap dancing came under the head of religious education."

"Soaks?" Marcy gasped.

"Miss Oaks, the deaconess at St. Luke's. The words sort of run together. She's been at the church a lot longer than Dr.

Harrison. I guess another reason the staff call her Soaks—behind her back, of course—is that she got the last two assistant ministers fired."

"Whatever for?"

David hesitated. Soaks had been in the one parish for twenty-five years, first as a girl just out of Deaconess Training School and then, as ministers came and went, she'd stayed on till she'd become almost as much of a fixture at St. Luke's as the high, carved mahogany pulpit. It was natural for her to feel she owned the church, not to mention the hired help. David confessed: "Dr. Harrison warned me when I first came on, 'She likes to be boss, David. If you can let her think she is and still do what you think best, you'll get along.'" David glanced down at Marcy uneasily. "It isn't very fair of me to be talking about her this way. After all, she's never done me any harm."

"She never will if I can help it!"

He smiled down at her indulgently but made no answer.

"We'll always tell each other *everything*?" she challenged.

"Of course," David agreed. He amended honestly, "Except something a parishioner tells me, in confidence."

"Oh," Marcy said, uncertainly. How could a minister's wife help him if he didn't tell her things? David was *hers*. Gently but firmly she'd make that clear from the very beginning, and, in the end, it would be better for everyone concerned.

It was raining when their train drew into the South Station at Boston. The station was gray, Marcy saw; the rain was gray and so were the people, faceless people slanting their black umbrellas against the driving icy wind while their cab splashed through the crowded wet streets up to Beacon Hill. "Reg'lar northeaster," the taxi driver said cheerfully as they turned up a steep narrow street between frowning brick or brownstone houses that seemed to Marcy to bend toward the cab, menacingly. So this was the Beacon Hill David had spoken of so proudly, Marcy thought breathlessly, this sunless alley, where people holed in like educated moles! As the cab turned into a wider street, the postage-stamp lawns were railed away by iron fences, carefully protected from dogs and Philistine viewers.

"Mount Vernon Street." David beamed. "Here we are, darling!"

The apartment house, red brick with a friendly white entrance and trimmings, was encouraging, but as Marcy, ducking her head against the rain, started for the front door, David grabbed up their bags, called urgently: "Come around back. We'll have to run for it."

Marcy followed him down the dripping brick alley too narrow to put up an umbrella, cringing as the torrents of rain ruined her new dove-gray hat, her high patent-leather heels catching in the uneven bricks as she tried to keep up with David's long legs. Empty garbage cans and a dirty wet mop stood by the back door as they dived into a dark corridor. Anyone'd think they were Jim Crow! Marcy looked, dismayed, down the long corridor where the dim electric light showed tall black letters on a door: SUPERINTENDENT. David, unlocking another brownish door, flung it wide. "Welcome home, Mrs. Gallant!"

Marcy stared about her, unable to speak as David switched on the unshaded electric-light bulb hanging from the ceiling, waited expectantly for her approval of the home he had provided. The bulb's white glare disclosed a large square room whose high walls, painted stone-colored gray, seemed to go up and up, airless and grim as a prison. The sparse furniture included a bare golden-oak center table upon which was a lamp whose transparent shade held unhappy butterflies imprisoned, one big chintz-covered armchair with the stuffing hanging down below the slipcover, four hard golden-oak chairs, and an iron bridge lamp with a soiled fluted paper shade; that was all, except for the green rug that covered the floor up to the brown linoleum at the edges. David beamed at the triple tier of white-painted hot-water pipes running around and round near the ceiling. "Never have to bang on the radiator for heat this winter!"

Did David really expect her to live here? There weren't even any windows, unless you counted those two narrow slits, high up, near the ceiling. . . . David went on dropping anxious words into her uneasy silence, "When we get our wedding presents, it'll look more homelike." He was like a little boy who'd brought his mother a slingshot for her birthday, but was afraid that, after all, she wouldn't like it. Darling Davey who loved her. She had to say something, quickly.

"Look at all those feet, Davey!" Marcy laughed hysterically, so that she might not burst into tears. "You can't see people in the windows, just disembodied feet!" How was she going to tell him, tactfully: *I love you very much but I can't possibly live here. It's a cellar. . . .*

"So you've come, have you?" a man's voice said behind them from the open doorway. "I didn't expect you till tomorrow. This your wife?"

"Yes. Brother Hicks is the superintendent, our good neighbor." David introduced the thin, slouchy man in dirty overalls to Marcy. Mr. Hicks needed a shave; the bows of his silver-rimmed glasses had been broken and were tied together with soiled string, and his sharp eyes peered admiringly at Marcy.

"Howdy, Mr. Hicks! What an enormous bed, David!" The brass bed with its pink-and-white crinkled bedspread all but filled the tiny bedroom, leaving only space for a chest of drawers, a curtained corner that must serve as closet. Was the low-slung bed really moving up and down in pink and white waves or was she still dizzy from the train? Marcy stared unbelieving as a big bulldog's ugly underslung jaw poked out from under the spread.

"Them dorgs!" Mr. Hicks grumbled as if he were as much surprised as Marcy. "Benjy, come right outa there! Abe! Jake! Git for home, you. My wife raises bulls," he explained, "but they won't bother you none if you keep your door shut."

He'd been using the empty warm apartment as a kennel! Marcy, furious, glared back at his shifty eyes behind their smeared glasses. Mr. Hicks blinked at her, predicting, "You won't stay here long, not a pretty little piece like you."

"I guess we will stay! I gave you ten dollars' deposit on our month's rent," David reminded him indignantly. "By the way, you didn't give me a receipt."

"Give it to you tomorrow," the janitor mumbled. He snapped his fingers at the dogs still milling about the corridor, "Come on, you!" He closed the door behind him, then opened it instantly to say: "If you folks do decide you don't like it, I kin rent this place in fifteen minutes flat. But you don't git your ten bucks back." The door banged shut finally.

"Cordial welcome." Marcy's voice wabbled in spite of all she could do. "What's behind that long curtain in the corner?" David pulled aside the limp brown curtain to display a windowless cubbyhole whose two wall shelves were piled high with battered pots and pans; a tin-covered table had a two-burner gas stove on top. The rusty iron sink had a rim of yellow scum near the edge. Remembering the huge, airy kitchen at home with its great fireplace full of leaping flames on a rainy day like this, firelight glinting upon row upon row of Aunt Riah's shining copper pans, Marcy simply couldn't stop the foolish trembling of her mouth. She quavered, "Aunt Riah couldn't even get a leg inside that. . . ."

David caught her up in his arms, sat down with her in the big chintz armchair, groaning: "I shouldn't have brought you here! Sam was right. He could have given you everything. Forgive me, beloved."

So Sam had talked mean to David, too! What right had he to criticize her very own husband? Marcy gathered David's

bright head in her two hands, drew his lips down to her own
soft, sweet-smelling ones. She murmured fiercely, "I have
everything. I have you."

It was after midnight when Marcy awoke in the big brass
bed beside the deeply sleeping David, decided she was thirsty,
tiptoed out toward the tiny kitchen for a drink. She snapped
on the light, then froze, horrified, for the carpet was no longer
green; it was a crawling silver flood, alive, moving, the dreadful waves rushing toward her petrified bare feet. She screamed,
"David, David!"

"They're bugs!" David was there in one leap, gathered her,
shaking and sobbing, up into his arms. "Millions of silverfish!"
He carried Marcy back to the comparative safety of their bed,
but neither of them dared sleep. They turned on the light,
watching fearfully lest the silverfish flow up the bed's legs onto
the pink-and-white spread. As she lay there, shuddering,
Marcy remembered what the miserable Hicks had said, "You
won't stay here long. . . ."

"He knew!" Marcy accused Mr. Hicks hysterically. "That
sneaky old janitor! That's why he wouldn't give you a receipt
for your ten dollars! He knew we couldn't stand these awful
bugs. . . ."

"Now, darling," David soothed, unwilling to believe the
worst about anyone. "Brother Hicks," Marcy knew, bleakly,
even if he wasn't a parishioner. "He may be all right," David
soothed reasonably, "but I agree we can't spend another night
like this. I'll look for another apartment as soon as I get
through with Dr. Harrison. I have an appointment with him
at nine tomorrow morning"—he glanced at his watch—"this
morning . . . but after that . . . You let me handle this, dear."

"Yes, David," Marcy agreed meekly, but inwardly she
warned the absent janitor: Don't think you're getting away
with this! You may hoodwink David, bless him, but not me."

She waited only until David had left for St. Luke's next

morning before she marched down the dim corridor, dressed
in a crisp blue gingham and with pink fire in her cheeks, and
banged on the superintendent's door. When the three bull-
dogs burst out, sniffing about her legs, they did not intimidate
her any more than Mr. Hicks. She demanded sweetly: "May I
use your phone? Ours is not connected yet." She walked without further invitation toward the black box upon the wall. "If
you'll just tell me the number of the owner of this apartment
house . . ."

"What you want to talk to Mr. Simpson for?" the janitor
demanded, worried.

Marcy's firm little chin came up. "You didn't give us a receipt for that ten dollars. You get the deposit, and then the
bugs come out and people move. Mr. Simpson might like to
know."

"Smart, ain't you?" The janitor should have blustered, but
instead his sharp little eyes were admiring. "Good cheap
places to live in this neighborhood are scarce. Seems like
you 'n' me ought to git along. If I call the exterminator, that
satisfy you?"

For a moment rabbity red-rimmed eyes stared into angry
violet ones. "If there's one bug left by tonight, I call Mr.
Simpson," Marcy issued her ultimatum finally. After all, they
couldn't afford to pay a month's rent on two Boston apart-
ments. "And you can keep your bulls out of our apartment,
hear? I like dogs, but not under the bed."

The exterminator came, saw, and conquered. That night
the floor no longer crawled. David, who had searched all day
with increasing panic for another vacant apartment he could
afford, pointed out happily: "You see, darling, it doesn't pay
to be hasty. The janitor meant well, but these old houses
spring surprises." Marcy opened her lips to tell him, then
closed them again. David might even consider it a matter of
principle to call Mr. Simpson, after all. She and David would

always tell each other everything, but it wouldn't hurt to wait until she could find a better, more suitable apartment. What was a wife for except to look after her husband?

"Dr. Harrison wants me to bring you over to see him when I go tomorrow," David told her. "You'd better drop by to meet Soaks, too. All right?"

"Of course." Marcy smiled at him through her long lashes. She was looking forward to meeting Soaks; there must be some way to make friends. She was only another woman, wasn't she?

Chapter Three

"DARLING, how about putting on a little speed?" David called to Marcy in the bedroom. Only one of them could dress in the small space available between the large bed and the dresser with its spotted mirror.

"I am hurrying!"

Marcy slid on the jacket of her dark-blue suit which looked less bridelike than her light gray, tipped the tricorn of the hat that made her eyes a darker blue but still had the gay little cockade of red on the side that matched her red handbag. "David, what's Dr. Harrison like, young or old?"

"Old. About forty-five, I think." David added proudly, "He's asked me to call him 'Jim.' He's tall, distinguished, with silver hair on his temples and a marvelous voice. The Sunday morning I was here, you could hear every syllable clear in the back of the gallery, even when he talked low, and that's something in a church big enough to seat twenty-five hundred. Marcy, it's three-fifteen and our appointment's for three-thirty!"

"I know. Just a second." Marcy rubbed a small piece of talcum-powdered chamois across her cheekbones, then scrubbed the powder off again with her handkerchief. She dropped a small ivory vanity case into her red handbag, and ran. David caught her hand, hurrying her along the sidewalk so fast her nose would get all shiny again.

"This is St. Luke's," David announced as proudly as if he himself were the architect.

"It's enormous! Almost a cathedral!" Marcy stared up at the great stone Gothic church, with its flying buttresses, its tall windows of richly colored glass, while at one end was the small chapel David had talked so much about, with its rose window jewel-bright in the sunlight. St. Luke's made you feel very small, almost lost. "A minister's wife can make or break a man—" Marcy paused on the top stone step to pull her vanity case out of her red bag, ran the puff hastily over her flushed face. David was laughing at her. "It's my slingshot," she grinned back, closing her red bag with a brave little click. "I'm Mrs. David, remember? Bring on your Soaks!"

"Miss Oaks to you," David warned uneasily, for he'd already learned that in this elfin mood Marcy was capable of almost any madness.

"You're ten minutes late," Soaks said reprovingly as David knocked at her already open office door, then introduced the uneasy Marcy. "Sit down on that straight chair, Mrs. Gallant."

David fled cravenly to his appointment with Jim Harrison, leaving Marcy, feeling like her first day at school, trying not to stare at Soaks' long head with the ridiculously small black cap tied on under her firm chin by two incongruously dainty white silk strings, at the black dress relieved only by tiny white collar and cuffs. Marcy had never seen a deaconess' uniform before. Soaks' stockings were black, too, as were her sensible oxfords which bulged for her bunions, and her middle-aged body was as uncompromisingly bulky as the heavy, scarred oak desk behind which she sat. Marcy, uncomfortable on the straight wooden chair, watched, fascinated, the mole with two hairs on Soaks' cheek go up and down, disconcertingly, when she talked. She had no eyelashes! That was why her eyes looked like two agate marbles.

"You're not twenty yet, I hear." Miss Oaks' gaze slid disapprovingly over the high red heels, the matching red leather bag, the gay cockade in Marcy's saucy hat. "I don't hold with ministers marrying young."

The red ran up Marcy's cheeks, but she kept her voice level. "Why especially ministers?"

"He should be thinking of his sermon, not of temporary things, of getting home to—er—you," Soaks told her bluntly.

"Temporary?" Marcy asked, bewildered. "I thought—"

" 'For in the resurrection they neither marry, nor are given in marriage, but are as the angels of God in heaven,' " Soaks quoted triumphantly. "Matthew 22:30."

You'd been married only four days, and already Soaks was getting you unmarried! The mole with two hairs quivered, and suddenly Marcy was sure how much Soaks had hated being an ugly little girl.

"I don't know exactly what angels do," Marcy admitted, "but flapping wings and twanging a harp all day would drive me loco. Besides, it wouldn't be heaven if I wasn't married to David."

"Young woman," Soaks gasped, "don't you believe in the Scriptures?"

"You make me think of Paw's story about the preacher he heard once at camp meeting," Marcy twinkled. "There wasn't enough cash in the collection plate to suit him, so the preacher told the ladies it was plumb wicked to spend cash money on the devil's fashionable hair-dos. 'Sisteren,' the preacher bellowed, pounding his pulpit, 'it says right here in the Holy Writ, "top-knot come down!" ' But when Paw looked up the verse later, it read, 'Let him which is on the house top not come down. . . .' "

Remembering Paw's shout of laughter at his own foolish joke made Marcy all at once homesick for that friendly sound. She could hardly believe it when Soaks gave a companionable little snort. Could she possibly be laughing, too? The two women were still beaming across the desk at each other when David brought Jim Harrison into Soaks' office to meet Marcy.

"This young lady knows her own mind anyway," Soaks told the men, chuckling.

"Delighted to meet you, Mrs. Gallant. Or may I call you 'Marcy'?" Jim Harrison was relieved to find the two were getting on so well.

"Of course." Marcy smiled up at the tall man with the heavy mass of dark hair frosted with silver gray at his temples. The deep lines beside Jim Harrison's mouth had been made by laughter as well as by discipline, and his wide, sensitive lips curved into kindness as if he knew pain but was not overwhelmed by it; Jim Harrison made you feel that you could tell him everything about yourself, good and bad, and that he might disapprove but also that he would understand. Perhaps his large tolerance was why he was so successful, had such a big parish as St. Luke's. As he released Marcy's hand, he urged: "Sara, my wife, wants you two for dinner tomorrow night. About six? We have to eat early, for I have a meeting afterward." He sighed, "As usual."

"We'd love to come," Marcy agreed, pleased. As Miss Oaks made a quick, impatient motion gathering up the papers on her desk, Jim Harrison added, "Why don't you come too, Emma?"

So her name was Emma. It fitted her, Marcy thought: austere but efficient. How could you tell what a baby was going to grow up to be, or did people grow to be like their names?

"I guess if I can go six months without eating at your table, I can wait a little longer," Soaks snapped. "Besides, I got calls to make."

"Perhaps I could make some of them for you?" David offered eagerly. "I'd like to get started. . . ."

"I have a cancer case—no nose—at the Home for Incurables. He won't see anyone but me," Soaks told him. "And Mrs. Ella Heinz has lost her first baby and she wants me to pack up the whole layette, give it away before she gets home from the hospital tomorrow. You wouldn't be any good."

David, flattened, let out his breath ruefully as Miss Oaks picked up her shabby black leather bag, her black cotton gloves with the neat darn in one thumb, and marched out of her office.

"Don't let her get under your skin, David," Jim Harrison advised, running his fingers through his thick grayed hair. "She's a good woman. She can even be gentle on occasion. Remember, her shut-ins are her family, Soaks' father, mother, her children she's never had. . . ."

"What she needs is a husband or a dog!" Marcy surprised herself by saying her thoughts aloud, and the two men shouted with laughter.

"She seems to have taken quite a notion to you, Marcy." Smiling back at him, Marcy knew a strange compulsion to win this man's considered good opinion. "We'll see you two tomorrow night."

Soaks was at the Harrisons' the next night for dinner, after all. Sara Harrison had seen to that in her quiet way. At first Marcy thought Sara the plainest woman she'd ever seen. She was slender, almost spare in her print dress that hung from her shoulders as limply as from a hanger, and her rimless glasses magnified her brown eyes so Marcy could not be sure what emotions they mirrored: but as the evening progressed, Marcy saw that the older woman's soft brown hair, drawn straight back to a knot at the back of her white neck, revealed the fine modeling of her head, her high, lovely forehead. The unobtrusive force of her personality crept up on you, Marcy thought, admiring the deftness with which Sara gathered up the reins of the conversation, guided it gently, never imperious but getting her own way because she expected to. "She comes from an old Louisburg Square family," David had explained. "But being wealthy and tops socially hasn't hurt her at all, because both are as natural to her as breathing." More important, Sara and Jim Harrison were still in love, Marcy knew, watching Sara's brown eyes seek Jim's waiting gray ones, down the length of the table, to talk to him without words.

The dinner was more formally served than at home in Fort Worth, but the damask tablecloth was no smoother than Momi's best ones, though the place setting the Irish maid in her black uniform was removing from in front of her was, Marcy suspected, a museum piece. Jim Harrison dealt with the thick steak oozing red richness upon a silver platter, gave the plates to the maid to pass instead of handing them around himself as Paw would have done, dear Paw urging in his loud, hospitable voice, "There's plenty more where this came from, folks!" The vegetables were also served from shining silver dishes, such as Aunt Riah had polished for the wedding. The mellow light from the dozen candles in two great silver candlesticks softened the faces around the table, sparkled upon the crystal bowl filled with blue and lavender asters. This was no austere parsonage but gentle, pleasured living. Why not? A minister was not a monk to embrace poverty as his bride. "Surely the lines have fallen unto me in pleasant places" was as true as John the Baptist eating his unappetizing locusts! Marcy caught back her wandering thoughts as Sara Harrison spoke.

"My dear, I hope you'll be very happy here." Her clipped New England voice belied the real warmth in her brown eyes. "I expect Boston's quite a change from a sheep ranch? In Texas?"

"Paw sold the ranch a year before the war, but he kicked himself all over the lot for doing it because, if he'd just held out, he could have made a fortune selling wool for uniforms," Marcy explained in one long breath, and then wished she hadn't. Would these Bostonians think it crude to talk about money? She rushed on, "Our house is in the city limits now, but when Momi was a little girl in Fort Worth the Chisholm Trail went right by our wire fence."

Would they even know what the Chisholm Trail was?

"That must have been something!" Jim Harrison exclaimed, eagerly. "Watching the thousands of longhorns go by on their way to Kansas! A great river of new wealth running north from the impoverished South!

Marcy rushed on eagerly, encouraged: "Momi says, when she and her sister were little, the cowboys used to lean over their fence, drop over the little calves too young to make the trek. Once they even gave her a day-old pony!" Marcy sighed. "I was born a generation too late for all the fun."

"I would have missed you fifty years ago," David objected, and everyone laughed. Bostonians might have a glazed, forbidding surface but underneath they were just folks. Marcy was proud of her Texas background but she wanted to be fair, too. She told Sara: "Your centerpiece is lovely. Momi can raise only little runts of asters in her garden for some reason. She'd give her eyeteeth for great gorgeous purple blossoms like that."

"You should take Marcy to see the fall display in the Public Gardens," Sara told David.

"I did, yesterday." David chuckled. "She didn't think much of them."

"That isn't fair, Davey! I thought the flowers were gorgeous." Now they'd all think her queer, not worshiping their sacred Gardens; but to anyone used to mile upon mile of rolling prairie to canter over, the Gardens, imprisoned in their high iron railings, were so shut in, so precisely neat. She tried desperately to explain: "I bet the gardeners measured from plant to plant with a ruler! All those cute little youngsters walking around the neat paths, and their nurses telling them, 'Don't touch, dear. Just look at the pretty flowers!'"

"But the children can ride in the Swan Boats!" Soaks protested.

"Sail around a puddle on a raft with a man on a bicycle, pretending he's a swan!" Marcy's hands in her lap, hidden by the tablecloth, were trembling as she tried to make them see as she did. "I wanted to yank up big handfuls of those lovely asters, throw them to the kids, and cry, 'Here!'"

"I see what you mean," Jim Harrison agreed, his face lighting up with a companionable grin that made him almost her own age. "How can these children help growing up into dull people if they never see beauty growing wild? Can't hold it in their hands?" Marcy beamed at him gratefully.

"We'll have coffee in the living room." Sara Harrison rose to lead the way into the long, luxurious living room overlooking the River. . . . The Charles didn't need a name to identify it to Bostonians, David explained, when Marcy went to slide her hand into his as they stood looking down at the hundreds of twinkling lights below. The river was beautiful, an inverted sky with man-made stars. And this was a lovely room, where your feet sank smoothly into the thick blue Chinese rug. The sofa was darker blue satin to blend with the rug, with several scarlet pillows for emphasis; the big coffee table had the patina which came only from generations of loving polishing; probably it was a Louisburg Square heirloom, as were the massive silver service, the delicate Limoges china at dinner. Marcy thought of their cellar apartment, their wobbly cardtable. She and David had a long way to go, but with both of them working together, sometime they would have a rich, beautiful home too. When David got to be a bishop, perhaps . . .

"Demitasse, isn't it, Emma? Black?" Sara asked, pouring coffee.

"Yes, thanks, Sara." Soaks accepted the cup David handed her, sitting stiffly erect without leaning against her chair back. Did she never let herself relax? Put on a bright becoming dress? A rich gray dress with those collar and cuffs would work wonders, round out her angles. Soaks had a high, fine forehead, straightforward eyes even if they did lack softening lashes. . . . You had to find out what made her tick, so she couldn't hurt David. Impulsively Marcy pulled a hassock to Soaks' feet, sat down, spreading her red wool skirts about her like a bright flower, and smiled up at the older woman.

"I don't know the first thing about being a preacher's wife, Miss Oaks," Marcy confessed. "I never knew before what a deaconess's job was. Did you get the baby things put away for that poor Ella—"

"Ella Heinz. I gave the clothes to another young mother in our parish who's expecting."

Marcy shivered. "I'd hate for my baby to wear another dead child's things! It would give me the creeps."

"You have to learn to be sensible when you're poor," Soaks told her briskly. "They were real pretty, and warm."

"I bet you know more about how the wheels go round than most ministers!"

Soaks admitted, well, she'd never preached a sermon, but she hoped if she did she'd have better terminal facilities than some preachers she'd heard. She'd known most of the young married people in the parish since they were born, when she'd written their names down on the cradle roll.

"Emma, could you go to the Christmas pageant committee meeting for me next Thursday, week?" Sara Harrison interrupted smoothly behind Marcy. "I'll be out of town." How long had she been standing there, listening? Marcy struggled up politely from her hassock as Sara, David, and Jim joined the group. "The meeting's at Serena Snow's," Sarah explained to the Gallants. "She's the student nurse from the Deaconess Hospital who has such a lovely soprano voice, better than any in the paid quartet, I think. She's to be Mary in the Christmas pageant that the students are putting on for the Sunday school."

"Snow?" David wrinkled his forehead. "I used to know a Serena Snow up in Maine when I was a kid, a funny little shrimp with red hair and freckles. Her father was keeper of the Gull Rock Light."

"She's got red hair all right, but she's no shrimp." Soaks' mouth had straightened into a thin line of disapproval. "She"

—Soaks searched for a word, found it—"she fairly *undles* down the aisle."

"Serena's singing the Offertory next Sunday morning, so you can meet her, David," Jim Harrison interposed deftly. "You're a member of that pageant commitee, too. You'd better go Thursday. Soaks will give you Serena's address: it's not far from your place. By the way, the church is having a telephone put in your apartment, so you'll be on tap." He held out his hand to Marcy. "I'm sorry I have to run, and I'm taking your husband with me; this official board meeting will be a good chance for him to get acquainted. Why don't you and Emma here stay around till we get back?" His eyes questioned his wife, and Sara smiled, nodded. "Do stay. We'll have more coffee and a chat."

Soaks said stiffly that she had work to do, and Marcy, terrified at the mere thought of hours alone with a strange Bostonian, pleaded that she wasn't quite settled in yet and that she'd better get on home to the apartment. To her relief, when the others left, Sara didn't urge Marcy, merely phoned down for the doorman to call a taxi, please. "There'll be at least five minutes' wait this busy time of night," Sara explained, so there was an awkward pause while Marcy stood there with her hat and coat on, wishing she could suggest waiting downstairs but not daring to.

"Marcy?" Sara Harrison laid an impulsive hand upon the younger woman's coat sleeve. "Do you mind if an old hand at this minister's-wife business—and it *is* a business—gives you a suggestion?"

Marcy looked up, startled, at the older woman. Had she done something wrong already, here tonight? "Of course not, Mrs. Harrison."

"You'd better say 'Sara,' since you call my husband 'Jim,' " dryly. "It's just what I wish some older preacher's wife had told me when I was your age," Sara went on slowly. "It would have saved me so much . . . heartache. I'm probably rushing in where I have no business to, but I do like you and your David so much. I want you both to stay, and Emma can be so—so prickly with young assistants. . . ."

When she hesitated, Marcy braced herself, urged bravely, "In Texas we say, 'Speak easy.'"

Sara flashed her an appreciative glance. "Very well. I should let David and Emma Oaks work out their own differences, if I were you. Be friends, if you like, but leave David out of it. He might resent your . . . helping . . . later on."

Did she mean you were a "managing wife"? Too ambitious for David? But Sara herself had made a lovely restful home for her husband! Fortunately the phone rang to announce the waiting taxi, and Sara Harrison held out her hand. "Do come again soon, Marcy. Drop in any time you want woman talk. Just come when you want to."

"It's been a lovely evening," Marcy managed. She fled toward the waiting elevator, her color high. To be criticized the very first evening by David's "boss's" wife! Just because you were trying to be polite to Soaks. How could you tell what to do? If you tried to help David, you were pushing yourself forward, and if you didn't make friends for him in the parish you'd hinder him too. If he made good here at St. Luke's, David could go anywhere, get a church of his own, maybe get to be district superintendent before too long. People *liked* David. . . . How could they help it? Paw said he "could preach the hinge off a church door," yet in other things David was childlike, too trusting. You'd been wise not to tell him about your victory over Mr. Hicks. You wouldn't tell him, either, what Sara Harrison had said about him and Soaks. Yet David was New England through and through, as Sara was, the same independent breed. Perhaps she did understand how his mind worked, better than you did. . . .

"This is the right number, Miss?" the taxi driver asked, turning his head to look back at her.

"Oh, yes! How much do I owe you?"

"Nothing, Miss. It'll be charged to the Harrisons; they pay by the month." He helped Marcy out the door, beamed approvingly, "Warm night for September."

"Yes. Good night." But as Marcy walked through the dark shadows to the back entrance, she shivered.

Chapter Four

MARCY sat in the next to the front pew with Sara Harrison next Sunday morning, looking up at David who was to read the scriptures and give the opening prayer. He looked almost swallowed up by the big red upholstered chair in which he sat; his dark-blue suit, newly pressed, fitted his broad shoulders, but his blond head did not lean back against the high chair back as Jim Harrison's did, his black impressive robe flowing about him, in a similarly red velvet chair on the far side of the platform; Jim could afford to be relaxed, his place here at St. Luke's was established. David's tenseness communicated itself to Marcy so that her gloved hand trembled slightly as she fumbled open her Order of Service, where the black type trumpeted proudly, *David Rand Gallant, Assistant Minister.* When he got up to pray, she lowered her head, reverently, hoping that Sara Harrison hadn't noticed how nervous she was. The offertory followed the prayer, and the black print read: "*Seek ye the Lord,*" *Serena Snow, soloist.*

"Shrimp with freckles!" Marcy thought, startled, looking up at the girl with the gorgeous red-gold hair, standing there quietly in her black gown, in the choir loft. Her skin was camellia white; her features were cut to classic perfection; and her glowing hair brushed the shoulders of her gown. She's the prettiest girl I ever saw, Marcy admitted uneasily to herself. Serena stood out from the rest of the vested choir like a cardinal bird in a flock of crows. Clasping her hands lightly before her, she began to sing with the natural sweetness of an unselfconscious child, yet her voice filled the great church easily. At the first notes, a candle seemed to have been lighted on the altar of her mind, for she glowed as she sang:

" 'Seek ye the Lord while He may be found;

53

Call ye upon Him while He is near. . . .
Let the wicked forsake his way and the unrighteous
Man his thought . . . and return unto the Lord. . . .' "

When the bright-haired singer finished, a muted sigh swept
over the congregation as if they had all held their breaths,
listening, but Marcy found to her surprise that she had been
twisting her handkerchief in her gloved hand into a little ball;
she dropped it hastily in her handbag. There were dangerous
depths in this girl, Marcy knew instinctively; somewhere,
sometime she must have suffered, to cry out so sincerely. But
perhaps—hopefully—this wasn't the little girl who had grown
up in David's beloved Bellport?

"Oh, yes, it was Rene all right," David assured Marcy that
noon at dinner. "I can't understand why she didn't stop by
the front door, where I was shaking hands, long enough to say
'Hello.' She must have got out of her choir robes, rushed off.
Maine people are so plagued shy. But I should have thought
she'd have grown out of it by this time. She certainly has
changed some from the skinny litle brat I used to go clamming
with at low tide! Wow!"

"Maybe she had a date," Marcy suggested, laughing. A girl
who looked like that would have plenty of men.

But David had already dismissed Serena as he demanded
anxiously, "How do you think I read the Scriptures this
morning?"

"Beautifully," she assured him. "I could hear every syllable." Then as he got up from the table and reached for his
hat, "Oh, Davey, you're not going out again this afternoon?"

"Just for a walk in the Gardens. To get my thoughts together," David told her. "I have to lead the young Adult Discussion Group at five-thirty this afternoon."

As he strode off, Marcy wished wistfully he'd asked her to
walk too; she wouldn't have said a word to disturb him.

Students, David had explained to her, were thick as raisins in the Boston pudding: students from colleges of art, business, drama, from universities, law and medical schools. One of David's chief jobs as Jim Harrison's assistant was to manage these young adolescents' activities, to see that their restlessness found focus, and certainly, not least important, that lonely Boy meet lonesome Girl.

"You can be a big help," he told Marcy, as they came into the big church parlor together later that afternoon. "Just circulate around, mix people up, will you? And see that the sandwiches and cocoa hold out."

Any girl born South of Mason and Dixon's line would find such a group easy to handle; in no time at all Marcy in her red wool dress, her curls and eyes dancing, had students three deep around her, laughing, teasing her about her thick Texas accent. One lanky Harvard law student demanded, What did she most miss here in the Land of the Cod, so far from home?

"White Southern fibs," she told him, smiling up at him through long, tantalizing lashes. "You Yankees think if you sweet-talk a girl, you've got to marry her! And you put your r's in all the wrong places. 'I'm at Havahd Lawr,' " she mimicked him gaily. "I'd give the whole herd of you for one Texas cowboy who'd tell me, pronto, 'Miss Marcy, you're the prettiest thing I ever did see!' He wouldn't mean it, of course."

"Sir, why don't you tell your wife pretty fibs?" the law student chuckled as David came up with a redheaded girl dressed in a green taffeta dress that whispered about her long legs.

David grinned down at his sparkling young wife. His smile said: "You're doing fine. I'm proud of you, darling!" Aloud, he introduced, "Marcy, this is Rene Snow, my old playmate." She was lovelier close to than from a distance. Her hair, which seemed at first bright copper, gleamed gold in the light as she moved her head to smile at Marcy. Soaks was right; Serena did "undle," moved so effortlessly she seemed to glide. Probably half the interns at the hospital were in love with her . . . you hoped. David, unaware of the currents flowing between the two girls, complained, "She hit me over the head once with a clam hoe because I told her her face was dirty."

"He hasn't changed a bit." Serena laughed. "Sorry I couldn't stop to say 'hello' this morning but I had a dinner engagement. Davo here always tells the truth, unflattering as it may be, doesn't he?" She explained to Marcy, "He was sixteen that last summer at Bellport, and I was twelve, when Davo taught me to swim. Only summer people are foolish enough to go into our icy water; most Maine people never try it." Her voice softened. "That was the year you sold the cottage, wasn't it, Davo?"

"I guess so, Rene."

Davo. Rene. Marcy was suddenly jealous of the years between these two she'd never known. Had Serena comforted young David that awful day when his preacher-father and his mother had sailed down the Kennebec to the sea, and had never come back to Bellport? Strange that David still thought Maine the closest place to heaven he knew! David shrugged his big shoulders as if to throw off a still almost unbearable memory, pulled out his dad's round gold watch and decided, "Time to begin." He raised his voice, "Find a chair, everyone!"

In the confusion of dragging the chairs into a big circle, Marcy found herself seated between Serena and the tall law student. How exciting David was, standing up there, drawing all eyes to him with his wide smile, with the "come-hither" look in his twinkling blue eyes, the upward tilt of his bright head! He mastered this big chattering crowd so easily, and he was her David.

"Our subject for discussion tonight is 'Are we victims of

inherited characteristics or free agents, able to work out our own salvation?' " David explained to the young lifted faces around him.

Marcy listened as the students ran over the universe with a fine-tooth comb, looking for the bugs left by their ancestors, delousing the centuries lightly, tracing the source of their own infection. She admired the deft way that David kept them all coming back to the essential question, led them toward what he himself believed so passionately.

"The yardstick of Jesus Christ can make us look mighty small," David said, "but it is also a challenge. Our genes may have determined what we are physically and mentally, but we can also be born again of the spirit. If we so choose, we can stretch to the divinity which belongs to us as sons of God. We may be limited in our capabilities, but He is not. I myself plus Jesus Christ equals infinity."

"But, David," the law student argued, "are Jesus' values so different from the Greeks'? From ours today? From, say, Freud's? Were they not all good psychologists? Take the case of the woman taken in adultery. The old Mosaic law was that she be stoned to death, but Jesus held back the mob by saying, with true Jewish shrewdness, 'Let him who is without sin among you cast the first stone.' How is this understanding of bodily weakness different from Freud's contention that man has many hungers that must be appeased? That appetite is neither right nor wrong, merely natural?"

Marcy felt Serena close beside her stiffen in her wooden chair as she waited for David's answer. Why, her hands in her lap were actually trembling!

"No similarity at all," David argued vigorously. "Jesus told the woman, 'Go and sin no more.' He admitted her sin, all their sins. But what a glorious relief it must have been for that terrified girl to look up into His pitying face!" David's own countenance glowed with reflected wonder. "We often forget that Jesus was a young man, too. He was tempted as we are, so He understood. The crying difference between us and Him was that He was always honest, with himself as well as others. It is not pleasant to see ourselves as we really are. What Jesus was saying tacitly was that *adultery of the spirit is even worse than that of the body.* . . ."

The rustle of green taffeta beside Marcy made her look up, startled, for Serena had jumped up from her chair, was almost running across the big room hurrying toward the vestry door, without explanation, or looking back. Was she ill? Should you go after her? But as Marcy hesitated, unwilling to interrupt the discussion further, the sound of the outer church door closing told her that Serena had fled out into the chill September night. She had even left her coat behind on her chair, Marcy discovered, too late. It was an expensive coat, of soft beige camel's hair.

"Queer, Serena's barging out that way while I was talking," David mused that night when he and Marcy were back in their tiny bedroom. "I gave her coat to the church janitor to lock up."

It hadn't occurred to him that he might have taken the coat himself to Serena, tomorrow. It was foolish envying her knowing David as a little boy. Marcy lay there in the light-blue flannel dressing gown on their big brass bed, admiring her husband's strong bare brown shoulders. Had swimming made them so strong?

Marcy asked, her tone carefully light: "Were you in love with Serena when you were sixteen? Don't laugh. I adored Sam when I was twelve. I was his squaw, Big Mouth."

"With Rene?" David chortled. "She smelled of fish most of the time. Move over. I'm bushed after all that talk." He grinned down at his small blue-flanneled wife whose eyes were at one moment so wise and the next as vulnerable as a small girl's. Nineteen was a lovely age. "You want to hear a nice white Southern lie? I'm in love with you! Only, I'll have to make sure those hungry students don't eat up the hostess!"

Marcy had little spare time to brood during those first weeks. Learning to cook a hamburger so that it didn't taste like burnt cardboard—David even made better coffee than she did—cleaning their apartment, so tiny that they lived in every inch of it every day, washing out clothes for the first time in her life, even if only blouses and underwear and socks in the inadequate basin in the bathroom with its loose plug that had to be fished out—such tasks occupied her mornings. And that awful phone . . . Jim Harrison or Soaks wanting to leave messages for David, parishioners excited over trivialities. Marcy wrote their numbers down on the little pad by the phone for David to call back. How could she possibly know what the hymns were for next Sunday night? Or how many certificates were needed for baptisms? When Marcy was anxiously baking her first batch of cookies for David's supper in the little tin oven on top of the gas burner, some strange woman called, went on and on about needing six more chairs for the kindergarten. The smell of burning cookies made Marcy panicky.

"Excuse me. Something's burning!" Marcy gasped. "I'll call you back later, Mrs.—er—" She hung up and forgot the whole incident. The kindergarten teacher called up two nights later, assuring David coldly that if he wasn't interested in the Sunday school's welfare, why should she be? Perhaps he'd like her to resign?

It took David fifteen minutes to calm her down, and when he put down the phone he looked so discouraged that Marcy, contrite, went to kneel beside where he was sitting in the chintz armchair, leaned her cheek against his, and let her lashes fan his cheek instead of kissing him with her lips.

"I'll listen the next time, Davey," she promised. "Even if they recite the telephone book. I'm so terribly sorry."

But the very next day Marcy got in wrong with Soaks. Marcy had invited the Harrisons for dinner. Maybe seeing this cellar and eating off a wobbly cardtable would urge them into paying the assistant minister more. . . . She was rushing out to do her shopping for that evening when the phone rang. She snatched off the receiver impatiently to hear a woman's voice high, shrill, and excited.

"This is Ella Heinz! I have to see the minister! Right now!"

"David isn't here," Marcy explained. "If you'll give me your number, I'll have him call you when he comes in."

The woman gasped something incoherent, and the line went dead. Just another neurotic woman having hysterics over nothing, Marcy thought impatiently, as she scrawled "Heinz" hastily on the pad by the phone. Should she have melon with ice cream for dessert or treat herself to one of those expensive but delicious apple pies at the bakery down on River Street? She decided upon the apple pie because it could warm in the oven while they were eating the duck with orange sauce such as Aunt Riah made. The phone was ringing again as Marcy came back into the apartment. She dropped her bundles on the oak table and picked up the receiver resignedly. "Yes?"

"That you, Marcy?" Soaks demanded. "David there? Ella Heinz, the one who lost her baby, tried to commit suicide with sleeping pills. If I hadn't happened to stop by her apartment—I figured something must be wrong when I saw her bedroom shades pulled down—she might have been in her grave instead of the hospital. Ella's come round: she says she phoned you. If David was out, why didn't you call me or Dr. Harrison?"

How were you to know Ella Heinz was desperate? She'd asked for David, not Soaks, and you'd promised to have him call Ella back. If Soaks told Jim what an idiot you were, this dinner you'd worked so hard to make nice would be a flat failure. Marcy asked anxiously: "Is Ella going to be all right? David's just coming in the door, I'll put him on."

David told Soaks that he'd drop by the hospital at once.

"But the Harrisons'll be here any minute!" Marcy wailed as David put down the receiver. "The duck's almost done; it'll dry up! Couldn't you go after dinner?"

"The Harrisons will understand. Go right ahead. I'll be back as soon as I can." He glanced down at the pad by the phone. "What's this hieroglyphic?" When she hesitated, his mouth hardened into a thin line she'd never seen before.

"Marcy, a minister's phone calls are as important as a doctor's. Surely you understand that."

"Of course I understand. I gave you the message. That's Ella Heinz. You're making a big thing out of nothing!" Her irritation with herself made her voice sharper. She should have realized how upset Ella was; if it hadn't been for her anxiety about the dinner, she might have. At any rate she'd told David about Ella the moment he came in. No matter how she tried, she seemed to make a mess of everything.

She flared, "Oh, go along to the hospital!"

Her nice dinner was ruined. When the Harrisons arrived, she explained brightly that David had been detained by a sick parishioner but that they wouldn't wait for him. The duck she'd spent all afternoon basting was a crisp brown, the potatoes crusty gold with butter, and the salad with stuffed dates for a body and slices of pineapple turned sideways for wings with stuffed olives for decorations was as exciting as the picture in the cookbook, but every bite was ashes in Marcy's mouth. Under her gay hostess chatter her whole attention was focused upon listening for David's step in the hall. One look at his face would tell her if Soaks had poisoned his mind with chatter about what Marcy should have done when Ella phoned. If Ella died, would Soaks blame her?

But when David returned just in time for dessert, he reported only that Ella Heinz had gone completely out of her head, that she hadn't even known him but that she would live. Poor Ella. Marcy's lips trembled. Being shut up somewhere in an institution wasn't really living.

"What a tragedy!" Sara Harrison murmured. "Women often lose hold emotionally after having a baby, but usually they recover."

"Anything left to eat, darling?" David asked hungrily.

As Marcy went to bring his heaped plate from the oven, Jim Harrison teased, "If you kids eat like this every day, we'd better cut down on your salary." David countered ruefully that they'd probably eat peanut-butter soup for a week, after this. When Marcy brought out apple pie à la mode, Sara said that she couldn't possibly manage ice cream but that she couldn't resist a nibble of that delicious-looking pie. Jim, however, ate everything on his plate. The dinner was a success after all. As the door closed behind their guests, David bent his head for a kiss; but Marcy hid her face in his big shoulder to murmur, muffled, "I honestly don't see how you put up with me, Davey!"

"The first hundred years are the hardest," David chuckled. "And the nicest."

Chapter Five

THE following week was the Foreign Missionary meeting at Louella Gratz's at the Hotel Vendôme where Louella and Henry, who had no children, lived in a large, expensive apartment. Soaks had warned Marcy that nobody ever missed the Foreign meeting at Louella's, she had such grand refreshments.

Marcy wore her dark blue silk with the write ruching at the throat which was vastly becoming; it gave her courage to ring Louella's doorbell, to face all the new faces. If only she could remember names! But walking into a roomful of strange women, most of them twice or three times her age, appalled her. But she did want them to like her for David's sake. When she saw Soaks, she'd know if she still blamed her about Ella Heinz.

"Marcy, darling!" Louella, a large woman dressed in purple, decorated with innumerable beads, necklaces, and bracelets that tinkled on her plump arms, enveloped Marcy in a perfumed, bosomy embrace. Louella loved anything pretty and new. She reminded Marcy of an Oklahoma Indian squaw in full bead, Marcy had giggled once to David; most squaws wore the family turquoise on their necks and arms as a sort of family safe deposit, but David had demurred that at least Louella washed her neck. Was Soaks here yet? Marcy wondered uneasily. She glanced down the rows of gilt chairs to where the deaconess's uncompromising black stood out from the other ladies' best plumage. Soaks was seated in the front row, as behooved her station.

"Come right down here, Marcy, beside Emma Oaks," Louella fluttered. "I was wondering, would you read the Scriptures? Pick out a nice short one, we've got so much business."

"Oh, my goodness, I couldn't!" Marcy gasped. "I never

63

read in public in my life." At the sound of Marcy's voice, Soaks turned, and her agate eyes running over the younger woman seemed to say: "That I can believe. You're a pretty poor excuse for a minister's wife." She was right, of course. Marcy begged Soaks, "You read, Miss Oaks!"

"You got to begin sometime," Soaks grumbled, but she reached for the Book beside her on the seat, got up, and stood there waiting for the gabble of conversation to die down. Marcy realized that even if she had been willing to read, it had been the right thing to suggest—for once. Relieved, Marcy let her glance slide around the apartment. It fitted Louella exactly. The walls of the enormous living room with its deep bay windows were papered in dark red with gilt pineapples rampant . . . or were they golden cabbages? The velvet draperies and thick carpet were also red. Living here must be rather like inhabiting a gilt bonfire, but the satin upholstered furniture pushed against the walls looked very expensive. Every small wobbly gilt chair was now filled; the ladies of St. Luke's must be devoted to Foreign Missions. But after the opening exercises, they discussed the coming church fair and whether to put candy canes or cornucopias of hard candies on the Christmas tree for the Sunday school. The only mention of missions occurred when Louella read a letter from a missionary in Tahiti, asking that the ladies hem and send her four dozen diapers. It was voted so to do. Marcy wondered idly if Tahitian babies normally wore diapers or if the missionaries were introducing them to the poor heathen as they had those hideous Mother Hubbards for their mothers.

The refreshments were as lavish as advertised, and the ladies certainly did justice to them. A long white-covered table had been set up in the library, a room papered in gold with red roses, where Louella sat at one end of the table pouring tea out of a vast silver teapot while Sara Harrison at the other end dispensed coffee from an even more ornate, glittering urn. There were also silver trays with sandwiches shaped as fans, circles, oblongs, anything but an honest garden-variety sandwich. The amazing array of cakes frosted with rosebuds, violets, and other unidentifiable blossoms tasted delicious, better than they looked. There were also vast silver bonbon dishes holding nuts, candies, mints, and chocolates.

Marcy, along with Soaks, as church staff, had been asked to pass the cakes, so the two of them were the last to leave Louella's apartment. As the door closed after their hostess's effusive thanks for their help, Marcy was startled when the deaconess's big black bag flew open and a paper napkin package fell out at their feet, opening on the hall carpet to expose half a dozen little frosted cakes. Soaks, her face very red, walked on down the corridor, pretending the little dropped packet had nothing to do with her. Was it kinder to ignore it? But she must know you'd seen. Marcy bent, then ran after Soaks to thrust the napkin back into the older woman's bag. "I wish I'd thought to bring a few home for David!" Marcy said warmly. "He loves little cakes."

Soaks said in a choked voice, looking straight ahead, "I know it was wicked of me. But I thought—the food at the Home is so—good for you!"

Did the poor thing get enough to eat? For the first time Marcy wondered how much salary a deaconess got? She dared to ask. "We get our room, board, and ten dollars a month allowance for incidentals," Soaks said reluctantly. "It's ample except that my stay-at-homes always seem to need little things. I usually leave old Mrs. Sampson, who can't get out of her wheelchair, a pat of real butter when I stop by; she hates the boardinghouse margarine so."

"You make me ashamed," Marcy told her soberly. She leaned to kiss Soaks' cheek; it tasted of soap and goodness. "Why don't you stop by the apartment, have tea with me tomorrow? May I call you 'Emma'? It sounds so much softer than 'Miss Oaks.' "

"If you like," Soaks told her, stiffly. She was still red, upset at having her little secret found out. "But Thursday's my hospital day. I'm sorry."

"So am I. But come soon, won't you?" It was comforting that Soaks was human, too. You learned to take people as you found them, and still liked them. Did that include yourself?

Marcy didn't tell David about Soaks and her pathetic little cakes but she did chuckle about Louella's earrings. "You should have seen them, about four inches long," she told David next morning at their late breakfast, which was practically their only time together when they were awake. Sometimes Marcy propped the receiver off the hook with a carefully careless look to make sure they were not interrupted. This morning in her pale blue negligee with a cerise ribbon belt, she sat enthroned in the big armchair, turning the toaster on the wobbly cardtable while David poured orange juice and made the coffee. She chuckled, "They were so heavy, her shoulders must be black and blue."

"Curious, Louella and Soaks being such pals," David said thoughtfully, munching a piece of toast. "They're exact opposites."

"Henry Gratz is Soaks' boss, almost as much as Jim Harrison," Marcy pointed out practically. "Henry's probably the most influential layman in the church. Forget it. That's mean of me, isn't it?" She must tell him proudly, "Soaks says I can call her 'Emma'! What are you doing today, Davey?"

"There's a Scout luncheon this noon. This afternoon I have to go over music with the organist, and tonight there's a committee supper in the vestry to map out the December programs for the student discussions. But I shouldn't be late —ninish. You going to take a nice walk in the Gardens?"

Marcy made a wry face. "I hate walking alone." Eagerly, "Maybe I'll hire a horse, go for a ride in the Fenway. Louella says it costs only three dollars an hour. I'll feel silly riding along a little bridle path, but at least I'll be in the saddle again."

David flushed, hesitated, but finally he had to blurt out, "Darling, this is all the cash we have till next pay day." He emptied his pants' pockets onto the cardtable. There were four dollars and forty-five cents and two two-cent stamps.

"It's my fault. I'm such an idiot about money," Marcy told him in a stifled voice. "We can make out all right, Davey, till next week. We'll have hamburg and scrambled eggs and cereal—and there's plenty of canned stuff. . . ."

David comforted eagerly, "I'll give you a hand with the dishes before I go."

"No. I'd rather do them alone, thanks." When she kept busy she didn't feel quite so useless, so inadequate for the job she had taken on. After the dishes were neatly shelved, the bed made, and the floor swept, there was nothing left to do but feel sorry for herself. She tried to read the newspaper, but it was full of pictures of ladies' committees for the Symphony or for fallen girls, advertisements of enticing clothes she couldn't afford to buy, murders, fires in East Boston, and politics. Not a familiar name in the paper; in Fort Worth she'd have known the whole society page. She sat there hunched miserably in the big chair, until she heard the rustle of paper sliding under her door.

Mr. Hicks was by now such a victim of Marcy's charm that he frequently collected the Gallant letters from the lobby, along with his own, and brought them downstairs. She grabbed up the thick white envelope from the floor; it was postmarked Fort Worth. Marcy ripped open the envelope impatiently, then read eagerly in Momi's precise handwriting:

"Pa broke his arm cranking up his model T. You know how impatient he is, if something doesn't work right off, he gets roaring mad. His arm's in a cast now and he's got him one of those newfangled self-starters so I hope we'll have some peace. Li'l Emily's learning to drive Sam's big Mercedes. Imagine, a woman driving. . . . But yesterday Sam let her drive all the way out to his Pa's ranch, and today they're going over to Dallas to a barbecue. I tell Li'l Emily, Sam'll think her unwomanly, but she and he seem to like going everywhere together. . . ."

The letter dropped from Marcy's suddenly nerveless fingers into her lap. Li'l Emily, of whom Aunt Riah'd warned, "What she wants, she gits. . . ." Don't be an idiot. If she loved Sam and he her . . . But how could he have changed so soon? Sam who had promised, "It's only three days and two nights to Boston. If you ever need me, Big Mouth . . ." If Sam could forget his promise so soon, Li'l Emily was welcome to him! Suddenly, Marcy felt stifled. She had to get out of there, get some fresh air. . . .

As Marcy went into the bedroom to dress, she stared at the little pile of soiled, crumpled bills upon the corner of the narrow chest of drawers squeezed in at the foot of their big bed. David had left her the four dollars and had taken only the forty-five cents for himself, for carfares and incidentals. Dear, darling, generous David . . . She flung herself across the bed, weeping bitterly.

Chapter Six

THOUGH Serena Snow's apartment was on the wrong side of Beacon Hill, the house was one of the lovely old faded brick ones, formerly a single dwelling, but now with a different tenant on each floor, as David found when he looked for the address Soaks had given him for the pageant committee meeting the next Thursday. She had added that Serena had asked them to lunch first. But there was no lobby and there were no name plates, so David stood there, hesitating about what to do next, when he heard Serena call to him from her open door. It was necessary for him to circle beneath the white stone steps to enter.

"You're the first one, Davo. Come right in."

She wore a simple black wool dress with imitation pearls about her throat and in her ears, but her bright hair and radiant smile of welcome lighted the dark doorway. Whatever illness or pique had sent her rushing out of the church vestry the other afternoon, she seemed to have recovered fully. It would be best to ignore the incident unless she herself brought it up, David decided. "I see you live in the basement too." David smiled as he tossed his hat upon what was obviously a studio couch covered with green corduroy and bright pillows by day, and by night emerging as a more or less comfortable bed. There were two more couches, but the room was enormous, running the whole length of the house, with three long windows reaching from ceiling to floor at either end. A fireplace with real logs burning brightly lighted the center of the long room. A chintz-covered davenport, deep, shabby, and comfortable, was drawn up in front of the leaping fire, where stood a low marble-topped table upon which had been laid out thin cups and saucers, a silver coffeepot, creamer and sugar basin. The silver-framed picture of a freckle-faced impish little boy smiled at the coffee tray, and from behind a slatted white screen on the opposite corner of the room a delicious smell floated.

"Lobsters!" David sniffed hungrily.

"Pa sent me down some. He sends 'em by the conductor, on the early train from Bath, and I always cook 'em the same day. He still hauls a few traps, but mostly because Ma likes a good stew." Her long green eyes twinkled at David, sniffing the good Maine fragrance as greedily as a hungry small boy.

"Shorts, I bet!"

She laughed. "Just over the line, maybe."

"I haven't had a good baiting of shorts since—since before the war, I guess. Do you live here alone, Rene?"

"No. Three of us, nurses at the Deaconess Hospital, use this for a base when we're off duty. I've been in training two years now. . . ." Her voice trailed off, for David wasn't listening. His glance had strayed up to the picture in the big gray frame over the fireplace, and there was a look of unbelief, almost of shock, on his face. The oil painting was by no ordinary artist, and had little in common with the well-worn furniture in the room. A slender young girl, obviously about to bathe in a small clear brook, was walking along the sun-flecked green bank. Orange shadows, reaching out toward the mocking silver shine of the water, wrapped the girl in the mystery of beauty only half revealed. She had thrown off her blue-green gown carelessly onto the grass, but her creamy bare back, her slender, childish legs looked curiously innocent, as if she knew herself alone, unobserved. Shafts of sunlight blazed down through the branches of the tall trees onto her white slenderness and made the bright hair loosened about her shoulders blaze into living flame.

"But . . . I mean . . . that's your hair, Rene!"

Serena smiled as David stared at the hauntingly beautiful painting. "That's why Dare bought that for me, the monkey,

a long time ago. He thought it was a great joke on me. He
has a juvenile sense of humor. But it's such a vivid splash of
color in this rather dim room, I like it. Do sit down, Davo.
The davenport is comfortable. I can't say as much for the
chairs."

"Dare?" David asked, doing as he was told, and Serena
sank down beside him.

"Dare Drexel. He and his family didn't come to Bellport till
after you left, did they? They bought Cap'n Poor's place after
he died, the big white house next to the church. They put a
fortune into making it just as it used to be two hundred years
ago when he sailed a clipper ship around the Horn. Chinese
wallpaper, fabulous antiques, paintings—this was one Dare
unearthed. . . . You remember Cap'n Poor's?"

Certainly David remembered the old Poor mansion; it was
about as conspicuous as the Lighthouse, although it stood
upon the opposite shore of the river, across on the mainland.
But the house had been pretty run down; to fix it properly
the Drexels must have had plenty of what it takes. What was
this Dare to Serena?

David could not bring himself to ask bluntly, for Maine
people were slow to speak about what really mattered to them.
To show he wasn't prying, David picked up the silver-framed
photograph of a small boy from the coffee table in front of
him.

"He's got the Snow nose, straight and short," David admired. "I didn't know you had a younger brother, Rene. He
must have been born after I left Bellport."

Serena drew a deep breath. "Riley is my son. He's six years
old. He lives at the Light with my folks."

So Serena was or had been married. To this Dare Drexel,
who could buy a valuable painting like that as a whim, give it
away like a box of chocolates? Then why was Serena training
as a nurse? Were they divorced? Something was very strange.

Serena was fidgeting beside David on the davenport, clasping and unclasping her hands nervously. She wanted to tell him something, but didn't know how, and he mustn't force her confidence. His dad, that wise old pastor, used to say that the hardest thing for a young preacher to learn was to wait till his people came to him, because only when they were really willing could they be helped. David smiled at Serena sitting beside him in her black dress; her long white hands were ringless, beautifully cared for but showing hard work in the hospital. Of what did she remind him? Salty wind in the treetops—that was it; the clean smell of pines in the sun.

"David," Serena burst out suddenly, "talking to a minister is a sort of confessional, isn't it? I mean, you don't tell anyone else?"

"No one else," David agreed.

She hesitated again. "Ever since that student discussion last week I've been upset," she confessed, picking up a tiny paper napkin from the coffee table, putting it back absently. " 'Adultery of the spirit' . . . Did you mean not being honest with yourself? Not facing facts—about yourself and—other people?"

"That's one way of putting it."

"I'm that—that woman Jesus saved from being stoned, David!" As David stared at Serena, appalled, she covered her shamed face with her hands, and tears began trickling down between her long fingers. She sobbed: "I thought when I came here to train, I'd hidden the past. How can I get away from it?"

" 'And return unto the Lord,' " David quoted from the song she'd sung last Sunday. "When you sang that, I could feel the whole congregation holding its breath listening, because it was sincere. It was a prayer, Rene, wasn't it?"

"Yes, oh, yes!" Her hands fell from her tear-stained face. "David, does prayer really work?"

"Of course it does," David assured her instantly.

"Don't just talk like a minister, Davo. I have to *know*." Her green eyes clung anxiously to his; David realized that if he said the wrong thing, her gaze would swoop away, frightened. Serena worried: "You can't possibly believe—no intelligent man could—that the Flinger-out-of-stars counts hairs and sparrows."

"Poetry," David explained, "often speaks more truly than the dictionary. A poet's way of saying that God cares. Even about small things."

"But there's no scientific proof of this?"

The proof of prayer was that it worked, David insisted. Did not the scientist, too, arrive at his "facts" by faith? If over and over he added two parts of hydrogen to one part of oxygen and the result was always water, this was a fact. In the same way when man reached up to take the hand God held out to him, the result was a reaction that changed his life.

"But He doesn't always give you what you ask for!"

"For the sun to come out at your picnic?" David smiled. "That's kid stuff, Rene. Asking to have the rules of the universe set aside for your whim! When the scientists comes to the deep chasm of his ignorance, he takes the calculated leap, and if he lands anywhere he's discovered an infinitesimal part of God's plan that was set up for the universe, since the beginning of time."

"You really believe that, don't you? Then how can terrible things happen to innocent people, to children? Like I did to Rye?" Serena's hands were shaking in her soft black lap, David saw, compassionately. "Oh, David, how do you find out what the Plan is? For you?"

"I'd better tell you about my 'stone-wall prayer,'" David decided cheerfully. "You remember the old tumbled-down stone wall that runs along the meadow above the pier at Bellport?" Serena nodded, wide-eyed, as he went on. "I was standing there the day after Dad and Mother were drowned, wondering how on earth I could go on, alone. The three of us had always been so close. A preacher can't save much, so I had almost no money to finish school, to go to college, no inheritance at all except a little insurance and the cottage where we'd all three lived together. It was my home, as precious to me as my own hand." He smiled at her, saw she was still trembling. "When you come to a stone wall you can't climb over or knock down, just do what I did. Close your eyes, jump blindly with faith. Just say, 'Thy will be done.' And it will be done." He warned her, "The answer's not always what you want or expect. Mine was to sell the cottage to go to college. But the answer comes. Always."

Tears were running unchecked down Serena's cheeks as she gasped: "I've made such a mess of my life so far! You think I could really change? Make things right for Riley?"

"Of course," David assured her. As she bent her head so that her shining hair fell in a bright screen across her face, she looked so forlorn, so like the skinny freckled child he'd known, that he laid his big warm hand over her small shaking one. "Try it, Rene. . . ."

"Well, my goodness, you two look cozy!"

David and Serena looked up, startled, to find Louella Gratz and Soaks standing there, staring at them from the open doorway. Louella said, rattling her bracelets nervously, "The door was ajar, so we just walked in." Her avid eyes were on Serena's flushed face as she drew her hand from David's and jumped to her feet. David stood up too. "You two must be awfully good friends!" Louella gabbled.

"Very old friends," David agreed, moving slightly away from Serena. Soaks, who hadn't spoken a syllable, was staring at the young people with her agate lashless eyes. Did she think he and Rene had been coyly holding hands? David wondered wryly. "I've known Rene here since she was twelve. Her father helped me bait my first fishhook. Hello, Miss Oaks."

"Good afternoon, Mr. Gallant." Not "David," and Soaks

did not seem to see his outstretched hand. Her face was
motled red and white. With embarrassment? Anger? She
would prefer to misunderstand, David realized ruefully; it
would give her a lever to make him do whatever she wished.
The silence went on and on, broken only by the nervous jingle
of Louella's bracelets as she stared first at David, then at that
redheaded girl. She'd always told her Henry that one was too
pretty to be up to any good in a choir. . . .

"Do sit down, Miss Oaks. Mrs. Gratz." Serena tried desperately to bring them back to commonplace, to break the
sinister spell of Soaks' silence. "Do you both like freshly boiled
lobsters? They're one of those things you either like very
much or don't. David and I were chatting until they were
done." Her voice shriveled before Soaks outraged little snort.

"Chatting! Well!" You might get away with this nonsense
with Louella, her tone added, but not with me, Emma Oaks.

"But, Miss Oaks . . ." When Soaks looked directly through
him, David had the queer feeling of being invisible. Well, she
could make a case against him, all right. New assistant minister holding hands with the lovely soprano. The way Soaks
would put it, her version would damn him in the eyes of the
official board. And she would have Louella, the wife of the
board chairman, to back her up. If only he could think of
some way not to have Rene hurt when she was trying to put
things right for her small son, but what could he say!

"Mm, those lobsters do smell wonderful!" Louella gushed.
"I always say, there's only one way to cook them: you plunge
them in, tail down, and sixteen minutes after they begin to
boil again, you—"

"We're not staying to lunch," Soaks announced, firmly. She
turned her straight black back, started for the door. "Come,
Louella!"

"But . . ." Walk out on an exciting moment like this? Not
if she could help it. "Don't you think, Emma—"

"There's too many lobsters for two of us," Serena urged

desperately, though she knew it was useless. But she had to keep trying, for David's sake.

The front door closing sharply behind the righteously indignant Soaks and the fluttering Louella put a period to her sentence. "Oh, David," Serena wailed, "they're probably going to tell Dr. Harrison and Louella's Henry that we're lovers! It's ridiculous! But I wouldn't put it beyond them. You'd better go now, get to Dr. Harrison before they do. . . . Why, David, you're laughing!"

It was true. David was leaning against the doorjamb in a paroxysm of unwilling laughter, and finally Serena joined him. It was funny, he insisted, Louella rattling her beads, and Soaks assuming the worst, like a bad Five-and-Dime movie, without allowing for any explanation. "But they can do you a lot of harm," Serena warned, wiping her eyes. "They can't hurt me, because I'm resigning from the choir anyway. David Gallant, are you hysterical?"

"No, just hungry," David told her.

"You mean you'll still stay?"

"Try to get rid of me. Only, lend me a bathing suit, will you? The only satisfactory way to eat Maine lobster is to go in, all over."

She tucked a white towel about his neck, brought in the rosy red lobsters on two plates, and put a big bowl between them for the shells. The shorts were just as delicious as he'd remembered them, still warm but not too hot to hold, to crack with the silver crackers, to push the warm meat out of the tail and then suck your fingers ecstatically. There were also melted butter, black coffee, hot rolls, and tomato and lettuce salad. No dessert, David approved, with a vast sigh of repletion: "It would take the taste of Maine away." He got up reluctantly. "I'm sorry to eat and run, but I promised to take Marcy to see the Old North Church. She's been deviling me for days, shouting, 'One if by land, two if by sea . . .' " His face sobered. He stopped his lighthearted nonsense as he put his hand on the girl's shoulder. "If I can help you in any way, Rene, let me know?"

"Will you please tell Dr. Harrison I'm resigning from the choir?"

"If I must. But I wish you wouldn't, Rene." She tried to smile at him, but her lips only quivered, yet the tenseness from the scene with Louella and Soaks had gone, David saw with satisfaction. Maybe Marcy could help Serena work this out; both of them needed a friend, and Marcy'd been restless, unhappy lately without enough to take up her time. All-women meetings bored her, and she was shy with new people older than she was. But if he explained about Serena's need, he could count upon the warmth of Marcy's loyalty. He asked Serena, "You mind if I tell Marcy about Riley?"

Serena hesitated. "Do you have to say he's . . . illegitimate? After all, it's not his fault."

"No, of course not."

"Then I don't mind her knowing I have a son."

It was a good thing he'd got it clear before he got home, for Marcy, with one look at his face, demanded, "What's wrong, darling?" When, trying to make light of it, he told her how Soaks and Louella had walked in on him and Serena, Marcy was worried. "One of them would be bad enough, but together those two are dynamite. We'd better go to see Jim Harrison, tell him what really happened."

"But nothing happened! Come on, darling. We'll climb the Old North Church tower, and then, if there's time . . ."

"Davey, how can you be so dumb?"

"It just comes natural to me," he said, so meekly that she laughed. But she insisted, "We're going to see Jim Harrison right now. The sooner, the better."

"But, darling, this isn't your fight," David objected. "You weren't even there when the unholy twins arrived!"

Marcy's eyes darkened stormily, "You're my husband! And what happens to you happens to me."

"Very well," David agreed reluctantly. Marcy wanted to take a taxi to get to St. Luke's quickly, but David pointed out it would cost at least fifty cents, plus tip; they could take the streetcar for five cents apiece. As they rattled along the busy streets, with the motorman clanging his warning bell incessantly, there was small chance for conversation. When they got off the streetcar, David, preoccupied, hurried ahead so fast it was hard for Marcy to keep up with him, but she was right on his heels as he leaped up the stone steps of St. Luke's and went down the corridor to knock at the older minister's study door.

"Come in! I've been expecting you." Jim Harrison grinned at David and Marcy standing there in the doorway like two uncertain school children before the headmaster. "Well, you certainly stirred up a line storm, young feller," Jim admitted, getting up to set a chair for Marcy. "What on earth did happen, anyway? From Soaks' and Louella's account, you and Serena cracked most of the Ten Commandments!"

David told him, ending, "I was thinking mostly of Riley, how much a little boy needs his mother. . . ."

"Mother!" Marcy gasped, her eyes wide violet pools of relief. "I didn't know Serena was married! But," doubtfully, "lots of singers use their maiden names."

David, glancing from Marcy to Jim Harrison, said slowly, "What Rene told me comes under the head of the confessional, I guess."

"Confessional!" Marcy gasped. "You aren't a priest!"

"Of course he's a priest, and a prophet, and a plain common garden-variety honest man," Jim Harrison interposed deftly, patting Marcy's shoulder reassuringly. Youth was wonderful, but starry-eyed, impatient and tiring. Naturally David wouldn't have been foolish enough to carry on with the soprano, especially when he knew Soaks and Louella were due at any moment. *Wise as a serpent, harmless as a dove* . . . Was anyone, ever? Jim listened unhappily to David offering Serena's resignation from the choir. "I certainly hate to lose her," Jim murmured. "Not only has she a gorgeous voice but she's easy on the eye. Probably the next soprano will have an operatic bosom and breathe heavily through her nose." When Marcy laughed, he added soberly: "Nonsense can be danger- ous as truth in the wrong places. This wouldn't do Serena any good at the hospital, either. She's a fine nurse. I'm on the board at the Deaconess and I see her sometimes when I'm calling there." The best way to stop Soaks and Louella from doing David any real harm was to make it abundantly clear that the senior minister took no stock in such tales about his assistant. If he, Jim Harrison, was to back David up, stand squarely behind him, publicly . . .

"I'm going to be in Minneapolis next week, David," Jim announced. "The district superintendent was to speak here but he's sick. How would you like to preach next Sunday morning?"

David opened his suddenly dry mouth to speak, but no words came. Preach here in this great church with twenty-five hundred listeners, stand up in the high carved pulpit where the silver voices of so many great orators still echoed? He was not worthy. Jim Harrison was doing this to prove that he trusted him. David was completely unable to speak his grati- tude.

"Jim Harrison, you're a darling!" Marcy's eyes were blazing with pride as she looked at her David. "You can use your 'Golden Sheaves for God' sermon, Davey! The one that was such a sensation when you preached at St. Paul's at Fort Worth." She told Jim, "My paw said Davey made more peo- ple cry than Taps on the Fourth of July!"

Why was Davey staring at her in that funny way? He told

Jim Harrison, slowly: "I'll be glad to preach. I think I'll speak about the 'Promised Land.' You know, Moses looking across wistfully and never getting there, like most of us." He drew a deep breath, "I can't thank you enough, Jim, but I guess you know how I feel."

"That's settled then," Dr. Harrison said cheerfully. His tone was dismissal; the incident was closed as far as he was concerned. But not, he feared, with Soaks. . . .

As David and Marcy went out of his study, walking so closely their hands touched, the older minister sighed. They wanted different things, those two, but they hadn't found it out yet. How far would Marcy go to realize her ambition for David to get ahead? Well, all married people had problems to adjust, to compromise. Marcy was very young, a child almost, and she was in love with her husband; she'd learn. David was older, twenty-five, wasn't he?—and he loved his young wife, passionately. But to him, born and bred in a parsonage tradition, the parish was bound to come first. Would his heart or his head speak when the final contest between them came? Just seeing them together, so much in love, made for nostalgia. Jim Harrison reached for his phone, called a number. "Sara? No, I don't want anything special. Just to hear your voice. Soaks is on the warpath again, and that's always wearing. Sara, I wish you'd ask Serena Snow and the Gallants to dinner next Sunday. Yes, I know I'll be in Minneapolis, but—Thank you, dear. Goodby."

Marcy was almost as nervous as David next Sunday when he marched up onto the platform at St. Luke's and took his seat in the great carved, crimson-velvet upholstered chair. David looked so different, wearing the flowing black gown Jim Harrison had lent him, instead of his dark blue suit. That he couldn't afford a gown yet didn't matter when he was only reading the Scriptures, not preaching, doing the whole service; but he looked wonderful, Marcy exulted, as if he belonged in high places. David would be a success; he had to be! Yet her own heart thumped nervously as she looked up at him sitting there, his blond head boyish against the crimson back of the great chair, his familiar figure swallowed up by the black gown. From her front pew she could see David swallow twice, run his tongue over his dry lips. Oh, Lord . . . She'd heard him preach only that once at St. Paul's, and he'd been more than good, compelling. Still, she was hardly a judge of sermons. She'd gone to service every Sunday because Paw insisted upon all the family filing into the family pew, no matter how late any of them had been out "dating" the night before. But it had been easy when the minister began, "My friends . . . " to turn off her attention, to think about last night, or just to sit, torpid, her eyes open but her mind drowsing in pleasant byways. But today Marcy was wide awake, every nerve alert, tingling, as she stared anxiously up at David. What if he mixed up his notes he'd worked on until midnight last night? If he rambled on like some preachers, saying "finally" in the middle of the sermon, then going on endlessly till everyone listening wanted to scream, she'd curl right up and . . . Oh, my goodness, it was time for the sermon! David was getting up from the big red chair, marching toward the winding wooden stairs that led to the high pulpit.

When David stumbled on his unaccustomed robe at the foot of the pulpit stairway, Marcy could feel the red of embarrassment flood up into her own cheeks; but David merely smiled at his own awkwardness, lifted his robe, and climbed on up. Now he was standing there, silent for an instant in the high pulpit, looking out over the congregation, with the great mahogany sounding board flaring above his fair head. The church was crowded. Nearly five thousand eyes were focusing, questioningly, on David. What had this very young man to say worth their listening to? After Dr. Harrison's magnificent ser-

mons, David Gallant had better be good. What would the
congregation decide about David?

*Please, dear Lord, help David to preach wonderfully, magni-
ficently, or I can't bear it. . . .*

"Let us pray," David muttered, so low hardly anyone could
hear him beyond the first pew. Then he did a strange thing.
Instead of bowing his head, David lifted his face joyously, his
eyes wide open, his whole sensitive face glowing as he spoke.
"Our Father who is nearer to us than breathing, speak Thy
words through my lips. . . ." As David talked face to face with
the Almighty who was his Friend, he seemed to grow taller, to
be no longer young but timeless. "Amen" David ended, and
Marcy could hear the satisfied rustle as the great congregation
sat back, relieved, in their pews; this young man was unusual,
anyway. But they were still waiting to pounce on any dis-
crepancy they could discover in David's words, like the Roman
circus where the crowd could save a man's life or condemn
him to death simply by turning their thumbs up or down.

"One day a man named Moses climbed a high mountain to
meet his God," David began his sermon, not even looking
down at his notes on the lectern. "I invite you all to climb
along with me for a few moments." Marcy heard no more for
some minutes because she was so limp with relief. David had
gathered the attention of the congregation into the palm of his
hand; *he was going to be all right.* She made herself relax, and
the gloved hands clutching her hymnbook loosened as David
went on: "We all have our mountain peaks, and it irks us
mightily when we have to come down again into the valley.
But we are never quite the same; we carry something of the
heights, a view of wider horizons down with us. When Moses
came back down from Sinai to his people after talking with
his God, 'he wist not that his face shone.' "

He had not once looked down at her. Did it not matter at all
to him that she was there? Looking up at him so high above

her, Marcy down in her pew felt a sharp contraction of her throat. For this David was not her intimate lover; he was indeed the priest, as he had said. When you married a minister, she wondered, in panic, did you have to marry the Church, too? And if you couldn't feel this passion for talking with God that David did, would it separate you? Would you go one way, and David, the priest, another? No, no. "A minister is a man, too," David had assured her, his lips on hers. But when David's sermon was done, Marcy realized she had heard very little of what he had said; the only thing she was sure of was that, like Moses, David's face had shone.

Chapter Seven

"DAVEY, what's so special about Maine?" Marcy asked one morning as she watched her tall blond young husband gathering up his papers and putting them into his green cloth Boston bag to carry to his office at St. Luke's. The green bag, she had discovered, was like the Swan Boats in the Gardens, so much a part of the lawyers, students, college professors, and clergymen that they were proud of its limp dowdiness, a sort of Boston Legion of Belonging. David had carried the handsome leather brief case she had given him hopefully for his birthday for only a week before reverting to his beloved shabby green bag with the black drawstring. He'd carried their lunch in it when he'd taken her down to Nantasket to see the ocean rolling in, a vast prairie of water frothing into endless waves that wiped out the sand castless of innumerable small fry equipped with pails and buckets while their elders munched popcorn and potato chips. The beach had seemed too cluttered, and when David had taken Marcy to lunch at T wharf she had remarked frankly that his beloved sea seemed to be mostly oily gray water and floating orange peels.

"I suppose it depends upon where you grew up," David told her absently. "When you meet the sea, you want plenty of it. The Harrisons have a nice place down on the Cape, but to me there's nothing like the rocky Maine shore. Our cottage was on the Kennebec, actually, but the tide runs so far up, the river is in effect an arm of the ocean." His eyes above the long paper he was folding grew dreamy as he told Marcy wistfully that the path to their cottage ran through a grove of tall pines, over a carpet of moss so soft and thick you heard no footsteps, only the rote of the water alongshore. You walked through sun-warmed silence, sniffing salt air, around to the front veranda, and the blue-green river was there, whispering or thundering on the bright yellow cliff. David drew in his breath sharply, nostalgically, "Suddenly you are home."

Marcy put her hand on his coatsleeve. "David, take me there?"

"The very first chance I get. But November's hardly the weather for Maine." As she stood there smiling at him, he noticed for the first time the dark circles under her eyes, the paleness of her face, the tightness about her lovely mouth which would some day be the thin relentless line of age. David asked, worried, "Darling, do you feel all right? You look—"

"Dreadful," Marcy supplied. "I'm not really sick anywhere special; I just feel mean all over."

"You'd better go to see Dr. Sturgis," David worried. Dr. Sturgis, a member at St. Luke's whom David especially liked, was a big blunt man with a rough tongue for hypochondriacs but strangely gentle with patients who were really sick. David worried, "We shouldn't have had all that gang in last night after the service."

"Oh, I like having them." One of David's schemes for working Marcy into the church program had been to bring back frequently to their apartment on Sunday nights a crowd of young people hungry for more good talk and (hopefully) food. So many mouths knocked Marcy's food budget to pieces, even if she did go long on the spaghetti and short on the cheese, but she throve on the excitement, being part of a young, gay, careless crowd. The students were nearer her age than his, David realized from the great height of his twenty-five years. Usually Serena was one of the group, for, though she had resigned from the choir, she still came to the student discussions when she was off duty at the hospital. Marcy reported, "Serena said last night she might be sent to Worcester soon, for her MH training at the state hospital—mental hygiene to you."

"We must have her over for dinner before she goes," David said absently.

"Sure. Only don't invite her right in front of Emma, as you did last Sunday. There's no use rubbing it in that you won out with Jim Harrison," Marcy advised. Davey was completely without guile. He knew perfectly well that Soaks was merely biding her time to get in a few more digs, although Marcy had tried to smooth things over by having a frank talk. Emma had asked Marcy coldly if she didn't mind her husband holding hands with another girl, and Marcy had retorted: "It didn't mean a thing, and you know it. David'd hold hands with you, Emma, if he thought you needed it. It's the way David is and the way I like him." Soaks had retorted that that Snow girl was a deep one, she could soften up a wooden Indian; but of course if Marcy didn't care . . . The gray-walled living room began suddenly to go round and round in such dizzy circles that Marcy staggered, and had to sit down in the big chair. David said firmly, "I'm going to phone right now for an appointment for you at the doctor's."

It was nice being taken care of. After David had made the appointment for three that afternoon, he picked Marcy up, carried her back to their bed, pulled the coverlet anxiously up to her chin. "Now, rest," he ordered. "I wish I didn't have to go to the hospital this morning, but Mrs. Huse, the contralto, is having an operation; she wants to see me before she goes upstairs at eleven. I'm having luncheon with Henry Gratz. . . ."

"Davey," Marcy asked out of the blue, "if someone in the parish were dying, maybe, and I needed you too, badly . . . which would you choose?"

"I wouldn't have to choose. I always take you with me." David bent to kiss her. Would he actually put his job first? Probably. She murmured, burying her face in the pillow so he wouldn't see her lips tremble. "Oh, run along Davey. I'm all right. I feel drowsy."

She waited until David had tiptoed out through the living room and had closed her door carefully before she rushed into the bathroom, and was ill. She remembered between gasps that she'd have to phone Louella Gratz she couldn't come to tea that afternoon. It was too bad, for Louella had hinted at church last Sunday that David should call more often; you had to get sick, Louella chattered, to rate a visit from the assistant minister. So Marcy had asked brightly, quickly, wouldn't she do? Was the church only for students, the poor and the sick? "The rich need religion too," Marcy had pointed out to David, but he'd only laughed, said that all Louella needed was to wash the kitchen floor to sweat off some of that fat. Marcy reminded him that Louella didn't have a kitchen; she and Henry ate downstairs in the hotel dining room. Louella wasn't selfish, really, just empty-headed, like Sally Lou at home.

That afternoon, Marcy, knee-deep in happiness, walked home from Dr. Sturgis's office on Commonwealth Avenue across the Gardens to Beacon Hill. "Nearly everybody has a baby," she scolded herself for feeling so special. But this would be Peter Andrew! She would wheel his carriage here on the smooth tidy walks; even if the frost had nipped everything so that the neat flowerbeds were bare, the children in their bright red, blue, and green snowsuits blossomed in the gray afternoon. Marcy smiled at a little boy in a dark blue suit with a red cap, riding the base of a dead statesman's proud statue, yelling, "Giddap, horsey!" to the iron mare high above him. Once she'd felt sorry for those hemmed-in city children, but now she understood that the horizons of childhood knew no boundaries. Peter Andrew'd play here, too, when he grew bigger. How was she going to break the big news? "Davey, you'll have to stay home tonight. I have something to tell you. This is our night. . . ."

Everything might have turned out quite differently, if

David had only come home alone that afternoon, if Marcy could have told him right off about Peter Andrew. Coming into the hot apartment from the cold air made her head whirl again, so she threw off her clothes, and flung herself in her dressing gown across the bed to wait for him. Wonderful and mysterious. Peter Andrew wasn't anywhere, then suddenly, out of your love, he was! She'd lie there quietly till Davey rushed in to ask what the doctor had said, and then she'd grin, "Davey, you remember about the twelve apostles? Well . . ."

The persistent knocking roused her from a sleep so deep it was almost a stupor. Drowsily, Marcy, her hair tousled, throwing on her old dark-blue dressing gown, sleepwalked unwillingly to the door. "Hi, there!" Serena beamed. She was still in her blue- and-white-striped uniform with her nurse's blue cape with its bright red lining flung over it. "I didn't have time to change . . . Oh, goodness," at Marcy's blank stare, "don't tell me David forgot to tell you he asked me to dinner tonight! He was over to see a patient at the hospital early this morning. My mouth's been watering all day. The salads for the hospital help are mostly hay."

"I did forget, and so what?" David beamed, coming up behind her in the dark corridor so that Serena looked over her shoulder to smile up at him; but his eyes were on the drooping Marcy. He asked anxiously, "Hello, sweet. What did the doctor say?"

It was all spoiled. You couldn't share Peter Andrew with Serena; you simply wouldn't. "I'm fine—just overtired, I reckon. Come in, you two. I look like a hag. I'm sorry; I haven't even started dinner."

"Think nothing of it," Serena caroled. "I have a mean hand with a can opener, and Ma's daughter couldn't help being a cook." She was hanging her cape in the closet, completely at home. Marcy drew her old dressing gown closer about her. Did Serena have to look so radiantly healthy in her starched uniform? Her bright hair was smooth, perfect, as if she'd just come from the hairdresser, Marcy thought, pushing her own tumbled damp curls back from her aching forehead. "Go lie down, Marcy," Serena urged. "David can show me where the things are I can't find."

Sure David could, Marcy thought miserably, lying there looking at her slightly green face in the dresser mirror at the foot of her bed. She felt worse and worse, listening to the two of them laugh in the tiny kitchenette. You'd think they were the ones who were married! "Give me that can of fish chowder up there on the top shelf," Serena was ordering. "Got any onions? Salt pork?" "Onions coming up," David boomed. "They're under the sink—hey, look out! Did I bump you?" They couldn't help rubbing shoulders in that tiny kitchen. Were you really jealous? Marcy wondered. Certainly you were. If you'd known that marrying a minister meant marrying the whole parish, so that even the most important thing that ever would happen to you and David had to be set aside till it was tasteless, flat as a bottle of unstoppered gingerale. . . .

"Soup's on, Marcy," Serena called. "Or do you want me to bring yours on a tray?"

"No. I'll come out." As Marcy slid into her place at the card table David had covered with her best embroidered lunch cloth it took hours to iron, she thought wearily that anyone with a grain of sense, seeing how she felt, would have gone along home . . . Serena proved to be a wonderful hand at whipping up a Lucullan feast out of cans. David took one taste, roared happily: "Real Bellport fish muddle! Tastes as if you'd just hauled in that haddock on a line!"

"I did," Serena assured him, her sea-green eyes sparkling. "He was a whopper."

David never ate anything she cooked that way, in great grateful gulps; Marcy regarded her own bowl with distaste. She'd never really liked the smell of fish. She dipped in her spoon, holding herself rigid, hoping she wouldn't disgrace herself by having to run from the table. Serena and David, unnoticing, were swapping stories about Maine. "Did you ever go to the Boothbay Harbor fish wharf when the tuna boats come in?" David asked, and she countered, "Did you ever get becalmed in a fog, out near Seguin? It's weird, like fighting a cloud." Serena explained kindly to Marcy that Seguin was a turtle-shaped rock, eleven miles offshore, but that the island had a first-class Light. David said all Maniacs were silent as rocks; once he'd spent all morning hauling traps with a lobster man in his dory, and all he'd said for five hours was, "Ayuh"; to which Serena retorted if you had nothing to say it was wiser not to say it.

David chuckled that there was nothing like Maine, but Marcy would gladly have given it back to the Indians, sight unseen. Serena finally sensed her hostess' growing uneasiness when they were left alone while David bought some chocolate ice cream for dessert at the corner drugstore.

"You didn't feel well enough for me to stay tonight, did you, Marcy?" Serena murmured apologetically. "Something you ate?"

"No. I just feel kind of queer, floating . . ."

But Serena wasn't really listening. She sighed, "Davo's such a dear!"

Sure, he was. Just because Serena'd known him before you had, didn't give her an option on him. The two of them tonight, laughing together, joking about a place you'd never even seen, leaving you out . . . his own wife, about to bear his child. A red mist of anger swirled about Marcy so that the words burst out before she could stop them: "You're a nurse; can't you see I'm going to have a baby? And I can't get Davey alone long enough to tell him!"

"I'm terribly sorry." Serena's face had gone very white. She stumbled toward the hall closet, flung her nurse's cape over her shoulders blindly, inside out, so that she looked like all the blazing beauty in the world. She told the miserable Marcy: "I hope you'll be very happy. Having a baby's the nicest thing that can happen to two people who love each other."

Marcy burst out, impulsively: "Then why do you leave your son up at the Light? Why don't you keep him with you?"

Serena wanted to scream at her, "It's none of your business!" But she mustn't make trouble between David and his wife. She moved swiftly toward the door before she said something she shouldn't. But she couldn't help the bitterness she felt looking at this woman who had everything, a husband, a baby she could own before the world. "Don't worry, Marcy. I won't bother you and your Davey again!"

She was gone down the hall before the penitent Marcy could get to the door, call after her, "Serena, forgive me! Come back . . . please, come back. . . ." Marcy, dizzy, held onto the doorknob, wondering what she was going to tell David. That she'd failed again in kindness, understanding? Oh, my goodness, she was going to be sick again! When David got back with the chocolate ice cream, she was too ill to tell him anything; all he could do was to hold her poor head until the attack passed. It was almost worth being so sick to have him thinking only of her; yet, Marcy had planned to tell him so gaily about Peter Andrew, but now she had to gasp out her big news between bouts of terrible nausea. He carried her, exhausted, back to bed, and lay down beside her, holding her hand until she dropped off to sleep.

Marcy was a strong, healthy girl; in a few weeks the sickness had passed, and she felt better than ever before in her life.

"There's a bloom on you," David told her, wonderingly. "You couldn't be prettier but you are!"

The nicest part of being pregnant was that he wanted to

be with her every moment he could snatch from his work. They bought a little tree, decorated it with bright balls from the Five and Dime, and piled the enticing packages from Texas beneath it. But when Christmas Eve came, David was furious because they were expected to go to dinner at the Gratzes. "If you could be just a little sick, we could phone," he told Marcy hopefully.

"Now who's telling fibs?" she teased him. "Of course we're going: Louella'd have your job if we didn't. We can open Momi's packages later. Did I tell you I waited to write to them about Peter Andrew? I told Momi, 'This is my Christmas present! To all of us.' "

"Momi'll buy out the whole baby counter," David prophesied happily. His eyes lighted. "Isn't that a new dress?"

She looked like the Spirit of St. Nicholas herself in her bright red dress, with her shining eyes, her curls that danced when she turned her head quickly so that the holiday earrings she had made herself out of tiny bells tinkled.

"It was Louella's," Marcy explained. "I made it over. She'll love it." Marcy whirled to let David see how the skirt flared about her slim lovely legs, full enough to hide anything.

What David didn't understand was that the parish *like* to give to the minister's family as long as it didn't really cost them much. It had made Louella feel warm, big-hearted, giving this dress she didn't need. Marcy flung herself against her big husband, fitted her curly head into the hollow of his shoulder where she belonged. "Give me a Christmas Eve kiss and then let's go."

The Gratzes' big apartment was overpoweringly noisy when they arrived at the second floor of the Hotel Vendôme. Nearly forty people were already milling around the huge red-papered living room when Marcy and David came in, late. Louella's bare arms, bulging out of her green satin sheath gown, rattled expensively as she greeted them, and the diamonds on her fingers and in her ears sparkled like Christmas tinsel, but of course they were real. Marcy looked around her at the mantel bright with poinsettias, at the Christmas tree filling the bay window, so thickly hung with silver and so blue with lights it was impossible to tell if it was a real tree or not.

"Just like a photographer's window! Where they stick that iron thing into the back of your neck and say, 'Smile, please!' " Marcy chuckled.

"Merry Christmas," David beamed at Soaks, who took his outstretched hand, then dropped it limply after a moment. Her black uniform had a new delicately hemstitched white silk holiday collar and cuff set.

Marcy admired, "How nice you look, Emma!"

Emma smiled at her. "They ought to put you up on the tree!"

"That's the nicest thing anyone ever said to me!" Marcy cried.

"Glad to see you here, folks!" Henry Gratz boomed, bustling up with Jim and Sara Harrison in tow. Henry was fat, boisterous, perspiring because of the loud green and red checked wool vest he wore under his jacket. "Round stomach with good capon lined," Marcy remembered vaguely from her schooldays. Henry was rather a dear.

"Hello, you two!" Jim Harrison greeted affectionately, and Sara smiled at Marcy and David over the din of conversation. Her brown dress had elbow sleeves and a modest V neck, but with the sprig of holly stuck into the knot of her dark hair she was quietly festive. Looking at Sara's perfection, Marcy wished she hadn't worn quite so red a dress, but Jim Harrison's gray eyes were twinkling at her admiringly.

"I hope David's going to take you up on the Hill for the carol singing later. It's one of our nicest local customs. Do you have carol sings in Texas?"

"We go you one better. We even have firecrackers! Tomorrow morning all the pickaninnies will wake the family up yelling at the back screen door, 'Chris'mas gif'! Chris'mas gif'!'" Her lips trembled suddenly, unexpectedly, and David's hand closed firmly upon hers. Marcy's first Christmas away from home; but it was their first one together, too. If they could only get out of this bedlam, be alone . . . David asked Jim abruptly, "How soon can we leave here, decently?"

"Not till after the presents, I'm afraid," Jim murmured. "Henry plays Santa after dinner, but Louella picks out the gifts for everyone. Last year I got a black velvet smoking jacket."

"But I thought . . ."

Jim's eyes twinkled. "No, I don't smoke. But the jacket must have cost a fortune. Louella's always generous."

So was the dinner, served in the big main hotel dining room with its many damask-covered tables, flashing silver, and its enormous wreaths at the windows tied with yards of red ribbon. Louella had outdone herself on the menu. Course followed course of magnificent food which came to a climax with a triumphant waiter bearing aloft a big silver platter upon which reposed a whole piglet with an apple in its mouth. Henry, stunned, said he wouldn't carve that little creature, he'd feel like a murderer; but Louella explained coyly, "You know my people are English, Henry darling!" She added hastily before he could argue, " 'Way back."

Marcy's head had begun to ache again, but after they were replete, glassy-eyed with too much food, they all trooped upstairs again for the tree. Marcy was wishing she'd sent Louella a twenty-five-cent Christmas card instead of a five-cent one when she heard her own name called.

"Marcy, darling, open up one of those silver balls on the tree, see what you find!" Louella shrilled.

"Me?" Marcy, feeling awkward but knowing Peter Andrew

could not possibly show yet with her full skirt, reached up and took down a silver ball. "Unroll it!" Louella ordered. Marcy did so obediently, stared down, startled, at the dollar bill in her hand. "Try another one!" There was a second dollar bill inside the next silver ball, and then another and another until Marcy lost count. Louella began to count aloud, and the others joined in, chanting, "Twenty . . . thirty . . . forty . . . forty-nine, fifty dollars in the silver balls!" Louella triumphantly announced her surprise gift for the assistant minister and his wife for Christmas. Marcy, standing there helplessly clutching dollar bills, torn between laughter and nervous tears, gasped, "It's too much! But, thank you, Louella." Suddenly the familiar dizziness came over her, and she swayed.

"Come on, darling. You're not well, we're going home!" David rushed up to take his wife's arm. He was scowling, his eyes black with anger. David seldom lost his temper, but when he did . . . She'd better get him out of here, fast. Marcy put up a hand to her head, murmuring to Louella, "I really do think . . . if you'll excuse us?"

Louella said stiffly, "Well, of course, if you're ill . . ." The giving of gifts from the tree had just begun, and the young minister and his wife were ruining her big surprise. Louella followed Marcy into the bedroom to help her with her wraps, but it was obvious Henry's wife was upset, disappointed. Marcy explained impulsively: "Louella, I want you to be the first in the church to know. It's a baby . . . but don't tell anyone just yet, will you?"

"Darling!" Louella gasped, placated. "How marvelous! I'll be silent as the tomb. Go right home and lie down. One can't be too careful."

Now she'd told Louella, the news about Peter Andrew would be all over the parish before midnight, Marcy thought ruefully as David guided her down the hotel's white marble staircase. The doorman had barely closed the big glass doors behind them before David exploded, "Why didn't that old harridan change the bills into pennies, make you crawl for them?"

"Davey!" Marcy gasped, trying to keep up with him on the snowy sidewalk. "She meant all right. I didn't mind."

"Well, I did! Charity makes me boil! You'd think a man wasn't worthy of his hire. This was worse that the 'pound parties' the parish used to have for my folks. At least they'd stay to eat up most of the food themselves! If St. Luke's wanted to raise my salary, why didn't they send us a check?"

Marcy had never seen him so upset. She slid her hand soothingly into his, reminding him practically: "Fifty dollars is fifty dollars. Look at all the crowds of people. . . . I hear carols! Let's walk down the avenue, up to the Hill. Davey, quit scowling. It's Christmas Eve!"

Beacon Hill was as magnificent as Jim Harrison had promised, Marcy saw, delighted, as she and David strolled along, hand in hand, stumbling over the uneven icy bricks. The stars shone frosty clear over the shadowy trees on the Common, and made wreath of jewels in the dark sky above the chimneys of the ancient brick houses. Most of the snow had been shoveled away, but there were patches of silver ice gleaming on the sidewalks where the lights from the solid blocks of housefronts spilled out, for each window in every house was ablaze with Christmas decorations. For once, staid Boston had not drawn down its shades but left them up, inviting every stranger's eye to come inside and be at home, to rejoice together in the birthday of a Little Boy. For whole blocks, every window up to the third or fourth floor shone softly with candles. "Prayers of the saints," David said, dreamily, watching the small pointed flames, squeezing Marcy's gloved hand warm in his. Wreaths and Christmas trees bright with expensive fruits of gold, silver, red and blue and yellow blazed in the windows, where heavy draperies were drawn back to show masses of red and white poinsettias. One breath-taking window of red and white roses and chrysanthemums was lighted only by a great Star.

> " 'God rest you merry, gentlemen,
> Let nothing you dismay,
> Remember Christ our Saviour
> Was born on Christmas Day. . . .' "

A group of heavily sweatered and snow-booted young people had stopped there to sing, laughing and friendly. David joined in eagerly, his golden tenor soaring above the rest so that a red-capped girl beckoned them closer, linked her arm in Marcy's. "Sing!" she cried. "Merry Christmas!"

"God rest you merry . . ." A queer old phrase, worn smooth by the centuries. English? Not Bostonian or Texan, surely; it belonged to everybody, like Christmas. As Marcy sang, too, she felt suddenly warm, wanted, and at peace. No longer a homesick Johnny Reb in a dam-Yankee town. Boston had opened its arms to her on Christmas Eve, and the age-old charm of its quiet houses shone out on the light of the candles. Beacon Hill wasn't a place, really; it was a feeling of permanence, of roots, of singing familiar carols with friends. The trouble had been, she admitted honestly, you had to open your windows, too, to let the candlelight in. You had everything tonight that a woman could want. Next Christmas, Peter Andrew would be here. . . .

> " 'O tidings of comfort and joy . . .' "

"Let's go home, David," Marcy urged as the carolers strolled on.

As they came in the front door, and snapped on the overhead lights, David bent to pick up the yellow envelope of a telegram pushed under the door.

"The folks saying 'Merry Christmas,'" Marcy sparkled, tearing open the yellow envelope with eager fingers. They hadn't forgotten her, after all. But as she read, the color drained out of her face.

"Anything wrong at home, darling?" David demanded, worried.

"Sam and Li'l Emily!" Marcy gasped. She handed him the telegram.

> "Emily and I married today. We want you two to be the first to know because you're responsible. Peter Andrew decided us. Every man needs a son. Love to you both.
>
> SAM

Chapter Eight

Aaron, Abaddon, Abagtha! David swore, fiercely, silently, as he sat numbed with fatigue and worry in the hospital lobby. Outside, the June morning was shouting with birdsong and sunshine, but in here was dim, lamp-lit silence, muted anguish as he waited for word from upstairs. It was criminal that Marcy had to bear this whole business alone, that he couldn't lift a finger to help her. . . . *Abana, Abarim, Abda* . . . David's cuss words came from the concordance of his Bible and from the depths of his seething anger at the unfairness of nature's inflexible loneliness for mothers. *Abdi, Abdiel* . . . It wasn't the actual words but the intent that made blasphemy, David had explained once to Marcy, and she'd laughed, "Sometimes you're an awful idiot but . . . oh, Davey, I do love you!" If only he knew what was happening to her . . . The nurse was beckoning! David leaped toward the desk where she sat, only to realize it was the tall man next to him twisting his newspaper to shreds who was wanted. "Soon, probably, Mr. Gallant," the nurse soothed. "She's in the delivery room." David sat down again, shut his eyes, made himself go as far as *Tabitha.* . . .

"Mr. Gallant? Congratulations!" David stared up at the nurse wildly, as if he'd never seen her before, as she smiled. "You have a fine boy: eight pounds, six ounces. Mrs. Gallant's in good shape too, but she's tired. The doctor says he'd prefer you didn't see them until later. All right?"

"All right?" David yelled. "It's wonderful!"

He rushed out of the lobby, down the steps where the sunshine, golden, glorious, was gilding even the hospital's sooty old walls, while up above the chimneys in the blue meadow of the sky little white lambs of clouds were woolly and soft as a child's toy.*Zorah and Zuzima!* He'd forgotten to

buy any birthday presents! He bought Marcy an armload of
tiny yellow roses and Peter Andrew a pink elephant with blue
bead eyes before he remembered to wire to Texas. Then,
clutching his purchases, he walked home across the Common.

"I have a son!" David marveled. He wanted to shout it to
the passers-by, their heads bent, hurrying, unseeing; to the
news vendor at the subway entrance; to the rheumy-eyed old
men shuffling their worn-booted feet along the concrete
sidewalks instead of merely polishing the wooden benches
with the seats of their shiny pants, as if, on this verdant
spring morning, new life had seeped into even their ancient
bones. That poor shaky fellow over there with the whisky-
veined nose and jerking hands . . . he hadn't much further to
go. Would he kick off his tattered body, his grimy, ill-fitting
clothes, to rise like that red balloon some child must have
loosed, bobbing and soaring ecstatically above the new green
leaves of the elms? "In this flesh shall I see God. . . ." But
surely not in that abused, shamed body. "But we shall be
changed . . ." Changed till we shall be able to hold up our
heads, worthy to face the Eternal. Perhaps babies like Peter
Andrew were sent, waving little blind hands helplessly, eyes
blinking but not focusing, depending completely upon loving
care, to remind us that spiritual growth starts blindly, too,
with only faith. Hey, you could preach that some Sunday!
Peter Andrew had already given you a text for your sermon,
bless him!

David hurried toward home to be sure that everything
would be ready when his wife and son came back. Momi had
sent enough baby clothes, blankets ,and sanitary equipment
to stock a store, let alone one small baby, but the crib Sara
Harrison had promised for Peter Andrew had not yet arrived.
How long would it be before it was needed? A week or two,
the doctor had said. If the crib wasn't there by then . . .
David found the door to his apartment open and Sara

Harrison, a serene brown pheasant in a brown suit and a hat with an orange feather, superintending the delivery man setting up the crib.

"Put it here in the bedroom between the big bed and the wall," Sara was saying as David came in. She took one look at his radiant face and came, beaming, to offer both her hands. "Congratulations! How are they?"

"It's a boy," David told her. "They're both fine. What a lovely crib! And it just fits."

"It ought to. I measured the space and had it especially made," Sara told him. "Jim's hoping to get you a raise with the board, by spring, so you can have a bigger apartment. See the little duck? Isn't it cute?"

The yellow fluffy duck painted on one end of the bed was so lifelike it almost quacked. It was a silly, adorable, crazy little yellow duck. . . . David was startled to see tears in Sara's eyes. "We always wanted a son. I suppose we could have adopted one, but Jim's away so much I was afraid to try to raise a child alone." She wiped her eyes, smiled at David. "Do you think Marcy will need a nurse when she comes home? I'd be glad to pay for—I mean, you wouldn't mind, would you? You two are almost part of our family."

David said gently, "It's very good of you, Sara."

"I'll call the hospital, as soon as you know just when Marcy is leaving the hospital," Sara planned. "I wish we could get the Snow girl, but she hasn't finished training. She hasn't been to church for ages."

David frowned. Though Serena'd been four months at the Worcester State Hospital, she'd been back in Boston for weeks. Her absence had worried him too, and not only at the church; he'd missed her gay visits to the apartment to see them. She could have given Marcy pointers on baby care. Even when he'd seen her at the hospital lately, Serena had always been busy: he hadn't really talked to her since that last

time when she'd made the chowder for their dinner. Student
nurses were terribly rushed, naturally; they had to study when
they had a little leisure, and they needed to sleep, but Rene
had always seemed to like coming to see him and Marcy. Rene
needn't have just walked out on them without a word; she
hadn't even sent a Christmas card. What was Sara Harrison
saying?

"Let me know the day before Marcy comes home, and I'll
stock up with food, milk, and things."

"I don't know what we'd do without you, Sara," David
said gratefully. Nevertheless, he was guiltily glad when Sara
left and he could be alone to hug his happiness to himself.
Having Marcy had been more than he deserved, but having
Peter Andrew safely here, too . . . He hadn't really understood the Trinity before, how three people could be one. How
soon could he go to see Marcy and his new son? "Later."
This afternoon, when Marcy was out of the anesthesia. He
didn't mind waiting too much. Very small babies had always
terrified him with their fragility.

Marcy was sitting up in bed that afternoon, proudly holding Peter Andrew, when David arrived. His son appeared to
be mostly blue blanket, small red face with monkey wrinkles,
closed eyes, groping tiny red paws. "Isn't he beautiful,
Davey?" Marcy's blue ribbon matched Peter Andrew's
blanket, held back her cloud of dark curls; her lashes were
fragile fans on her flushed cheeks as she stroked back the dark
fuzz from Peter Andrew's damp little forehead and smiled up
at David radiantly. "See how close his ears are to his head? And
he has your long artist's fingers. . . . Here, you hold him,
Daddy!" David held out his arms gingerly, and the warmth
inside the blue blanket made his son real, at last.

"Hasn't he got an awfully big mouth?" David asked to
hide his overwhelming pride. "Look at him yawn! Practically
a manhole you could fall into."

"David Gallant, he has not! He's just starved, and no wonder: they don't give him anything to eat for twenty-four hours. The doctor says I'll have plenty of milk for him; thank goodness, we won't have to fuss with formulas. Open your eyes, sonny, so your doubting father can see how beautifully blue they are."

David bent lower to look as Peter Andrew blinked rapidly, said "Yah!" and hit his father in the eye with his tiny red fist. Both parents laughed proudly. "He's hungry and mad and I don't blame him," Marcy crooned, holding out her arms. David gingerly kissed the dark fuzz on his son's small head, and handed him back as if he were a cobweb. Marcy murmured, "Isn't it nice, being a family?"

The nurse came for Peter Andrew, then appeared with a basin, and David took the hint that he was in the way. As he left, reluctantly, Marcy called after him: "Come in about ten tomorrow morning, why don't you? Pete will be trying out his new built-in lunch cart."

David spent the evening scrubbing the little apartment so that it would be spotless when Marcy and Peter Andrew came home. Momi, Paw, and Li'l Emily would want to come North to visit the first grandchild. You couldn't take Peter Andrew there, Texas was so hot in the summer. . . . Camp Bowie used to broil in the sun. David, glancing around the tiny space, decided that a cellar apartment had one advantage; in hot weather it would be cooler. He tried the tiny crib with the duck painted on the footboard in one corner of the living room, then in another, and finally put it back in the overcrowded bedroom. Foolish little yellow duck with no quack.

David went to sleep smiling, and slept so deeply content he didn't hear the phone ring at first. When the sound finally got through to him, David staggered sleepily into the living room, and lifted the receiver. "Yes?"

"Mr. Gallant? David?" It was Dr. Sturgis! Was anything

wrong at the hospital? David came wide awake instantly, his heart beginning to pound, his throat so dry he could hardly gasp, "Marcy? Is she—" Dr. Sturgis broke in hastily to say that Marcy was fine but that the baby was having difficulty breathing, so the nurse had sent for him. He'd put the baby into an oxygen tent but he wasn't satisfied. "I'd like to call in a pediatrician, if you agree?"

"Of course," David mumbled, terrified. If another doctor was to be called in after midnight, Peter Andrew must be pretty sick. "I'll be right over as soon as I can get my clothes on," David said, and flung down the phone.

Later, David had no memory of dressing or of running down the Hill toward the hospital, only of how the cruelly bright light over the desk in the waiting room hurt his eyes when he rushed inside. The doctor was there waiting. The older man looked drained, tired, as he laid his hand compassionately on David's shoulder. "How is he?" David gasped. "What does the pediatrician—"

"My dear boy, I'm so sorry," Dr. Sturgis interrupted heavily. "We really did do everything we could." He ought to be steeled to this, he thought, but he never was.

Did. David was falling into an icy well that froze his whole body, his thoughts. He tried twice before he could croak, "You mean—Peter Andrew's—"

"Yes. He's gone, David." There was no way to gloss over the terrible truth, and this boy had to take it. He was a preacher, wasn't he? It was "Physician heal thyself," and God knew that wasn't easy. The doctor rubbed his tired hands over his eyes in order not to watch David's lips move in and out, his fight to control himself. Dr. Sturgis murmured: "His lungs filled up. We don't know exactly why. The nurse went in to check, and the baby was choking. Perhaps in twenty years we may know the answer to what happened."

David's hands were clenched so hard they ached. "Marcy . . . Mrs. Gallant . . . does she know?"

"No. We let her sleep. She's not too strong. Do you want me to tell her when she wakes?" the doctor offered.

The roaring in David's ears made it hard to concentrate. "No," he decided finally. "But thank you." He straightened his big shoulders. "I—I'll take a little walk. Then I'll . . . Marcy and I had better be together when she hears."

He stumbled down the hospital steps into the early morning. The sun was pink behind the chimney tops, a banner of light, but inside David it was still night, black, unreasoning panic at the thought of telling Marcy that Peter Andrew was dead. He'd been so much alive, hitting you with his tiny soft fist. You'd held him only once in your arms, and now . . . It couldn't be true! It was too cruel. "Father, if it be possible, let this cup pass from me. . . ." But even as David prayed, he knew, as had the Man at Gethsemane, that it wasn't possible. The chalice was already at his lips, and he must drink its bitter brew with faith or else his whole ministry was a mockery. How smugly he'd preached to other panic-stricken parents! But why did He have to take back *Peter Andrew*? If what David believed was true—and it *had* to be—*the Lord was holding Peter Andrew right now in His arms.* Why was this such small comfort? So hard to believe? Thomas had waited to be convinced, had had to have something tangible. "Lord, I believe; help thou my unbelief." David cried in his heart, one tender father to another, "Into thy hands I commit my only son. . . ." But he still felt numb, heavy-hearted. His prayer seemed to mount no higher than his head; he might have been mumbling to himself.

David was unaware that he hadn't shaved, that a lock of his fair hair stood up on the back of his head and that there were dark shadows under his eyes as he walked into Marcy's room later that morning. "Hi, Davey. You're a few minutes

early. The banana wagon with the babies hasn't come yet."
Her blue nightgown made her eyes deeper blue as she smiled
up at him; the smile faded. "Davey, what's the matter with
you?"

How could he tell her? But he had no choice. David held
both her hands as he told her as gently as he could that Peter
Andrew wouldn't be coming for his first breakfast. Marcy
stared at him, her eyes dilating as she pulled away her hands.
"No, no!" She was trembling all over. "The wagon's coming
down the hall now. I can hear him yelling. . . . I reckon I'd
know my own baby's voice!"

"Oh, my dear . . ."

"Nurse! Nurse! I want my baby!"

Marcy shook off his detaining hand, started to get out of
bed, to run into the corridor as the head nurse and Marcy's
own ward nurse came hurrying into her room. The pity she
saw in their eyes convinced her as no words could have done.
"Now, Mrs. Gallant," the nurse urged, "just lie back down."
Marcy twisted away. "Leave me alone!"

David picked her up, laid her back on the bed, held her
with his big soothing, gentle hands. "Listen, my darling . . ."
The nurse slid something shining into Marcy's arm, and
gradually her gasping breaths that were tearing at David's
own throat grew slower.

"She'll sleep now," the nurse murmured. "It's the best
thing for her." She glanced up at the haggard David. "You
should get some rest, too, Mr. Gallant. She's going to need
you when she wakes up."

But Marcy didn't want David later; she didn't want anything except to be left alone. It was almost as if she herself—
the part of her that mattered—had gone away with Peter
Andrew, David worried uneasily, looking down at her lying
there so still, refusing to talk, even to eat. She'd lain there
that way all day, with closed eyes, her lovely color gone and

her face strangely shrunken so that he saw how she'd look when she was old, haggard, but with the bones of her face still beautiful.

"If she doesn't relax soon, we're in for trouble," Dr. Sturgis said to David. "If she'd only let go, cry . . ."

He had to get through to her, David knew desperately, tell her that having Peter Andrew for just a short while, for only twenty-four hours, wasn't wasted. Did he really believe this himself? Nine months, and then this . . . David stroked back the wet curls from her hot forehead, murmuring, "But we're still a family. 'For this my son who was dead and is alive again . . .' "

"Spare me the texts, David," Marcy interrupted wearily. When she opened her eyes they were almost black with drugs, the eyes of a stranger.

Had he been smug? He hadn't meant to be. He was lonely, confused, begging with every fiber of his being for her to come back to him, for certainty in his own mind. Telling yourself the same things over and over didn't make them real.

Marcy murmured: "Would you mind going now, David? I want to sleep."

David, not Davey. But the little cross still hung on its slender chain around her neck. "October 18, 1917." Did it seem eons ago to her, too?

If only she could sleep again, deeply, quietly, David worried as he tiptoed out of her room; but not all the drugs science had discovered could reach this dreadful aloneness, hers and his. But Marcy would have to find her own God for herself. Not even he who loved her so desperately could help her. There was no rest that did not come from within.

Yet, in spite of his own turmoil of mind, David kept doggedly trying to prick Marcy alive. It was kinder to give her pain than to let her shut herself up this way in bitterness. If only they could search for comfort, together . . .

"What do you want me to do with the little crib with the duck, darling?" he asked her, deliberately, a few mornings later. "Lend it to someone? Or put it into the storeroom till we need it again, maybe?"

She shuddered, "I'll never go through this again. Give it to Emma for someone."

"Momi'll be here tomorrow," David announced, not arguing. He couldn't say, "for the funeral"; the words wouldn't come; they were too final, too cruel. "We'll have to decide. . . . Do you want Peter Andrew sent back to the family lot in Fort Worth? Or shall we buy a lot here?"

"What does it matter?" Marcy said stonily. "He's dead."

"He's alive," David told her, trying to convince himself, too. " 'Their angels do always behold the face of my Father. . . .' "

Marcy's eyes were enormous, empty. "You really believe that, don't you? Well, I don't. Peter Andrew was too little. It's wicked, I tell you." Her lips twisted bitterly. "You say the Lord is kind. How could He be if He took Peter Andrew? Why did He send him at all, if He was going to snatch him right back? *I don't believe He knows anything about it . . . or cares. Aunt Riah was right; we are animals. We're born and die like them. What's the use of kidding yourself?*"

His poor darling. . . . Marcy was frantic with shock, with loss, her poor breasts swollen with milk which was now no use to her small son. She looked so white, so small and ill. She didn't mean what she'd said. But as long as she thought this way, for her Peter Andrew was indeed dead. Was the reason he couldn't get through to help her that he himself was not sure? Was he only mouthing his faith, God pity them both? David, shaken to his soul, walked out into the corridor so blindly he almost bumped into Jim Harrison waiting there.

"Son," was all Jim Harrison said, but the rest was all in his voice. He laid his hand on David's shoulder, went quietly into Marcy's room, but came out at once, strode over to the desk urgently. "Nurse? I think she's fainted."

Marcy was unconscious for a week, too sick to know that Momi had arrived from Fort Worth or that the quiet little funeral had been held in St. Luke's chapel, where the sunlight fell through the high rose window in a coronet of red, blue, and purple onto the stone floor. Only Jim and Sara Harrison, Momi, Soaks, and David stood beside the mound of flowers under which Peter Andrew slept before the altar. "He isn't there," David's mind kept telling himself fiercely. "He isn't there. Oh, Marcy, my dear, my dear . . ." Someone was sobbing aloud, David realized dimly as Jim closed his book of prayer, ended the service. Of all people, it was Soaks!

David put a comforting arm along her shaking black shoulders. "You know, Soaksy," he soothed, "you've got the biggest family I know—sixty babies on the Cradle Roll!" Soaks sniffled, jerked away from him, and fled out the chapel door.

A few days later, when Marcy was more herself again, David told her how strangely Soaks had acted. Marcy asked, curious, "What did Soaks say when you said that?"

"She said, 'Do you have to be a complete fool?'" David reported ruefully.

"You don't know much about women, do you? Can you nurse a Cradle Roll? Rock it to sleep nights?"

David swallowed. This cynical, bitter stranger was not his Marcy; she didn't seem to care any more if he came to see her or not. As David, his big shoulders drooping, came out of her room, Momi was waiting for him, led him to a davenport in the hospital lobby.

"Sit down, son." It was the first time she'd ever called him that. "I want to talk to you about Marcy. She's only a child herself yet, David. She's still in shock, but she'll get over this. You'll have another child, but he'll never be quite the same as the first one." She hesitated, then went on slowly, feeling her way. "The doctor says Marcy's going to need care for quite a while. He says she can go back to Texas with me and

—and Peter Andrew when I go Monday, if we take her to
the sleeper in an ambulance. He thinks the complete change
of scene would be good for her right now. I'll be glad to pay
her fare. You've had a lot of expense you didn't count on."

"I can take care of my wife!" David flared. But could he?
Marcy'd been in the hospital so much longer than he had
expected, and the funeral expenses were piling up. Sara
Harrison had offered to lend whatever they needed; David
could pay her back, if he must. How could he let Marcy go?
Yet how could he not? Marcy needed sun, pampering, good
food, Aunt Riah's kind of loving care. . . . If only he could
go home with her! But someone had to go on earning cash
to keep the family going, pay the bills.

David told Momi stiffly, "I'll pay for her ticket and for
Peter Andrew." Momi's kind eyes met his with understanding, and he added, "But thanks, Mother." So the bonds were
sealed between them; it was the second wedding, that of two
generations.

The next day Marcy roused for the first time, asked the
nurse to call Dr. Harrison, to see if he could come to see her
at once, before she left for Texas. Would he be able to get
through the hard shell she'd crept into? David wondered
anxiously, pacing up and down the corridor while Jim was in
Marcy's room.

Jim Harrison came out into the corridor with pity in his
fine eyes, running his hand distractedly through his thick
silver-flecked hair. "Her mind is sick as well as her body,
David. But don't worry, she'll make it. Now's the time to
humor her . . . to love her."

David stared at the older man. Was he actually urging you
to love Marcy, you to whom she was dearer than life itself?

"She says she's tried, but has just made a mess of things.
She says she's no preacher's wife, no help to you. She wanted
you to get ahead, but she didn't believe especially in your job

in the church. She believed only in you, David Gallant. She says Sara warned her, but she just barged right ahead. I don't quite know what she's talking about; she's not very coherent."

"What does it matter?" David said heavily. But what Soaks thought did matter at St. Luke's, Jim Harrison knew. It mattered with Henry Gratz, urged on by Louella, probably. Henry and Soaks both had been at Jim to get "some well-known orators" to preach this summer while Jim and Sara were vacationing in Italy. "Big men who would fill the church, not just a green youngster," Soaks had insisted; but Jim had pointed out that David needed the money desperately, that to let him down now would be wanton cruelty. He must preach, go on acting as assistant minister, in fact as well as in title. Jim had won out, but he was willing to bet Soaks would find some pretext to make life hellish for David this summer. Jim Harrison sighed. Well, he had to go; he'd let Sara down so many times, promising her a real vacation and never giving it to her, and she had set her heart on seeing Rome again. He advised the troubled David: "Just give in to Marcy, no matter what foolish thing she says. It's all you can do for her just now."

But David could hardly believe it when Marcy announced firmly, that night: "I wish you wouldn't come to the station tomorrow, David; it'd be easier for us both if you don't. The ambulance and—and everything—will be fuss enough."

"Not come to see you off!" David gasped, so appalled that she shrugged. "Come if you want to."

"Naturally I want to! I may not see you again for weeks!"

But David and Marcy had very little time alone at the train, although Momi kept tactfully away from them as much as possible. As Marcy lay there in the narrow lower berth, her nervous, twisting hands were much too thin, almost transparent. David, impatient of the porter bustling up with more blankets, of people pushing by in the aisle, sat down on the edge of Marcy's berth to protect her as much as he could from curious eyes, but there seemed nothing to say. It was difficult to chatter trivialities with the knowledge heavy between them that up in the baggage car the small body of their son rode to his only inheritance from proud generations of other Mintons, a little plot of Texas earth. As the conductor yelled, "All Aboo-oord!" Marcy spoke feverishly, in a rush:

"David, I may never come back. I can't promise. If I can't believe what you do . . . honestly . . . it's no use going on. But I'll write, let you know."

"Not come back!" he gasped. He caught himself. He mustn't argue, upset her now, with the long journey ahead of her. "You're just worn out, darling, not yourself. . . ."

"Hurry, David!" Momi rushed up anxiously. "The train's moving!"

He had time only to brush Marcy's cheek with his frantic lips, run down the aisle, swing off the steps to the platform. He stood there, waving, a mechanical man, till the train was out of sight, though Marcy lying flat could not possibly have seen him through the window. She was sick; she didn't know what she was saying. But what if she did? The train was out of sight; *Marcy was gone.* David rushed blindly through the vast gray arches of the South Station, brushing people aside ruthlessly till he was outside, plunging into the street traffic while drivers yelled angrily and the Irish policeman roared at him in a rich brogue. David saw nothing but Marcy's white face, heard nothing but the incredible words echoing and re-echoing in his mind: "I may never come back. . . . I may *never come back. . . ." If he lost both Marcy and Peter Andrew . . .*

David walked and walked, tramping, plodding along for hours, not caring where he went, till finally, trembling with fatigue, he looked about, found himself on Tremont Street near the Common, under the brownstone shadow of St.

Paul's Cathedral. As the doors swung open, with people going inside, he could hear faint organ music; and because his legs would hold him up no longer David went into the strange church too, sank down upon the yielding red cushions of a dim pew. The organ stopped playing, and people slid to their knees as the priest began to pray aloud up at the high altar, his words falling richly upon David's ears: " 'Almighty God . . .' " Like most Methodist preachers, David didn't hold much with "canned prayers," but the words intoned from the Book of Common Prayer might have been meant especially for him since the beginning of time. " 'We entrust all who are near and dear to us to thy never-failing care and love. . . .' " The priest's voice swelled till it filled the nave of the great cathedral with faith and sureness, "both for this world and for the world to come, knowing that thou art doing for them better things than we can desire or pray for. . . .' "

"I am not alone," David realized humbly. "Despairing people have been praying thus for centuries. Age upon age has found the same need and the same God." When you looked down the long dim arch of the ages, your little self seemed very small, indeed. God's love, never-failing, infinite, enfolding your smallness in His greatness . . . *He was here. He was yours.* David slid to his knees upon the unaccustomed bench, covered his wet face with his big hands. He murmured humbly, "My Lord and my God . . ."

Chapter Nine

> "Out in the wind
> The dead leaves blow,
> Dry water running in a brook
> Of empty air;
> So in my heart is all desire dead.
> Yet days flow on,
> Dry leaves rustling November:
> Nor is there dawn nor dark,
> But only dusk. . . ."

"READY fo' yo' brekfus, Miss Marcy, honey?"

Marcy let the pad of paper with its scrawled verse slide from her languid fingers onto the white organdy bedspread as Aunt Riah's enormous bulk sidled through her bedroom door. Long, sleepless nights had taught Marcy to keep either a book handy, or paper and pencil to jot down the rhymes that she'd made desperately to keep from thinking. In the dark, memories could grow to nightmare strength she could throw off only by filling her mind with a spate of words. "Goodness, it's hot, Aunt Riah!" Well, August was almost gone. Marcy had been lying here seven—no, eight weeks.

Aunt Riah set the silver tray with the best rosebud china, and a lace-edged napkin, upon the bedside table, lifted the round silver cover, announcing, "Sarah September's Ruby snatched them aigs from the haylof' not ten minutes ago; 'n' I done make you a nomlet lighter'n a baby's bref."

Sarah September, Aunt Riah's eldest daughter, was just Marcy's age; Aunt Riah always named her children for the month they were born so she could keep track: Julia January and Freddy February. Marcy said firmly, "I just want coffee, black, please."

"Ain't nobuddy gwine git strong on coffee, coffee, coffee,"

Aunt Riah grumbled, stubbornly pouring the cup half full of cream, adding sugar, buttering cornpone lavishly. "Black coffee," Marcy insisted. Grumbling, Aunt Riah poured another cup, watched Marcy drink thirstily. The daily letter from Boston was right there on her tray, but Miss Marcy had made no move to open it. Aunt Riah asked, "How Mistuh David?"

"Fine. He brings God a big red apple every morning!"

"Quit talkin' dat way! Lightnin' strike you down, chile!"

Aunt Riah folded her big arms, glowered down at her charge, miserable among her lace pillows. "I done bury me four chilluns in the col', col' groun'. De Lord give, de Lord tuk away. Huccome you blame yo' man?" Marcy stared, unbelieving, as Aunt Riah rushed on, "It's true time I had ma' say. Ain't you ma baby? Same as Sarah September? Didn't I brung you into this worl'? Maybe ole Doc he'ped a mite, but 'twas me whopped you till you bawled, wrop' you in a blanket. . . . Home is where yo' man is at," Aunt Riah rolled on, stubborn as a tank. "You 'n' Mistuh David is young yit; you kin have you a whole passel o' young uns. . . ."

"Get out of here!" Marcy gasped.

"Yas'm." This was the first time her baby'd showed any spunk since she come home. Praise de Lord. "Yas, ma'am!" Anything was better than her just lying there, stiller'n mud. Aunt Riah picked up her silver tray, pushed her white cap further awry, and lumbered as far as the door before she said: "Miss Sally Lou downstairs. She brung you some mighty pretty posies. Shall I ask her to step up?"

"You know perfectly well I don't want to see anyone. Now get out of here!"

Marcy lay back panting, wiping her wet face; the stove-hot breeze ruffling the white organdy curtains gave promise of an even hotter day. She simply couldn't stand answering people's questions about her and David's future. How could she tell them anything when she didn't know the answers herself?

So the doctor had told Momi to humor her, to leave her alone
till she wanted to see her friends. She hadn't even seen Sam,
no one but the family. She glanced around the flower-filled
room, at the new books overflowing the shelf on the wall; it
was nice of the neighbors to send her things . . . and to stay
away themselves. That huge wilting bouquet of red roses on
the table came twice a week with no card, but she suspected
they were from Sam. She'd like to tell him not to send them,
but perhaps they came from Sam and Li'l Emily both. What
did it matter?

Marcy glanced wearily again at David's letter lying there
on her bed. She knew what was inside without opening it.
David loved her. When was she coming home? Yesterday
he'd caroled about the bright red geraniums in the Public
Gardens, flaming fire softened by the blue smoke of ageratum.
Marcy remembered walking there last fall, after the first surprise frost, when everything had turned black overnight. One
day the beds had been full of late asters, chrysanthemums,
pink, white, blue, pale lavender; to look at them was to soak
in color at every pore, but the very next day the beds held
only black sticks. A little girl in blue leggings had walked by
Marcy, asking her mother, "Where did all the flowers go,
Mommy?" and her mother had answered, "There was a black
frost last night, darling." A black frost had fallen on the magic
between Marcy and David, too.

Marcy shivered in spite of the heat, wishing the piping of
Sarah September's brood out in the back yard didn't hurt her
head so, but it was too much effort to get up, to call down to
them to play somewhere else. Sarah September already had
four children, two boys and twin girls, and she was exactly
your age; the two of you'd been close as sisters when you were
little. Aunt Riah had fed, scolded, petted you both im-
partially, put you together into the big white tub in the bathroom, a black baby at one end and a white baby at the other,
soaped you till you both yelled. She'd order, "Now splash

yo'se'fs clean, you calliopes!" You'd never even bathed Peter Andrew. You'd never run to pick him up, needing you, nor tucked him into his crib with the little yellow duck to keep him company in the dark. It wasn't fair. . . . Marcy buried her hot face in her pillow, clenching her damp fists.

"You awake, honey?" Li'l Emily's voice by the door was cautious, uncertain. "I knocked," she apologized, "but you didn't answer."

"I must have dozed off," Marcy murmured, turning over to smile unconvincingly. She'd given them all a bad time but she couldn't help it. Little things irritated her, a sudden noise, a curtain flapping.

A horn, as melodious as in an orchestra, blew impatiently outside the window in the back yard, and the children shrilled excitedly, "Do it again, Mistuh Sam!"

Li'l Emily told Marcy: "He shined up the brass on his car till it puts your eyes out. It's such a pretty day even if it is hot. A ride would give you a breeze. Won't you come with us to see the new house?"

"No, thanks." At the relief on Li'l Emily's face, Marcy said gently: "Don't worry, darling. I don't envy you your house. Or—anything. I'm glad for you."

Li'l Emily's face flared into sudden beauty, as she said steadily: "I love Sam; I always will. I want to ask you something. Have you really left David?" Scanning the unhappiness on Marcy's face, Li'l Emily added quickly, "It's none of my business, really, only . . ." Her dark eyes added: Sam is my business. But looking down at her sister lying there, Li'l Emily's eyes softened, and she laid her hand on Marcy's. "I feel like a pig being so happy while you . . . Do you still love me?"

"Of course," Marcy said wearily, patting Li'l Emily's hand. "Run along, darling. Have fun."

Marcy heard the Mercedes roar out of the yard. Maybe she should have gone, faced up to Sam and the rest once and for all. But she seemed to have lost all vitality, all urge to go on. She could look at David's letter lying there beside her on the bed where Aunt Riah had put it pointedly and feel nothing. Whatever magic she and David had known had dried up, tumbleweed in the wind. Would it have been any different if she'd married Sam? They had grown up together, liking the same things, riding, dancing, excitement. David's excitement was his preaching, his parish, things quite apart from you; he lived in other people's lives, rejoiced in their being born, baptized, married, yes, even in their dying with the faith that they were merely being born again. *Raw drama, only you couldn't go home when the curtain came down; tragedy lived intimately with you and David, night and day.* Why couldn't the parish let the parsonage be a real home, a place to retreat to, to lick your own wounds? A minister's wife had to laugh and cry to order, to be all things to all men no matter how her head or heart or feet ached; she had to go from a wedding to a funeral, from laughter to hot tears, and feel both sincerely. Marcy knew this now; knew that if she went back she'd have to share with David his eternal patience . . . listen to other people blurt out their troubles, push her own weariness aside; she would have to share her husband night and day till there was small energy left. Could she take this half-marriage again? Perhaps, if she cared enough for the things David did, had the faith to give. But she couldn't pretend; and she was so tired, so terribly tired.

Marcy reached for David's letter. He wrote every day, whether she answered or not. She slid her finger under the flap of the envelope.

"DARLING, I have news!

"The committee from Silverton were here today and asked me to be their new minister! Salary $2,500 and house. I told them I'd have to consult my good wife.

What do you say? Isn't it marvelous? A church of our own! Could one of Aunt Riah's brood come back with you, maybe, to wash dishes? Just imagine us able to afford a maid! Wire me, won't you?

"By the way, I met Serena on the street today and she says Dan Drexel, the chairman of the committee at Silverton, is the guy who bought Cap'n Poor's big house in Bellport. It's a small world. Serena got her nurse's cap and she's proud as Punch.

"Oh, my darling, when are you coming home?

"Your own DAVID"

He was so loyal, so good, so much better than she was. But being ashamed of yourself didn't warm you; it only made you colder, lonelier. What was she going to say to David? She saw then that there was another letter hidden under David's larger envelope, which she hadn't noticed before. She picked it up; Louella's bold scrawl was on the envelope. What could she want?

"DARLING LITTLE BRIDE:

"My heart bleeds for you! I asked your husband last Sunday when you were coming home and he said, 'When she's well enough!' I didn't need to be told that meant 'Never.' There's something you ought to know. Soaks and I saw your David yesterday with that *Snow woman*. They were on the sidewalk by the hospital, bright as brass, *laughing and talking*. My Henry says he wouldn't blame you at all if you got a divorce. Naturally David would never get another church, not here in New England. Soaks says she warned Jim not to let David preach this summer, but Dr. Harrison is *so kind*. . . .

Marcy's hands were shaking with anger. Louella was a fool. Give her a grain of sand, and she made a whole beach out of it. But if the Silverton committee got even an inkling of Louella's and Soaks' foolishness it would kill David's chances of getting the Silverton church. He needed her now as he never had before; nothing could scotch such crazy, underhanded whispering except his wife's going back to him. *Even if you couldn't bear to have David touch you any more, did you have any right to ruin him? Yet if you went back, feeling that way, David would know it at once. What were you going to do?*

"I brang you a neggnog, honey," Aunt Riah's voice coaxed behind her, holding out the brimming glass. Dear Aunt Riah, she'd always love you no matter what you said to her; she was earthy, kind and good. As Marcy sipped the eggnog to please the old woman, she asked abruptly, "Aunt Riah, do you believe in heaven? As a real place, I mean?"

Her baby must be feeling better, funning this way. Aunt Riah chuckled. Her laughter was rich as her Christmas fruitcake, as she sat down in the rocking chair by Marcy's bed and folded her hands in her vast white-aproned lap. "Honey, does I believe in home? De main streets where de quality folks live is gol' and de little streets is jasper where de po' folks got dey mansions. But de doorknobs is all pearl lak on dat shiny cross Mistuh David done give you." She rocked faster and faster, caught up in her heavenly dream, her black face shining, her tired feet with the shoes with holes cut out to ease her feet pushing the floor harder and harder as the glory grew in her, as she worked up to the climax of all good gifts. She crooned, "Ain't no black souls nor no yaller souls. . . . Dey all white . . . 'count dey washed deyselfs in de blood o' de Lamb!"

She began to croon, high and true as a flute:

> "In the land of fadeless day
> Lies a city, four-square.
> It shall never pass away

For there is no night there.
God shall wipe away all tears;
There's no death . . ."

"It isn't true!" Marcy pounded upon Aunt Riah's white-aproned knee, crying hysterically, "My baby died and so did yours! And He didn't care. . . ."

"Shut yo' mouf on dem black words!" Aunt Riah seized the small white fists in her big ones, warning sternly, "Ole debbil, he right ovah der in de cornah, listenin'."

Poor Aunt Riah with her jasper streets and her devil in her corner, and her heaven where her skin would be white . . . But even if it were only a child's fairy tale, what right had you to rob her of it? "I'm sorry," Marcy gasped, lying back, spent. "Sing if you want to, Aunt Riah."

"God shall wipe away all tears;
There's no death, no sighs, no fears,
And they count not time by years
For there is no night there."

Marcy's tired eyelids were drooping. She sleep so bad, nights, po' l'l lamb. . . . Aunt Riah, watching anxiously, hummed on and on, rocking and singing verse after verse, drifting finally into a hum. Hum soft as a bee, as a butterfly's wing . . . Bress de Lord, ma baby's asleep.

Marcy simply couldn't decide what to write back to David, so she sent him no word at all. *By the end of the week,* she promised herself, *I'll send him a letter.* The next day the thermometer soared again over a hundred; it was too hot to think. When Li'l Emily came upstairs to Marcy's room to show her some camisoles she was edging in real lace, Marcy asked her why she didn't cool off by going riding with Sam. Li'l Emily said Sam was away; he'd gone East on the train on business for his father. But the roses continued to come.

Neither Marcy nor Li'l Emily mentioned them—another thing better left unsaid, Marcy knew, like telling David she couldn't come back to him.

And yet the thought of David waiting for her wire that never came was a weight, pressing down on her, a guilt almost too heavy to bear. But how could she give him what she did not have? No one could force her emotions. If she went back to him, still sick in body and at heart, what good would she be to him? Their ideas of being happily married were so far apart. Was a quiet place to be together too much to ask? A parsonage might as well have no door! "A priest never belongs to himself, darling," David had said. "Then they should pay you enough to live on comfortably," Marcy had retorted; David had insisted money wasn't as important as the satisfaction of being needed. Maybe not. But it cost money to live decently just the same, and to be sick. The hospital bills must have set David back almost six months' salary, and all to no good.

"But Peter Andrew *is* alive! Still ours, my darling. We're a family living in two worlds!" David's voice spoke in Marcy's mind as clearly as if he had been standing here beside her in her bedroom. If only he was right; if only she could be sure . . .

Restlessly Marcy got out of bed, threw on a thin white negligee, fastened its cerise ribbon carelessly about her too thin waist, went out onto the veranda, and leaned her hot cheek against the grateful coolness of the clematis leaves. David's God was kind, loving, even when He hurt you. How was this possible? She knew very little about Him really. Oh, she'd gone to Sunday school when she was small, wearing her white dress and blue sash; she'd mouthed obediently all her life, "Our Father who art in heaven . . ." But she'd never really thought of Him as her father, Marcy admitted to herself. A child's faith learned by rote, so that when a hard fact of life had hammered her senseless there had been nothing left.

Yet David and Aunt Riah both have something to hold onto, Marcy knew, twisting her cerise sash round and round in her thin, nervous fingers. They're both too honest to pretend. There must be something wrong with *me*.

She pushed the damp curls back from her weary forehead. The blossoms on the clematis vine smelled too sweet, cloying. If there really was a living God, how did you find Him? Through a chink in the glossy green of the leaves she stared dully up at the hot blue of the August sky where a little white cloud floated serenely. The cloud had faith it would not fall. Perhaps if she said the words, faith would come to her, too.

"Oh, God, I believe. Help thou my unbelief!" She waited breathlessly, she didn't know what for: to feel different, perhaps to glow all over as David's face had when he had preached his first sermon at St. Luke's, but nothing unusual happened at all. In the stable below her a horse neighed; a child laughed in the kitchen garden; a bee buzzed importantly into a creamy blossom by her ear, drank up the nectar, went on about its business. Even the white cloud drifted away beyond the chink in the clematis leaves, and there was only hot blue sky, empty as she was.

Hearing the bedroom door open behind her, Marcy called listlessly, without turning her head, "I'm out here, Aunt Riah."

"It's me, Big Mouth."

"Sam!" Marcy gasped. She whirled to face him. What was he doing here? Li'l Emily's husband . . .

"You're so doggone thin." Sam stood there in the veranda doorway, running his fingers through his thick red hair as he did when he was upset, his round face so white, shocked at the way she looked, that the freckles stood out like pennies. He said abruptly: "I went to see David. I went to knock the living daylights out of him for doing this to you, but—"

"You saw *David!*" Marcy's shaking fingers grabbed at the balustrade as she swayed, and Sam took a step forward, but he didn't touch her. She gasped, fragile as her white gown with its sash the color of her ripe mouth, "You went clear to Boston?"

Sam nodded. "Paw's business could've been done by mail. I wanted to tell that psalm singer of yours he either had to come and get you or to let you go. What's so important about a church, a man has to put it before his own wife?"

Sam had gone two thousand miles for you. But he belonged to Li'l Emily and you were married to David. The blood roared in Marcy's ears as she gasped: "Did you tell David that? What did he say?"

"I didn't even speak to him. Listen, will you?" Sam explained he'd arrived in Boston on Sunday morning, found David didn't answer his telephone, and so, anxious to see David as soon as possible, Sam had gone to St. Luke's to morning service. Sam said he'd hardly heard the music, the prayers, he was so full of what he was going to say to that do-gooder up there in the pulpit, smug in his popish black gown.

"I gave it to him for his birthday!" Marcy quavered, protesting. "He looked nice in it!"

It seemed as if Sam didn't hear her. He was back in Boston watching David go up into his high pulpit to pray. "He acted queer," Sam explained helplessly. "None of this 'What-a-poor-worm-am-I' stuff. He didn't bow down. He lifted up his head when he prayed . . . and his face kind of shone. . . ."

"I know." How well Marcy knew that faroff shining mountain-peak look! Pain stirred in her, the agony of remembering, like a hurt that has been numbed by drugs but still aches unbearably, underneath. From afar she could hear Sam going on about what David had preached that morning.

"Beloved, now are we the sons of God" had been David's text, Sam told her. But David had insisted that since we were the sons of a King, we had the divine right to choose what we wanted to be. *God couldn't do anything for us unless we agreed.* (It sounded so like David that Marcy could almost hear his voice instead of Sam's.) The story of Abraham and his son Isaac had never made good sense to him, David admitted, until last spring when he'd lost a son of his own. What monster could ask a father to cut his young son's throat for sacrifice? But that wasn't what God wanted at all. He was trying to point out that death didn't matter any more than being born; they were both parts of the Plan. *God could make Isaac great in Israel only if Abraham was willing to give his son up.* "A terribly hard thing," David had said, "for a father to do."

David was talking about himself and Peter Andrew! He hadn't been resigned to his son's dying at all; he'd had to fight, too, for strength to go on. . . . The veranda whirled about Marcy's dizzy head; the sweetness of the clematis vine was choking her. She tried to cry out to Sam, "Why are you tearing me apart this way?" But all she could manage was "Why—why—"

"Because David still loves you," Sam told her. "You know what he said? He said heaven was what you wanted most, he guessed. He knew an old mammy who thought heaven's streets were paved with gold and jasper . . . and why not? Others thought heaven and hell were inside a man's mind. But for you and him and Peter Andrew, heaven was just the three of you being together, for all eternity. . . ."

Davey, you lost a son, too. But I thought only of myself. . . . Tears were salt in Marcy's mouth and her knees crumpled; but Sam caught her up into his arms, held her safe. She was sobbing like a child, but the ice was melting about her frozen heart; she could feel again. *Davey, I can't believe as you do. Peter Andrew's dead. But you're alive and you're my husband.* . . .

"Shall I call Momi?" Sam was asking wildly. "I'm the one should be called 'Big Mouth'!"

"No, no, I'm fine." Marcy's wet violet eyes shone gratefully up into his anxious ones as she stood erect alone.

Sam said awkwardly, "There's another reason why you must go back to David." He mumbled, looking over her head, "Li'l Emily . . . I mean, she's two months along."

Li'l Emily was going to have Sam's baby. Why hadn't she told you? You knew why. Marcy murmured, her face suddenly radiant for him: "I'm so glad for you, Sam. You wanted a son. And Li'l Emily adores you."

"Yes. She's wonderful." He was lucky, all right. Li'l Emily, born wise as well as plain, knew that love was never static, that you had to go on fighting for it. Marcy was so impulsive, so waywardly generous . . . and so dear. David's wife.

"Sam?" Marcy begged him. "Will you wire David for me? This is Saturday. Just say: 'Coming home. Meet me Tuesday morning train.' Is that ten words?" If you had to take one step, you might as well go all the way. "Is there room to say, 'love'?"

"There's room. I'll go right now."

Tasting the bitterness of his success, Sam moved blindly toward the veranda door, but Marcy, her tear-stained face lifted to the hot blue of the sky beyond the clematis vine, hardly knew he was gone. She would try to be the "good wife" David wanted, and if she failed, at least . . . But she mustn't fail. Love, duty. Where did one end and the other begin? Or were they the two sides of the same bright coin?

Chapter Ten

SERENA SNOW lay dreamily content in her own white-painted iron bed with the brass knobs that shone in the morning sun blazing in through the open window, and tried to think how she would break her news to Pa and Ma. Serena was grateful to be away from her roommates, to be alone again if only for a little while. She liked her nursing job, but a hospital had no privacy; often she ached for the peace and aloneness of Gull Rock Light where she had grown up. A crisp breeze stirred the ruffled curtains at the windows, and Serena sniffed contentedly. Familiar noises outside her window told her what was happening: the silly clucking of the hens as Ma threw them some feed, the tinkle of the bell of the Jersey cow, Mollie, as she moved from one tuft of grass to another in the tiny meadow—Pa'd have to begin lugging hay for her from the mainland at Bellport soon—the staccato barks of the two dogs, Penny and Useless, her pup, waiting at the back door because they smelled the breakfast bacon.

"Lookit, Gram!" Riley's shrill treble rose excitedly under Serena's window. "John's caught him a cunner!" John was Rye's pet seagull to whom he fed table scraps daily. "Hear him, Gram? He's laughing at the rest!"

"Ayuh. Some cute to watch, ain't they?" The air was so still Serena could hear Ma's softly slurred words. "But I don't think much of their manners. The mother walks off 'n' leaves her young ones soon's they're born almost and they go after her, yelling, 'Please wait, please wait!' "

In the lazy stillness, Serena could hear even the whisper of the river against the yellow rock outside; then Rye's clear voice shattered her peace. "My mother leaves me, too."

Serena stiffened, waited breathlessly to hear what Ma'd say. Her voice was calm as molasses as she pointed out, "I'm your mother, too, your grandmother. Rene left you here to take care of me and Pa. What would he do without you to help him with the Light?"

Serena let out her breath slowly. Ma was wonderful, just the one to handle a high-strung young one like Riley; she never got flustered, upset. Serena knew she should have talked to Riley before, tried to explain to him why his name was still Snow, why his father never came to the Light. David had warned her that she'd have to be careful how she told Rye, to make him feel he was loved. Maybe she'd better have it out with him today. If only David were here to help her! But it wasn't right for her to depend so upon him. Maybe, Serena wondered uneasily, she shouldn't have stopped to talk with him on the sidewalk, in front of the hospital. Those snoopy twins, Soaks and Louella, *would* go by, see them together. Neither Serena nor David had planned their meeting; it had been one of those bonuses like the New England morning, sunny but deliciously cool because the east wind was blowing off Boston Harbor. After the first leap of pleasure at the sight of David's broad shoulders, of his bright head that would never wear a hat unless forced to, Serena had tried to slip unnoticed through the swinging hospital door. But David had come hurrying after her. "Rene, you got your cap!" His vitality, his pleasure had been an electric current between them. "Under what stone have you been keeping yourself? You might have written us a line." He meant when the baby died, but she could hardly tell him that she hadn't wanted to remind Marcy of their bitter words, that she'd known about Peter Andrew before David had. . . .

"How is Marcy?"

"She's been very ill." Was David choosing his words too carefully? "Not only physically but emotionally. But her letters sound better. Did you hear I'd been offered the Silverton church?"

"Yes. Dare Drexel told me. His father's chairman of the committee." But Dare's father, Dandy, was a martinet about other people's morals; his own were his own business, but if the minister stepped the least bit out of line ...

Lying there in her brass bed at the light, Serena hoped uneasily the rumor she'd heard that Marcy was not coming back to Boston and that she was leaving David had been untrue. He mustn't be hurt this way; he didn't deserve it.

"You ready for a mugup, Pa?" Ma's voice came in through the open window, and Serena knew if she didn't get downstairs soon they'd think she was sick. How was she going to tell them that Dare Drexel was coming to the Light today to ask her to marry him?

Better get down to Pa while he was still good-natured from Ma's hot cinnamon rolls, fragrant even up here. This was Pa's second breakfast, really. He set the coffeepot on the stove when he got up at sunrise to put out the Light. The Light had been his whole life for the fifteen years he'd been the sole keeper here; he slept with his window looking out on it, waking up heaven only knew how many times a night to be sure it was winking, "Danger! Look out!" He went across to the mainland to go to church, to get provisions, to take Riley to the school bus, but he hadn't stayed all through a movie up to Bath in ten years; he got so restless.

Yet his and Ma's was a good life, a full life, here at Gull Rock Light. "Don't you ever get lonesome?" summer visitors would ask when they came aboard the tiny island. One of the favorite Bellport summer sports was to row over to Gull Light and climb the winding iron tower steps to look down at the river. "We ain't got time," Ma would explain. "I got my vegetable and strawberry beds to take care of. I can pretty near everything we eat, winters." There was just room for the garden and the small meadow where Mollie nibbled sweet grass all summer on the narrow end point of land jutting out

into the turbulent river; on one side of the little peninsula lay
impassable swamp, and on the other the current ran so swiftly
that when the river yeasted up not even Pa's powerful outboard motor could make it across to the mainland. Even in
calm weather he had to outwit the strong current by pointing
the dory's bow upstream, then letting her drift back down
toward the lighthouse slip. But if you were stormbound here
for a month, you'd never go hungry. Ma had hundreds of
shining jars down cellar, stuffed not only with vegetables and
fruit but with chickens, canned lobsters, and deer meat Pa'd
shot in season. There were great jars of candled eggs, pounds
of golden butter churned from Mollie's rich milk. Ma could
feed a regiment if she was put to it! Queer that Riley was so
skinny with all the creamy milk she poured into him; maybe
it was because he was never still a minute. . . . Serena heard
his shy tap on her door.

"Rene? You awake?"

"Well, I am now anyway, Rye." The door burst open, and
Riley catapulted onto the foot of Serena's bed. She smiled at
him and patted his faded blue dungareed knee, but he drew
back, as always. Even as a very small boy Riley had never liked
to be touched; but he was glad to see her, his brilliant eyes
shining shyly, Dare's eyes, but innocent. Riley was small for
six, his hair bleached almost white by the sun, which made his
eyes startlingly blue in his thin, heart-shaped face. He was a
pixie child, at once old and young, and forever eluding her
who loved him. What was that dark blotch under his left eye?

"You've been fighting, Riley!" Serena said sharply. He'd
just started first grade, and Pa ran him over to the mainland
every morning to get the school bus.

"Ayuh," Riley agreed, kicking her bed nervously with a
small worn sneaker.

"What about?"

Riley squirmed. "Kid at school called me a bad word. It
was a lie, and I made him swaller it."

Coldness ran over her whole body, and the bitterness of fear was in her mouth. So it had come, the inevitable question. Trust the school kids. . . . He was too young to understand the whole bitter truth, but the shame must somehow be made hers, not his. How was she going to comfort him, she who had robbed him of his good name? This was the terrible stone wall of her sin she couldn't climb over. Unless . . . unless what David had told her about prayer was really true! She closed her eyes, no longer able to watch her small boy's face, and prayed: "O God, it isn't his fault! Please give me the right words not to hurt him more. . . ." As she waited a melody sang in her frightened mind, words she had sung so many times in the choir:

> "O love that wilt not let me go,
> I rest my weary soul in thee. . . .

Love was the answer. The only good thing that had come out of all this was her love for Riley; the saving grace was not for you to be loved but for you to love. But how did you explain that to a six-year-old? Serena drew a deep, shaken breath as she asked: "Remember that picture book I gave you on your birthday, Rye, dear? Where Jesus had His arm around a little boy?"

"Ayuh. They all had on nightgowns," Riley agreed.

"When people called Him bad names, He didn't fight back; He forgave them. He loved them."

"But I love you! That's why I hit him!"

"I know. And I love you, too." O Lord, I'm making a mess of this; help me. . . . "Hurting people hurts you too, Rye— more than it does them, maybe. But love makes a magic circle. Everyone inside the circle is safe. No bad words can hurt you." Please make it true. . . .

"Oh," Riley breathed, relieved. He was so little, and he had to grow up to face injustice; she couldn't stop that. But perhaps she could. . . . Had they told Rye, too, who his father

was? If she married Dare, even too late, gave Rye a name he
could be proud of, got him out of here into a new place where
they could begin again . . . But did Dare want Rye or only
her? Dare might arrive at any minute; she'd better dress. She
smiled at Rye, saying: "Now scat. I'm getting up. I bet Ma
sent you up here to tell me breakfast was ready."

"I forgot." His adoring eyes added shyly, "I forgot looking
at you." She bent to kiss him even if he didn't like it, and
Riley, embarrassed, roared off down the stairs, pretending he
was an outboard engine. Serena slid quickly into her clothes.
She swung a full green skirt over her head, pulled on a white
wool sweater, ran a comb through her bright hair so that it lay
in ordered waves upon her shoulders instead of being caught
into a net as at the hospital, and dashed cool water over her
face from the basin. But Pa was already pushing back his chair
from the table from his second breakfast as she came into the
kitchen, glowing.

"Lally-gaggin'," Pa snorted, glancing up at the alarm clock
on the mantel which said eight-thirty as Serena slid into her
place at the oilcloth-covered table beside the black iron stove.
Pa was a small man, yet tough and wiry enough to put any
man in his place, but his gray eyes, which could be steely,
were unexpectedly gentle when he looked at his beautiful
daughter.

"How you talk, Pa! No call for everyone to slide out before
sunrise, jest because you do." Ma's cheeks were pink as her
starched gingham dress; she was plump, not fat; medium, not
short; *comfortable* was the word for her. Ma said, "It's gonna
be a pretty day." She pushed the spoonholder closer for
Serena, added three slices of crisp bacon to Riley's plate, and
put butter and homemade strawberry jam lavishly upon his
toast before she poured Serena's coffee black from the gray
enamel pot. Pa liked it "strong enough to git up 'n' walk."

"When you git through stuffing your face," Pa told Riley,

"you might dodge up to the tower with that new polish I left in the shed. I got to take a run up to Bath, 'n' the inspector's due tomorrow."

"Sure thing," Riley promised. Pa glanced down at his daughter as he passed, and she smiled back at him, affection between them as warm, as nourishing as Riley's toast, in the quiet kitchen. Pa took down his plaid mackinaw from the hook by the back door, and Riley, cramming the rest of his breakfast into his mouth, rushed after him. In his own mind, Rye was the assistant keeper the government was too poor to supply Pa with after the war.

Now, Serena thought uneasily. *I must warn Ma now.* But it was hard to break the peace that lay warm as the sunlight on the well-scrubbed kitchen floor. Wood crackled in the iron stove as Ma put a new stick in. Penny stretched her brown-and-white mongrel body, and Useless, so named by Pa who'd have drowned the pup except for Rye's pleading, bit his mother's tail, happily. Ma was stacking dishes in the sink, the clink of china and dime-store silver making a homely sound, when Serena spoke suddenly.

"Ma, Dare wants me to marry him. He's coming here today in the *Sans Souci III* for my answer."

The cup in Ma's nerveless hand crashed to the kitchen floor. She gasped: "After all these years? Oh, dear, that's the first cup I've broke since we was married!"

Serena bent to help pick up the pieces, explaining: "It was a shock to me, too. He called the hospital. I told him I'd be spending the weekend up here, and he said he had to come up anyway, to see about taking up the *San Souci* for this winter."

"You wouldn't take Riley away!" Ma sank, shaking, into a hard wooden chair, her brown eyes as pleading as the pup's. "He's like my own!"

"But if the kids at school are deviling him, perhaps a home

with Dare and me in a new place where no one knew
him. . . ."

"A boy wouldn't have no home with that jellyfish! If you
wasn't good enough to marry seven years ago, you ain't now!"
Pa roared from the kitchen doorway where he'd come back,
unnoticed. "He didn't have the guts to buck his folks."

"They offered to take Rye," Serena reminded Pa. They'd
been over this so many times, but Pa always got red hot. Dare
would have run away with her, married her anyway, if she
hadn't been too proud when his folks didn't want her for a
daughter-in-law. Dare had been Daniel Drexel III, just home
from St. George's School, and she had been a river-bred girl
who sang in the choir in the church next to the big white
mansion where the Drexels lived. If Dare hadn't been made
to come sulkily to service that morning when Serena had sung
the solo, and if he hadn't invited her that hot July night, with
the stars and the river blazing with romance, to come out with
him in the *Sans Souci*, the cruiser his folks had given him for
a graduation present . . . Why was she looking for excuses
when there weren't any? Only that she'd been sixteen, only
ten years older than Rye was now.

"His folks know Dare's comin' here to make an honest
woman of you?" Pa demanded of Serena.

"I don't know," she admitted.

"Want me to git shet of him for you?" Pa asked with longing. "No need for you to see him."

Pa never could forgive the Drexels for offering to put Rye
in a home. "No!" Pa had roared. "Named for me, ain't he?
Riley Snow. He's stayin' right here with Ma 'n' me. I guess we
can feed our own flesh and blood."

"No, Pa. I'd better see him, find out what's in his mind.
He—he's got a legal claim on Riley, I guess even if he's hardly
seen him. We wouldn't want any trouble."

"Trouble!" Pa snorted. "He's never been anything but."

"You'd better redd up your room, Rene," Ma changed the subject tactfully, but Pa made a swear word of slamming the back door.

Serena went obediently upstairs, though actually there was little to do except spread up the sheets, the hand-blocked red-and-white quilt, the tufted bedspread. There was no dust on the dresser nor were there kitten curls under the bed; the white curtains were crisp as ballet skirts and you could eat off Ma's rag rugs. All Ma's days fell into three parts: clean, keep her man satisfied with good food, get a good night's sleep. She was probably busy right now planning a hearty lunch for Dare, even if she hated to set eyes on him. Serena sighed, wishing she could see her own way as clearly. Rye needed his father's name, all right, but Dare'd never give him what Pa had. Financial security, yes; but not a sense of responsibility. How could Dare, when he didn't have it himself?

After she'd finished redding up, Serena went out to sit with her back against the jutting yellow cliff to watch upriver for the *Sans Souci III*. Ever since she could remember, the river had been a part of her life, the focal point of the whole family's existence. Its swift-flowing waters, deep blue in the sun or an angry gray when it breezed up into whitecaps, were hauntingly, dangerously beautiful. Only the river people know how fickle a tidewater river could be. The risks the summer people took, blithely, unknowing! People had to get a license to drive a car, Pa lamented bitterly, but any fool could buy a boat and push her off into the stream as long as he could start an engine. When they ran themselves up on a rock or into the whirlpools, Pa had to roar out in his high-powered dory to the rescue, and if he couldn't handle it he called for the Coast Guard picket boat from Popham. Strong binoculars were kept on the window sill above the sink, as well as up in the tower, so that Pa or Ma could scan the river constantly, and sound the bell to greet the knife-prowed destroyers on their trial trips downriver to the sea. Pa rang greetings, too, for the sailboats and other small craft that tooted back "Hello!"

Serena glanced up at the roar of Pa's powerful outboard motor, headed toward Bath. He must have decided to make himself scarce before the *Sans Souci* arrived, which was a mercy. It would be easier to handle Dare if Pa wasn't here to needle him. Were you justified in marrying just to give Rye a name? But marrying without love, could you build happiness for any of the three of them?

As she sat there, troubled but soothed by the river rote as familiar as her own breathing, the sun coming out from behind a cloud reflected dazzlingly upon the polished brass of the *Sans Souci III* as it rounded Mark Island in the river and came on toward the light. Rye had heard the engine too. Serena watched the small figure in the rubber boots exactly like Pa's except for size, run clumping down the path to the boathouse so that Rye could give Dare a hand at the slip. Rye adored boats; ships were in his blood, and the big cruiser was powerful beyond a boy's dream. Like everything about Dare, the *Sans Souci III* was expensive, dashing. It disappeared behind the boathouse slip, and presently Dare's tall, debonair figure came up the path, alone. Rye would stay to admire the cruiser hungrily, to touch its smooth shining mahogany, to sit behind the wheel maybe, pretending he was navigating her.

"Hi, Rene!" Dare called, waving his white cap with the gold braid, and she waved back, amused.

Always the perfect yachtsman, with his immaculate white trousers, his blue coat with the brass buttons. Most summer people around here preferred dungarees and sweatshirts, but Dare didn't mind being conspicuous; he liked it. Or was it as the prospective bridegroom he'd dressed the part? But he was tall, well built, a husband you need never be ashamed of. As he climbed toward her over the rocks, his cropped-close brown hair showed how well shaped his head was. Riley hated his own "sissy curls," plastered them down with water; he had Dare's eyes too, blue, long-lashed. As Dare came up, eagerly, Serena smiled, patted the warm yellow rock beside her.

"Sit down, Dare. Isn't this a marvelous day?"

"You look marvelous," Dare told her, settling down obediently beside her. "But you're too thin. This nursing nonsense, I suppose."

"I like it," Serena told him. "I have to stand on my own feet sometime, so it might as well be now."

"Why do you have to?" Dare objected. His eyes ran appreciatively over her slender figure, her bright hair. He was admiring her as impersonally as he did the brightly painted picture he'd given her so long ago, that hung in the Boston living room, pleased that she was beautiful. "I didn't come to talk about the weather," Dare said. "Rene, we've known each other long enough to talk sensibly. I've never denied Rye is my son."

"How could you?" Serena bristled. "But why, after all this time. . . ."

"I'll be twenty-five next month. I get what Gramp left me then. Gramp made a will. He left me half a million, to be paid to me when I'm twenty-five, but I don't get it unless I'm married. Gramp was old-fashioned; he thought marriage settled a man." Dare grinned, apologetically. "It's quite a hunk of cash. For both of us to spend—if you want to, Rene."

The blood pounded angrily in her veins, rushed to her cheeks. Was he—trying to buy a wife? She was only a convenient phrase in his grandfather's will.

"You're not very flattering. It's rather like being proposed to by a—a safe-deposit box!"

"I don't have to marry you; I could marry anyone," Dare pointed out. "It would be to Rye's advantage, too. He's growing up. Could you send him to college on a nurse's pay?"

When she did not answer, staring down at the swift river beneath them, Dare rushed on, pleading: "I swear I won't cramp your style, Rene. You can do as you please, and so will I."

"That I can believe," bitterly.

"Don't be that way," Dare begged. "Dandy heard you sing at St. Luke's and he said you'd come a long way. You were stunning looking—darned if he wasn't proud of you! If he'd been alone, and not with the committee, he'd have taken you out to some swanky joint to eat." Serena thought: Like father, like son. Did too much money warp you?

"When was your father at St. Luke's? I didn't see him," she asked Dare, playing for more time to think.

"Oh, I don't know. When the Silverton committee were scouting for a new minister. Ours is leaving to be president of some jerk college out west. You know how Dad is, in church business up to his eyelids. Listen, Rene, he and Granny agreed that if I married anyone it'd better be you. Granny said she'd build a new wing on the Silverton house so we could have an apartment of our own."

Everything was neatly arranged. Dare would have his half a million, but Granny could still keep him under her eye; Serena would be made an honest woman, and Riley would have his father's name. The only drawback was that she'd be tied for life to a man who hadn't grown up yet. Could she afford to pay that price for Rye's future? As if her thinking of him had called him, Riley's small figure shot out of the boat-house door and ran up the path toward Ma's kitchen. He did not look up at them at all, but Serena knew that he had seen her and Dare sitting there. Probably Rye'd come up to them eventually, making a game of it, creeping up behind them. Rye was shy, sensitive; what had happened to him at school had already left a deep scar.

"Is there a good school for Riley in Silverton?" Serena asked suddenly.

"Be reasonable, Rene," Dare flared. "How could we be married one week and show up the next with a long-legged kid of six? It simply wouldn't wash. But we could send him to a good school, St. George's where I went, if you like, send him to college, then a year abroad, maybe."

"No! I won't marry you if I can't have Riley!"

"What can he hope to learn here on the Rock? Clamming, fishing, maybe. I don't love anyone else, nor do you. Be sensible, Rene. You don't want to go on emptying bedpans all your life!" When she didn't answer, Dare took her by her slim shoulders, shook her gently. "I've got a right to look after my own son!" He was tacking into the wind, watching her face closely as he wheedled. "If it doesn't work out, we can get a divorce later. . . ."

"You leave my mother alone!" A small whirlwind, coming up behind them, hurled itself against the startled Dare so that he had to take his hands from Serena's shoulders to ward off the small anguished fists pounding at him.

"Riley!" Serena gasped, grabbing for him. "Stop that!" He must have heard the whole conversation. His blue eyes were blazing and he was sobbing mad, beating with his small clenched fists against Dare, kicking and yelling: "You are *not* my father! I hate you."

As Serena pulled the little boy away from Dare, Rye hid his face in her shoulder, mumbling, "*Is* Dare my father?"

"Yes," Serena told him, holding him tightly.

"But he doesn't want me!"

"Of course he does." Serena's eyes flashed over the small tousled head at Dare, begging him: Help me! Do something!

Dare rubbed his leg ruefully where Riley had kicked him, but the kid had guts. He invited, "Hey, young feller, how'd you like to take a ride in the *Sans Souci?* Steer her down-river?"

Exactly how he bribed me, Serena remembered bleakly, stroking the small shaking shoulders; but Riley's smarter than

I was. She stared unbelieving at her son's tear-stained face
lifting from her shoulder, damply radiant.

"You kiddin', Dare?" Riley demanded. "Could I take her
wheel for a little while?"

"Sure." Dare threw Serena a triumphant glance. Who said
he didn't know how to manage kids?

"Well, gosh," Riley gasped. "Let's go! Can Rene come
too?"

"Of course. The three of us will go," Dare promised triumphantly. He urged Serena: "We can run up to Bath. I
don't know exactly how long it takes to get a marriage license
in Maine, but. . . ."

"Riley!" Ma's voice called from the foot of the Light as she
stood there in the doorway. "Where in tuncket's that polish
Pa asked you for?"

The light died out of the small boy's face. He drew a deep
quivering breath of regret, looking down at the cruiser drawn
up on the slip, its brass and paint shining in the sun, at the
great wheel for which his small fingers yearned. "I can't go,"
he told Dare, fighting back his tears. "The inspector's comin',
and I promised Pa, if he went up to Bath, I'd polish the
brass." He fled up the path toward the great white Light that
had to be kept shining and clear for the big new destroyers
knifing downriver, the Light that was his job, too.

Serena was so proud of him her throat hurt. So very proud.
She watched the small figure leaping on sneakered feet from
rock to rock, going back to his job. Pa had taught him to think
like a man. She knew that she could never let Riley down; he
was all that mattered. He's right, she thought. It's where we're
needed that we're happiest. No one but me can give Riley
back his birthright. As she turned back to Dare, her mouth
was quivering and her eyes were too bright, but she said
evenly: "I'll marry you, Dare. As soon as you like. But if I do,
it's for keeps. There'll be no divorce."

Dare gave a sigh of relief. "That's my girl." No need to argue details when he'd won. "You and Rye'll have all Gramp's money when I'm gone."

"I don't want a cent!" Serena cried passionately. "Only for Rye to be looked after, for his education." If this was to be a business marriage, they'd work it out that way. She told him: "Uncle Ben's a lawyer up in Bath. You can make a will, put Riley into it. We can stop by there when we get the license."

"Sure, if it'll make you feel any better."

When he bent to kiss her to seal their bargain, she did not resist, but her lips were unfeeling under his. At least Dare hadn't pretended either; he'd been honest with himself and with you; that was the important thing. From now on, Riley would be safe; you would have done your best, given him all you could. You mustn't cry. But people always cried at weddings, didn't they? Not the bride. When you made a mistake you paid and paid—

A bell rang down below them, silver in the clear air, and Serena's mouth curved into a wry smile. "Lunch is ready. Ma has chicken lobsters." Dear Ma, she thought there were few sorrows that hot boiled lobsters, biscuits melting with Mollie's rich golden butter, and homemade strawberry jam would not ease. Maybe Ma was right. "Come on." Serena held out her hand to Dare. "Let's go down."

Chapter Eleven

THE late afternoon sun gilded the small white houses and tangled bright fingers in the green hair of the elms and maples that lined the street of the New England town of Silverton, where Marcy and David were driving in Heinrich, their second-hand flivver upon which David had made a ten-dollar down payment. They were going to have dinner at the Drexels'. The Silverton parish was spread out over so many miles, David had to have a car, but so far he'd had spent nearly as much time under the Model T as in the driver's seat. The Gallants were not yet settled in at the big square white parsonage, but when the chairman of the official board issues an invitation the minister and his wife accept. Marcy had bought a new dress for the occasion, a dark-blue chiffon, very long in the waist and so short in the skirt that the blue wisps had to be pulled down over her knees every time she sat down. David had been scandalized, but Marcy had demanded, was there any law that a preacher's wife had to be dowdy? Any more than people had to put such odd things into missionary barrels? Did piety consist in running about Africa in someone's old corsets and evening slippers? David's doubts had dissolved in laughter, but not before he and Marcy had had the nearest thing to a quarrel since she had returned from Texas.

That afternoon, after having tramped all the ancient cowpaths of Boston, Marcy had burst in the parsonage door, dropped a large silver-striped box upon the hall table, calling up to the study, excitedly, "Davey? Come see what I bought!"

"He ain't here. The Bates twins're terrible sick. He phoned not to wait dinner. I'm fixin' to go over to my sister's when I finish the dishes," Mrs. Minnie Moran had announced from the kitchen doorway. She was a large woman with masses of oily hair, knotted at the back of her neck, and a long, lined face. David had engaged her to help around the house until Marcy felt stronger, but Marcy had the suspicion that Mrs. Minnie as she'd asked them to call her (a compromise that subtly underlined her status as a parishioner, not a maid), had enticed David into letting her set up a listening post for the parish. When the phone rang, she usually beat the Gallants to the receiver, and spent most of her spare time chatting over the wire.

"Come, set right down." Mrs. Minnie seated herself at the table and shook out her napkin as Marcy sniffed unhappily. Finnan haddie. Mrs. Minnie knew Marcy hated the smelly stuff, although David smacked his lips over it. If only the parsonage wasn't such an enormous ark of a house with two parlors, five bedrooms, and a dark kitchen designed more for entertaining the Ladies' Aid than for a family of two . . . Marcy needed Mrs. Minnie, and both of them knew it, and compromised.

"I think I'll just have a tray of tea and toast in my room," Marcy decided, suddenly exhausted at the thought of facing both Mrs. Minnie and finnan haddie across the supper table, for when David was at home Mrs. Minnie served them, but when she and Marcy were alone the helper sat at the dining-room table as a matter of right. As Mrs. Minnie's lips tightened, Marcy added hastily: "I'll fix it myself. Go right along to your sister's when you're ready."

A few minutes later, when the kitchen door slammed, Marcy decided she wasn't hungry, after all. She was trying on her new dress when she heard the front door open downstairs. "Davey? Come up here, sugar. I've something to show you." She smiled at him in the mirror, a vision of long silk-clad legs amid panels of blue chiffon. "Like it? I got it for Drexels'! I want to do you proud."

She'd been right to get the blue instead of the beige, Marcy decided, pirouetting for David so that the chiffon billowed out in blue wings. "My, that color makes your eyes gorgeous, dearie!" the svelte black-clad salesgirl at Delmonico's had said.

"How much did that cost?" David demanded.

"Only fifty dollars. I opened a charge account at Delmonico's."

"Fifty dollars!" David yelled. "That's nearly a week's salary! You know how I feel about charge accounts. If we can't afford something, we don't buy it; otherwise, we'd get buried so deep we'd never dig our way out. . . . For Pete's sake, what're you crying about?"

For Marcy, in tears, was slipping the blue chiffon dress from her white shoulders. She stepped out of it, tossed the new dress in a heap onto a chair. "I don't have a single thing that fits me since I was sick! But of course if you don't think I should . . ."

"Sure, you need new clothes," David agreed.

Any mention of Marcy's sickness made him weaken. She was only a child, after all, his lovely child trying to grow up, and his job was not to discipline her but to love her. He went to pick up the blue dress, to put it up on a hanger, carefully, in the closet. Even a blue rag that cost fifty dollars was worth taking care of.

"Both Bates twins have scarlet fever," he took her mind off his outburst. "What one gets, the other always has. Their mother couldn't go with them in the ambulance to the hospital, so the boys were both howling, scared to death. They're only ten. I stayed with Mary and Jim Bates till the doctor's sedative made her drop off. Tough on her, poor girl."

"Oh, Davey, I'm sorry!" Marcy wailed. Would she never learn the signs when the parish had battened off Davey's emotions? Left him empty? "I bet you haven't had any dinner."

"Cup of coffee and a ham sandwich Mary made."

"Come on. The Minnie bird's flown to her sister's, thank heavens. I'll scramble some eggs. I haven't eaten either."

The dress was becoming, all right, David had to admit, grinning down at Marcy sitting beside him on Heinrich's black leather seat with the blue-green chiffon scarf showing at the neck of her white coat as they rattled along toward Drexels'. The night was so warm, one could hardly credit it was October; but that was New England for you, golden when you expected ice, as unpredictable as his lovely wife. Life with her was never dull, anyway.

Marcy moved closer to him, laid her warm hand over his on the wheel. "You know something, Davey? You don't just get married once. You fight, make up, get married over and over, as many times as you need to."

"Just so long as you keep on marrying me." David grinned, bringing Heinrich to a stop in the road in front of an enormous white house. "This is the Drexels'. Some place, isn't it?"

The big house, standing on a high hill with several acres of green lawn sloping down to the road, was enormous, white and imposing, with two wings, one of which was part of the original house and the other, glistening with new paint, was plainly recently finished. "For the newlyweds," David explained. "Dan Drexel's son Dare and his bride; they were supposed to be back from Bermuda today. Granny Drexel built and furnished the new wing for them so they could have a place of their own and still be near her. Granny's the one who has the money; she keeps house for Dan—Dandy they call him: you'll see why. . . . His wife is dead. Granny's over eighty, but she's spry as a cricket, and sharp-witted. She's quite a gal."

Heinrich groaned on up the winding drive, to stop with a final protesting grunt in front of the wide veranda with its high white pillars. As David helped Marcy down, the front door was opened by their host. "Right on the dot, David!" he beamed. "Granny'll like you. She's particular about meals being on time." Dandy Drexel was a small man, but everything about him was fastidiously correct: his dark-blue suit, his immaculate stiff white collar, his dark tie and shoes; Marcy suspected the only reason he hadn't worn a dinner jacket was that he knew David wouldn't own one. As Dandy took her hand in his, his eyes slid over her with a shrewdly appreciative glance. "Why didn't you tell me, David, that your wife was a beauty?"

David grinned proudly at Marcy. "That big building out back, darling, is for the famous Barnstable Players."

"Players?" Marcy murmured, taking back her hand, smiling up at Dandy apologetically.

"They're only amateurs, but they put on some pretty good shows," Dandy Drexel admitted. "My son, Dare, is the producer, stage manager, and stagehand too, I guess. Granny built him the barn to keep him out of mischief. He's the restless type, Dare is. Do come inside. Here's Granny."

"You're prettier'n they said you was, but I hope it ain't gone to your head," Granny told Marcy, reaching out to her the free hand that wasn't holding her heavy black cane. Granny was small but erect, with a shrewd, wrinkled face out of which black eyes were bright as a girl's.

As Marcy followed Granny's slow limp across the great entrance hall, the old lady's black taffeta gown rustled crisply and the heavily jeweled rings on her thin old fingers sparkled. Granny'd be a difficult woman to fool.

A door opened, and Granny beamed: "Here's the children. Dare, make you acquainted with Mr. and Mrs. Gallant—" Her voice stopped as David made an inarticulate sound in his throat and Marcy gasped, both of them staring incredulously at the two young people advancing toward them across the thick Oriental rug.

"Rene!" David cried, but Marcy was speechless, looking at

the girl in the pale beige dress with the peacock blue scarf over her shoulders, a dress strangely, unbelievably familiar. Rene being young Mrs. Drexel was bad enough without—

"I meant to phone you, Marcy, this afternoon, but I got involved," Serena apologized. "Hi, Davo! You look marvelous, Marcy, that dress . . ." Her green eyes, puzzled at first, crinkled into laughter. "Goodness, where did you get yours? Delmonico's?"

Marcy's face flamed. Her new dress was exactly the same as Serena's, except for the beige color!

"I made them give me a blue scarf like yours because it was more becoming," Serena chuckled. "Twins, no less! But we don't have to wear them to the same places."

But Marcy hadn't anything else to wear, literally. Not for dinner, anyway. It wouldn't matter to Serena, who was a Drexel now and, who could buy anything she wanted. Marcy looked bleakly at Dare, Serena's husband. Why, out of all the men in the world, did Serena have to choose one in their new church?

"Nice to get to know you, Dare," David said, heartily. Naturally Rene wouldn't advertise her marrying Riley's father at this late date, but David approved.

"Come in to dinner, folks," Granny ordered irritably. These pesky young ones should have told her Serena knew the new minister and his wife. She didn't like being taken by surprise, and neither had young Marcy. What was the tenseness between her and Serena? More than a dress . . . Granny hobbled ahead of them into the big dining room where Dare swung out her big chair at the head of the long table. "Anything I hate, it's cold vittles. Rene, you sit next to David. Dare, you'll have to put up with me. Your Pa won't be satisfied unless he's got the prettiest girl next to him. I'll call you 'Marcy'; I'm old enough to be your grandmother."

"Do, please," Marcy agreed, sliding into her chair. "I miss my own folks. Texas is a long way off."

The dinner seemed endless. Marcy ate the delicious food, parried Dandy Drexel's heavy-handed compliments, answered Granny's queries automatically. Yes, she agreed the parsonage dishes were nice with that little green-vine pattern, and the oriental rug Granny had sent over when she discarded it from the living room had warm and gracious colors; the rug sort of drew together all the orphan furniture.

"Orphan?" Granny bristled.

Granny was jealous for her parsonage. "I just mean the chairs and sofa don't match," Marcy explained hastily. "I'm scared to death I'll get a scratch on something. . . . I've never lived in a house where none of the furniture belonged to me —us—before. All David and I own are our linen and our wedding presents!"

Dandy Drexel said dryly: "Well, I guess you needn't stay awake nights, worrying. Most of that stuff people in the parish threw out of their attics."

"How you talk!" Granny glared at her son. "The Aid gave six suppers to earn the cash for that parlor sofa! It's real good rose velvet."

"Rose is my favorite color." Marcy was rewarded by an approving glance from David, looking up from where he'd been chatting with Serena. To judge by the light in both their faces, they'd been discussing Maine again. Where was her little boy with the queer name—Riley? Had Serena got a divorce from Riley's father? Did David know? His surprise at seeing Serena had seemed genuine. There was something very strange going on. . . .

Serena suggested, as they rose from the table, "Would you like to see our new apartment, Marcy?" When David asked, eagerly, how about showing him too, she put him off easily.

"When I get things settled, I want you both to come to lunch. I have a kitchenette where I can cook, but Dare and I have dinner with the family. We won't be long, Granny."

The wing apartment boasted a long living room whose east wall was mostly windows, hung with flowered chintz draperies; the rose and green were repeated in the coverings of the deep-cushioned chairs and of the sofa. Quite a change from Serena's old basement apartment, Marcy thought, but the vivid picture of the girl bathing was up over the fireplace. Already the room looked lived in; Dare's pipe lay carelessly on the little table of translucent Italian marble and a book was flung onto the seat of the big armchair. The rug was Chinese, and Granny had picked it up in Hong Kong, Serena chattered, and that ugly, fascinating little black god on the mantel she'd bought in Mexico.

"You're wondering why I married Dare and what's become of Riley." She faced Marcy at last, her green eyes alert. She wasn't going to have her decision to give Rye a family spoiled before it began. "The first is none of your business, if you don't mind my saying so, Marcy. Rye is still up with my folks at the Light. For a while. No one in Silverton knows yet—that he's mine. And—and Dare's."

Marcy drew a deep, sympathetic breath. So that was what was worrying Serena. "I won't breathe a word, not even to David."

"David already knows—oh, not that Dare and I were married, but about Riley."

So David had known all along that the little boy was illegitimate but he hadn't trusted her to tell her, his own wife! The hurt struck deep as Marcy watched Serena, looking into the gilt-framed mirror on the wall, tuck a strand of her bright hair into place nervously.

Serena said suddenly, as if she'd made up her mind she had

to: "I'm glad you decided to come back. You very nearly ruined David by staying so long in Texas."

"*I* ruined him!"

"If you'd stuck by him, Louella and Soaks couldn't have talked. It was sickening, the things they said. Soaks wouldn't hear a word against you, poor little wronged wife. . . . You'd think David had walked out on you, instead of the other way round!"

"But I went home only because I was ill." Why did she have to explain to Serena? Marcy caught her breath for the enormity of Serena's accusation; her passionate bitterness could mean only one thing. Marcy burst out, "*You're in love with David!*"

Serena stared unbelieving, stunned. She had picked up a small framed picture from her dresser, as if she'd been about to show it to Marcy, but now she gripped the silver frame so hard her knuckles were white. Suddenly there were tears in her eyes, and Marcy wondered uneasily if she had made a fool of herself? If she was wrong, it was unforgivable to accuse Serena. Would she never learn to curb her tongue? She glanced uncertainly at the picture in the other girl's hand, a photograph of a little boy with freckles but with Serena's cleanly cut features. It must be her Riley. How stupid could she be? Of course he was the answer. Overcome by remorse, Marcy faltered, "You—married Dare for Rye's sake, didn't you? So he'd have a father? Forgive me. It—it was a brave thing to do."

Serena defended: "Dare's a good egg. Half the silly things he does are because his folks always treated him like a kid. Too much Granny and too much money. But I keep hoping, now he's got Rye to take care of—"

Marcy finished the sentence for her silently "—that Dare will grow up."

Serena married to Dare, Li'l Emily having Sam's son who

might have been yours, and you and David lacking the old magic but trying to work it out—marriage wasn't simple; it had innumerable bypaths where you could get lost. Marcy said slowly: "You're Maine and I'm Texas. I reckon we both know how to keep our mouths shut."

"You really mean that, Marcy?" When the other girl nodded, Serena wiped her wet eyes, then glanced in the mirror to murmur ruefully: "I can't go back in there. Granny's too sharp. She'd want to know why I've been crying."

"Don't worry. I'll settle Granny."

Serena flung herself down on the chaise lounge. She was gorgeous, lying there with the lamplight making a halo of her hair. She must love her Rye as you had Peter Andrew. That Serena's son had been born under a cloud would make her feel even more responsible for him. Well, this was one conversation you wouldn't repeat, even to David. People who urged that husband and wife should share every thought were simply being childish. Momi had managed Paw for thirty years without his suspecting it; however much he might rant and roar, he always did what she wanted in the end. If that wasn't being successfully married, what was?

Back in the Drexels' big living room, Marcy announced that Serena was feeling under the weather and had gone to bed.

"Sick to her stomach?" Granny asked eagerly.

Dare scowled, "Granny!"

"Been nearly two months, ain't it?" Granny figured. It was obvious she hoped for a new grandchild as soon as possible. Marcy wondered how she felt about Riley. The answer to that was that he wasn't here and Granny managed this household.

Marcy said slowly: "It'll be nice to have someone I know here in Silverton. Do you suppose Serena will pour for me next Thursday at the Ladies' Aid tea at the parsonage?"

"Of course she will," Granny accepted for her, pleased. "You're smart and pretty. You can call me 'Granny' if you like. But don't make any passes at my grandson. He's spoken for."

"Pay her no mind," Dare begged, but Granny tapped him with her cane, ordering:

"Take Marcy 'n' David into the parlor and show 'em my gimcracks. My leg's too tired to stand around."

The parlor was French with long windows hung with gold embroidered draperies, a pale flowered carpet, delicate satin sofa, and gilt chairs with spindly legs. "Not a comfortable seat in the lot. Granny entertains here only the people she wants to get rid of." Dare grinned. "Or else she has big parties for those she wants to pay off. But she's proud of her loot." He waved at the little gilt-edged, glass-topped tables filled with the treasures Granny'd collected in her travels all over the world. They must be worth a fortune, Marcy thought, awed, looking down at jade earrings from China, alabaster from Italy, unbelievably delicate fans from Japan, carved edelweiss from Switzerland. When she admired a tiny ivory Chinese coolie drawing his delicate-wheeled rickshaw, Dare insisted upon taking the trinket out of the case. Was it entirely accident that, in showing her the exquisite toy, Dare's hand had brushed hers?

"You ought to join our Little Theater group," Dare told Marcy, close to her ear. "The players in the Barn are strictly amateur, but we do charge admission to pay for the sets and stuff. We're casting this week for *The Second Mrs. Tanqueray.* His voice rose excitedly. "You should try out for Paula!"

David's arm jerked, and Marcy said hastily, "Oh, no. I couldn't." She handed Dare back the ivory toy nervously and he put it away, shut down the glass lid carelessly.

"Why not?"

"Mrs. Tanqueray wasn't exactly a surburban parson's

wife," David suggested dryly, but Dare brushed his words aside impatiently, insisting to Marcy:

"You have everything Paula had—charm, mystery, beauty . . ."

"Don't let him talk you into playing that tart," Granny snapped, hobbling up behind them.

Dare protested: "You wouldn't want us to play trash, Gran. Pinero may not be Shakespeare, but his stuff is real."

"So's chewin' tobacco, but I don't hanker after it," the old lady said tartly.

Marcy interposed quickly: "I'm afraid I'm much too busy getting settled, to take on anything more just now. Why don't you ask Serena to play Paula, Dare?" It was a mean thrust but she couldn't resist it. There was a limit to how noble you could be. She smiled up at her tall listening husband: "Davey, we ought to be going. Thank you for a lovely evening, Mrs.— Granny."

"Come again soon," Granny urged. "I like young people around."

"I'm glad you sat on that young squirt," David remarked as he and Marcy rattled home on Heinrich's black leather front seat. "I hear some of the young set who act in his Barn are quite fast. But of course hens will cluck. Lots of people still think the devil owns the theater." When Marcy didn't answer, he looked at her anxiously. "Not that I think that, but still . . ."

Marcy patted his arm. "Davey, you're sweet. You'll be proud of me yet."

"I'm glad you asked Rene to help you with the tea. She's going to be at a loose end. I bet she won't even have to make a bed, with all those maids at Drexels'."

Marcy murmured, "I wish Mrs. Minnie would wear an apron serving dinner. Serena's beautiful, isn't she, Davey?"

"Sure. What were you talking about so long in her apartment?"

"Nothing much." Was it possible he had no idea of the way he could charm lady parishioners? It was a good thing that David had her to look after him.

Chapter Twelve

WHEN Marcy woke in the big double bed with its bunch of wooden walnut grapes hanging heavy over her head, David was gone, as usual. He must have crawled out of bed carefully, and taken his clothes from their closet with infinite care not to wake her. Marcy yawned, looked at the small gold wrist watch Paw'd given her, and knew that by now Mrs. Minnie had cooked David's breakfast and he had left for hospital calls, committee meetings. . . . It had been this way ever since they'd come to the new parish where he'd felt he had to get to know all his people as soon as possible. Preaching was fine, he explained, but what people really wanted was a pastor to whom they could tell their troubles. A pastor was a safety valve, if he was any good. Marcy sighed. They never had time now for a leisurely breakfast together, as when they were first married, at St. Luke's. All officers of the organizations in the church had wanted "a word from the new minister." The phone and doorbell rang constantly, even during meals. Practically the only time she got David to herself was when he was asleep, Marcy thought ruefully. Maybe she ought to print calling cards. *Mrs. David Gallant at home to Mr. David Gallant.* 11 P.M. *Thursdays* . . .

A knock on the door was followed abruptly by Mrs. Minnie appearing with a tray of coffee, toast, and a boiled egg.

"Why, Mrs. Minnie!" Marcy beamed, surprised. "How kind of you."

"Easier for me than you messing up my dining-room table in the middle of the morning," Mrs. Minnie explained, but her gray eyes gleamed, pleased. "You mind if I use the best tablecloth for the Home Missionary Tea this afternoon?"

"Heavens, no. I mean, yes, do use it." Marcy reached avidly for her coffee. "I'll get right up and help you."

"The barrel come," Mrs. Minnie reported. "The one they're goin' to pack for the missionary's family in Idaho." She glanced disapprovingly at the blue chiffon dress on the back of a chair, and then at Marcy lying there, a rosy child with pink cheeks and disheveled brown curls, and reported, too carelessly: "Miz Drexel called, the young one. She asked if she could see David this morning, in the church study."

Under Mrs. Minnie's avid eyes, Marcy's color rose in spite of all she could do. "This *is* Thursday, isn't it?" On Thursday and Tuesday mornings David kept office hours at the church so that anyone who wanted to consult him about personal or church affairs would be sure of finding him. There was a note about it on the bottom of the church calendar.

"Janitor's there on Thursdays too," Mrs. Minnie reassured, and Marcy knew the older woman had recognized the tension in her. Deliberately Marcy relaxed her fingers on her coffee cup. She stared at the dress Mrs. Minnie was putting upon a hanger. Why couldn't Serena have come here to the parsonage? Because then she'd have to see you, make small talk, when all she wanted was to see David.

"Never mind putting that away." As the startled Mrs. Minnie stared, Marcy ordered recklessly, suddenly determined to put out of sight the dress that was twin to Serena's: "Put it into the missionary barrel for me, will you? Before the rest come."

"But it's your good dress! It ain't even paid for!"

So she had listened to you and David arguing over charge accounts. "It'll be paid for. Why shouldn't I give it away if I want to? You think the missionary's wife will die of shock at getting something new?"

"I suppose she'll like it, poor thing," Mrs. Minnie agreed. As she smoothed out the dress doubtfully, the delicate chiffon caught in the cracks in her rough fingers, and a spot of color appeared on the thin, yellowed skin of her cheeks. "It's a pretty color, ain't it?"

Marcy offered impulsively, "Would you like to keep the scarf?"

"My gracious, no," Mrs. Minnie gasped. "What would I do with it?" But she laid the softness of the chiffon against her cheek for a moment. Poor soul. She must buy Mrs. Minnie a bright new scarf for Christmas, rose perhaps? Mrs. Minnie folded the blue-green scarf and laid it carefully in the top bureau drawer. "You can wear that with most anything. Your husband won't pay for nothin', anyways." She started for the bedroom door, the dress in her hand. "This all?" Mrs. Minnie could hardly wait to get to the phone, to tell her sister the latest crazy thing the new minister's wife had done. "You want I should polish the teaspoons?"

"Please. I'll rinse off the china cups," Marcy promised. "After my bath."

The bathroom was like the rest of the parsonage, enormous, hard to heat. The zinc tub stood so high on four iron legs, you had to leap to get inside, but the water was hot, soothing, and the gardenia bath salts gave off a subtle fragrance. Marcy leaned back, relaxing, planning. The ladies could put their wraps in the north bedroom; there were twin beds to hold all the coats. They could overflow into the blue bedroom if more came than you expected, and very likely they would, if just to see how well the new preacher's wife kept their parsonage. Marcy sighed. That first morning when she and David had arrived straight from the train from Texas, with Marcy exhausted by the soot and roar of the Pullman, David had looked around happily. "Four bedrooms. We can put up the bishop and the district superintendent and their wives, if we ever get the conference to meet in the Silverton church!"

David always thought of the parsonage in terms of his job, never as their home, a secure retreat. Anyway, with Mrs.

Minnie there, they might as well have lived in a telephone booth. David could never understand why Marcy objected so strenuously to having her around, or why Marcy disliked having him introduce her as his "good wife." "It sounds as if I wore tatting on my underwear!" Marcy had explained that first morning when Mrs. Finkelsetter, president of the Aid, had been waiting for them to arrive at the parsonage with a friendly late breakfast keeping warm in the oven. "Doesn't 'good wife' sound smug to you, Mrs. Finkelsetter?"

The Aid president had stared at Marcy, uncomfortably; she was a plump woman who looked rather like the first doll Aunt Riah had made Marcy out of a baby pillow tied in the middle, with the face painted on. "Oh, I don't know. Maybe." Her cheeks now were so roundly pink that Marcy realized wildly that doubtless Mrs. Finkelsetter crocheted her own tatting. Oh, dear. But the Aid president had come through splendidly. "You mean, if you are good, no need to underline it?"

Marcy chuckled, remembering, and the fragrant bath water slid caressingly about her white neck. Mrs. Finkelsetter was a dear, and even Mrs. Minnie had her moments. But it would be nice to have some say in what went on in her own home. Mrs. Minnie had proved as adamant in her menus as the laws of the Medes and the Persians; Sunday, a roast of beef, lamb, or chicken; Monday, cold meat; Tuesday, hash; Wednesday, omelet or cheese soufflé; Thursday, stew; Friday, fish, which she knew Marcy loathed; Saturday night, beans and brown bread indigestible to anyone but a New Englander. But Mrs. Minnie was economical in her buying, and, as David said, they'd just have to put up with her till they were sure Marcy was strong enough to take care of the house herself. It was the principle of the thing, Marcy retorted; was she or was she not boss in her own kitchen? When Marcy made a cake, Mrs. Minnie resented being asked even to wash up the cake pan,

Marcy reported indignantly. "The Minnie Bird told me: 'I don't hafta work for nobuddy! I'm jest accomodatin'.'"

David laughed, "Humor her," he advised. "It won't hurt you to wash a pan, and it gives her a big kick."

David was right as usual. Marcy sighed, got up out of the fragrant water, and reached for a big towel with the entwined monograms that she had to fight Mrs. Minnie to let her use instead of keeping for "company." "I'd better ask Mrs. Finkelsetter to pour, this afternoon," Marcy decided. "She's in charge of the reception next Friday."

The reception was the church's formal welcome for the new minister and his wife. Marcy wondered anxiously if her wedding dress would be too elaborate to wear? Or should she wear a suit and silk shirtwaist? She'd call Granny Drexel, Marcy decided, stopping at the telephone on her way downstairs to the kitchen. Fortunately, Granny was at home. "Has it got long sleeves?" Granny demanded when Marcy suggested the wedding dress.

"Long sleeves and a lace bertha."

Granny approved, "Flatters folks when the minister's wife dolls up some."

But as she came into the brightly lighted vestry on the evening of the reception, Marcy saw that the satin dress Momi had embroidered with the pink roses around the neck and a spray on the skirt to make it look less bridelike was the most elaborate in the big noisy room. The very walls were bursting out with bustle, heat, and conversation, for nearly all the four hundred parishioners had tried to crowd into the long, low-ceiled room. To accommodate the crowd, the folding doors had been rolled back so that the two side rooms, the kindergarten and the Ladies' Parlor, could be used. Even then the tables had to be set so closely together that when one diner sat down or got up, the whole line of diners had to move, too. Each table was covered with immaculate, shiny white paper, brightened at intervals with tight bouquets of fall asters or autumn leaves stuffed into water glasses. Yellow candles, looking a bit the worse for wear, stood at varying angles in low glass candlesticks.

"We never light 'em except at the headtable, so we can use 'em again," Mrs. Minnie explained at Marcy's elbow. "They look real pretty, don't they?"

"Lovely." Marcy turned to smile at Mrs. Finkelsetter bustling up with a large platter of ham for the table. Mrs. Minnie, feeling her importance as a member of the parsonage family, warned, "When you set up the head table, Mr. Gallant don't like no fat on his ham."

"I expect he can cut it off, then, for himself," Mrs. Finkelsetter snapped. After all, she'd been peeling potatoes here in the kitchen since nine this morning, but if all the ladies who'd promised to help had come . . .

"Can I help serve?" Marcy offered eagerly. Something to do instead of just standing there while people inspected her out of the corners of their eyes.

"Not in that dress." Mrs. Finkelsetter eyed the gaily embroidered white satin dubiously. "You got no apron. Besides, this is your reception. There's Mr. Gallant beckoning you, now. I guess he wants you to meet the Curtises. My goodness, what a pretty bouquet of roses Winnie Mae's got for you!"

Dr. Curtis and his wife looked nice, her kind of people, Marcy thought gratefully, smiling at the tall, dark-haired, but rather tired-looking man in a well-cut tweed jacket. His pretty wife, Cecily, wore a dark-blue silk dress with a white satin binding at the neck which Marcy saw instantly was exactly the demure sort of dress she should have worn herself. Knowing she was overdressed made Marcy feel rather on the defensive, but no one could resist for long the warmth in Cecily Curtis's wide-set brown eyes.

"I'm so glad you're young," Cecily confessed to Marcy. "The last minister's wife was over sixty and she always made me feel as if I ought to recite my catechism. Winnie Mae," she urged the elf of a child with blond hair, startling with her mother's brown eyes, who was nervously flirting the two ruffles which made up the skirt of her pink organdy dress, "what are you going to do with those roses, darling?"

"Give them to *her!*" Winnie Mae gasped, clutching the large bouquet, and delving deeper into her mother's skirt. Cecily gave the three-year-old a gentle push. "Well, go on!"

Winnie Mae gulped, and stared up at Marcy with glazed brown eyes; but even when Marcy bent down, smiling, and reached for the roses, the child backed away, terrified at all the beaming parish watching her. David came to the rescue. He grinned down at Winnie Mae, then made a buzzing sound in his throat. "It's a bee, Winnie Mae," he said. "He wants to steal honey from your roses. Listen!" The bee buzzed again, and Winnie Mae began to giggle. As the bee buzzed right down and landed in her bouquet, the child thrust the flowers suddenly at Marcy, then ran to throw her arms around David's leg.

"Do it again!" Winnie Mae begged.

David picked her up and perched the tiny girl, a pink organdy butterfly, on his big shoulder as he made the bee buzz again. This time the bee landed in the soft place in the back of Winnie Mae's plump little neck.

"He has a way with children, hasn't he?" Cecily Curtis beamed to Marcy. "Do you have any of your own?"

"No. I—we—"

David answered for Marcy, glancing quickly over Winnie Mae's head: "We have a son, but he lived only one day."

"Oh," gasped Cecily, "I'm sorry!"

Dr. Curtis interrupted, "I think they're waiting for you two up on the platform, Mr. Gallant."

"David," he corrected. He and Dr. Curtis exchanged smiles. "Phil, then, David."

At the long table set upon the platform in the front of

the room the candles were lighted in celebration. Granny and
Dandy Drexel were already up there, as was Mrs. Finkelsetter's
husband—in all the time they lived in Silverton, Marcy was
never to think of him as anything else, he was so thin and
apologetic, with his six brown hairs smoothed over the top
of his bald head and his anxious smile of a nicely brought-up
rabbit. Places were also set for the Sunday-school superintendent and his wife, and for Marcy and David, but when he tried
to give Winnie Mae back to her mother the little girl wailed,
"I want to stay with my beeman!"

"Now listen, Winnie Mae," Cecily began to urge, embarrassed.

"Do let her," Marcy begged.

But Mrs. Finkelsetter said flatly, "There isn't any room."

"I'll give you one of my roses," Marcy offered hastily as
Winnie Mae's mouth puckered into a wail.

"She can sit on my knee!" David decided, keeping her small
hand in his as they started up front. As it turned out, Winnie
Mae couldn't stay with David, for an emergency message from
the hospital came for Dr. Curtis and he and his family had
to leave even before David said the blessing. Cecily explained
she couldn't drive the car, and in any case they had only one.
It was always this way, being a doctor's wife, she sighed; and
Marcy said the life of a minister's wife was worse, and do
come to see her soon. She liked the Curtis family the best of
any parishioners she had met yet. She felt they might laugh
at the same things.

As she skirted the little paper cups full of lukewarm fruit
salad to her place at the head table, Marcy saw that Dandy
Drexel had saved the seat for her next to him, with David
next to Granny, who was already sitting down at her place.
"My knee hurts," she explained. "I guess the Lord'll excuse me if I don't stand up for the prayer." David told her
he didn't think prayer had much to do with posture. Granny

said, No, for the Mohammedans she'd seen in Tunis had prayed with their heads on a rug.

"You look like a bride tonight, Marcy," Dandy Drexel admired. "It's my wedding dress made over," Marcy confessed. As she looked out over the crowd down below, staring up at them, waiting for David to say the blessing so they could sit down, she wondered, almost panicky, if she'd ever be able to remember all these names? Eight hundred eyes . . . All at once they seemed to merge frighteningly into the Eye of God on her Sunday-school card when she was a little girl at St. Paul's.

"Good evening, Marcy," Dare's voice said behind her. He looked as if his dark-blue jacket and gray trousers had grown on him. He murmured, "I can tell you the menu with my eyes shut: ham, potato salad, pickles, melting ice cream, and five kinds of pie. But Granny always insists on the whole family gathering round. . . . You haven't changed your mind about doing Paula? We're having the tryouts tonight at the Barn."

"Sh!" Granny hissed fiercely. "Quit your foolishness, Dare, and go back down where you belong. With Serena."

Dare melted away like the ice cream, as Mrs. Finkelsetter, very pink and trembling, announced, "Our pastor will now say the blessing." Marcy bent her head. She must warn David later he musn't pray so long when everyone was hungry. She looked under her almost closed lids for Serena. She and Dare were standing at a table just below the platform. "With the other goats," she could almost hear Dare chuckle. Serena's pale green organdy dress looked simple, but it was artfully cut to show her long, perfect body; it must have cost plenty, Marcy knew enviously, but money didn't matter to that family. The Drexels even had three cars, a big Mercedes-Benz, a Packard with a roll-down top, and a black limousine about a block long for Granny, driven by James, the chauffeur. A

Pierce-Arrow? "Amen," David said, and Marcy sat down with the rest.

The dinner was exactly as Dare had warned, but it was also delicious. If the fruit cup was lukewarm from waiting too long, the ham was pink and spiced, the potato salad had some sort of luscious mustard dressing, the pickles were homemade, and the currant jelly delicate and rosy. There were also hot rolls, mountains of butter, and afterward ice cream in vari-colored slabs and homemade pies so mouth-watering Marcy was hard put to it to select a lemon meringue dripping with brown beads of sweetness. Mrs. Finkelsetter's husband, she noticed with awe, took all five kinds of pie offered him. She waited for his thinness to bulge out or for him to burst, but he did neither; he merely sucked coffee loudly through his false teeth. Marcy, smothering a giggle, saw that Dare and Serena down below her were getting up and striding toward the door, and envied them. If only she could miss the speeches! The Sunday-school superintendent, an eager man in a gray suit and spectacles, looked as if he would talk forever; he did. Then Dandy Drexel as chairman of the board rambled on above the clinking of coffee cups, the rustle of crushed paper napkins. David, bless him, simply added a postscript: "My wife and I are very happy to be here and we want to meet you all. You'll have to forgive us if we don't greet you correctly the first time." He used to have a system for remembering names, David explained, but the system was so much more trouble than the names that he'd discarded it. Polite laughter. They would now adjourn to the Ladies' Parlor. Everyone clapped, and the noise of chairs being pushed back from the tables was deafening as they surged toward the Parlor where they had to wait endlessly for the tables to be removed to make room for the receiving line.

Marcy shook four hundred damp hands, smiled fixedly at four hundred faces, and by the end of half an hour her feet hurt, her hand hurt, her smile hurt, and she wanted to go home. But David was in his element; he already knew most of the people from calling in their homes, and their faces would brighten as he greeted them. The new minister was, as Mrs. Finkelsetter put it, "common, like us."

Even church receptions end, however. Back home at last, Marcy, kicking the white satin slippers off her aching feet, was ready to fall into bed, but David was eager to talk. Several people this evening had promised to take over church school classes, and David hoped, though he had got away before he had a chance to put it up to him, that Dare Drexel would take the leaderless troop of Boy Scouts.

"Scouts!" Marcy gasped, peeling off a sheer stocking. Anyone less fitted to teach boys to tie knots . . . How could David be so obtuse?

David went on, unnoticing. "Rene hates theatricals but she's planning all the incidental music to be played between the acts of *The Second Mrs. Tanqueray*. Where did you put my clean pajamas?"

"Try looking in the drawer where they belong." Marcy yawned. "I was Rosalind in our high-school senior play. Of course, that wasn't anything, but . . ."

"You aren't considering playing Paula!"

"I don't know, I might." She laughed at his dismayed face, leaned to lay her soft cheek against his. "You're too easy to tease, darling. I'll make a bargain with you, Davey. I'll skip Paula if you'll stop calling me your 'good wife.' I don't like being branded, even by you."

Chapter Thirteen

THE Phillip Curtises were the only couple in the church with whom Marcy felt perfectly at home; she and Cecily came together as naturally as two drops of water running downhill. The Curtises lived only three doors down the street from the parsonage, so that Cecily was always grabbing up Winnie Mae, opening Marcy's front door without ringing, and calling in her clear fluting voice, "Mar? Anyone home?" Cecily was the nearest to a warm-blooded Texan Marcy had met up North, and Winnie Mae was a darling; she not only looked a life-sized doll but was good-natured, able to play happily by herself. The two girls shopped together mornings, following Mrs. Minnie's list; fed Winnie Mae candy bars, and made her ridiculously small ruffled dresses. Every now and then they bribed Mrs. Minnie to baby-sit so that they could go up town to window-shop. Because Dr. Phil was just beginning his career, as David was, the girls couldn't afford the clothes they wanted, but they could decide what they would have bought if they had the money.

"Dr. Phil," as Marcy and David called him, found the young new preacher equally congenial. They met frequently at the hospital on their respective rounds of patients, but Phil and David did not become really close friends until the night at the shabby boardinghouse where Dr. Phil, deathly tired and knowing his bill would never be paid, was standing by the old lady who was fighting for every breath. David had come at 2 A.M. because the old lady knew she was dying, and had asked wistfully for "her pastor," the only family she had left. She held tightly to David's hand until her fingers loosened, and Dr. Phil, his hand upon her quiet pulse, snapped shut his watch.

"She's gone. It was good of you, David. She hated living

here. Lonely old age is tragic." His doctor's eyes slid over David's drawn face, his heavy eyes. "What do you do to let off steam, feller?"

"I ought to take up golf or tennis, I suppose," David said soberly, "but there hardly seems time to eat, let alone hit a ball around."

"Come home with me and have some breakfast," Dr. Phil offered, closing up his black bag, then, at David's hesitation, "Cecily won't mind. She's used to meals at all hours." As they went together down the shaky wooden steps of the shabby boardinghouse, the sky blazed with banners of crimson and yellow. "What a gorgeous sunrise!" David murmured. Was the old lady up there, welcomed by that blaze of glory? He hoped so.

Cecily got up, looking sleepy and yet deliciously fresh in a rose-colored woollen dressing gown. Winnie Mae in her pink sleepers fell upon David with shouts of joy. "My beeman! Do it, David!"

"Leave him alone, baby, he's tired," her father told her, but David swung the little girl up on his big shoulders; she grabbed at his bright hair, and hung on, crowing with delight.

"I like being bothered," David explained. "My Peter Andrew'd be almost her age."

Cecily fussed over David, urging hot biscuits and honey upon him, while Winnie Mae sat on his knee, eating alternate bites.

"We would have called you to come over, if it hadn't been crack of dawn," Cecily told Marcy later that morning at the parsonage. Marcy said wistfully she wished they had called; she hardly ever saw David. He was getting terribly tired. These night calls wouldn't be so bad if Heinrich could be depended upon to start; but even with hot water in his radiator the cold fall nights made him stubborn. Sometimes Marcy would have to go out in her warm dressing gown, with a coat over it, and sit shivering on the front seat, running that little jigger on the wheel up and down with David cranking, until Heinrich took a notion to roar into action.

"You need a decent car," Cecily worried. The telephone interrupted, and Marcy came back to report that Granny Drexel wanted her to come over for tea, which was, of course, a command performance. Not that Marcy wouldn't have liked Granny if she hadn't a cent; she was exciting, unpredictable, and not old in anything except her body. the undisputed head of the Drexel tribe. "It does seem redundant, the Drexels having three cars and Davey's having only an excuse for one," Marcy told Cecily as she came back to pick up her coffee cup. She and Cecily drank quarts between them, Mrs. Minnie grumbled. "Did you know Serena's learning to drive?"

"What for?" Cecily's eyes widened. "They have a chauffeur, James."

Marcy made a wry face. "I asked her. She said, 'To get places.' Dare was furious because she'd dented a fender." Marcy broke off as David, his face smeared with oil and dismay, came into the living room where the girls were chatting.

"Heinrich's laid down and died," David reported. "I'll have to take the streetcar over to the Gowdys. Hank's on the loose again."

"Not so early in the afternoon!" Marcy frowned, for David's preoccupation with that persistant drunk Hank Gowdy who neglected his five children who sat, shining faces washed, clothes neatly mended, each with a penny clutched in his or her hot little hand every Sunday morning at service beside their mother, Ruth Gowdy, was a main bone of contention between Marcy and David. Hank was a big man with red hair and muscles of steel; sober, he adored his family, but after a few drinks he was quite capable of beating up his wife if he suspected she'd hid out a few dollars on him to feed the children until next pay day. Ruth should call the police, Marcy insisted, not David.

"Ruth just phoned that Hank's down in the corner saloon, fixing for trouble unless I get him out of there, soon." David sighed, rubbing his cheek with oily fingers. Hank was one parish problem he ought to have licked by now, but he couldn't let Ruth have more patience than he did; she took in sewing, and kept their three-room apartment over the grocery store as immaculate as possible with seven people living there; she loved Hank, and David could see why. In spite of his great bulk, there was a sensitive streak in him, a yearning for something better than his grade-school education had afforded him, with a consequent tendency to strike out at an unrewarding world. David had seen Hank look at his wife with a dogged yearning for forgiveness that he could not put into words but that Ruth understood. It was this sensitive child to whom she clung as she would have to her other five.

"Well, I'm off," David told the girls cheerfully. "Don't expect me back until you see me, Marcy."

Marcy murmured, drat Heinrich, she'd hoped David would run her over to see Granny Drexel. Now she'd have to take the streetcar, too. Cecily soothed that she and Winnie Mae would walk down to the corner with her.

Granny obviously had something on her mind when Marcy arrived that afternoon at the big Drexel living room to find the old lady sitting upright in a stiff-backed chair, with her bad leg stretched out on a hassock in front of her. Granny motioned Marcy to a comfortably cushioned armchair and told the uniformed maid fussing over the tea tray: "Pour and then git. I want to talk to Miz Gallant, here."

"I'm sorry to be late," Marcy apologized. "Heinrich was on the blink again—as usual."

But Granny wasn't listening. After the maid had scurried away, Granny told Marcy abruptly: "I'm worried over Rene. She don't act right."

"Is she sick?" Marcy stirred her tea, avoiding Granny's sharp black eyes; she'd have to be careful, Granny was so keen.

"If you mean, is she expectin', she ain't," Granny snapped. "That's just the trouble." She shot Marcy a glance that asked: How much do you know? "You ever hear tell of a bride 'n' groom who slept in two rooms?"

Marcy sidestepped a direct answer. "Maybe Serena misses Riley."

"That's why she's learning to drive. She wants to run up to Bellport by herself," Granny admitted. Her black eyes snapped. "I guess Rene told you and David about Riley?" As Marcy nodded, the old lady dug into her pocket of her black silk dress, adding proudly, "He's a Drexel, all right. Some smart for six." She handed Marcy a slip of ruled white paper with printed words slanting crookedly across the page. It read:

"DEER RENE: I caught a heering. Jon et it. When are you coming up to see me? I need fishhooks.
"RILEY SNOW DREXEL."

The third name had been erased and then written in again so hard it cut the paper. *Riley Snow Drexel.* Did you have to adopt an illegitimate son to give him your name? This was enough to upset Serena, all this uncertainty. Marcy handed the paper back. "What's a 'heering'?"

"Herring, of course. John's his pet seagull, Rene says. Oh, I don't blame her for wanting the boy, but if he come here folks'd talk. We'll have to wait a spell." She changed the subject abruptly, "Where's David? Why don't he stop by more often? Parishioner, ain't I?"

"He's down under the Model T," Marcy explained. "Heinrich's always losing a gear or something. David spends more time on that wreck. . . . It nearly drives him crazy, all these new people moving into town. He says the Unitarian minister's usually been there before him. Not that one church isn't as good as another . . ."

Granny bristled. "Different. I never could see how folks

could celebrate Christmas if they don't believe the Baby was God's Son. Ought to dance around the Maypole or something. What's worryin' you?" as the little maid slid in through the door and stood waiting to speak.

"Mr. Dare says, do you and Mrs. Gallant want to come out to the Barn?" the maid reported. "They're rehearsing."

"I'd love to," Marcy said eagerly. "I haven't seen the Barn yet."

"Git your coat. Mine's in the closet," Granny ordered.

Granny leaned heavily upon her cane as she hobbled down the path toward the playhouse she'd built "to keep Dare busy." As they stepped inside the wide door, Marcy saw that the Barn was large enough to hold a couple of hundred spectators. Although the seats were only wooden benches, the stage boasted all the necessary equipment: footlights, spots, flats, a stage setting showing a comfortable living room bright with English chintz and flowers. As Marcy and Granny tiptoed down the aisle, the spot was on a tall blond girl on stage, with Dare down below, berating her.

"Nancy, for gosh sake, stop hamming, darling! *Feel Paula.* She loves the guy!"

The girl called Nancy stiffened, glared. "If you don't like my interpretation, darling, you know what you can—"

"Hi Granny. Hello, Marcy!" Dare interrupted with relief, turning to beam at his audience. "I'm afraid you've come at a bad moment. We seem to be getting nowhere but fast." He ordered, "Time out, everyone," and came down the aisle to meet his grandmother and her guest. Granny coughed, and Dare said anxiously: "Is it chilly in here? I hadn't noticed. The footlights and spots warm up the stage. I'll have James open up the furnace."

"You will not," Granny snapped. "Be like burning up dollar bills. I'll git along back where it's warmer. You show Marcy around."

As Dare looked after her hobbling away, he said: "She won't be able to get out of bed tomorrow if she gets chilled. She hates like poison being eighty. In some ways, she's younger than any of us. She loves rehearsals. You want to meet the cast?"

"Oh, I don't want to interrupt. I'd rather listen," Marcy demurred, but for the first time she really warmed to a Dare who could worry over his grandmother. She sat down in a front seat as he called, "Ready, folks? Everyone in the wings, please, except those onstage."

The rehearsal went like all amateur first attempts. Dare and Nancy, who had the lead parts, had their lines fairly well, but none of the bit players seemed to know their entrances or exits; stage business had to be worked out to avoid players bunching up or peering blankly for a speaker who wasn't there. Queer how different Dare was here—no longer the adolescent showoff, but the firm director. He made instant decisions that were invariably right, and handled his actors expertly, cajoling not ordering them, getting from them finally what he wanted. Even the blond Nancy played up to him finally, using her body and eyes, subtly, as he suggested. So Dare wasn't stupid, just lazy, Marcy decided. What had his mother been like? Had she made Dare wear Little Lord Fauntleroy velvet suits to greet her guests in the drawing room before dinner? Strange that this play world seemed to be the only place where he'd learned to face reality. He had real talent.

"Curtain," Dare called finally. "Good show. Come on up to the house for tea and sandwiches. Coffee, too, I expect. How about you, darling?" he asked Marcy.

"Darling" didn't mean a thing except that you belonged to the gang.

She said impulsively, as they walked up the aisle: "You're

good, you know. Why don't you go to New York, Dare? Try for a real stage job?"

"I tried." Dare shrugged. "But Granny wouldn't hear of it. Amateur theatricals are all right as a sideline, but real grease paint's too sissy for a Drexel. You see before you the future President of 'Drexel and Sons, Designers of Fine Bathrooms for Luxury Living.' There must always be a Daniel."

"You should go anyway," Marcy urged. "You're bigger than the Barn." It was equally absurd to imagine the elegant Dandy Drexel, Senior, as a plumbing executive. But the business was probably so well organized it ran itself, no matter which Daniel's name was engraved on the letterhead. Money bred money, and Dare could hardly be blamed for not tossing away his heritage by bucking Granny; still . . .

"Hi, you two." Serena was sitting behind the tea urn, pouring for the players who were milling around the big living room, when Dare and Marcy arrived. "Milk or lemon? Have you joined the cast, Marcy?"

"No, thanks—to both questions," Marcy told her. "As Mrs. Minnie says, 'I've et.' With Granny earlier." As Dare led her around, introducing her to the players, Marcy was conscious of Serena's green eyes following her thoughtfully. Serena looked lovely in her black velvet dress; the lace around her square-cut neck must be real. As Granny hobbled into the room, Dare rushed to ease her into the big chair and make her comfortable. Marcy murmured that she must go, but Granny wanted to know what her hurry was. Surely that Minnie snooper could fix supper.

"How many fenders did you crash today?" Dare asked his wife.

Serena grinned. "No paint off, for once. James says I'm doing so well he thinks I can apply for a license next week. Can I have the Packard tomorrow, Dare? Or are you taking it to the office?"

Dare said that not only was he using the Packard but that the pater had to drive to Worcester in the Mercedes and that Granny'd need both James and the Pierce-Arrow. Tomorrow was her Boston Symphony day.

"Seems like three cars ought to be enough for one family," Granny grumbled. "I figured on loaning David a car tomorrow, if his was still passed out, but I couldn't miss Symphony."

Marcy reassured her quickly: "David hates borrowing. He says it's the easiest way to lose friends." She glanced at her wrist watch. "Heavens, I really must go. There's a streetcar at the corner at six, isn't there?"

"David shouldn't be usin' shanks' mare when the parish is so spread out," Granny worried. Then her face cleared, and she patted Marcy's shoulder. "There's time to talk and a time to act, I always say." What might Granny mean by that?

"Come on, Marcy, I'll run you home in whatever Rene's left of the Packard," Dare offered. His hand ruffled his wife's smooth bright hair. "Want to come along for the ride, Red?" Granny must be imagining things, Marcy saw with relief.

"I've had enough for one day, thanks." Serena, glancing around at the cast, obviously good for another half-hour of arguing over the play, made a rueful mouth. "Someone's got to play hostess to your gang, and Granny's all in. Run along, you two."

Marcy dropped an impulsive kiss on Granny's cheek as she went by, let Dare drape her warm coat over her shoulders, and followed him to the garage. As she slid into the front seat of the luxurious car, she remembered Sam's big freckled hand tucking the robe about her feet, and sighed.

"Rabbit run over your grave?" Dare asked.

"I used to have a friend who had a Mercedes in Texas. It seems good to ride in a real car."

"Kid stuff?" Dare asked, interested.

She explained, "Oh, yes. He married my sister." The engine

was a pleasant murmur, as they slid out into the street. Marcy commented, ruefully, "Not much like our Model T. It shakes so it rattles your back teeth, and the radiator's cracked, so Davey has to get out every few miles to give Heinrich a drink."

"Why don't you get a new Henry, then?"

"Three guesses." Didn't he even know how much the Silverton church paid its preacher? Probably not. "I wonder how David made out this afternoon with Hank." She told Dare, "He takes the parish troubles so to heart. The Old Man in the Shoe. I worry about him getting too exhausted."

" 'Live and let live' . . . that's the only way to be happily married, I tell Rene."

As they neared the parsonage, Marcy begged: "Let me out here at the corner, Dare, please. Mrs. Minnie'd broadcast it to the entire congregation if she saw us drive up together."

"So what?" But Dare slowed obediently at the corner, and stopped. Marcy opened the car door for herself, and jumped out without waiting for him to help her. She waved, smiling, as he drove off, sounding his horn in farewell, with its unmistakable three-note chord. Oh, dear, did he have to sound that trumpet?

Marcy's cheeks were becomingly flushed as she ran up the parsonage steps; Mrs. Minnie was in the kitchen, thank goodness, and the sound of the typewriter came from the open study door. David was home. If that was his sermon, it must be full of fire and brimstone, the way he was pounding. He didn't look up as she tiptoed by, so she went into the bedroom and shut the door, feeling suddenly deflated, the gaiety of the afternoon gone.

Next morning while Mrs. Minnie and Marcy were both polishing silver in the kitchen, she shot Marcy a sharp glance over her chamois. "You mind if I say something, Miz Gallant?" Marcy was still "Miz Gallant," though her husband was "David"; it showed their respective states of grace in Mrs. Minnie's affections. She rushed on, "That Dare's a wild one."

She'd heard the Packard's horn yesterday. You were in for a lecture. "Why does everyone call him 'Dare'? I thought his name was 'Daniel,' like his father's."

"And his grandpa's," Mrs. Minnie agreed, scrubbing away at a tarnished fork as if she wished it were Dare's mischievous grin. "Folks've called him 'Dare' ever since he was twelve. Some kid bet him he couldn't walk along the ridgepole of the Drexels' barn, so of course he did. Fell off and broke his leg. When they took him to the hospital he kept yelling: 'It isn't my fault. He dared me!' " Mrs. Minnie glanced at Marcy bent over her polishing cloth. " 'Twa'n't the last time he took a dare, neither. In college they bet him he couldn't go eighty miles an hour in his car, and he got his license took away for a year."

The tooting of an automobile horn in the street broke into Mrs. Minnie's homily about how any woman who had the sense the good Lord gave her would steer clear of Dare Drexel's nonsense. Maybe there wasn't no real harm in him, but still . . .

"Who's making all that racket out front?" Mrs. Minnie demanded irritably, carrying her polishing rag to the dining-room window to look out. "I declare, if them Drexels ain't got them a fire engine!"

Marcy went to the window too, and stared out at the bright red Stutz convertible, flashing brass and new paint in the morning sun, and drawn up in the parsonage driveway behind the decrepit Heinrich. "Davey!" Marcy called upstairs to the study, "Granny and Dare are here!"

"Saturday morning!" David grumbled. Once he got into his sermon for tomorrow, he hated to be interrupted. He came reluctantly downstairs, flung a coat over Marcy's shoulders, and followed her out to the street where Granny was sitting in the front seat of the bright red car beside Dare, who smiled sleepily. Granny wore her black fur coat and her hat with black bows that always reminded Marcy of a large family of crows, nesting. "Well, David, how do you like your new assistant pastor?" Granny asked.

"Assistant *what?*" David gasped.

Granny patted the car door with her black-gloved hand; still David didn't understand. Marcy was quicker.

"You mean the car is—is for us? *Oh, Granny!*"

"Can't let the Unitarians git ahead of us." Granny grinned, nodding her old-fashioned hat; she refused to change styles every year; given time, the styles caught up with her again. "I woke Dare here out of his beauty sleep this morning, made him go down town shopping with me for this here firewagon. The car people didn't seem to want to part with it immejit, but I told 'em: 'For sale, ain't it? You ain't in business for your health, are you?' So we drove off, and here we are. Like it, David?"

"But I don't understand. . . ." David stared at the bright car and then up at Granny's satisfied grin and at Dare's stifled yawn as he sat there behind the wheel.

Granny urged, impatiently: "Git in, git in, both of you. Dare, show David how to work all them gadgets. If that new-fangled starter don't work, we'll send the fool thing back."

David was quite pale. "But we can't possibly let you buy us a car!"

If he won't take it, I'll just die, Marcy panicked. He would refuse, of course. He wouldn't be "beholden" to anyone.

"You ain't accepting anything," Granny snapped. "This is in your name only to save a lot of fuss. It's the new assistant pastor at Silverton Church. If you got to git somewheres in a hurry because someone's passin' in his raincheck, this'll do it. Now hush up and git in that front seat, David Gallant, before I freeze to death. I never did like cars with cloth tops, but

Dare said you would. Dare, show David how to push them buttons, then git into the back seat with Marcy. David kin drive us back home."

Granny'd done it; it was going to work; David was getting into the driver's seat. Marcy drew her heavy coat anxiously about her as Dare slid in beside her; even now David might balk. He was pushing down the starter. As the powerful engine drew them down the street she heaved a deep breath of relief. No more cranking, or filling up Heinrich's cracked radiator, Marcy exulted; no more wondering if you'd make the next hill! You could hardly hear the engine back here, it ran so smoothly. Davey looked thrilled, in spite of himself, as the big car moved obediently under his hands.

"Like it?" Granny asked David, pleased.

"It's like having wings," David agreed, almost reverently. "But—"

"No 'buts,'" Granny ordered. "Jest git me home before I freeze my innards. When everybody else's too all-fired busy to take me where I want to go, I'll give you a ring, David."

"You do that." David flung her a grateful glance. "The Silverton Church thanks you."

"Who is the church? You 'n' me 'n' the other feller," Granny reminded him. It was impossible to argue with Granny, bless her; Marcy hugged her happiness. Let Dare sit there beside her, trying to catch her glance with his, amused and a little bored. He was only Granny's little boy, but Davey was a man.

When they left the Drexels at their big white house, Marcy got into the front seat beside Davey and let the shining window down to feel the rush of wind through her hair. Driving was like flying in this great bright car! She murmured dreamily, "I reckon this was what Granny meant when she told me yesterday there was a time to talk and a time to act."

"Marcy Gallant, if you dared hint to Granny—" David

slammed on the brakes so hard Marcy shot forward in the seat and had to grab at his arm to save bumping her head on the windshield. His eyes staring down at her were suddenly blue ice. "If you planned all this . . . I've a good mind to drive this straight back to Granny!"

"Go right ahead, if that's what you think of me!" Anger at the unjustness of his accusation flared so brightly that Marcy gasped, "Let me out of here!" She fumbled at the door handle, furious at the tears which blurred her eyes.

David's icy gaze melted into concern. "Darling, I'm sorry." He reached for her hands, held them struggling in his own. "I didn't mean—but you sounded as if . . . I know you'd never ask for anything for yourself, but perhaps for me."

"You don't trust me!" Marcy sobbed. "This must have been in your mind for ages. You've been bottling it up. You don't even like me!"

"That's nonsense and you know it! But we've been brought up in such different ways. I admit I've resented your trying to get in with the right people. . . ."

So Sara Harrison had been right about David's being rigid New England. But you'd only tried to help him. "Is that what you call my getting up at four in the morning to make coffee for your Hank Gowdy? A drunk I don't give a hoot about?"

"That's just it. You just do it for me, and he—well, he feels it." David certainly must have thought about this for a long time, Marcy knew bleakly. "I'd have taken you with me calling on shut-ins, except—oh, I know you have a block about sickrooms after what happened to Peter Andrew, but . . ."

"I can't help it!" she wailed. "Hospitals give me goose eggs all up and down my spine. They smell of ether, dead flowers, pain, despair." Marcy's voice thinned to a despairing whisper. "I can hear the banana wagon coming down the corridor, and Peter Andrew isn't there."

"I know, darling." He melted completely into contrition. They drew together again, his cheek leaning down upon her soft curls. What demon drove you on to hurt the one you loved most? Or was it a compliment that there was one person in the world to whom you could show your whole mind and she would understand?

"I reckon I did complain a little to Granny," Marcy admitted honestly in a small voice. "But I never dreamed of her giving us a car. Honest, Davey."

"I believe you." Was he reassuring himself as well as her? "Your hands are like ice. We'd better get on home."

As they flew along, Marcy suggested, "Let's call the new car 'Jehu.' You know, 'He driveth furiously.' What are you going to tell Mrs. Minnie? About the car, I mean?"

"The truth. That Granny gave it to the church."

"She'll probably want you to taxi all the old ladies in town to church."

That was exactly the idea, David said happily. Now he'd be able to pick up old Aunt Lottie Hard and the lame Mr. Cox on Sunday mornings, on his way to service. He could crowd in the Scouts; they wouldn't mind sitting in each other's laps. Davey would be taxi driver and chauffeur for the whole parish, Marcy realized; probably they'd never get to go anywhere themselves, just for fun. Well, that was David. She wouldn't change him if she could. She smiled at him through wet lashes. Her eyes slid along the shining bright hood of the new Stutz, the brass fittings of the headlights, as she told the Jehu silently, "Well, at least David didn't send us back."

Chapter Fourteen

WE look like a bride and groom in a slick magazine, no depth, Serena thought wryly as she and Dare sat at the Sunday-morning breakfast table in their own apartment, her green chiffon negligee fluttering as she poured out the coffee from the elaborately chased yet delicate Georgian silver coffeepot Granny had collected in England. Dare's light brown hair, mirror-smooth in the sun, his chiseled profile against the window, his shoulders broad in the dark-brown dressing gown with his monogram on the pocket would thrill the lady reader who'd wonder why her own husband never shaved on Sunday morning. The only thing wrong with the too perfect picture was the shaking of Dare's hand as he reached for his third cup of black coffee, refusing waffles and honey with a shudder.

"Heavy party last night?" she murmured. She knew he'd arrived after three this morning in the guest bedroom next to hers, but she had no idea where he had been, nor did she really care; but, as Ma had warned, "Politeness greases wheels."

"Boring," Dare admitted. "At Nancy's. I see enough of the cast at rehearsals." He ran his fingers through his crest of hair irritably as he burst out: "Why the devil can't Granny let us sleep Sunday mornings? You'd think the earth would quit turning if we didn't march into the front pew across from the minister's at 11:00 A.M." He cast Serena a speculative glance. "Have you noticed that silly little hat of Marcy's with the cockade? It's a kind of thermometer. If she wears it cocked over one eye, all's well with the world; if she wears it on the back of her head even her curls pop with temper. She's cute."

"You can watch your thermometer unimpeded this morning; I'm singing 'Ave Maria' at the offertory," Serena told him. David had talked her into joining the choir. She might as well: even rehearsals were something to do. Once she'd have thought that having all that money to shop for anything she wanted would have been heaven, but lately she'd even been wondering if she couldn't do some kind of volunteer work at the hospital. Imagine being homesick for bedpans!

"David has more luck with my wife than I do with his. Granny says you're going to act as his secretary." Dare was getting back at her because Marcy still refused to come near the Barn and because he resented James teaching Serena to drive the Packard.

"Only Thursday mornings. Don't worry; the church is always full of people wanting David. I hardly see him."

Lately Dare was getting more and more restless. Well, so was she. Now she had her driving license, there seemed no place to go. She didn't feel sure enough yet of her skill to drive the car into Boston traffic to shop, or up to Bellport, a trip of two hundred miles, with long distances between garages to change tires. Serena knew all the cast at the Barn, of course, and many of the Drexel's older friends had entertained Dare and her; but Maine people didn't fit into new places easily. She was desperately lonely for Pa and Ma, and for a small towheaded boy who didn't like to be touched but who loved her shyly with his eyes.

She asked, suddenly: "Dare, couldn't we have Rye down for Thanksgiving? I haven't seen him for almost three months."

"We've been all over this before," Dare reminded her, his face darkening as he set his cup down in his saucer with an exasperated click. "Even if he does call you 'Rene' and me 'Dare,' we'd be sure to give the show away in front of the servants. What's been eating you lately?"

"Is it so peculiar of me to want to see my own son? My family has some rights, too. Couldn't you and I go up to the Light for Thanksgiving, maybe?"

"Granny'd raise merry hell."

Serena asked bitterly, "Is Granny always going to run our lives for us?"

"So long as you two ain't got the sense of a ruffed grouse," Granny's voice announced from the doorway behind them, "I have to." The two young people turned, startled, and Dare leaped to his feet to help Granny to a chair. She was ready for church in her black silk dress, wide-brimmed bowed hat, and warm black karakul coat. Her eyes went disapprovingly from Serena's fluttering gay negligee to her grandson's dressing gown. "Ain't you two going to service? Not sick, are you?"

"No, just lazy, I guess." Serena smiled affectionately at the old lady. Dare muttered hastily that he was just going in to shave; it wouldn't take a jiffy.

"Wait a minute. I never seem to get you two alone. I got something I want to ask you about." Granny unsnapped her large alligator bag and drew out a white envelope, explaining, "I opened this by mistake." As Dare's eyes began to twinkle mischievously, she snapped: "Don't be impertinent. It was addressed to 'Mrs. Daniel Drexel'; that was me before Rene was born. Why wouldn't I open it? What I want to know is, what in tuncket's goin' on here?"

As Granny handed her the envelope, Serena didn't dare look at her husband; her hand went cold, for the letterhead was that of Uncle Ben up at Bath, and when she unfolded the paper reluctantly under Granny's sharp black gaze, the paper inside was headed: *Revised copy of the agreement between Daniel Drexel, Third, and his wife, Serena Snow Drexel.* If Granny had read this, she knew. . . .

Granny accused Serena bitterly, "I didn't figure you for a schemin' hussy, Rene."

"Granny! Wait a minute. Don't talk that way to Rene!" Dare rushed to his wife's rescue. "We both signed that agreement. If we choose to have a legal arrangement, it's our own business. It doesn't mean we can't both be—er—fond of each other."

Serena was so pale the freckles stood out upon the bridge of her nose; it made her look childish, forlorn. Granny demanded flatly, "You wanted to marry him? Answer me, Rene."

Serena stammered, still not looking at Dare, "Of course. I . . . we . . ."

"Just because we faced the fact that I may not live forever . . . Oh, Granny, be reasonable!" Dare turned on his charm, smiling at the old lady, but a quick pulse was beating in his throat, and Serena knew that he was terrified of what his grandmother might do. Serena continued to stare with miserable eyes at this old lady who had bent all her family to her will.

"If I thought she'd just married you for Gramp's money, I'd bust that agreement wide open if it was the last thing I done!"

"You can't," Dare told Granny triumphantly. "It's my will!"

"I can cut you out of my will, young man." Dare's face went blankly unbelieving, then worried, as she went on grimly, "I've a good mind to leave every cent I have to the Silverton church!"

"Why don't you?" Serena had had enough. She sprang to her feet to face Granny. "I married Dare so Riley could have his father's name. You ought to understand that—you who think the Drexels are so high and mighty! The Snows go 'way back too—there was one in Bellport in 1672. Probably he wouldn't own me, but Riley's not to blame!"

"Rene, take it easy!" Dare begged.

But Serena brushed him aside. "If you read that paper, Granny, you saw that I didn't ask a cent for myself. . . . Is it so terrible to want Rye to have what belongs to him? He's Dare's son, too, and your own great-grandson even if you are scared to death someone in Silverton will find out."

Dare had come up to put a restraining hand upon her arm, but she flared at him: "Granny's right about one thing. Either we live as a family or I'm through!" Tears were running down her cheeks and she was trembling all over. "I'm not going to church!" She ran toward the bedroom door and slammed it behind her. The click of the key turning in the lock was a period to her hysterical outburst.

"She must be sick, Gran," Dare excused his redheaded wife; but the old lady's eyes were not angry, merely hooded as she watched him knock anxiously upon the bedroom door. "Rene, you got to come! You're singing the solo. What'll I say?"

There was no answer. "She means it," Granny decided. "If you was any man at all, you'd make her love you. Maybe she's right about Riley, too." Her eye began to twinkle maliciously, "Maybe I'll make *him* my heir instead of you."

"Granny, you wouldn't!"

"Oh, go shave. Go to service and cool off. Then we'll see." What had got into Granny and Rene? Hysterical women! Disgusted, he went off toward the bath between Serena's room and the guest room.

Serena had flung herself across her bed, shaken by the storm that had risen inside her, but the outbreak had been building up for a long time. She had to think things through, to decide what was the right thing to do next. She'd made one mistake already, now two; no use rushing into a third.

She waited until she heard the car roar out of the yard with the reckless abandon with which Dare always drove before she unlocked her door, went to the bathroom to bathe her swollen eyes, and settled down upon the chintz-covered chaise lounge to wonder if she should apologize to Granny.

No, what she'd said might be rude, but it was true and Granny knew it. Let there be truth between them and no truckling, for once. If only she could talk this over with David! But she couldn't talk to him about herself and Dare any more after Marcy's accusing "You love David!" The very thought was bile in Serena's throat. David was as far above her, as shiningly untouchable as the Light was above Gull Rock. He was the wisest man she'd ever known, and the kindest. He'd taught her the "stone-wall prayer," the words you said only when you were up against a wall too high for you to climb over, when you were desperate. As you were now.

She wasn't even sure what to ask for . . . to love Dare as passionately, as blindly as she used to? No one could go back to being sixteen. But one thing was certain: she and Dare couldn't go on living this way, married and yet not married. Either they had to become a real family, and make a home for Rye, or this whole experiment was a mistake. And yet if Rye came here while there was still tension between herself and Dare, might not the little boy grow up as unstable, as adolescent emotionally as Dare was? If only she knew what was the right thing for all three of them—but that would need someone far wiser than she was. Serena bent her bright head upon her despairing palms, and cried silently, Oh, God, make me wiser, more tolerant. . . ."

"Rene? Can I come in?"

"Granny!" Serena gasped, rushing to unlock the door. But it couldn't be Granny standing there in the doorway, Granny who'd never missed a church service unless she was flat on her back, hobbling over there to the chair, grimacing as she sat down and thrust her bad leg out in front of her.

"I dug up the well-buried headache." Granny grinned.

"Granny, I'm sorry I was so rude. I was upset. . . ."

"I like spunk!" The old lady waved aside her apology. "Especially when it's the truth. I've rotten-spoiled Dare," she admitted. "But it ain't his fault. Maria, his mother, was a weak woman, and she gave in to him. After she died, I guess I put on the finishin' touches. Little motherless boy kinda gits under your skin." Granny apologizing! Serena stared, unbelieving, as the old lady demanded flatly, "You aimin' to walk out on Dare?"

"No!" Serena flared, and suddenly she knew it was true. "When I make a promise, I keep it, Granny!"

"Good girl," Granny approved. "You're what Dare needs, someone to stand up to him, make him toe the mark after I'm gone. I didn't figure on tellin' nobody this but . . ." She hesitated, then said astonishingly, "I didn't love my Daniel neither—not that way—when we was first married." Serena's eyes widened as the old lady went on slowly: "But I came to it. When my Daniel died, I wished I could go, too. 'Till death do us part' ain't all laughin' and carryin' on. There's times in every marriage when all you can do is to hold on, tight. Maybe you don't go all hot 'n' cold over your husband but you kin be faithful—*Faithful to yourself*. Then, maybe, if you're lucky like I was . . ."

Why, Granny's eyes were wet! Serena wanted to go to her, but she knew the old lady would hate it if she put her arms around her.

Granny snapped, "This advice don't cost nuthin'." When Serena didn't speak for fear of saying the wrong thing, the old lady changed the subject with characteristic abruptness. "You think you could pilot the Packard as far as Portsmouth, Rene?"

"Why, yes. Of course I could."

"I ain't seen your Riley since he was old enough to talk back."

Your Riley. Granny hadn't really accepted the little boy yet, but she was trying to be fair. Serena said carefully, "He has Dare's eyes and his hair but the Snow nose." What could Granny be leading up to? With her, you never knew.

"I ain't quite up to driving eight hours to Bellport. If your Ma was to put Riley on the Pullman at Bath, you think he'd be old enough to git off at Portsmouth? The porter'd look after him. If we started early from here, the three of us could have lunch together."

"Oh, Granny darling!" Whether she wanted it or not, Serena threw her arms around the old lady's neck and kissed her cheek. "Riley'd love it! He's an independent little boy. I'll write Ma tomorrow. It'd take a day to get the letter there and another to get one back. . . . How would next Friday do?"

"Good's any other day." The old lady patted Serena's shoulder. Nobody had called her "darling" for thirty years. Who knew, perhaps she might even like the young rascal! Granny hoped she'd be able to get out of the car after riding clear to Portsmouth; she wasn't as young as she used to be. But a woman should know her own great-grandson by sight.

Meanwhile Dare had been having his own troubles at the church. All the way to service in the big Packard, his father had clucked and fussed over both Granny and Serena being too sick to attend: Granny couldn't have a headache; it must be one of those newfangled flu bugs. Didn't Dare think so? They'd better ask Dr. Phil to stop by after church. Dandy bustled into the choir room as soon as they arrived to warn the choirmaster that Serena would not be able to sing the solo that morning, before settling down beside Dare in the Drexel pew. Dandy nearly drove Dare frantic, the way he kept opening and shutting his hymnbook, looking blankly up at David as if he weren't hearing a word of the sermon. His father knew as well as Dare did that Gran was up to something. Did she plan to pump Rene further? If so, what would she say? Would Gran actually go so far as to disinherit him?

Dare moved restlessly on the cushioned seat, wishing he could start for home, find out what was happening. He glanced across the aisle at the right front pew where the minister's wife sat, demure in her dark-blue suit with the white stuff at her throat, her curly head tipped to look up at her husband in the pulpit. But Marcy wasn't as demure as she looked; she'd make a good Paula because she threw her whole self into whatever she did. But she wasn't as handsome as Rene. Darned if he hadn't been proud of her, talking up to Granny that way! Rene didn't have red hair for nothing; there was banked fire in her. Once, this flame had been lighted for him, Dare, had been gorgeously beautiful. Perhaps it could be kindled again. . . .

"Amen," David said. Dare bent his head for the benediction, startled that the service was actually over. If he went out the back door, Dare thought hopefully, he wouldn't have to face David shaking hands with the departing congregation in the front lobby. But Dandy insisted upon his son's going out with him. Dare tried to slide by unnoticed, but David reached over, put out a restraining hand.

"I'd like a word with you, Dare." David then turned to the older man calmly: "While you're bringing the car around, Dandy, why doesn't he come into my study for a moment?"

There was no excuse not to go. Dare, scowling, impatient to get away, followed David into the small, crowded study and watched the other man shrug off his flowing black robe, then hang it carefully up on a hanger. David asked abruptly, motioning Dare to the more comfortable armchair: "Dare, what's wrong with Rene? She isn't happy."

"Has Rene been bellyaching?" Dare leaned forward in his chair, ready for battle.

But David answered quietly, "She hasn't told me anything, except that you two have a boy up in Maine. I've been thinking, maybe if the three of you took a trip, went off somewhere together . . ."

Dare interrupted. "Rene got what she wanted. The kid'll get every cent I have, when I'm through with it."

"Naturally, as your only son," David pointed out. "Maybe if you did something with him, even if you don't exactly hanker to . . ."

People were always on the child's side; parents had problems too. "It isn't easy," Dare burst out, "making friends with a half-grown kid. How do I know he'll even like me?"

"You don't, but you can try. You're right. Whether you succeed or not, it won't be easy. The most successful man who ever lived didn't have a very easy time of it."

"Who was that?"

"They crucified Him," David said softly.

The frantic tooting of the Packard's horn at the front door of the church came, faint but imperious, to the study, which was suddenly very still. Without a word of farewell, Dare went to answer its summons. What right had this man to tell him how he should treat his own son? *His* son . . . The words had a strangely appealing sound. Rye looks like me, Dare thought, with a new sense of pride. Riley Snow Drexel . . . Why not Daniel Drexel, Fourth? If they gave out that he and Serena had adopted him, who in Silverton would know different? The Gallants wouldn't tell: being kind was their business. Rye was a spunky little cuss. Dare remembered the small fists pounding against his arm, the way the boy had fought for his mother; yet there had been his radiant smile when Dare had offered him the wheel of the *Sans Souci*. He had a way with kids, if he did say so; he'd understood his son better than even Rene. Perhaps a trip, the three of them together, might really work out, at that. . . . They couldn't go till after the production of *The Second Mrs. Tanqueray*, but over the following weekend he and Rene could take Rye down to New

York for a few days to see the Christmas lights and decorations: they could go down to the docks, go aboard one of the big ships; Rye'd like that and so would Rene. When Rene was mad, her eyes flickered sparks like sputtering green candles and the glory of her hair was a fire to warm a man's hands. The trip would be worth a try, anyway.

Chapter Fifteen

DAVID gave Marcy no hint of his efforts to bring the young Drexels together; he considered it unethical to discuss his parishioners, even with her. But he laughed at her fear at his going into homes where some member had come down with an infectious disease. The unusually mild fall weather had dragged out the poliomyelitis scare in New England. The newspapers had been careful not to call this an epidemic, but there had been twenty cases in David's parish alone. The latest had been Tommy Gandy, a Boy Scout who had a crush on David. He hung around every Sunday after service, carried David's books and papers home proudly, dropped by afternoons after school on the chance his idol might be there or have a word for him. He even tried to walk the way David did, swinging his short legs in a ludicrous imitation of the older man's long, easy stride. The night Hester Gandy phoned, hysterical, to report that Dr. Phil thought Tommy had polio, David had stayed with the Gandys till nearly daylight.

"But what can you do?" Marcy had wailed, sleepily, when David came into their bedroom the next morning. "Change every stitch of your clothes, hear? You're not a doctor like Phil."

"I told Tommy stories about Texas till the ambulance came," David reported, obediently reaching for a clean shirt. "His mother being so upset scared Tommy worse than being sick." He knotted a fresh tie about his throat and reached for the hairbrush, explaining: "The family need me to make coffee, answer the phone. Who wants to say, over and over, 'We don't know yet if he'll be paralyzed'?"

Marcy stared at her young husband with round frightened eyes. Doctors didn't know how polio was carried, but the newspapers said fatigue made you more susceptible, and

David, rushing around night and day, was always tired. If he wasn't afraid for himself, he might think of her. But he was doing a fine job of drawing the congregation together, making them work as a unit. Even Mrs. Minnie admitted, "My sister says you're a hustler, all right, David!"

"Davey," Marcy asked abruptly, "who appoints the district superintendents?"

"The bishop." He held the comb in his hand to stare at her in the dressing-table mirror. "But don't get ideas. He'd never appoint anyone under thirty, that's for sure."

"You're going to be the youngest bishop ever elected," Marcy stated firmly. "You'll see!"

"But I don't want to be!" David laid down his comb, whirled to face her lying there. She was lovely enough to distract any man; but he had to make her understand that success for him meant helping Hank Gowdy to find himself, making Tommy Gandy laugh when he was scared to death. "I like *people*. I don't want to be shut up in an office, do nothing but press buttons and dictate to secretaries, make speeches, pontificate! If I'd wanted to be an executive, I'd have gone into business!"

"Sara Harrison says the church is a business," Marcy said mildly. "I'd better get dressed to please Mrs. Minnie. She thinks a negligee at breakfast is 'sloppy.' Winnie Mae had a cold yesterday, a little fever that worried Cecily," Marcy reported as they went together down the stairs to the dining room where the smell of Mrs. Minnie's bacon was enticing. "Phil told her that if she got upset every time the kid had the sniffles, she'd always be in a tizzy. I suppose he's right. Are you going to be home for lunch? I'd see more of you if I were sick in the hospital so you had to come to visit me!"

"No lunch but I'll try to make dinner."

"Where you going this morning, Davey?" She was irresistible in her gray wool gown with the wide white collar, her soft dark curls falling in a childish lock down onto her forehead, her blue eyes wistful. "Can I tag along?"

"Sure, if you want to. Good morning, Mrs. Minnie." They sat down at the table, where Mrs. Minnie passed crisp bacon, orange muffins, and poured delicious coffee. David told Marcy, buttering a muffin lavishly, "I'm taking Hank Gowdy to the psychiatric ward at the hospital."

"Oh, no!"

"He and Ruth have agreed it's the only thing to do, for him to have treatment." He glanced at Mrs. Minnie, then decided the incident would be all over town by now, after the shouting last night. "On my way home from Gandys' at 3:00 A.M., I drove by the Gowdys' flat on Main Street. I noticed people's heads sticking out of windows and a light in Hank's, up over the grocery, and heard the kids yelling, so I ran upstairs. Hank was standing behind the baby's crib waving a knife, and Ruth and the kids were cowering in the corner of the room, terrified. I had to paste him one on the chin, to knock him out. When he came to, Hank hadn't the foggiest idea of what had happened."

"It's terrible!" Marcy gasped, wide-eyed. Mrs. Minnie had all but dropped the muffin plate. "You might have been hurt. Hank's a big man. You shouldn't take such chances. . . ."

The telephone interrupted as usual, but Marcy beat Mrs. Minnie to it, for once. "Oh, hello, Mr. Watts." She made a wry face at David and motioned him away. Mr. Watts, the organist, was always feuding with the tenor; the organist insisted the tenor sang offkey, while the singer retorted the organist tried to drown him out when he should have played *pianissimo*. It was bad enough for David to have to worry over real troubles, without having to waste his days on petty spats. "Yes, I'm sure Mr. Gallant must have picked out the hymns for Sunday. The list is probably up on his desk. I'll find it and call you right back." She hung up hastily, the two dimples in the corner of her mouth deepening. "How am I doin'? What hymns do you want?"

" 'Fight the good fight' would be appropriate." David grinned. "Good grief . . ." For the phone was again shrilling. Marcy made frantic motions with her hand, urging David to get out while he could. He actually had his hand on the front doorknob when she called after him, urgently: "Wait! It's important. Yes, Nurse, Mr. Gallant is on his way to the hospital right now. He'll be there very soon." Marcy hung up, her face sober. "It's old Aunt Lottie. She's on the danger list. The nurse at the hospital says she's asking for you."

Aunt Lottie Hard, as everyone in the parish called her, was almost as much a fixture at the Silverton Church as the pews, the lectern, and the organ. She'd been baptized and married in the church, and very likely would be buried there. A wisp of a little old lady in shabby black clothes, she hobbled down the aisle every Sunday as regular as the first hymn. She always wore the same shapeless gray felt hat, decorated in summer with pathetic gray-blue flowers, but this fall she had substituted assorted moulting feathers. David used to stop by the Old Ladies' Home in Jehu to pick Aunt Lottie up every Sunday morning until she had gone to the hospital with "a tired heart. . . . Just wearing out," Dr. Phil had reported. But flowers or feathers, Aunt Lottie had always held her gray head high and she had a smile as brightly innocent as a child's. She always said the same thing to Marcy after church, whatever the weather.

"Ain't it a nice day? The Lord's Day."

"I'm going with you—to see Aunt Lottie," Marcy decided impetuously. "Get my coat, Davey."

"Sure you want to go?" David asked dubiously, as she stood at the hall mirror tilting a gay red beret on her brown curls. He suspected Aunt Lottie might be ending her long walk down the aisle. Marcy had never, he was sure, seen anyone die.

"Of course I do. Aunt Lottie's a dear."

Marcy would have to face reality some time, and it might as well be now, David decided, tucking her into Jehu's front seat and wrapping the rug about her small high-heeled slippers. "We'll pick up Hank on our way. He'll be all right—just black-sunk, I expect. He's crazy about Ruth and the kids, actually." Seeing the rising dismay on his wife's face at sharing the car with a repentant alcoholic, David changed the subject. "Aunt Lottie told me that she sets such store by the church because when she comes down the aisle she hears wedding bells! She still meets her Johnny there. I'll sure miss the old lady."

"Miss?" Startled.

"Until she gets back," David told Marcy hastily. No need to upset her, until it was inevitable.

Hank was waiting for them on the sidewalk in front of the wooden stairway that led up over the grocery store to their tenement, pacing up and down, his hands thrust into the bulging pockets of his shabby gray overcoat. He hadn't shaved and his red hair needed a cut, but he seemed reasonably sober. Marcy glanced at Hank apprehensively, for the deep lines about his mouth were frightening, and then up at the apartment window where Ruth was waving, the baby tucked under her arm. Marcy waved back, admitting honestly to herself: I don't see how she stands it. If I had to live in that awful place with those dirty windows and gray lace curtains, and five rackety kids, I'd go nuts too, I reckon. Hank got into the back seat, his red-rimmed eyes avoiding Marcy's uncertain glance. What did you say to a man who'd tried to kill his wife but didn't remember? Marcy was glad when they reached the hospital and David took Hank off somewhere down the corridor, leaving her to wait in the discreetly lighted lounge.

Marcy perched nervously on the edge of a deep couch. Quiet was necessary in a hospital, naturally, but did everyone have to act as if you were already buried? The smell of ether, strange antiseptics, and dying flowers which the busy nurses had had no time to water penetrated even here to the outer rim of the hospital. I shouldn't have come; David was right. . . .

"Coming, darling?" David was back, smiling down at Marcy's heart-shaped face shadowed by bitter memories crowding back. She hoped they wouldn't have to pass the maternity ward to get to Aunt Lottie's. "She's been moved from the ward to a private room," David reported, holding open a swinging green baize door.

"Is she really very ill, Davey?"

David looked down at his small wife compassionately. Well, she had to know. "They always try here to give someone privacy, at the end."

"Oh!" Marcy drew a deep, quivering breath. Think of Aunt Lottie, nothing else. Aunt Lottie with the brave faded flowers on her hat. Poverty was cruel: the only way Aunt Lottie could afford privacy was to die. Marcy drew herself up, smiled bravely up at David. "Well, what are we waiting for?" She followed him into the small room where the nurse, who was bending over the old lady's high white bed, soothed, too brightly, "Here's Mr. Gallant, Mrs. Hard."

"Marcy's come to see you, too," David amended.

Marcy hardly knew Aunt Lottie without her black dress and hat; she seemed to have shrunken frighteningly, almost to nothing. She lay there, a tiny skeleton of an old lady in a hospital nightgown too large for her, propped up by pillows, drawing deep, rasping breaths. Her brown face was wrinkled, brown as a walnut; the nurse had tied her wispy braids of white hair with incongruous bits of pink ribbons, tiny bright banners against despair.

"I brought Marcy with me, Aunt Lottie," David said again, but the old lady didn't seem to understand; she was absorbed in the vast effort of inching her small brown clawlike hand across the taut white bedspread toward his. David took the groping fingers in his big warm clasp, sat down in the chair the nurse slid toward him beside the bed.

"Preacher!" Aunt Lottie gasped. "Stay . . ."

"I'll stay as long as you want me," David promised. Unnoticed, Marcy shrank gratefully into a chair as far from the sickbed as possible, her shaking legs giving way under her; she couldn't have walked out if she'd tried to. Fascinated, yet terrified, she was conscious of slow, dark, invisible wings moving in the quiet room. Aunt Lottie's chin was quivering so she had to put up one thin hand to steady it as she asked, a child afraid of the dark, "Am I . . . going, David?"

"You'll mount up with wings," David promised surely, gently, his big warm clasp holding her hand safe. " 'Those who wait upon the Lord shall mount up as eagles.' "

So now she knew. Crouching in her hard seat, Marcy watched Aunt Lottie's mouth twist, straighten bravely. Was dying like being born, a frantic struggle not to leave the sheltering womb for the frightening unknown? Marcy closed her eyes, opened them again to see the sunlight flooding in through the hospital window. As she looked at David's bright head, the wonder grew on Aunt Lottie's face; the wrinkles smoothed away till her smile was young, radiant. She whispered, "Remember, Johnny, how the organ played . . . the day we were married?"

"I remember, dear," David said.

But he isn't your Johnny, he's my David! Marcy fought down her rising panic. Davey, Davey, how can you sit there, smiling? Aunt Lottie's dying! Do something! Unconsciously Marcy drew deep hard breaths herself, trying to help, but the rasping, tearing sound in Aunt Lottie's throat went horribly on and on. Death might be as natural as birth, but why did both have to tear you apart?

"It's so . . . dark," Aunt Lottie gasped. "I can't see. . . ."

But the sunlight still flooded the bare room, making bright lozenges on the bedspread. The darkness was the shadow of the black, waiting wings. . . . Marcy saw David reach down, raise the light body higher into his arms, saw the old lady settle her head into the hollow of his shoulder with a sigh of sheer happiness. "Johnny . . ." The thread of her voice snapped as her mouth opened in a dreadful yawn. What was that curious rattling sound? It filled Marcy's own throat with terror, so she could hardly breathe, either. She had to get out of here, now, at once. As she rushed for the door, neither David nor the nurse noticed, for he was laying the tired frail body back upon the pillows, and the nurse was smoothing the sheet up over Aunt Lottie's dreadful yawn.

"It was a glorious passing, Nurse." David's voice followed the fleeing Marcy into the corridor.

What was glorious about losing the very breath of life itself? Death was ugly. You would die, everyone would die, brutally, helplessly. . . . "Marcy?" David's feet came hurrying after her down the corridor, and when he reached her he cupped her white, frightened face with his comforting hand.

"It was horrible!" Marcy gasped. "That awful rattle in her throat—I'll never stop hearing it, never!"

"I shouldn't have let you come," David berated himself. For him to see the worn empty shell of the body shucked off as the spirit rose, free and shining, was a triumph that never ceased to awe him; but to Marcy, unprepared, vulnerable, the whole rebirth had been as much of a shock as Peter Andrew's going. He should have warned her, David realized, prepared her a little, explained that the crudities of the body no longer had validity, that the eagle-winged spirit alone was real. He'd been cruel; he had expected too much of her. David reached down, gathered up the small bewildered girl who was his wife, and carried her out to Jehu's bright red-leather front seat.

"We haven't been anywhere together for weeks. Let's play hookey," he suggested. "We'll take the day off, drive up to a little inn I know in the hills. It used to be an old mill, and the food is wonderful. You'll love it."

"Oh, Davey, do you mean it?" Her suddenly ecstatic face shamed him anew. If she'd been as lonely as that . . . She'd tried so desperately today to back him up, to help with Aunt Lottie, and it had cost her dear. Her innocence, poor darling.

"Let's go."

They had a glorious day together. The sun gilded the brown New England meadows, their riot of autumn color subdued by frost, and lighted the far blue dreaming hills. Inside the Stutz the bright-red seats reflected their mood where Marcy, almost hysterically gay with relief, sat close to Davey, who was warm, alive, and hers. They found a milk bar still open beside the narrow winding country road, ordered sandwiches and coffee and chocolate ice cream in thick white saucers. "Don't eat too much," David warned her. "We're going to blow our-selves to a real dinner at the mill." The fall landscape deep-ened into violet dusk, then into early evening as they drew up at the old inn. Above the dim sloping roof the stars were bright new pennies in the hand of night. But inside, all was gaiety and color, with the delicious smell of food for hungry people. The tablecloths were red-and-white checked, and over their table hung a cage with a wise blue and gray parrot who ducked his head to one side to regard them hopefully: "Polly's hungry. Cracker?" Marcy gave the bird a lump of sugar while they waited for their dinner, which was delicious—it ought to be, it cost enough, David grumbled. They held hands under the table like a couple of high-school kids.

"Davey, I've never been so happy in my whole life!" Marcy told him as they climbed back into the Stutz. "Darling, let's run away often. We need it. It's like—who was it—Antaeus, touching Mother Earth, growing strong again. At least, I need it."

"So do I," David confessed. "I didn't know how much until we came away."

Marcy's fragrant head lay against his shoulder most of the way home, and when he grew perilously sleepy she made him sing with her to keep awake:

" 'I dream of Jeanie with the light brown hair . . .' "

When they reached home, Mrs. Minnie had long ago gone to bed, but the light was on in the front hall and her list of phone calls was lying there on the telephone table. Without reading it, Marcy snatched up the white paper gaily and thrust it into the front of her dress. "No, you don't, Davey," she insisted. "Tonight is yours and mine."

"But there might be something important!" David argued. "Give."

He held out his hand for the list of calls, but Marcy demanded, "Are Mr. Watts and his silly hymns more important to you than I am?" She moved closer, and rubbed her soft cheek against his. It would have taken a stronger man than David to refuse her when she smiled up at him, her luminous eyes lazily inviting, "Love me, hm-mm?"

David reached for her, hungrily.

They had their most wonderful night together since they were married. They came down to a late breakfast the next morning, Marcy dreamy-eyed and glowing in her pale blue negligee, her hand unabashedly in David's as she smiled at Mrs. Minnie. Poor thing, it had probably been years since anyone had held hands with her. She had never mentioned Mr. Minnie. What had happened to him? She stood there in the dining-room doorway, her vinegary face long and sober, the cleft in her chin deepening as she demanded, "How was Winnie Mae?"

"Winnie Mae?" David stared at her, uncomprehending.

Mrs. Minnie bridled. "Didn't you find my note? I marked it *important*. The Curtises wanted you should come over, no

matter how late you got in. She's got bulbar polio—the kind
you can't breathe with. She kept asking for her beeman, Phil
said."

"Not Winnie Mae!" Marcy gasped. "Oh, Davey, poor
Cecily . . ."

David's face had gone so white it scared Marcy as he
dropped her hand and ran for the telephone. While they'd
been laughing together, having a second honeymoon, maybe
little Winnie Mae, who loved David and whom they both
loved, had been breathing like Aunt Lottie. . . . She was the
reason Davey hadn't phoned last night! Marcy's mouth was
suddenly dry. He would never forgive her if . . . She stood
there, straining her ears for David's voice on the telephone,
trying to make out from his conversation what had happened. One look at his face as he came back was enough.

"She's gone. They did a spinal puncture at the hospital, but
she died at two this morning." David's face was a deathmask
too, his eyes burning through its stiffly held stillness.

Winnie Mae was gone. Poor, poor Cecily . . . Poor David.

Marcy grabbed dizzily for a chairback, held on. "Don't look
that way, Davey! It was my fault!"

"I could have got the list away from you if I'd really wanted
to," David said harshly. He looked sick; he was sick.

Marcy cried: "Davey, where are you going? You haven't
shaved yet or had breakfast!" She ran after him out into the
hall. "You aren't a doctor, darling. You couldn't have changed
anything, really."

But David was already shrugging on his overcoat; his un-
shaven face under the stubble was the color of ashes. "I should
have been there. Cecily, Phillip—they sent for me. And
Winnie Mae . . ." He faltered; then his voice rose in anguish,
"My own people needed me, and I failed them!" As he
slammed out the door, Marcy stood there in the front hall,
coldness spreading throughout her body. If it had been anyone

but Winnie Mae . . . David had loved her like his own. Phil and Cecily were their best friends. David shouldn't have gone alone. There might be something she could do, too. But Marcy, going upstairs to change her clothes, moved slower and slower. What could she say to comfort Cecily and Phil when she knew that Winnie Mae was gone forever, like Peter Andrew? David would do better alone. He would crucify himself, and for what? It wouldn't bring Winnie Mae back. "My own people needed me, and I failed them." David would forgive her, but he'd never forgive himself. When the front door had closed behind him, sharply, a door had closed in David's heart, too, leaving her frighteningly alone.

Chapter Sixteen

THE New England maples on the parsonage lawn had flamed into brief beauty, fallen into bright mounds, and were gone. On the morning of Winnie Mae's funeral, when Marcy looked out her bedroom window, the trees flung bare skeleton arms against the gray sky, moving as restlessly in the wind as her thoughts. At home there would still be a few roses in Momi's garden, but here December meant dull skies, bitter winds, snow falling, magnificently beautiful one day, the next melting into dirty gray lumps on the city streets; winter meant flapping overshoes, ugly and hard to walk in, the heavy footsteps of winter. Marcy shivered, glanced over at their rumpled bed where she had slept alone for the past week. David had come down with a heavy cold and had used the excuse to move into the guest room.

"No sense in your getting my bug," he'd explained.

The truth was, David wanted to be alone. When Marcy went down to breakfast, Mrs. Minnie explained, glancing disapprovingly at Marcy, that David had gone to the Curtises to check on some last-minute arrangements. All the ladies she had worked for before came down to breakfast fully dressed, not wearing a kimono so thin you could see through it. The house had to be kept as hot as August. Since the church paid the coal bills, anyone would think . . . Mrs. Minnie sniffed, then banged out through the folding doors to slam her kitchen pots into the sink, for it was obvious that Marcy wasn't listening. What was going on here, anyway, with the preacher sleeping in the guest room and his wife away off someplace where she didn't hear anyone talking right at her? Mark her words, there was trouble brewing.

Why hadn't David taken her with him to Phil and Cecily's? Marcy wondered briefly. They could have gone to the church together. She'd been over to see Cecily yesterday, and she and Phil had been wonderful. David had no right to shut her out. They were her friends, too, as much as his.

Winnie Mae's funeral was held in the church, and not a seat was vacant. As Marcy came down the aisle to where the Curtises sat, hand in hand unashamedly, in the front pew, the heat of the crowded room, the sickening sweetness of the mass of flowers covering the white coffin, pathetically small in front of the altar, struck her like a blow, so that she swayed.

"You feeling all right, Mrs. Gallant?" the usher whispered anxiously at her elbow.

"Yes, thank you." Marcy drew herself together. If Cecily and Phillip could take this, certainly she could. If only she could put her arms around Cecily, hold her close, murmur, "I know. I lost Peter Andrew, too!" Both parents nodded at Marcy as she slid into the pew beside them. Cecily wore a dark-blue suit with touches of white at the throat, and Phillip's suit was dark brown, wrinkled as if he'd just come from a sickroom, as doubtless he had. Cecily had explained that to wear all black would have terrified Winnie Mae. Marcy couldn't understand how Cecily could sit there, without a tear, with only her lips trembling when the choir sang, as Winnie Mae used to, smiling and flirting her short skirt, " 'Saviour, like a shepherd lead us. . . .' "

When the brief service was over, Cecily continued to be wonderful. As they waited for the cars to take them out to the cemetery, she even noticed other people. "Thank you very much for the lovely carnations. . . . How is your little Johnny?" The price Cecily paid for her self-control was evident only in her hands, which shook unless she clasped them tightly, a knot of dark gloves. After the committal service Cecily and Phillip returned to the parsonage, where Marcy insisted they come in for coffee, instead of going straight home to their empty house. It wasn't until Cecily went up to Marcy's bedroom that she broke down, and flung herself into her friend's arms, sobbing bitterly. Marcy held her close, stroked her hair, her own tears running silently down her cheeks. There were no words for such grief, such aching emptiness.

Cecily sobbed, "Winnie Mae and Peter Andrew are about the same age, aren't they? Maybe they'll play together."

"Yes."

Marcy ran her tongue over her dry lips. She could hardly tell Cecily that Peter Andrew was buried in Texas and Winnie Mae in Massachusetts and that was that.

Later, Cecily went to powder her nose, to search the mirror anxiously. "Are my eyes very red? I mustn't worry Phil. He's a tower of strength, but underneath he's crushed." She took up Marcy's silver comb from the dresser, ran it through her dark, rumpled hair. "Phil says we must have another baby, right off."

Oh, no! But everyone had a right to decide for herself. Marcy managed, "I suppose that's the right thing."

After Cecily and Phillip had had a cup of coffee and some of Mrs. Minnie's nut cakes, had gone on to face the loneliness they must, Marcy glanced over at David's face, white, drawn, not triumphant as when Aunt Lottie had "mounted up with wings." He sat there, crumpled into the big armchair as if he couldn't bring himself to move.

"This was the hardest service I ever conducted," David confessed, running his hands up over his weary face. "And this morning, at the hospital, I had to tell Tommy Gowdy that he'll never walk again without crutches. The muscles of his legs haven't responded to treatment; they're destroyed."

"Oh, David, no!" Marcy was appalled. "Why did you have to tell him?"

"Phil thought that Tommy'd take it better from me."

Tommy who used to walk back with his idol to the parsonage after service, to hang around until Marcy produced cookies or a piece of cake, when David usually had some, too. She asked faintly, "How did Tommy take it?"

"He went white. Then he said, 'Well, I can tie square knots, anyway.' " David's face creased into deep lines of tenderness. "Tommy'd be all right if Hester—if his mother'd only let him alone, not cry over him every five minutes. . . ." His own mouth tightened as he admitted, "But I couldn't help thinking, I'd rather Peter Andrew had gone than be like . . ."

"*David!*" Marcy cried, appalled, but he only stared at her dully, yawned, then let his head drop into his hands. He was at the end of his strength. She begged, tugging at his arm, "Come upstairs and lie down, Davey. You're exhausted."

He went without a murmur, and was asleep almost before she drew the quilt up over him. She tiptoed out, closed the door carefully, and went back downstairs to sit by the living-room window, to stare out at the brown grass of the lawn. He hadn't kissed her since they had failed Winnie Mae. Perhaps Soaks had been right that a preacher should not marry young, that he should keep his mind on "higher things." But what was higher than two people loving each other? Yet love did die, Marcy knew bleakly; she not only read about it in books but she saw it in the enduring faces of middle-aged people who obviously lived together merely from habit . . . like Louella and Henry Gratz, for example, because it was the thing to do. But she and David mustn't go on living under one roof merely in order not to shock the neighbors! She had discovered, after Peter Andrew died, that love could change. Into pity? Duty? Were these enough? No! She and David had been so like old times that evening at the old mill, holding hands under the table like a couple of kids. Perhaps, if she waited, the same David would come back to her. "And when he came to himself, he arose and went to his father. . . ." She was getting mixed; David was no Prodigal Son. But she could stand anything if he would only come home to her.

She tried to argue it out with David that evening. "How long are you going on punishing yourself for being human?" she demanded.

David scowled at her, his brows drawn together. "Is repentance old-fashioned?"

"Well, you're always preaching forgiveness for sinners who repent. Doesn't that include us?"

His eyes looked dull, his face flushed, tormented, as he murmured, " 'If he offend one of these little ones, it were better that a millstone were hanged around his neck. . .' "

"Oh, Davey, you loved her! Almost as much as Phil and Cecily. If they don't blame you—where are you going?"

"Out for a drive," David muttered. When Jehu roared out of the yard, Marcy watched from the window, then flung herself across her bed and burst into tears. If you couldn't comfort David, what good were you? If he kept on this way, he'd really be sick. The hours went by, and David neither came home to dinner nor phoned. Marcy kept his food in the oven long after Mrs. Minnie had gone upstairs to her room on the third floor. David had been almost out of his mind. Had anything happened to him? An accident with Jehu? When the phone finally shrilled at ten, she yanked the receiver off the hook, demanded, shrilly, "Davey, where on earth—"

"Don't you ever talk to anyone except your husband, Marcy?"

"Dare!" Marcy gasped. "Is—is anything wrong?"

"It sure is! I'm yelling for help," Dare told her. "Nancy, our leading lady, has the flu. The doc says she won't be out of bed for days, maybe, and the play's next Thursday! The tickets are all sold, and there's no way of sending them back. You've got to help us out, Marcy. How about reading Paula's part for the rehearsal tomorrow night? If you don't, we're sunk.

Nancy'll probably make it. All doctors are calamity howlers. And she's a real trouper. She'll come if she can stagger on-stage."

Marcy drew a deep breath, hesitating. Her relief that it wasn't bad news about David was so great she felt light-headed. Tomorrow night was Saturday; David would be finishing up his sermon anyway. He must know she'd be worrying; if he didn't care enough to call her . . .

"I'd love to help out," she agreed. "What time is rehearsal?"

"Eight, sharp." The relief in Dare's voice was flattering. "You've saved my life, Marcy. I'll stop by for you at a quarter to eight."

"Fine. I'll have my hat on."

As Marcy laid down the receiver, the front door opened and David came in. He made no excuse for being so late, merely walked heavily to the hall closet to hang up his coat. He muttered, "I hope that wasn't another call for me?"

Not a word of apology, of explanation. Her face lifted hopefully for his kiss might have been another piece of furniture. She said stiffly: "No, it was Dare. His leading lady is sick and he wants me to read the part tomorrow night. I knew you'd be working in the study, so I told him I would. I didn't think you'd care. . . ."

"Do as you please," David said shortly.

Was he punishing her or himself? "Your dinner's in the oven. I've eaten." She turned, ran upstairs to her room. David could at least have told her why he was so late, where he had been. He was being childish, ridiculous. Perhaps if she went ahead, made a life of her own, it would shock him into realizing that he missed her.

The play rehearsal was exciting, and being the center of interest for a while was soothing to her ego. The rest of the cast welcomed Marcy warmly, gratefully, and did everything they could to help her with her lines. By this time they knew their cues; their task was merely one of interpretation and characterization, but when Marcy faltered in her reading they threw her a line eagerly so that soon she began to feel the part of Paula, rather than merely mouthing it. Dare handled them all delicately but firmly, playing on each actor's mood to bring out the best that was in him. Or in her. Paula was a woman deeply in love, Marcy understood, so that her performance took on warmth, understanding, and pity.

"Marcy," Dare suggested, "don't you think perhaps just a shade more hesitation before you say . . . 'and I wanted so much to sleep tonight?' Remember, the audience has to sense, *right at that moment*, that you are wondering whether or not to kill yourself!"

"I can't put all that into a gesture! The way I talk!"

"Of course you can," Dare encouraged. "You're not killing yourself wantonly, you know, but to release the man you love. He is more important to you than life itself. Make the audience realize that."

To release the man you love. Marcy stared at Dare, letting her script drop with her hand. What were you doing here? You should be at home with David. No matter how difficult he was, he was your husband and you loved him. She told Dare flatly: "I'm sorry but I have to go, Dare. I'm dead on my feet. I can't feel the words any more."

"But you will be here tomorrow night, at eight?"

Marcy stared at him, at the beaming, waiting cast. It was obvious Dare had told them that Marcy was actually taking over the part for the sick leading lady. Dare murmured urgently: "Nancy's still flat in bed. If you don't help us, we're licked, Marcy. The house is sold out for the show. There's an ad in this afternoon's paper with your name as the lead!"

"You had no right—"

As the cast burst into cries of: "You were fine, Marcy! We'll all help you," she glared helplessly at the unrepentant Dare, at the mischievous twinkle in his blue eyes. He taunted her, "You scared of David?"

"Of course not." Her chin came up. "But I'll have to talk it over with him before I decide." She glanced at her wrist watch. "It's after midnight! I must phone Davey to come get me."

"I'll run you home."

"No, thanks. Davey's waiting up to hear from me." But when she finally got David on the wire, his voice sounded stupid, muffled.

"What time is it? I'll have to dress. . . ." He'd forgotten her!

Marcy snapped, "I'll wait for you at the end of the drive so you won't have to come in." If it had been Hank Gowdy who needed him, or Tommy, he wouldn't have forgotten. It would be too humiliating to let Dare drive her home after refusing him. She was chilled through, waiting at the street corner until David arrived, yawning, his hair every which way. She hated to have to tell him about her playing Paula, but there seemed to be no way out.

"David, I'm stuck. There isn't anyone else. They'd have to pay back the tickets. Besides, Dare, the fool, put my name in the paper this afternoon, so the damage is done. The parish will read about it."

"Dare's a smart cookie," David admitted dully.

If he hadn't yawned again, acted so bored, Marcy might even then have called the whole thing off; but if David didn't care any longer what the parish thought, why should she? The queer thing was that once she'd told him, she felt relieved, almost gay. She went to sleep at once, as she used to do when David was there, a warm shoulder in the big bed to lean against.

The next morning was the Sunday of the Every Member Canvass. David and Dandy Drexel had had a hot argument about how to conduct it. Dandy explained that as chairman of the finance committee he usually set up a blackboard in the front of the church at the morning service, called for subscriptions from the pews, then crossed off the amounts given until the year's budget was met. But David had retorted that there'd be no moneychangers in his service; it was for worship only. The two men had finally compromised upon setting up the blackboard in the back of the church, Dandy's making a short speech before the sermon, and then taking subscriptions quietly as people went out.

David kept to the agreement. After the second hymn, he announced coldly, "Mr. Drexel, our finance chairman, would like to say a few words." Uncertainly, Dandy stammered out that he would be at the back of the church after service to take any subscriptions people wished to give, and that that afternoon the committee would call on any who hadn't had the opportunity to donate to the year's budget. Then he sat down again. David not only did not mention the canvass but he preached on what seemed to Marcy an entirely alien subject. She could have shaken him for being so perverse. His text was Judas at the Last Supper, demanding, "Lord, is it I?" We still today go on betraying both ourselves and each other, David insisted, his face pale and stern above his black gown. When we read in the newspaper about a neglected boy stealing a car, a drunken derelict thrown by the police into jail, we should ask ourselves, "Lord, is it I?" Marcy, glancing across the aisle at Dandy Drexel, saw his waxed mustaches still moving up and down irritably. Though David preached the sermons here, Dandy gave or raised the money. They'd never had a serious disagreement before.

On their way up the aisle after service, the worried Marcy bumped into Serena, chic in her black suit and butterfly of a hat. Her laughing green eyes went from Dandy's unhappy scowl at his blackboard to David shaking hands at the church door. "Men never grow up, do they? Dare says you're playing Paula, Marcy. I'm glad he found someone." Serena added proudly, "Did David tell you that Dare and I are taking Rye to New York, the day after the performance?"

"He never tells me anything. . . ."

Dare said behind her, his hand on her elbow: "There's only three more days for you to learn your part, Marcy, so I've called a rehearsal for tonight. I'll stop by here for you right after evening service."

If David was going out of his way to antagonize his leading family in the church, the least she could do was to smooth them down. "Very well," Marcy told Dare. She reported to David at dinner that noon, half defiantly, that she was going to rehearsal tonight after the evening service, and waited for the lightning to strike. But he surprised her.

"Good luck," he told her. "I'll be there next Wednesday night, rooting for you."

David was coming to the play! Before Marcy could catch her breath, say anything, he got up abruptly from the table, went to his study, and closed the door. At least she was real to him again, not just a ghost walking about his house. David was rooting for her! It looked as if she were on the right track at last.

As the two leads in the play, Marcy and Dare were together almost constantly during the next two days, sometimes rehearsing at the Barn where Serena was certain to be fussing with records, trying out music for the intermissions, or in the front parlor of the parsonage with Mrs. Minnie keeping a sharp lookout through the half-open kitchen door. But Dare seldom spoke to her as Marcy Gallant; to him she was *Paula*, the woman he was trying to help her create. They were as impersonal as two well-chaperoned wax figures, Marcy thought, pleased and yet piqued at the same time.

Marcy was entirely unprepared, therefore, for what hap-

pened at the Ladies' Aid meeting. Since Tuesday was the day
of the dress rehearsal, Marcy had planned to spend most of
the morning in bed, with cold cream on her face, for she must
be rested, glowing for tonight. In the afternoon she'd rip out
the lace bertha in the neck of her wedding dress; it didn't
look much like Paula, but it would have to do for the last
scene, as it was the only thing remotely resembling a dinner
dress that Marcy owned. She was still in her negligee, hunting
around for the nail scissors after lunch, when Mrs. Minnie
asked, uneasily, "You getting dressed? It's almost two." When
Marcy stared blankly at her, the older woman bristled, "Aren't
you goin' to Aid this afternoon? They're fightin' it out about
the new kitchen cupboards. Miz Finkelsetter wants them
wooden because her brother is a cabinetmaker. . . ."

Marcy wailed, "I simply can't go! Not this time."

Mrs. Minnie regarded her ominously, then tightened her
lips; after all, she was an official member of the parsonage
family; it was her duty to speak. "You might stop all the
loose talk that's floatin' around." She exited hastily to the
kitchen, the door wagging behind her like a loose tongue.

What, exactly, did Mrs. Minnie mean? She wouldn't give
her the satisfaction of asking, Marcy decided; she'd call Cecily.
Her friend was evasive, at first. Yes, she'd go to the meeting,
Cecily advised; the minister's wife was expected to be there
if she wasn't flat on her sickbed; of course the rumors going
around didn't have an atom of truth in them, but still . . .

"What isn't true? Cecily, talk sense."

"That you and Dare are . . . carrying on," Cecily admitted.
"I know it's ridiculous, but you know how people are; they
watch the parsonage with a spyglass, and it wouldn't be the
first time for Dare."

"Are you joking? I'm not a teen-ager," Marcy scoffed. "I
ought to rest for the dress rehearsal tonight, but if you think
I should go, for David's sake . . ."

"I'm afraid I do." Cecily had grown up in the Silverton church, knew all the danger signals. "I'll stop by for you, darling. We needn't stay all through. When they start the refreshments—how I loathe 'tea and little cakes'—we'll slip out. You can still get a nap before dinner."

This was Mrs. Minnie's doing, Marcy knew grimly as she dressed; doubtless by now the whole parish knew that the preacher and his wife were sleeping in separate rooms and that Marcy had been the one to tear up the note about Winnie Mae. Even if Cecily and Phillip didn't hold this against her, it would scotch the rumor of any rift between the two families by her and Cecily appearing at the Aid together. How small could people be?

The vestry was already crowded when the two girls arrived. There was a sudden expectant hush as Mrs. Finkelsetter swooped down, a beaming mountain of brown silk, to boom: "I told 'em you wouldn't put play-actin' before the church, Miz Gallant. Not that I hold against goin' to a good show. 'Any play our minister's wife's in, 'll be all right for the kiddies,' I told 'em. Miz Gallant, will you read the Scriptures for us?"

Oh, my goodness, Paula and the kiddies— Marcy protested, "But I never . . ."

She stopped, as Cecily nudged her. "Of course I will, if you want me to, Mrs. Finkelsetter." As Marcy and Cecily sat down together, the vice president, Mrs. Henriette Crakes, a sharp-eyed little woman, handed Marcy a black-bound Bible, open at very small print. Mrs. Crakes suggested: "I marked the place. If you 'n' your girl friend can stand bein' separated a few minutes, won't you move up front, Miz Gallant? So everyone can hear you?"

Marcy murmured to her friend, "What did she mean by that?"

Cecily, very pink-cheeked, whispered back, "Oh, dear, I

hoped you wouldn't hear that one. . . . Mrs. Minnie's sister thinks we spend too much time together. She says a minister's wife is supposed to belong to *all* the people, not play favorites."

Marcy's cheeks burned red, but Cecily pushed her, gently, begging, "Go on up front. Please." Marcy, seething, sat down in the front row, with vacant seats on either side. How dare they talk that way about Cecily so soon after Winnie Mae's going? She'd see Cecily twice as often, after this. Marcy sat there, outwardly calm but inwardly furious, while they sang "Peace, perfect peace, with sorrow surging 'round," while the secretary's report was read and accepted, while the treasurer's report was read and accepted, and while everything except her and Cecily was read and accepted.

"Our pastor's wife will lead us in our worship program," Mrs. Finkelsetter announced, "and maybe say a few words." About what? Marcy wondered frantically. She'd been so upset, she hadn't even looked at what Mrs. Crakes had chosen for her to read. Panic froze her to her chair; she couldn't bring her cold hands to lift the Book from her lap. Curious rustles were already rippling over the chairs behind her; she had to begin, say something. In her extremity, words she had once learned for Sunday school at St. Paul's came to her, as clear as if they were printed on her mind. She got up and, looking beyond all the blank faces, recited blindly:

" 'Create in me a clean heart, O Lord; renew a right spirit within me.' " Strangely, her fear, her anger slid away from her; she could bow her head and say quietly, "Dear Father, help us to know Your plan for our lives. We try very hard to do the right things, but we make mistakes because we are not big enough to see the whole design. But you know the pattern, however badly we misweave, the knots we make in our thread. Please guide us to find Thy beauty in our lives. Amen."

She sat down, breathless, to find Mrs. Finkelsetter beaming

proudly at her; so she must have done all right. Well, she meant every word; the prayer had been for her, too. She could feel perspiration in the palms of her hands, but apparently she hadn't disgraced David entirely. She dimly heard the discussion of "new business" raging about her, between Mrs. Crakes, whose husband ran a hardware store, and Mrs. Finkelsetter, whose brother was a cabinetmaker, as to whether the new church cupboards should be wooden or steel. Mrs. Finkelsetter said that wood, painted brown, wouldn't show the dirt so much, and Mrs. Crakes bridled that if dirt was there it should be washed off anyway. At which, Mrs. Finkelsetter flared angrily: She wasn't one to save herself; hadn't she worked her fingers to the bone for this church? Oh, dear, she ought to stop their quarreling before one of them resigned from the Aid, Marcy knew, in panic; a real minister's wife like Sara Harrison or David's mother would have known what to do.

"I move we adjourn for a cup of Mrs. Finkelsetter's wonderful tea," Marcy said loudly, surprising even herself. It worked, too. The argument was laid upon the table, and everyone cooled off with a steaming cup of tea. Mrs. Finkelsetter asked Marcy to pour, so she and Cecily had to stay till the last cookie was gone, but they walked back home together as they had come. If anyone in the parish thought they could pick out her friends for her, Marcy sputtered to Cecily, they were quite mistaken. "You're sweet, Marcy," Cecily said. "May I come in a minute? I don't know how I could have stood our house without you to come to when it gets so quiet I can't stand it any longer."

Chapter Seventeen

THE dress rehearsal seemed to Marcy utter bedlam. The first set, "a richly decorated room," had been easy enough for the Drexel household, but the property man had forgotten to provide any food for the table where the four men were enjoying dinner; several actors missed cues because they were backstage trying on their costumes for tomorrow night, which enraged Dare; and the spotlight dimmed during the second act, flickered, and finally went out. "I'll bet James is using that big trouble light again!" Dare fumed. "The garage is on the same circuit as the spots. I've told him again and again ..." He rushed out the door that led from the Barn to the garage, roaring, "James! James!" The big Irishman emerged from under the Packard, muttering that them brakes wasn't working just right, but if nobody here wanted him to do his job it was no skin off his nose. Dare roared back to leave the electricity alone, but James muttered he wasn't no cat to see in the dark.

"Wait for daylight," Dare ordered. "Serena and I both used the Packard today. It's all right."

It didn't help Dare's triggered temper that Marcy, who'd been reading her script frantically while he was gone, did the very thing she'd been terrified of, skipped a line, and consequently became so panic-stricken that Dare made the whole cast begin again at Act One, Scene One, so it was after midnight when they finished going through the play for the first time.

"We'll simply have to run through that last act again; it stinks," Dare decreed, running his distraught fingers through his hair so that it stood up in an angry crest like a cockatoo's. He was exhausted enough to tell Marcy bluntly, "You look like the farmer's daughter in that white rig—Rosebuds, no less! Haven't you something a trifle more sophisticated?"

Marcy flushed hotly, and Serena spoke up quickly from the front seat where she'd been watching the rehearsal: "I have that slinky black dress I wore in Bermuda. I'm sure it would fit Marcy."

"Time out, everyone," Dare ordered, relieved. "Go see how you like it, Marcy." The cast sank wearily down upon the stage sofa, chairs, even flung themselves down upon the thick oriental rug which brightened the set as Dare called after the two girls, "Try slicking her hair up on top of her head— no baby curls."

Close to tears, Marcy was sure she'd never be able to play Paula sensitively enough to amuse an idiot child. Glancing at her set face, Serena soothed: Everyone knew about dress rehearsals being pure hell; Dare didn't mean anything; the artist in him upset himself more than anyone else. You'd think she was his mother, excusing a child's temper tantrum. As Marcy followed Serena into her bedroom, she couldn't help an involuntary indrawn breath. Any girl could be beautiful with a background like this, white and gold, glowing with diffused lighting. The dull gold-papered walls gleamed from the two crystal lamps on Serena's white dresser; the carpet was white too, thick and comforting to bare feet; and the twin beds were covered with dull-gold silk. No orphan furniture here that didn't match. On the dresser, another picture of Riley had been framed in elaborately carved ivory.

"He looks a little like Granny," Marcy murmured.

"They're both as independent as cactus," Serena told her, ruefully. "When we had lunch together the other day, she bought him a fishing rod he adored, but he wouldn't call her 'Granny.' He called her 'ma'am.'" She was rummaging in her well-filled clothes closet, and hauled out triumphantly a long black silk dress, tight at the hips but flaring around the ankles to show a froth of white chiffon. "Try that, Marcy. I wore it only once in Bermuda, so no one here's seen it."

She hated wearing Serena's things, but the dress was perfect for Paula. Marcy was a trifle more rounded than Serena in all the right places so that the black silk fitted her as if she'd been poured into it, and the white chiffon swished about her high-heeled white satin slippers, sighing luxuriously when she moved. There were no shoulder straps, and her perfect shoulders emerged as if sculptured in ivory. Marcy gasped, "I feel naked!" Serena tossed her the blue-green scarf from the dress they'd both bought at Delmonico's. "My jade would go wonderfully with that." She selected from the gold-tooled white leather jewel case on her dresser a necklace and earrings so exquisitely fashioned, so cool that as the green lotus-flower pendant lay in the hollow of Marcy's throat she caught it in her hand to warm it. The jade earrings were slim, long, lovely; with her brown curls slicked up on top of her head with two silver-tipped combs Marcy hardly recognized the glamorous woman in the mirror.

"I feel different," she murmured, and Serena laughed, "I am proud of you!"

The admiring murmur that greeted Marcy when she came back on stage brought red to her cheeks, lighted her eyes. She lifted her long lashes in a slow, languorous smile at Dare, who stared at her, unbelieving. He smiled back, moving closer so that she could feel his breath on her cheek.

"You are Paula! I knew you could look like this but . . . Take off that scarf. . . . Not bad, not bad at all. Just toss it beside you on the sofa for color. Rene, you should give her that jade; it suits her better than you."

"If you want to give her your wedding present to me, go right ahead!" Serena snapped.

Marcy filled in the awkward pause quickly: "Don't talk

nonsense, Dare. What time is it? It must be getting terribly late."

"Last Act, Scene One," Dare called, the imperative director again.

What the dress did for Marcy wasn't nonsense; its silken whisper as she moved made her feel smooth, too, exotic, a woman desirable and desirous. Playing Paula was going to be fun after all. Suddenly Marcy saw how she could complete the transformation from the inside out; to act the love scenes satisfyingly all she had to do was to think herself back into that crazy, wonderful moonlight night in Texas when she met David. . . .

"Curtain!" Dare called, and Marcy turned to him, radiant, poised, completely sure of herself at last. . . . The scenes "marched" magically. What Marcy said, did, had nothing to do with herself at all; she was inside Paula's mind. The long earrings swung lightly against her cheek as she turned to meet Dare's hot gaze, yet he was not Dare, but Aubrey Tanqueray, her husband; she had become in truth the unhappy, passionate woman who found the price of flouting public opinion too high, not for herself but for her lover to pay. The whole cast were sparked into brilliance by the lightning flashing between these two so that tension rose higher, became more brittle. Marcy's heart was pounding, her breath coming faster, unevenly, as she swept offstage in her last exit. There was an awed silence after the final curtain, and then the cast began to applaud loudly.

"It's for you!" Dare told Marcy proudly, dragging her back onstage.

Marcy had an intoxicating feeling of power. David might be proud of her yet!

"Want to know something funny?" she confessed to Dare. "I pretended you were David!"

His face darkened so, she was afraid he was going to strike

her. She remembered too late that no one could dare this adolescent; all his pride would be aroused now to prove he was as much a man as David. For an instant his angry eyes held hers so that she couldn't look away. Serena broke the spell by calling, "Sandwiches and coffee in the living room, everyone!"

Thankfully, Marcy gathered up her long froth of black-and-white skirt and all but ran down the stage steps and up the aisle; but Dare was only a grim step behind her. Her heart pounding, she wondered, breathless, how she was going to get rid of him. As they came into the living room, she moved quickly toward the telephone on the tall mahogany desk. "David told me to call him when I was through . . . My goodness, it's after two!"

"I'm driving you home." She pretended not to hear Dare as she listened with growing concern to the bell ringing and ringing in her ear. There must be something wrong with the phone. David must be there. . . .

Serena said, coming up behind them: "If David's as tired as he looked last Sunday, he'd sleep through a fire alarm. He looks terrible lately; it worries me."

"Suits me if he wants to play Rip Van Winkle." Dare walked away toward the door to the garage. Surely, Marcy thought, Serena didn't want Dare to drive you home in this mood! She must know him well enough to see he was at a high pitch; but if Serena didn't worry why should you? Lovely secure Serena tossing you her castoff clothes. . . .

"I'd better go change," Marcy murmured.

"Keep the dress on, why don't you? You'll need it for to-morrow anyway," Serena told her negligently. "But maybe you'd feel safer if you gave me the jade. It's quite valuable."

Speechless, with shaking fingers, Marcy ripped off the jewelry, dropped it into Serena's palm. If only David would come, get her out of here where she didn't belong . . .

"The Packard's out front, Paula!" Dare had come back with her warm coat over his arm, taking it for granted he'd get his own way as usual.

As Marcy pulled the blue-green scarf closer about her neck, she invited anxiously, "Why don't you come too, Serena? Get a breath of fresh air?"

Serena looked from the sudden scowl on Dare's face to the heightened color in Marcy's cheeks, and hesitated. Marcy was to think later that the course of all their lives might have been different and that scandal might never have touched them with its black wings if only a trifle hadn't tipped the scales.

"The coffee's all gone, Rene!" someone called.

"More in the kitchen. I'll get it!" Serena called back. The tension between the three of them had been broken. She decided, "Both of us can't leave with all this gang to feed."

"Of course not. I'll be right back, Rene."

Dare steered Marcy triumphantly toward the front door, out to the drive where the great Packard's engine was already purring contentedly. The top was down, and behind the great lighted house the dark sky was spangled with stars, a stage setting of awe and beauty. It was a night for romance. Marcy, pushing aside the thought, slid into the front seat where Dare tucked the heavy velvet robe about her white satin slippers. She shivered, "It's cold!"

"Don't worry, I'll keep you warm." He slid in beside her, teasing, "The stars are applauding you too, darling. Clapping a million silent hands."

There was poetry in him as well as childishness: "darling" didn't mean anything in the theater crowd. He slammed his foot down on the accelerator so that the big car leaped ahead, roaring out into the night. If she hadn't known that the yellow liquid in their glasses tonight on stage had been tea, she'd have suspected Dare was intoxicated. Perhaps he was, but not with wine. With the success of his play? He reached for her gloved hand under the velvet rug, but she snatched her hand away.

He made no effort to touch her again, but he begged, "Relax, can't you, Paula?"

Paula, not Marcy. So he felt the strangeness too, as if they were still playing at being someone else. Just for tonight. What harm could it do? David certainly didn't care how she got home. A delicious warmth was stealing over her, a sense of living in a world different from that of every day. As her eyes went up to the stars over Dare's head, the heavens made her feel small, floating in space. Two such little motes in a vast universe, she and Dare. The Packard ran like a dream. As a blazing pair of headlights lighted up their two faces like spotlights, Dare swerved the car toward the left off the state highway. Marcy didn't realize what he intended until the car lurched into the sandy road that led down toward Silver Lake. Though the lake was only a few blocks from the parsonage, it was a world away—the Lake where lovers parked in summer, to be alone.

"Dare, I must go home!" She had to be careful not to arouse his adolescent perverseness. But she could handle him all right, appeal to his pride. "This is the nicest car I've ever been in. But it'll be freezing cold down by the lake. . . ."

"We're going to do what I want for a change." His tone was masterful, exultant. "I'm mad about you, Marcy!"

"Dare Drexel, you turn this car right around!"

But he only laughed, and the car slewed again, throwing her against his arm as she cried, alarmed, "You're driving too fast!"

There were no lights in any of the cottages, but the starlight on the water made the lake gleam icily silver, menacing behind the tall pines bordering the banks. The pines were coming rapidly toward them.

"Dare, slow up, will you? This is dangerous!"

He put his foot obediently upon the brake, but the car did not slow, and for the first time she was really terrified.

"Stop! Please stop, Dare!"

At the hysteria in her voice, he slammed his foot on the brakes again; but instead of slowing, the car, now on the downgrade toward the lake, accelerated sickeningly. When Dare's foot went clear to the floor, he shouted: "The brakes are gone; Open your door, Marcy! Jump!"

Marcy fumbled at the door handle, but her hands were too numb with terror to obey her. A big pine leaped toward them frighteningly as Dare yelled again, desperately. "Jump, quick!" There was no time to think, little time to act. The car door miraculously flew open, and she hurled herself free, rolling over and over on the soft pine needles. Almost instantly there came the sickening sound of steel crashing into wood, making her heart stop beating with horror. Then, mercifully, darkness closed over her.

She came back to consciousness moments later with the sound of whimpering in her ears, a pitiful, childlike sound. It was she herself who was crying that way in the dark, breaking the heavy, ominous silence. Slowly she tried to move her limbs, her body, she rolled over, sat up, painfully; she was bruised but nothing was broken. Then full realization flooded back. *Dare . . . had jumped, too? Was he . . . all right?* She stared fearfully over at the silent crumpled body of the car against the tree trunk, a dark mass against the dim light; everything was very still in the shadows. There was no sound at all. She had to find out what had happened to Dare. . . . She got to her feet and ran, staggering on her high-heeled slippers across the pine needles, to look inside the car, crying hysterically, "Dare!"

His head was lolling forward like a rag doll's, and as she scrambled desperately up into the seat beside him she saw that only the steering wheel kept his body from falling for-

ward. She put out her hand, trying to prop up his head, but
when she took her hand away his head fell forward again,
inert, dangling like a broken doll's, limp and horrible. She
struggled against waves of nausea. Just an instant ago he'd
been alive, laughing, calling her "darling" in that mocking
voice she was never quite sure was sincere, but now . . . *What
was she going to do?*

She sat there, very cold, even her thoughts numb, on the
seat beside him, so deeply in shock she wasn't conscious
that her coat had been nearly torn off her bare shoulders until
she began to shiver and the need to draw her coat about her
brought her back to reality. She had to get a doctor for Dare,
but she couldn't seem to make her legs move, to wade out of
this terrible nightmare. She ripped off her glove, made herself
take his limp wrist, wait; but there was no pulse she could feel.
But she wasn't a nurse. She must get a doctor quickly, be
sure. Dr. Phil! She caught at his familiar name; he would help
her. She'd walk back to that last house on the state road,
pound on the door to wake them up, phone Dr. Phil to come
quickly.

Slowly she forced herself to climb out of the wrecked car,
to start back up the road; but since the sand made hard going
for her thin slippers, she kept to the side of the hard ground
where the pine needles made walking easier. Later she was to
bless this lucky chance that had left no trace of her high
heels. She pushed back the disheveled curls that had fallen
down over her forehead, stumbled, and saw that the white
ruffle of Serena's dress had torn, was hanging down. It didn't
matter; nothing mattered except getting hold of Dr. Phil at
once. If he wasn't home, Cecily could reach him. Cecily, her
friend . . . Suddenly the eager, inquisitive faces of the Ladies'
Aid yesterday came back to her. If they made such a foolish
fuss over her and Cecily being close, over Dare's merely driving
home the minister's wife, what would they say if they could

see her now? If she and Dare were found here together by
the lake, she with her torn dress and with Dare dead, no
matter how innocent they were there'd be headlines in tomorrow's paper; she could see the words printed against the darkness already:

MINISTER'S WIFE AND SOCIETY MAN IN LOVE PACT?

If she went on, waked up those people in the middle of
the night, that was what would happen. Dare's death would
be made ugly, and David would have to give up the Silverton
church. Dare was dead, but David was alive and her utter
stupidity had dragged him into this horror. She'd been wrong
to let Dare drive her at all, but actually what had happened?
She and Dare had held hands, had driven down a country
road together at night. That was all. Hadn't they been pun-
ished enough? A scandal wouldn't help anyone. Not Serena,
Dandy, or Granny, and certainly not David. But she couldn't
just walk out and leave Dare alone. She had to call Dr. Phil.
She might have made a mistake but she wasn't a monster.

As she stood there, alternately sweating and freezing with
fear such as she had never before known, the sound of sirens
on the state highway came to her. *Fire?* Then she saw through
the trees that the lights had gone on in the house up above
her. *Not fire, police sirens!* The people up there must have
heard the crash down by the lake and phoned for the police.
She wouldn't have to call Dr. Phil after all! The police would
look after Dare. Relief flooded over her warmly, so that her
mind began to function again, swiftly, desperately. If they
didn't see her, if by any miracle she could get home before
David did, who was to know that Dare hadn't taken her home
first? Before the accident? She had to get out of here, fast.

She began to run toward the bushes at the side of the road.
Somewhere nearby was a shortcut back to the state highway
that the young people's fellowship had used last summer when

they came here on a picnic. Was that the break in the bushes? The police sirens were nearer now. Hurry, hurry! She flung herself up the path, into the thickness of trees, as the police car roared behind her down the sandy road, its sirens still screaming, toward the lake. But they hadn't seen her; they hadn't been looking for her. She was sobbing with relief as she stumbled on up the path. She had to get home before David. If he saw her this way, he'd get the whole story out of her; she had to save him in spite of himself. Her high heels held her back, so she snatched off her shoes and began to run in her stocking feet. She never could remember later if any cars passed her on the highway or not; she knew only that after eons of walking on frozen, aching feet she stood in front of the parsonage steps, stared at the study's dark windows, and knew that she'd won. David wasn't home yet. She still had a chance.

Her head hurt and she ached all over, not only in her body but in her mind, as she staggered into the front hall and reached for the white pad on the lighted telephone table. Her hand shook so the scrawl was barely legible, but it would have to do.

David: Have gone to bed. Please do not disturb. Marcy.

Upstairs, safe behind her own closed door, she flung herself across her bed, crying hysterically. But she had to stop; she musn't wake Mrs. Minnie asleep upstairs. She was icy cold. She drew the blanket up over her shaking shoulders, over her head; but she couldn't shut out the terrible picture of Dare's lolling head. He was dead, dead, dead. . . . He hadn't even held her hand, but as a man "thinketh in his heart so is he." He'd paid a terrible price. Could she get away with pretending he'd brought her home before the accident? Maybe not, but she had to try. Not for her own sake—she deserved whatever punishment came—but for David's. "Davey, Davey, I'm an awful fool but I love you. . . ."

Chapter Eighteen

IT was after three-thirty in the morning; David felt drained, exhausted, barely able to keep his eyes on the road unrolling darkly under Jehu's headlights. All day, most of the past week, actually, he had been dizzy, heavy with a queer lassitude; he suspected he had a fever, but Marcy musn't know or she'd worry. Surely by now she was safely home, asleep, he hoped, for he was too tired to talk, to tell her that Tommy Gandy was dead. Tommy, who'd been David's small, adoring shadow, had unexpectedly stopped breathing about two hours ago at the hospital; it was, perhaps, better than crutches all his life. But David could hardly say this to Tommy's frantic parents, Hester and Hector, called out into the night. Hester had been hysterical, Tommy's father stoic, showing his agony only in his eyes, but this was all the more dangerous because repressed. David must get over to see them at home the first thing tomorrow—today, he amended wearily. Strange for him to feel so depressed, so leaden. He needed Marcy, her freshness, her gaiety; to feel her soft coolness against his hot weariness would be heaven. This rift between them lately had been his fault, but he couldn't help himself. After Winnie Mae's going so suddenly he had felt numb, drained, afraid to let go lest he give way to his own dark emotions; but it was wrong to blame Marcy. She was what she was, impulsive, loving, outgoing: as soon blame a meadowlark for singing— Good grief, that had been close! As the car jerked, righted itself, he realized he had run over the curbstone at the last turn toward the parsonage. He musn't fall asleep!

To keep himself awake, he began to count the houses he passed in which the friendly lights had all blinked out, the little lights of home. If only he could make Marcy see that here, on as many small stages, the drama of life was being

played, birth, love, death; real tragedy and comedy, not like
Dare's make-believe stage, bright with the tinsel of excitement.
Had Dare brought her home from rehearsal or had Granny
sent her back with James tonight when David hadn't answered
when she called him? When he explained about Tommy,
Marcy would forgive him. His eyelids had grains of sand under
them, and his head was burning up. If he could just slide in
beside Marcy, take her in his arms again, he could rest. . . .
But as he drove into the yard and glanced up, her bedroom
window was dark. He musn't wake her; she'd want to be
rested for her big performance tonight, which was important
to her. He'd just open her door, make sure she was safely
home. . . . But as he came in the front door, the telephone
began to ring shrilly.

I can't answer it, I can't take any more tonight . . . But of
course he must answer. As he reached for the phone, he saw
Marcy's note, read it quickly before he lifted the receiver,
said wearily, "Yes?"

"Davo?" It was Serena's voice, but he could hardly hear
her. She gasped, "Is Marcy home? Is she—all right?"

"Why, yes. She's upstairs, asleep. But why—"

"Are you sure?" This was queer; he could hear Serena
breathing hard over the phone as if she'd been running.
"Thank God. Dare must have brought her home before—
before he—" Her voice broke, steadied again. "Davo, the
police just called. Dare's had an accident, a bad accident."

"Was he seriously hurt? I'll come right over," David offered.
"Where did it happen?"

"Down by the lake. The Packard crashed into a tree. They
don't know how he lost control yet, but—oh, Davo, Dare's
dead!"

For an instant David couldn't reply; disaster tonight had
been piling up too fast. He was sick, overwhelmed. "This will
be a terrible shock to Marcy. I'll wake her."

"No, no. What can she do? Tomorrow'll be time enough. But I would like . . . I mean, could you come over for a short time? It's more than I can handle, here. Dandy's beside himself, and Granny . . . She pretends to be tough but actually she's old and frail."

"I'll come at once."

He tiptoed back out the front door; he even let the Stutz coast down the small incline of the driveway to the street before he started the engine lest he wake Marcy. Rene was right; let her sleep. Pity this had to happen when Dare and Rene were getting close to each other again. Dandy would be horribly maimed by losing his son; however the older man might grumble about "artistic nonsense," Dare was Dandy's future, the part of himself that would go on. Granny would be shattered. Dare, restless, greedy for life, might have matured sooner if he hadn't been so shackled by his wealth, his family, if he hadn't been Granny's one ewe lamb. . . . Ironic that she who wanted his happiness most should be the one to destroy what he yearned for, real achievement in the theater. Well, we all had our blind spots. As David drove into the Drexel driveway he saw that nearly every window in the big house was blazing with light. Several cars were parked in front of the door, including Dr. Phil Curtis's dusty model T. Poor man, he must have just got home from the hospital too. What was that State Police car doing here? Of course; they'd found the crashed Packard; every violent death had to be investigated, reported. Poor Rene.

She met David in the spacious front hall, with its fireplace where the blazing logs had been replenished by the frightened servants. With its comfortable chairs and thick oriental rugs, the hall was actually a small living room. Serena wore a negligee of changeable silk, flung carelessly over her nightgown; the silk shimmered as she moved, and her hair fell in bright, unheeded waves about her shoulders.

"Davo, the police are here!"

"Yes, I know. It's just routine. It doesn't mean anything, Rene." She looked like a little girl with her hair down that way, but she'd come a long way since they'd gone fishing together; there was strength in the curve of her lips. Her face was pale; though she had been crying, she controlled herself as he led her to a chintz-covered armchair, made her sit down, and settled himself across from her. It might help her to talk it out. "Tell me what happened."

"They don't know yet. They think the brakes must have failed. James says they weren't working right, but Dare wouldn't let him check them tonight. Dare must have decided it was such a lovely night he'd come back by way of the lake." Her green eyes slid away from David's uncertainly. "Dare was at a high pitch after the rehearsal, excited. He often drove around at night. He said it rested him to drive fast." Her voice shook. "It was a blessing he got Marcy home before—"

"Yes." David's own throat tightened. In his weariness he blurted, without thinking how it would sound, "Without Marcy . . . I wouldn't want to go on." He listened, horrified, to his own voice. If he hadn't felt so dizzy . . . "I'm sorry, Rene, talking about myself. This must be terrible for you, coming just now, especially."

"Because we were married only a few months?" Serena's slim hands were twisting the gold belt of her shimmering negligee. Her eyes met his honestly. "It isn't that so much; it goes back much further. Dare and I were a couple of crazy kids together. That summer I was sixteen . . . I didn't know there was so much happiness in the cock-eyed world." She smiled briefly, a little grimly. "Or that you had to pay for it. But Dare was planning to make it up to Rye, to make him the fourth Daniel legally. We were all three going to New York. If only they could have gotten really to know each other . . ."

Her eyes filled with tears that were good for her, that really must come if she was to stay sane.

"Rene? David here yet?" The door from the corridor opened and Granny come hobbling toward them, using two canes as David jumped up to help her. Bent over that way, she looked every one of her eighty-odd years; but when she lifted her head her eyes were dry, angry, full of bitter hurt. "Don't preach, Pastor," she croaked. "I couldn't stand it. Dare wasn't a very good boy, but I loved him. Sometimes I think it's a sin to love anyone like I do—did—that boy."

As David helped ease her down into the big chair, her tortured old eyes staring up at him reminded him of another father's lament for a wayward child, "*O my son Absalom, my son, my son Absalom! would God I had died for thee . . .*" Granny would gladly have died for Dare.

"He always drives too fast," Granny admitted bleakly, as if talking in the present tense made Dare real, not just a broken body carried away somewhere by the police. "You can't stop him. Any more'n you could stop him climbing up on the barn roof when he was twelve. Dare's headstrong but he ain't mean." She looked sharply at David, reverted to the past tense. "It was a mercy he was alone. Folks would have talked."

"I suppose so," David agreed. "I didn't wake Marcy; she'll come over tomorrow. . . . Hello, Phil, I thought we'd said 'good night.'"

"Granny Drexel!" Dr. Phil gave one horrified look. "I told you to stay in bed. Off with you," he ordered, lifting Granny easily from her chair, half carrying her toward the door. "You're next, Serena. I'll bring a sedative to your room."

"You'd better get some rest," David agreed as Dr. Phil and Granny disappeared. "Today'll be hard enough. People will be phoning, flocking here to see what they can do. You'd better do what Phil says, Rene, dear."

He wasn't aware of what he'd called her, but color

flooded her pale cheeks. He was thinking of the freckled little girl with red pigtails who'd grown up with him and who was now so badly hurt. She got up at once. "There's nothing anyone can do. But thank you for coming, Davo." As she went swiftly out the door, David wondered, picking up his overcoat, if he should try to find Dandy or just go? He was still hesitating when Dandy himself came into the room followed by two state police who said, "Good night, sir," and went out the front door. Dandy sank down in a chair close to the fire as if he were cold.

"Don't go yet, David." Dare's father's face was lined, chalky, and his hands were trembling as he ran them over his tired eyes. Yet he'd taken time, David noticed, to fold a white scarf into the neck of his loudly patterned red silk dressing gown. "David, why did this have to happen to me?"

"Two thousand years haven't been long enough to answer that," David told him gently. "I asked it myself, once. My own son lived only one day, but you had Dare for—"

"Twenty-three years," Dandy admitted. "It seems only yesterday he was learning to talk, trying to say 'Dan-Daddy,' shortened it to 'Dandy.' " He pulled the scarf closer about his throat. "I can't seem to get it through my head that he won't ever come walking through that front door again. They took . . . the body to the undertaker's. I suppose it's best. But they might have let Dare . . . come home."

"He is Home," David said quietly.

"I know, I know," the other man agreed irritably. "I've said it and now I've got to live it." He glanced sharply at David, who had swayed slightly in his chair; in spite of all he could do the dizziness was coming on again. The room was going round and round his head in vague circles, till he forced himself to concentrate on Dandy. "You look dead beat yourself, David. I'm a selfish old man. Go on home." He got up, held David's overcoat for him, patting him on the

shoulder. "I'll be over tomorrow morning to talk about arrangements for"—rejecting the word "funeral" he substituted
—"services. I expect Granny will have ideas." He added
hastily, "Serena, too."

"Any time," David agreed. "Bless you."

But he wasn't to get away so easily. "David?" As he put his
hand on the handle of the front door, Serena came up behind
him with a rueful smile. "Granny wants to see you. She won't
go to sleep till you tell her she can have the full choir for the
funeral. Phil says you'd better come in for a minute. . . . Now,
who— It's almost morning!" For a knock had sounded on the
front door. David opened it, and the three of them stared,
startled, at one of the police officers standing there with something dangling from his gloved hand.

"I'm sorry to disturb you again," he apologized, "but one
of our men just brought in this, and I saw your lights were
still on." He was holding out a long, twisted, bedraggled rag
of chiffon, blue-green in the light. He explained: "It had slid
down behind the front seat of the Packard. It doesn't look like
a man's scarf. We thought you might be able to identify—."

"Let me see that!" Serena leaned over Dan's arm, snatched
the scarf from the officer's hand, and stood staring down at
it. She had been pale enough before, but now there was not
even any color in her lips. She could not look away from the
dark stain on one end of the scarf. She whispered, "That's . . .
blood!"

"Yes, ma'am. The scarf must have been there when Mr.
Drexel was—when the accident happened. That's why we
showed it to you."

Serena shuddered, and dropped the scarf back into the
policeman's hand. "Then he couldn't have . . ." She stared
wildly at David, then swayed; but as Dandy and David sprang
to support her, she straightened. "I'm all right. Leave me
alone." Serena drew her shimmering negligee closer about

her, shivering. "I'm sorry. It made everything real. I know Dare
was—hurt—but I hadn't realized . . ."

"Can't you leave us alone until morning?" Dandy said
sharply to the officer, who backed out hastily, closing the front
door.

It had been stupid of the officer to show Rene that bloody
scarf, David thought as he drove home half an hour later.
What had she meant, "Then he couldn't have . . ."? David,
driving along in a mist of fatigue, was suddenly too tired to
care what she had meant or that the blue-green scarf had
looked vaguely familiar. He left the Stutz outside in the driveway. Too dizzy even to undress, he flung himself across the
guest-room bed and fell instantly into a sleep of sheer exhaus-
tion.

Breakfast was very late next morning at the parsonage because David, for once, overslept. When he opened his eyes,
he didn't move for a moment, for his whole body felt hot,
his eyes leaden. How could he possibly get up, start another
day?

"You look like death warmed over, Davey," Marcy said
worriedly from the open doorway of the guest room. "I'll
bring you up some breakfast. Mrs. Minnie told me about
Tommy. I called Hester. It must have been horrible for you."

"Don't fuss." David's voice sounded irritable, unreasonable
even to himself, but he was glad he didn't have to go into
long explanations about last night. Did Marcy know, too,
about Dare?

"Telephone, Miz Gallant!" Mrs. Minnie called up the
front stairs. "Serena Drexel wants to talk to you, poor thing."

If Marcy didn't know all the details about Dare's going, she
soon would, David realized gratefully, for a buzzsaw seemed
to be grinding in his forehead. He heard her say, "Serena? I'm
so sorry. . . ." Then there was a long silence before she spoke
again, her voice shaking, uncertain: "Yes, I'll be here. We—

we can talk up in my room." More silence. David got dizzily to his feet and went into the bathroom to douse his head in cold water; it helped, but it didn't clear away the queer mist completely. He went carefully downstairs and sat at the breakfast table where Marcy was crumbling toast, pretending to eat.

He asked, "What did Rene want?"

"She and Dandy are coming over here to plan about the funeral."

"You both need something inside you," Mrs. Minnie ordered from the dining-room doorway. "Git on with them hot cakes and syrup and good strong coffee. I got plenty to do, if you haven't."

Her sharpness was a bracing astringent. Marcy and David tried obediently, but he could manage only fruit juice and black coffee, and after one mouthful of hotcake Marcy put down her own fork, too. "They're delicious. But—I—I simply can't swallow, Mrs. Minnie." She jumped nervously as the doorbell rang. "That can't be Dandy and Serena already!"

"I'll go," David told Mrs. Minnie. He opened the front door, then stared, surprised, at the state police officer standing there, erect and unsmiling in his immaculate uniform.

"Reverend Gallant? I met you last night at the Drexels'. Lieutenant Ryan."

"Oh, yes, good morning, Lieutenant. What can I do for you?"

"Is Mrs. Gallant in? Could I speak to her for a moment?" As David's face went blank, the officer explained: "We have to get out a report. She was the last one to see Mr. Drexel before—"

"I see," David said doubtfully. "She's having breakfast, but I'm sure she'll be glad to help you any way she can. Mr. Drexel drove her home here before the accident, so I don't quite see. . . . Go into the parlor, won't you? I'll call her."

But Marcy was already in the hall. Moving woodenly, she followed David and Lieutenant Ryan into the front parlor, and slumped gratefully into the big armchair. She had worn a long-sleeved soft gray wool dress this morning which David liked especially and which hid the bruise on her left arm. Pinned to her shoulder was a silver butterfly which she fingered nervously. She had to be very careful what she said; David knew her so well. She murmured, "Yes, Lieutenant Ryan?"

The lieutenant asked, obliquely, watching her, "Did Mr. Drexel seem upset about anything when he drove you home last night, Mrs. Gallant?"

"Upset?" Marcy repeated the word carefully. "Why, no. He was excited, of course, and tired. We all were. We'd rehearsed so late for the play." She locked her hands closer in her gray wool lap to keep them from trembling. "Dare—Mr. Drexel—and I had the leads. It was to be given in the Barn tonight—*The Second Mrs. Tanqueray.*"

"They made me read it in high school," the lieutenant commented dryly, but his eyes never left her.

David was frowning. He demanded sharply, "What's that got to do with the accident, Lieutenant?"

"Nothing, perhaps. Only we wondered why Mr. Drexel should slam on the car brakes so hard if he wasn't—well, angry. The first time he used the brakes, you can see how the car left skid marks. They were frayed, all right, but if he hadn't slammed them on so hard the second time they might have held."

The brakes were gone the first time he tried! He was scared; we were both terrified! The words screamed in Marcy's sick mind, but she said nothing. But she couldn't stop the flush creeping up her neck, or the way her hands were shaking.

David was angry at her being heckled this way. He snapped, "Lieutenant, Dare Drexel was a very close friend to us both.

His death has been a bad shock. My wife was here at home, when the accident happened. The Drexels phoned me minutes after they heard from the police, and she was already asleep here, in her own bed. Do you doubt my word?"

"Of course not, Reverend, but—"

The doorbell ringing startled them all into silence. Marcy, frozen with fear of what was happening to her and David, could hear Mrs. Minnie say: "You poor people, come into the dining room, won't you? David and Miz Gallant'll be through in a few minutes. The police is here, that young Mike Ryan."

But Marcy heard no more. She was watching, paralyzed, the blue-green scarf that the lieutenant was taking out of a brown paper parcel. "Is this yours, Mrs. Gallant?"

None of it had been any use; she'd failed. She wanted to scream at him: Yes, yes, yes! I was there. Take me away, why don't you? It would be a relief to have it over with, finished.

"That's my scarf, Lieutenant!" Serena said sharply from the parlor doorway. Her black dress emphasized her pallor, made her face look as white as the ruching at her throat. Dandy, coming up behind her, put his arm with the black armband around her waist and scowled at the lieutenant. "You again!"

Marcy, agonized, stared at Serena. She must realize that the whole cast of the play knew she'd worn Serena's scarf last night. . . .

Serena rushed on: "I'm sorry, Lieutenant. I remembered after you left. I drove the Packard yesterday morning. I must have left the scarf on the seat."

What Serena said was partly true and yet it was all wrong. . . .

Mrs. Minnie stared at the scarf, then cried: "Miz Gallant's scarf like that is right upstairs in her top bureau drawer. I saw it this morning. You want I should go git it?"

"That won't be necessary—"

Mrs. Minnie rushed on: "None of us here is criminals, Mike Ryan, and don't you act like we are—you that used to shoot a BB gun at my cat!"

The lieutenant's eyes were twinkling, and relief was growing on David's face as the policeman apologized, "Sorry, sir, but we have a job to do."

As David ushered him toward the front door, Serena said quickly, "Could we go upstairs to your room, Marcy, while Dandy and David talk?"

Going up the stairs behind Serena was the hardest thing Marcy had ever done, because at the top she'd have to face Dare's wife, who knew the truth, or part of it, anyway. Serena sank down into a chair, and Marcy closed the bedroom door sharply, then leaned against it, her breath coming in sharp gasps.

"I wouldn't have left him if there'd been anything I could do! You've got to believe that, Serena!"

"You think I don't know that?" Serena pushed back her dark veil, and her words were bright coins dropping into the tin cup of the room's stillness. "When I saw the scarf with blood on it, I knew you must have been with him when the accident happened." She told Marcy bitterly: "Dare always liked crowds about him, telling him how wonderful he was. For him to lie there, alone, to have to be picked up by strangers—" She caught her lip between her teeth, let it go again.

"You've got to understand! I was going to phone for Dr. Phil when I heard the police coming." Tears were running down Marcy's cheeks, and she wiped them off with the back of her hand, childishly. "I knew they would take care of him. Oh, Rene, I didn't know what to do! It happened so quickly. If we just hadn't been down by the lake, people might not have—imagined terrible things. There'd be talk; the newspapers—" She shivered, adding honestly, "It was David I thought of. Dare was gone but David was alive!"

"It's the living who matter," Serena agreed, harshly. "I don't blame you. Any woman would lie for the man she loves. Sometimes lies are truer than the truth, in their results, anyway. A scandal wouldn't help anyone."

"You think I ought to tell David?" Marcy demanded, anxiously.

"No!" Serena said sharply. She went over to the window, stood looking out blindly, looking inside herself instead of at the black, frost-bitten parsonage lawn. She was silent for so long Marcy wanted to cry out: Say something. Don't just stand there! Serena turned to face Marcy. "You know what I'm going to do right after the funeral? I'm going to take Rye to New York, tell him Dare and I planned it that way. Take him to the park, the theater. . . ."

So Serena was pretending too, pretending that Dare had been a father to be proud of. But she'd given herself away. Or didn't she realize herself what it meant? Downstairs, Serena had lied to the lieutenant, not for you, partly for Dare, but mostly because she couldn't find it in her heart to hurt David!

Hysteria, long curbed, mounted in Marcy's throat. She might have spoiled everything even then, if Mrs. Minnie hadn't pushed open the bedroom door without knocking, carrying a tray upon which was the silver teapot, sugar and creamer, and two of the best wedding cups.

"There ain't nuthin' more comfortable than a nice hot cuppa," Mrs. Minnie said briskly. "I'm gonna stay right here, see that you two girls drink up."

There was, fortunately, no further chance for private conversation. Presently, Dandy called up and Serena went away, and Mrs. Minnie ordered: "Get your things off and lie down; git some sleep, Marcy. You look plumb tuckered. That fool Mike Ryan! I guess I cooked his goose. I'll set right here till you drop off."

Marcy. She belonged for the first time. Marcy reached over,

caught the other woman's rough hand in hers, gratefully.
"You're a grand friend, Mrs. Minnie." She might broadcast
Marcy's and David's failings to the whole parish, but just let
a stranger attack either of them, and she'd claw and scratch.
You were her family. Marcy wouldn't sleep, but to please her
friend she undressed, got into bed, closed her eyes.

She slept for hours. When Mrs. Minnie woke her apolo-
getically, the room was so dark she had to snap on a light.
Marcy looked, dazed, at her wrist watch. "Why, it's after five!
Where's David?"

"I kep' his lunch warm in the oven, but the spaghetti's all
dried to strings and he ain't come back. He went over to see
Tommy Gandy's folks," Mrs. Minnie said. "Dr. Phil's downstairs. I told him you was asleep, but he said I'd better wake
you. You want your kimono?" She draped the blue chiffon
over Marcy's white shoulders.

What could be important enough for Phil to wake her
out of a sound sleep? Oh, dear, perhaps Cecily . . . Marcy ran
down the stairs, dark-blue chiffon floating out behind her in
wings, her anxious hand outstretched as she cried, "Phil? I
hope nothing's wrong with Cecily."

"No, it's David, Marcy." As her hand froze, dropped to her
side, he added hastily, "It wasn't Jehu. I've worried over the
way David streaks along, writing his sermon in his head with
his foot on the accelerator and heaven help the poor pedes-
trians. . . ."

"*Phil, what's wrong? Where's David?*"

"At the hospital. They called me from Gandys' when he
collapsed, and I took him there, for tests. David didn't want
me to tell you, but when I saw the lab report . . . Marcy,
David has polio!"

Chapter Nineteen

It was hard for Marcy to breathe through her unaccustomed white gauze mask as she followed Dr. Phil in his white coat, with the stethescope sticking out of his pocket, down the long hospital corridor. She felt sick, empty, as Phil explained, "We have to wear masks because patients like David are extremely susceptible to respiratory infections." And she had thought the mask was to protect *her!* He glanced at her wide, startled eyes, reassured, "There's nothing for you to worry about, Marcy. There's very little danger of infection, with proper precautions. Not one of our nurses has got the bug yet. Here we are." He knocked lightly upon a closed door, opened it at once, and the nurse stood aside from the high white bed as the doctor came up. "This is Mrs. Gallant, Miss Neal."

David was so still lying there, with his eyes closed, wrapped in a white shroudlike sheet, and the sound of his difficult breathing filled the small room. Marcy's heart began to beat in frightened thuds, but Dr. Phil, incredibly, smiled.

"He's better. Isn't he, Nurse?" As she nodded, pleased, too, Phil explained to Marcy: "Bulbar hits hard at first, but sometimes the patients come out of it quicker, without any bad aftereffects."

Were there different degrees, then, of this horror? Marcy asked thickly through her mask, her eyes never leaving David's too-flushed face, "What do you mean, 'bulbar'?"

"An infection of the gray matter of the brain," the doctor told her, watching David closely. "The patient may lose the impulse to breathe, and then his lungs cease functioning." His voice sharpened. "Like . . . Winnie Mae. Or the infection may center in the spine. Either way can cause paralysis of the motor nerves, of course."

He meant that David might be paralyzed. This was *David*

243

you were talking about so calmly, David who might never walk again, whose mouth might be drawn down in that terrible caricature of laughter you'd seen in a pitiful woman in the streetcar. . . . Marcy shuddered, "Can't you do something?"

"We're doing all we can at the moment," Dr. Phil soothed. "The nurse will begin hot packs soon. We can't do much to stop the paralysis, but we can make David more comfortable and hope that his clean living and the good Lord will do the rest." As David's eyelids fluttered, Phil added, "He knows you're here."

David's eyes widened at the white-masked apparition that was Marcy. With a great effort he gasped. "Go—home." His eyes closed again, but even at the door of death itself his thoughts were of her. Before anyone could stop her, Marcy bent to kiss his cheek; it was burning with fever.

"You'd better go now," Dr. Phil ordered, drawing Marcy hastily away. "You can get a taxi in front of the hospital. I'll stay a while." As she hesitated, her frightened eyes wide over her gauze mask, he pushed her toward the door, promising, "I'll call you if—if there's any change."

Marcy went back to sit beside the telephone. When she refused to go to bed, Mrs. Minnie drew up the great armchair from the front parlor, made her lie back in it, and put her feet up on a hassock. Mrs. Minnie herself lay down on the sofa; thus the two women spent the restless night, waiting for the call that, mercifully, did not come. At daylight they both went to bed, and at 7:00 A.M. Dr. Phil woke them to say David was holding his own; if he went on in this way, in two or three days he'd be out of danger. Out of danger of dying but not out of danger of paralysis, Marcy reminded herself bleakly.

For the next few days she lived intimately with fear, a leap of terror every time the phone rang, which might be the hospital saying David was worse; of shrinking from the shocked sympathy of the parish, who flocked to the parsonage. They came in great numbers to inquire, in too low voices, how David was, sometimes leaving a covered dish so that Mrs. Minnie, who rushed from door to phone all day and half the night, wouldn't have to cook. Sympathy can be practical and nourishing, Marcy thought dully; you can eat it. She saw each caller herself, mumbling over and over, "Thank you, but we don't know yet. . . ." One evening, because Marcy had left the night light burning in the hall beside the phone, her next-door neighbor thought she was awake, alone, and impulsively knocked on the door at 1:00 A.M., to share her vigil.

"They'll have you in the hospital, too," Mrs. Minnie worried, after she'd flown down the stairs, ushered out the zealous comforter, and tucked Marcy back in bed. "People should use the sense the good Lord give 'em. Just look!" She gestured toward the kitchen table. "How we gonna eat five apple pies?"

"They mean all right," Marcy offered wearily. "Everyone is so kind."

"Kind to themselves or us?" Mrs. Minnie sniffed grimly. The following morning she tackled the problem firmly, asked Mrs. Finkelsetter why each member of the Aid couldn't take turns, feeding the parsonage family? Why couldn't one take Tuesday, another Wednesday? "Of course," the Aid president agreed. She also arranged efficiently a system of relay phone calls, whereby each church member reported to another how David was. As if anyone knew. But Marcy was touched almost to tears by Hester Gandy's gift for David and by Ruth Gowdy's unexpected request when she came to call one morning.

When Ruth arrived at the parsonage, her good dark-blue coat was carefully brushed, but there was a neat darn in her thumb of her cotton glove. She carried a sort of coop of chicken wire. "Hank made it," she explained proudly, "to hold David's book, so he can read in bed when he gets better."

Not *if* he gets better but *when*. . . . "David will love it." Marcy kissed Ruth's cheek, which flushed happily.

"Hank says for you to tell David he hasn't touched a drop since he got home from the hospital. He feels terrible about David. For six weeks Hank's brought me home his pay envelope, without opening it!" Ruth patted the contraption that David wouldn't use because the hospital had its own bed tables, if he ever got well enough to use one. Ruth beamed, "Hank's real good with his hands. He's making a play pen, too, for the new baby!"

New baby! That was all Ruth needed, with an unstable husband and five children already. "It's a beautiful book rest," Marcy managed. How could Ruth possibly be so radiant? Marcy asked, "When do you expect the baby, Ruth?"

"In April." Ruth's face was eager, yet shy. "You think David would mind if we named him 'David Gallant Gowdy'?"

"He'd be proud," Marcy assured her. No need to tell Ruth that David was still too sick to talk or that he might not be here in April himself. After the other woman had gone, Marcy felt strangely comforted, for these were David's people, who loved him; they would not let him go.

But the gift almost too precious to accept, even for David, came from Hester and Hector Gandy. Hester wouldn't even come into the parsonage, just stood at the door, insisting: "I can't stay but a minute. I know how dead tired you are. . . . Here." She pressed a small white envelope into Marcy's hand. "Jim and I want you to have this. To use for whatever David needs. We know too well what hospitals cost. . . ." Her voice broke, explaining, "It's Tommy's college money."

"But we couldn't possibly take—" Marcy began, but Tommy's mother interrupted fiercely.

"You've got to take it! Jim and I couldn't bear to spend it for just anything! I think I'd have lost my reason if it hadn't been for David. When Tommy went, he stood right by, nearly all night. It wasn't so much what he said; he was just there. And he came the next morning when he was so sick himself. . . ." She reached out, patted Marcy's arm. "Here I am keeping you in the cold doorway. . . . I must go. But don't you worry: the Lord wouldn't let a good man like David down. If he never takes another step, he'll 'walk in the light.' "

He'll walk in the light.

As Marcy closed the parsonage door behind Hester, the words were like a benediction. This was the sharing he'd done with his parish, compassionate, suffering with them; and he was right; it was more important than she was. Yet David had tried to make her understand that he hadn't chosen the parish instead of her; he'd explained: "But I don't leave you behind, my darling; I take you with me." And she had been too stupid to know that this was true, that their love walked with him wherever he went. In any way that mattered, he had never left her alone. It was she who'd failed him by not understanding. If he would only get better, come back to her, she'd never be jealous of his work again. As it was, she woke with a start each morning, wondering, "Is he still here? Is he alive or—" She always leaped out of bed without finishing the sentence in her mind.

One good thing about this eternity of waiting was that with David so sick, no one expected Marcy to go to Dare's funeral. Henry Parker, a professor at Boston University School of Theology where Dandy was a trustee, conducted the service at the Silverton church. Mrs. Minnie sat proudly in the front parsonage pew, and reported to Marcy everything down to the last rustle and tear of the congregation. The church had been "jam packed" with people and flowers, but Mrs. Minnie was rather disappointed that they'd left the coffin lid down; she supposed it was to hide how Dare's face had been cut up. "But his face wasn't marked at all. . . ." Marcy caught back her

dangerous thoughts as Mrs. Minnie rushed on that "that professor" had talked fine about Dare, called him a "son of the
morning, that shall shine in his place forever." Dare hadn't
been any star, except maybe in his own Barn, but of course
the professor didn't know him very well. The quartet had
sung, "Lead Kindly Light." Marcy wanted to scream, "I
don't want to hear any more!" but she had to go on listening
while Mrs. Minnie said Serena had held up real good; she
hadn't cried, though you couldn't see her face very well under
her thick veil. But Granny had collapsed on the way back up
the aisle, and had had to be taken home by Dr. Phil and put
to bed. After the service, more people had rushed up to Mrs.
Minnie to ask how David was than had gone to the cemetery,
she ended triumphantly. Dear Lord—

When Marcy phoned next day to ask how Granny was,
Serena said she was just worn out, body and emotions; she
didn't seem to want to go on; that was the real danger, Phil
said. How was David?

"Phil was afraid, at first, that all his extremities would be
involved. But now David can move his hands a little. They
may be able to 're-educate' his leg muscles; they can't tell
yet; it's too early."

Serena drew in her breath sharply. "Marcy, David said
something the night of the accident; he told me, 'If anything
happened to Marcy, I couldn't bear to go on.' But you have
to, for him. It seems to be a woman's job, to go on."

David had told Serena how much he loved her. A great
shout of happiness rose inside Marcy; it was generous of
Serena to tell her that. "Did you take Riley to New York, as
you planned?"

"I couldn't leave Granny," Serena pointed out, adding ruefully: "And Rye's got the measles. Wouldn't you know a kid
would spring something like that? Ma'll take good care of
him. . . . She brought me through measles, mumps, and

goodness knows what . . . but I'm anxious to get up to the Light. Well, good-by. Give David my best."

"Tell Granny I'll stop by as soon as I can," Marcy said.

Marcy went to the hospital to see David every afternoon now he'd been moved into the ward; stayed through the visiting hours. The ward was a large well-lighted, pleasant room, with the beds well apart but near enough for conversation. Phil said that David would be better off there than in a private room with nothing to think about but himself. The patients were of all ages. There was a litle boy, ten, with a cast encasing his whole body, only his arms free, who kept turning his head back and forth on the pillow. Another older boy lay upon an oscillating bed which went up and down, up and down, all day and all night, never stopping, or his breathing might stop, too. There was talk of a new iron lung that breathed for you, but few hospitals had one yet or could afford one. The adolescent girl with short dark hair and the angry mouth had one arm hung up over her bed with a heavy weight upon it; and there was another man whose throat muscles were affected so that he couldn't talk, and could make only thin chirping noises, rather terrifying to hear. But the others talked to him exactly as if they could understand what he said.

"If you can't be cheerful, stay at home," Dr. Phil had warned Marcy. "Families can play the devil with a patient's peace of mind. Worry can raise a temperature, too, don't forget. Help David look ahead."

What was there to look ahead to, with David paralyzed? Marcy pinned on a smile as securely as her hat whenever she went into the ward. The days slid by, lengthened into weeks, and still David showed only tiny gains; he could use both hands now, feed himself, but the muscles of his legs had not as yet responded to treatment. As David grew better, he also grew more difficult, unreasonable, irritable, and quite unlike his usual self. Marcy would never forget the awful Christmas afternoon when she'd brought him his presents, the dark-blue dressing gown with his initials on the pocket for when he was able to sit up, handkerchiefs, and pajamas, and she had told David gaily about the big box of Christmas fruitcake and pecan nuts from Momi, the generous check from Paw to help out with the hospital. Marcy chattered on brightly: Granny had asked her to come to the Drexels' house for Christmas dinner, but she could hardly walk out on Mrs. Minnie, who'd sent David a pair of bedroom slippers she'd crocheted herself.

"Wait till you see them," Marcy chuckled. "They've got life-size pansies on the toes!"

David, his face grim, unwrapped the slippers, stared at them for a moment . . . and then threw them petulantly down onto the polished hospital floor. "I'm never going to walk! When I ask Phil, he shys off, says, 'Give us time, feller!' None of you are kidding me!" The eyes he lifted to Marcy's were tortured, lusterless, with a flicker of fear. "I—I still can't feel my legs at all!"

"It takes time, Davey."

"You aren't being 'tactful,' God help us?"

"No."

"Everyone lies to me," this new, childish David complained. "I asked the nurse if I had any temperature this morning and she said, 'Whatever made you think that?' But a guy in a wheelchair came in to see me, and saw my chart on the foot of my bed. My temperature was up again half a degree!"

"He shouldn't have told you," Marcy murmured.

"Why not? I want to know the truth."

But if he wasn't well enough to stand the truth. . . . David's lips twisted bitterly as he looked around the ward, at the big tree in the corner, sparkling and shining with its ornaments, at the nurses, fewer than usual, as all who could had gone home to celebrate; at the patients with their families grouped around smiling too brightly, at the once tidy beds covered with torn tissue paper and red ribbon. David said, incredibly: "Why don't you go, Marcy? This is a devil of a way to spend Christmas. You don't have to stay here." The nurse was coming up with a tray in her hand, on which was a tiny glass cup with something white inside. "Is that my medication?" he asked eagerly.

This was another world of bitterness and pain in which Marcy had no part because she could walk, breathe, and run. The professional glued-on smile on the nurse's lips must be catching. Was there any medication for a frightened heart? Marcy picked up her gloves and laid the discarded slippers upon the bedside table. "I'll be in tomorrow," she promised David.

"Don't bother. You look all in. I'm fine. They look after you here, don't they, Nurse?"

Didn't he really want you to come every day? Marcy rang for the elevator, realizing wearily that it was true that lately there didn't seem to be much for her and David to talk about. She came daily into the ward, sat down by his bed and asked, "How are you today?" "I'm fine. How are you?" "Oh, I'm fine." And then they just sat. Perhaps David was right. Tomorrow, Marcy decided, she'd go to see Granny instead of to the hospital.

A telegram had been pushed under her front door when Marcy got home; she threw off her wraps, then sat down in the big chair in the empty front parlor to open it. It was from Li'l Emily and Sam: *Glad to hear better news. When David is able why don't you two come home? Make us a long visit? Little Sammy's going to need an aunt and uncle. Love . . .* Let's see, Li'l Emily must be seven months along now, but Sam had sent the lavish telegram. *Come home.* Where was home? Marcy put her head down upon the arm of the chair and wept bitterly.

Granny, who was sitting up in a big chair with the tea table in front of her when Marcy came in that afternoon, took one look at the girl's drawn, anxious face, and rang for the maid. "Git more tea 'n' scones, Hilda, 'n' make the tea strong enough to sit up and shout." Granny ordered Marcy: "Sit over there by the window where I can see you. I'm kinda tuckered out these days."

She'd aged terribly. Marcy felt contrite that she hadn't come before, but walking in this front door, seeing the empty, unused Barn out back, brought back everything she wanted to forget. What must it be like for Granny? The old lady snapped: "That professor's sermons is dry as Melba toast. He came to see me, prayed over me till I told him, 'Don't bother tellin' the Lord what I need; He knows anyways!' "

Marcy giggled; she could just imagine Henry Parker's startled, studious face with spectacles. He probably was glad to get the extra money for preaching at Silverton, for professors were notoriously underpaid, almost as poorly as preachers. As if Granny could read her thoughts, she asked Marcy flatly, "How you makin' out for cash?"

"Oh, all right. Paw sent me a check, and the church treasurer is prompt with David's salary every two weeks. . . ." Her eyes widened, as she realized suddenly, "The church can't go on paying for two ministers!"

"I've increased my weekly envelopes to cover the extry salary," Granny explained. "Lemon or milk? Now, git that hot tea into you. That Parker ain't much shakes, but he'll do till David gits back."

Marcy's cup was shaking in her hand so she had to set it back onto the saucer, "No one could take care of this big parish on crutches, Granny!"

"Why not? Still got his brains, ain't he? You don't preach

with your legs." Granny picked up her knitting needles and
the bright ugly squares of yellow and red she was knitting into
an afghan for the poor heathen. Her loyalty was a fire at which
to warm your coldness.

Marcy gasped, "David'd have a fit if he knew you were
paying extra, Granny."

"Who's to know if the treasurer don't talk? I told him I'd
stop payin' if he did." As far as she was concerned, the subject
was closed. "Dandy's goin' around the world. Says it's business, but he's just got the heeby jeebies. Rene is gone too, up
to the Light. She didn't want to leave me here alone but I
made her go. She needs her ma." Granny shot Marcy a keen
glance. "Git her out of that hospital nonsense."

"Hospital nonsense?" Marcy faltered.

"She wants to go back to work at the hospital," Granny
told her. "She ain't got the black ribbon on her cap, and Dr.
Phil says they're short-handed and need her."

Serena working at the hospital, seeing David every day,
taking care of him intimately. . . . Granny said, her sharp old
eyes on Marcy's dismayed face: "Lots of females fall in love
with the minister. It don't mean a thing, so long as they say
it with neckties and potholders."

Granny knitted for a few moments without speaking, and
the room filled with the warm fragrance of tea, of understanding. The old lady said finally: "Marriage ain't no picnic. You
can't walk out on it when it rains or when the bugs bite. But
any two people with good manners can make a go of it."

"Then you don't think there's just one man for one
woman?"

"Of course not. You can't tell me that the Lord just sits up
there on a gold throne and picks out Jane for John . . . or
Marcy for David. Marriage, religion, too, for that matter, are
mostly being polite, treating the other fellow like you want

to be treated. . . . You're not going already?" as Marcy got up, precipitately.

"Mrs. Minnie wants early supper so she can go to her sister's."

"You oughto git rid of that Minnie snooper," Granny snapped. "Save you five dollars a week 'n' keep. Why don't you move in here with me? This place is big enough. You needn't see me all day, if you didn't want to, 'n' if you was lonesome you could bunk in with Serena."

"Oh, I couldn't! Mrs. Minnie's been wonderful. I couldn't just fire her. . . ."

"The Parkers have three boys. They'd be better off in the parsonage than in that little apartment in Boston," Granny went on inexorably. "Minnie could spy on *them*. I bet they'd jump at the chance. You could store all your stuff in the Barn."

The room was closing in on her. How was she going to refuse Granny, who was paying David's salary? Keeping you both?

"I—I'll think it over," Marcy compromised. "I really must go. Thank you for everything, Granny." She bent, kissed the old lady's withered roseleaf cheek, and all but ran out of the room. If she gave up her and David's home it would be the end of everything; she'd be really adrift. Granny was a generous but persistent woman. If only she could talk this over with David! But he musn't be worried. What was she going to do?

Like so many worries, the matter was settled without her volition. She had taken to gathering little bouquets of the parish news, taking them to David to amuse him before the deadly hospital lethargy of their just staring at each other, wordless, began. She told him one afternoon, "Dandy's going around the world. He'll be gone a year, Granny says."

"Are Granny and Rene going too?" David demanded, alarmed. "Rene hasn't been in to see me for four days."

"Didn't she tell you? She's gone up to see Riley. He's had measles, then pneumonia. No, Granny says she's too old to give up her comfortable bed."

"Granny's a fighter," David said, admiring. "She's an oak." He sighed. "Dandy's only a willow."

Did he think you were a willow, too? Marcy watched his face light up at the rattle of cart wheels in the corridor. "Must be temps." He looked at his wrist watch. "No, it's the nurse with medications. Visiting hours are over."

Suddenly Marcy's words poured out, a torrent she could not stop. "Davey, what's come over you? For heaven's sake, don't you think of anything but—but pills?"

"A lot you care what happens to me!" David shot back. "I lie here all day, and all you can do is to bawl me out!"

White with shock, Marcy rushed out of the ward before she should say something else she shouldn't. This couldn't possibly be David talking that way. . . . The rustle of crisp skirts came after her down the corridor and the nurse told her, "Dr. Curtis wants to see you a moment before you go, Mrs. Gallant. He's there in the doctors' room."

Marcy's thoughts were whirling. She demanded at once, "Phil, will David walk up into his pulpit? Ever again?"

The doctor got up from his chair to face her, said levelly, "I don't know, Marcy. But I think so. It may take a year or two to bring that left leg back. Or he may have to use crutches all his life or wear a brace."

Two years! Marcy caught her breath, appalled. They couldn't possibly go on taking Granny's charity that long. David who was to be, as she used to tease him, "the youngest bishop ever elected." His bright career was finished before it ever started.

"Marcy, you're a sensible woman," Phil Curtis broke in

upon her bitter thoughts. "It's a compliment, really, that I can tell you. . . . I think you should go away for a while."

"Go away!" She looked up at him blackly. "But, David—"

"Doesn't need you just now," Phil completed the sentence for her. "His mind, his emotions have had a shock, as well as his body. He has to adjust to his new capabilities as a baby does, learn to walk in more senses than one. The nurse reports he's always depressed after you've been in. No, don't take it that way," at the stricken look in her eyes. "The feeling isn't against you, personally. You remind him of the work he can no longer do, of the mounting bills, maybe. . . . Incidentally, we've arranged for his way here to be paid here for the next few months. He might as well have it as anyone else." Dr. Phil patted her shoulder, "You need a little vacation."

David didn't want her any more. When she still couldn't speak, Dr. Curtis added briskly: "This is a very normal reaction, Marcy. The people you love most are apt to be the ones who most irritate you when they are strong and you are helpless. It won't last."

"I . . . see."

"No, I don't think you do, quite, not yet. But you will when you think it over," Phil promised. "Sometimes all we can do for those we love is to let them go." He glanced at her sharply. "You feel all right? If you'll wait for a few minutes, I'll drive you home."

"No, thanks. I have an errand to do." She had to be alone. *David didn't love her.* As Marcy went blindly, agonized, down the hospital corridor, trying to keep back the flood of her tears, the elevator door opened, and she collided with a nurse in uniform.

Serena said alarmed: "Marcy! what's wrong? David's not worse?"

Marcy gulped, forcing back her tears, faltered painfully,

"Phil says, 'Take a vacation.' But where? I could go back to Texas, I suppose."

Serena put her hand reassuringly on Marcy's arm. "Don't worry too much, Mar. I've seen this happen with lots of patients, but it passes. Texas is too far away. Davo's liable to want you badly almost any day." Her face lighted up with a sudden inspiration, warmly friendly as her sympathy. "Why don't you go up to the Light? Ma'd love to have you; she gets lonesome for woman talk. You could help Rye with his lessons; the doctor won't let him go back to school this term. I'd bring him to Silverton but Granny's not up to having a noisy kid around. Besides, I'm nursing here. Do go, Marcy. It makes sense for everyone."

Her offering of refuge was the ultimate humiliation. Yet it was good of her. Serena was kind.

Serena urged: "The Light has no doorbell, no phone; you could really rest, Mar. You need it. How soon could you get ready? Granny says you can store your stuff in our Barn. Will next Thursday do?"

So she and Granny had already talked her over. Was Dr. Phil in on this, too? She had no money to speak of; this wouldn't cost anything but her fare up to Maine, and she'd see David's precious Bellport, which he loved. Perhaps she'd love it, too, but she doubted there was that much emotion left in her. She felt empty, useless. Marcy said dully, "Thursday's all right, I reckon."

"Marcy, this is encouraging, really," Serena comforted her. "It means that underneath his weakness, Davo hasn't given in. He's still fighting."

She and her Davo. Well, she'd have him to herself now. No, that was unkind. If you were born a little person, could you ever change? Grow into tolerance. What did it matter? What did anything matter?

Marcy did not have much to pack, actually, only her and David's clothes and personal belongings, his books, typewriter, their wedding linens, silver, blankets. But it took all of the time and strength she had, even with Mrs. Minnie's help, to get them stored in the Barn. For three days Marcy did not go to the hospital at all; but finally, after she'd crammed her two suitcases with the warm clothes Serena warned she'd need for the March winds at the Light, Marcy could put it off no longer; she had to go, say goodbye to David. What, she panicked, was she to tell him? She could hardly blurt out, "The doctor says you'll be better off without me." Nor could she let David think that she *wanted* to leave him, or that she was just taking a jaunt to his beloved Maine when he couldn't go. She was still wondering what to say when she got off the hospital elevator at the sixth floor, stood there a moment, startled, listening.

They were singing down in Convalescent, in David's ward!

> " 'There's a long, long trail awinding
> Into the land of my dreams,' "

How could they possibly sing? The boy in the cast, the girl with her arm anchored up over her head, chaining her fast, the boy in the bed that never stopped oscillating. . . . That queer chirp must come from the boy who couldn't talk. And yet they sang, softly, almost humming. When David's tenor soared above the rest, the lump in Marcy's throat swelled so she could barely breathe:

> " 'Where the nightingale is singing
> And the white moon beams.' "

She could no longer see the hospital corridor for her tears. "Stop it!" she told herself sharply. The last thing to offer was pity, to these gallant young who no longer knew the miracle of walking, talking, or even of breathing normally; but who held fast to the greater miracle of just being alive. There was indeed a long, long trail ahead of her and David, and where it would lead she could not see; she knew only that you couldn't stop walking; you could never stand still. She lifted her chin and went in to David, humming too, under her breath.

Chapter Twenty

"Here, John! Here, John!" Riley was calling his pet sea gull to breakfast to show Marcy how tame he was. She stood there on the yellow cliff in front of the soaring white tower of the Light, her hands in the pockets of her warm winter coat, smiling at Riley, thinking of another little boy. The salt air was crystal clear, cold, exciting; across the sparkling river the village of Bellport was white against the dark pines. The little boy in his warm plaid jacket, his high hip boots, and cap whose visor perched over one ear held the pan of scraps, shook it invitingly. "Come here, you!" Out of the vast blue sky came the answering rush of great wings, a hungry squawk as the big gull who had been hovering overhead, circling in wide sweeps, swooped down, screaming triumph, to snatch a scrap of fish from Riley's hand.

"If you keep your big yap shut, you'll git more," Riley advised John. The big bird, gobbling greedily, flapped his wings angrily to discourage the other gulls who had heard his loud exultations and had come to investigate. Seeing the food, they descended in a gray and white cloud, waddling awkwardly over the yellow rock, snatching at whatever they could, soaring away. The instant they spread their wings, their awkwardness left them, Marcy saw with wonder; they became shining and glorious in the sun.

"I could almost fly myself!" she told Riley, hugging her arms together to keep warm. That vivid blue of river and sky, unpaintable because it was always changing, made her feel as if all she had to do was to raise her arms to soar with John and and his friends.

Past and future didn't seem to exist here at the Rock; there was only the lovely today where nothing was expected of her. Perhaps it was the river that spun the spell, the river whose voice was never still, now loud, now soft, but always there, the "rote," Ma Snow called it, the water singing against the rocks. Behind her the Light was a white finger, topped by a shining circle of glass, where the yellow curtains were already drawn against the sun; at her feet was the small white building that housed "Carrie" the foghorn; and to her right, bolted to the rock against the wild winter winds and connected with the light by a sturdy wooden walk, was the square white keeper's house, freshly painted, as immaculate as anything with which Pa and Ma Snow had to do.

Riley, watching the gulls swoop and sail across the sky, asked suddenly, "Miz Gallant, can Dare fly now as good as John can?"

Marcy, startled, wondered what Serena had told him. Rye rushed on, "What does God look like?"

You never could tell where conversation with Rye would swoop, gull-like. "I expect He looks different to different people."

"I seen a picture—"

"Saw."

"I saw a picture of Him once in a book. He was sitting on a cloud in his nightgown. He had a beard like Pete Epps." Peter Epps was the postmaster at Bellport across the river, who ran the village store also; a big-boned, bearded man who looked as if he'd slept in his clothes, but the gray eyes behind his silver-rimmed spectacles were keen but amused, as if he saw life's absurdities clearly but was not perturbed by them.

"Ma thinks God looks like a sunset," Riley was chattering on. "Her 'n' me were looking out the kitchen window last night when the river was breezing up, and the sky got all bright red, real handsome. Ma said, 'I think God must look a little like that, Sonny.'" Riley demanded earnestly, "How could God look like Pete Epps and a sunset?"

Marcy laughed. "I'm freezing. Let's go in. It's time for your arithmetic, anyway."

Ma's immaculate kitchen was deliciously fragrant with the

cake with generous lashings of maple sugar warming in the oven, with the smell of coffee always brewing, black and hot, in the big gray pot on the back of the black iron stove with its nickle as brightly polished as the Light was, every day. Pa put on the coffeepot mornings at sunrise when he got up to turn out the Light, and the dark brew was always there when needed, hot and comforting as now. Sipping at her white mug of coffee, Marcy glanced up at the organdy curtains freshly laundered at the windows, at Ma's red geraniums blossoming on the windowsill. The wind and the call of the gulls screaming outside, the murmur of the river rote made it seem even more cozy inside; she was in another world from any she had known, a safe world where no one would criticize or hurt her, a world where she was content merely to be sipping coffee. Ma took the maple-sugar cake out of the oven just as Pa came into the kitchen from the Light, with timing perfected by long practice in listening for his boots on the wooden walk that led from the Light to the house.

Pa was a small man, really, but his belief in himself, that he could do anything, made him seem big in this little island world that was his. His face was brown, wrinkled soft leather, out of which his very blue eyes twinkled; he wore shapeless brown pants, a gray wool sweater Ma had knitted for him, a brown-and-white checked wool jacket which he hung up on the hook by the kitchen door, his high fisherman's boots thumping across the floor. His only concession to a uniform was his cap with its tarnished braid, which he wore, summer and winter, on the back of his head. He didn't really need any insignia of office when his father before him had been a lightkeeper and *his* father before him; knowledge, authority were in the sure way he walked and sat down in the creaking rocking chair in front of the stove.

"I declare, I think this cake lacks salt," Ma worried, passing Pa a well-filled plate and a mug of coffee. Pa murmured that she'd been saying that for thirty years, and Ma smiled at him. "How you talk!"

Ma was a winter apple, round, rosy, appetizing in her crisp gingham housedress. Pa adored her, though he'd never think of telling her so. He snorted: "Rye, git outa that woodbox. What you messin' up the deck for?"

"I lost a nickel," Rye scrabbled around among the kindling, then drew out his coin triumphantly. "Pa, when you go git the mail, kin I buy a choc'lit cone?"

Ma glanced quickly at Marcy and then away. She hadn't missed the way Marcy looked for mail daily, and then how her face fell. She'd been here a month, and not one letter from David, but Serena wrote Ma often, telling her how well he was doing. His hands weren't paralyzed. Then why didn't he write? Maybe today . . . Ma said hastily, "Let's take a run over right now, Pa." She needed some baking powder, and it was such a pretty day. The four of them crunched down the frosty path to the boathouse with Useless, Rye's Heinz-variety yellow pup, dancing and barking about them, leaping into the bow of the big dory. It was bitter cold on the river but better than brooding. As their bow cut the icy blue water, Ma pointed out to Marcy: "See that little place with the red roof, up there on the cliff? That was the Gallant place before foreigners from Boston bought her."

Why hadn't Ma told her that before? Did she think that today there wouldn't be any mail either and that she must take her mind off her disappointment? Marcy looked up at the low brown cottage with the red roof, perched on the high cliff, with pines a dark fan behind it. David had been a little boy here. She said wistfully, "Sometime I'd like to see inside."

"Go today, if you want," Ma offered. "Pete Epps's got the key. Place ain't been lived in for two years. I hear tell it's up for rent."

The store was warm from the potbellied redly burning

stove with the usual fringe of lanky fishermen seated around it who moved over to give Pa room, and Riley raced to buy his choc'lit cone. Marcy hurried to the little mail window, surrounded by boxes through which she could see Pete Epps' bearded face.

"Nuthin' for you, Miz Gallant, but there's one from Rene for her Ma." Pete sounded apologetic, handing over the letter which Ma opened at once, and read aloud. Everyone here knew Marcy was waiting for the letter from her husband that didn't come, was speculating about it, she knew, her cheeks flaming. David was better, Serena told Ma; one leg was responding to therapy and they had good hopes of the second. He was using a wheelchair now, wearing his blue dressing gown; tell Marcy it looked fine on him. "Sometimes all we can do for those we love is to let them go." But not forever—

Ma glanced at Marcy's dismayed face, told Rye, "You stay here with that cone till we git back with the key. No use freezin' your outside as well as your inside."

Miserable, wishing she hadn't asked to go, but not knowing how to get out of it, Marcy followed Ma "down the road a piece" and up the mossy path through the pines to the back door of the small brown house. Marcy murmured, "Queer they still call it the Gallant place."

"The Gallants was always real neighborly," Ma explained, fitting the key into the back door, shabby with its faded paint. "They used to cruise around more with the village people than with summer folks. The Boston foreigners called this place 'The Barnacle,'" Ma snorted as she stepped into the damp cold of the kitchen, which was large for so small a house, with a sink and pump, a black iron stove, a couch over by the window, and a rocking chair with a flat turkey-red pillow in the seat. "Ain't changed much; jest kind of shabbied out," Ma opined. "Brr-rrr, it's tomb-cold in here! David's Ma used to set in that window waitin' for her pies to brown. She was some good cook. They always ast her to make her pecan pie for the church suppers, and folks fought for a piece."

It made David's mother come alive, people fighting for her pecan pie, but the coldness bit into you. Marcy followed Ma past two small bedrooms, with a bed, washstand, and a chair, into the enormous living room, and stopped, surprised. "Why, it's all windows! What a gorgeous view!"

You could see all up and down the sparkling river, the ribbon of yellow cliffs, the far-off pointed pines piercing the bright blue sky, and the swift darker blue of the water, foaming around the point beyond, off on its mysterious journey to Popham Beach, to the sea. Pa had taken Marcy down to Ocean Point in his dory, but the sea had frightened her; there was too much of it. It was not quiet like the Texas prairie, but moving, threatening, looming high over the dory, tossing them helplessly. Marcy had been glad to get back safely to the river mouth. Ma came to stand beside her. "Some handsum', ain't it? David's Ma used to say if heaven was any prettier than this she didn't want to stay." Ma sighed, because now David's mother knew the answer. She glanced over at the cold, empty maw of the big graystone fireplace. "The little tikes used to have sings, Sunday nights, around that fireplace, and toast marshmallows, all village young uns with David, Pete Epps, Janey Tikes, Rene, Cap'n Eri's Timmy 'n' Hezzie. . . . That was early on, before the Drexels come, of course, and David sold."

No wonder David's and Serena's roots went deep.

Ma said, "Pa'll be itchin' to get back to the Light, but there's one thing I'm bound to show you if Pa toots his whistle off." She led the way into the shed attached to the little house and pointed to a tall upright of unpainted pine with a series of notches with dates in black pencil. "That's where David's folks used to measure summers how much he'd growed. He was only minnow-high when he first come."

Little David, only minnow-high. Suddenly Marcy wanted him so badly she almost cried out: I've got to go home, Ma. Will Pa drive me up to the train in Bath? But she couldn't go, till he wanted her. "Wait till David sends for you," Dr. Phil had warned when she left. "The initiative must come from him, Marcy."

Marcy was glad she had Riley's school homework to help him with; it gave her some way to pay back Pa and Ma, who were so good to her. When she'd offered to pay board, they'd been almost insulted. Ma'd pointed out that Marcy's keep cost them practically nothing: with Mollie's milk, all the stuff Ma'd canned downstairs, and Pa hauling his traps nearly every day, they bought very little at the store. The government furnished coal, kerosene for the keeper's icebox, lamps, and for the Light. Anyways, they weren't allowed to take boarders.

Pa made it ashore daily for the mail, but the weary weeks went by; it was April, and still no letter from David, but Marcy continued to write gay weekly letters to him with nothing much in them. What was there to write about except gulls and river and how Ma'd made an angel cake? The burning query, What's the matter, Davey? Don't you love me enough to use a pen? couldn't be asked. On April 2nd Pa brought back from the post office a telegram, but when Marcy's face went white, Pa reassured her at once, "It's from Texas, not Boston." He squinted down at Pete Epps' black pencil scrawl on a piece of brown wrapping paper, and asked Marcy, "You know someone name of—Samuella?"

"Li'l Emily's baby's come!" Marcy snatched the paper from Pa's reluctant hand. "She's my sister. She must have named her for Sam—too bad he didn't get the boy he wanted. But— Samuella! It's outlandish!"

Ma beamed, planning: "We'll knit her a sweater. You say, she's named for her Pa?"

Marcy nodded. "But I can't knit!"

"I'll teach you," Ma promised. "Pa'll git you some pink yarn. He's cruisin' up to Bath today to git some new parts for the icebox." When Pa looked mutinous, she ordered: "You stop by Etta's. She's Pa's cousin, runs a little store."

"Giftie Shoppe!" Pa snorted, "With painted clamshells!"

He took Marcy's money for the yarn, however, and presently, from the warm kitchen they could hear his powerful engine roaring upriver. Ma went to the window, worriedly. "River's too calm. Makin' up for a bad blow. I wisht he'd waited till tomorrow."

"There isn't a ripple," Marcy protested, coming to look out, too, over the flat, icy water. Ma said doubtfully, well, it wouldn't take Pa more'n half an hour upriver, an hour to buy his stuff, and half an hour back; he'd be home by three o'clock most likely. "I think I'll make me a batch of sugar cookies."

She was too nervous to sit still, but Marcy couldn't see why. Idly she watched Ma put wood into the black wood stove, open the dampers, get out her shining mixing bowl. Marcy had never seen a place so immaculately clean, ready for inspection in every corner at any minute. "Shipshape," Pa called it. He as well as Ma cleaned every day, scrubbed the kitchen floorboards white, blacked the stove and polished the nickle, besides milking Mollie, feeding the hens, taking care of the Light.

This kitchen was the living room, actually; the parlor was a museum where treasures too precious to use were kept. Marcy watched Ma roll out dough without spilling a speck of flour. She didn't let anyone but her dust the mantelpiece with the big pink shell which held a velvet pincushion too good for pins, the white vase shaped like a lady's hand which never held water, the paper fan from Japan opened to show the girls in bright kimonos dancing there, the priceless luster teapot which had been a wedding present of Ma's great-great-grandmother, and the painted tin mug that said "Having a wonderful time at Old Orchard Beach." The center table protected by a "piece" embroidered with daisies and love knots held the other treasures, the big family Bible with its gilt clasps, and a pile of postcards of Niagara where Ma and Pa had gone thirty years ago on their honeymoon. All these were valued equally because of memories so real that the object itself was never actually visible. After all, Marcy thought, isn't the value in the eye of the beholder? What made a diamond more expensive than a piece of glass except the arbitrary price set upon it? Both glittered magnificently in the sun.

"Ma? Cookies done yit?"

Rye and Useless came roaring into the kitchen, scenting food. His cheeks were red from the wind, and the warmth of the kitchen made him yawn; then Marcy caught it from him, yawned too, and Ma suggested, "Why don't you two take a nap?" She herself went to the kitchen window again, peered out. "Tide's turned. It's breezin' up. But Pa should be back before the river gets persnickety."

Rye was asleep almost before Ma finished tucking him up on the couch. Marcy went gratefully to her own bed: it was wonderful how she could sleep here; she just laid her head down on the pillow. . . .

The knocking on her bedroom door woke her out of a deep sleep. Her window was dark, she saw drowsily; she must have slept for hours. "Come in." At the sight of Ma there in her doorway, the kerosene lamp shining upon her anxious white face, Marcy was out of bed in an instant, demanding, "Is anything wrong?"

"It's six, deep-dark under the table, and Pa ain't home yet," Ma said. "He musta had trouble findin' them machine parts. I wisht he'd come. It's makin' up for a real northeaster!"

The wind and rote were making such a racket alongshore Marcy could hardly hear what Ma said. Every now and then the wind would take the sturdy square little house in its teeth and shake it; it was comforting to know it was bolted to the rock. Staring at the black pane of glass, Marcy was startled to see a bright finger cross the dark sky. "The Light!" she gasped.

"Darkened up early tonight," Ma agreed. "Rye's out there."

Both she and Rye knew how to start the Light, tracing its warning in the sky, but a seven-year-old out there alone, with the rain and wind beating about the lonesome tower . . .

"Supper's on, Marcy," Ma said. "Rye's had his." She went back down the stairs holding the kerosene lamp high so they both could see. She'd waked her because she couldn't stand any longer waiting here alone. Marcy shivered. Surely Pa wouldn't try to make it home in this terrible storm; yet he'd never rest easy away from the Light. Ma fretted, "I hotted up the lobster stew and made biscuits. They're in the oven."

"You eaten yet, Ma?"

"I ain't hungry."

Marcy ate because she knew it would worry Ma more if she didn't, but her ears kept straining, too, for the sound of Pa's powerful engine, fighting the roar of wind and water.

The Light and Ma and Rye were his life, his duty, his reason for being; he would chance anything to be sure they were safe. There was where the danger to him lay: but there was nothing you could do to change Pa. Seven o'clock, eight o'clock, and still no Pa. Ma had the oven door open, as if she found it hard to get warm, and Marcy was cold, too, remembering what David had said about how few of the fishermen knew how to swim. If Pa's engine stopped and his boat was tossed violently up onto the rocks . . .

Once, Ma put on Pa's yellow oilskins, went out to the tower to tell Rye to come in, have a cup of cocoa, but she came back without him. Her face was drenched, her hair hanging in wisps as she put the oilskin back upon its hook by the back door.

"Rye all right?" Marcy asked anxiously.

"Ayuh. He says he'll be in when Pa comes," Ma reported. There was iron in these Maine people; even little boys did their jobs, were allowed, no, *expected* to. Ma sat down stolidly again by the stove, her hands locked in her lap, her chin lifted for the sound she both wanted to hear and feared. "If he rides the rollers in right, onto the slip, he'd make it, easy," Ma explained. And if he didn't ride the roller right . . . Marcy felt a thousand years old, as if she'd sat there forever, watching the lines deepen around Ma's mouth. She said: "Marcy, I got to tell you; I wrote David I'd showed you his old home, the Gallant place. And you missed him, terrible."

"Oh?" Marcy said. Writing to David was pouring water down a well. Why didn't Pa come?

It was after nine before he came stamping in the back door, water draining from his cap, his clothes, his boots making a squelching sound. Marcy waited for Ma to run to him to throw her arms around his neck, to ask what had happened, but all Ma said was: "You'd best git shet of them wet clothes. Rye's at the tower."

"Ayuh," Pa said. He chuckled wearily. "Thinks he's an admiral, no less."

Naturally he'd gone to the Light first. Ma's relief was too great to talk about. "You'd best sit here by the stove to eat," she told Pa when he came down in dry clothes. He put his gray socks she'd knit for him obediently into the oven, took the steaming hot lobster stew she handed him, and began eating hungrily, warming his big gnarled hands on the bowl.

"Home's pretty snug on a night like this," Pa admitted. "Not that you 'n' Rye couldn't manage, Angie." Her name was Angela; it was the first time he'd called her by name before Marcy. His eyes met his Angie's and something flashed between the two of them, something so proud, bright, and shining that Marcy's throat tightened painfully. This was it, the peace that passed understanding; maybe two people came to it only through storm and trouble. After the wind and the fury died away, a man and his wife could come at last to this wonderful shared peace in a quiet kitchen.

Davey, I need you! Marcy's heart cried. Loneliness was a sharp pain.

The glowing letter from David came in the next day's mail, telling Marcy that he'd walked six steps on his crutches! He was glad she'd seen his home, admired the river peering in its front windows, for now she knew why he loved that rocky coast. He envied her living there at the Light. He'd been too homesick for Maine to even write about it. He was homesick to see her, too. Terribly. Couldn't she take a run down to Boston? As she read on, David's letter trembled in her hands. If he could just see her, it would be like getting a breath of the good Bellport air; he'd be O.K. in no time, David wrote wistfully. When the hot, happy tears came, Ma asked anxiously, "David worse?"

"No, he's better." Marcy managed. "He's lonesome for— for Maine." Perhaps she could get a train for Boston this afternoon.

Ma said calmly: "Why don't he come up here for a spell? Won't he git shet of that hospital pretty soon now? It's eatin' into April."

It would cost money to go down to Boston, money you couldn't spare. What David needed most was hope, a plan for the future.

Marcy stared at Ma. Maybe that was the better plan, since the parsonage was occupied. David loved this place so. Ma went on in her practical way: "Why don't you two rent the Gallant cottage? If you took it for the spring and summer, Pete Epps'd let it go, cheap. It's be some chilly right now on the cliff, but you could shut off the big front parlor and up-stairs, heat the kitchen and the two downstairs bedrooms with the wood stove."

"That would be wonderful!" Then her face fell. What

would they live on? David would never stand for Granny's going on supporting them when he knew. "If I could only get a job . . ."

"Etta's lookin' for help at her Giftie Shoppe," Pa said. He took off the stove lid, spat, disgusted. "Calls it 'The Laughing Cat.' She told me when I was up to Bath she wanted a likely-lookin' gal to take stock now, wait on customers this summer. She allus opens Memorial Day, the first weekend cottagers start sloshin' down the deck." He shot Marcy a sharp glance. "Etta can't keep help long; got a knife-edged tongue, cuts at both ends and in the middle, but she pays reg'lar. Twenty-five a week."

Marcy gasped, "But I haven't had any experience selling!"

"Don't need no college course to sell a painted clam shell," Pa snorted. "I'll run you up to Bath tomorrow."

To Marcy's surprise, but not to Pa's, who knew how desperate Etta was for someone attractive to customers who didn't want all outdoors for pay, Marcy got the job. Pete Epps offered to rent her the cottage for twenty-five dollars a month, seein' there wasn't any bathroom and she was takin' it for the whole season, spring 'n' summer. Then Marcy dared to write Dr. Phil, and got his enthusiastic approval. He thought Maine an excellent idea if she could keep David warm; David was ecstatic, wanted to start the next day, but Dr. Phil had arranged with Serena for her and James to bring David down to Bellport in Granny's big car where he could lie down with pillows on the back seat. Serena wanted to see Rye, anyway. It was probably safer for David to have a nurse along, Marcy realized, but were she and David never to be alone?

Pa and Ma Snow and Marcy worked, scrubbed, to get the cottage ready. Pa donated a woodpile that all but filled the back shed, and stopped by every day to start a fire in the kitchen stove to dry the place out. Marcy and Ma polished windows, cleaned, and aired bedding they found in the bureau drawers. Even the weather cooperated, warming up to an early spring. Marcy went around singing, laughing at Rye heating up the ends of candles, sticking the ends onto the stones that jutted out on the gray fireplace. "But we aren't going to use the living room for a while," she protested; but Rye said it was just like Christmas, wasn't it? Lighted candles for David and a light inside Marcy too.

But on the day David and Serena were scheduled to arrive, Marcy got scared. She stood there alone in the toasty warm kitchen and wondered frantically what she was going to say to David after all this time. She musn't notice his bad leg with the brace. He wore only one now, he wrote, but had to use crutches. It'd be too cold for him out in that icy shed, so there was a china arrangement with a pink rose on the lid, in the downstairs bedroom. If he got sick again, what would she do? She must have been crazy to chance it, with no doctor nearer than Bath. . . .

"Ahoy, Marcy!" It was David's voice. She flung open the back door, tried to call back to him, but only a croak came. She was so appalled. David was only a ghost of himself! She wanted to run to him, to help him, but would he want her to? But would it be kinder to pretend not to notice?

David and James were coming up the path, with James' arm under one of David's, while he limped along with a crutch under the other arm, hobbling painfully on his leg heavy with the brace. Oh, God, will he ever walk alone again?

"David, welcome home!" Marcy gasped. "James, how nice of you! Didn't Serena come?"

"Too long a ride for him just out of the horsepiddle," James grumbled, easing David up the short flight of six back steps, into the kitchen. "She went out to the Light. Where'll I put him?"

"Like a log of wood!" David gasped. He was so paper-white, so thin.

"Right there on the cot by the window," she babbled, terrified.

"Be—all right—soon as I've rested." David fell onto the cot exhausted, closed his eyes, and Marcy pulled the comforter over him. That dreadful brace . . . How was she ever going to take care of him and work, too? She urged, not wanting to be alone with this frighteningly fragile David: "You'll stay for supper, James? There's plenty of lobster. And apple pie." But James said, No, he'd better get a move on; Granny'd given him money to eat at the hotel in Bath.

Then for the first time in five months Marcy was alone with David, and he was a stranger, a pitiful stranger. He looked so terribly ill. Had he fainted? She rushed to kneel beside him, and he opened his eyes, smiled at her. She must be strong like Ma.

"Marcy? *Marcy! I'm home!*" David opened his arms and they closed about her, thin but reassuringly real. She leaned her head down against his shoulder and, to her horror, burst into tears.

Chapter Twenty-one

THEY were together again, he and Marcy, and yet so far apart. Was it her fault or his? David wondered that glorious July Maine morning as he sat there on the ancient wooden pier soaking up sunlight and splendor thirstily after arid months in the hospital. The grayed wooden floorboards were broken here and there so he could see the blue-green water down below sloshing among the piles, while across the river lay the Light with its cluster of white buildings, the Light which was by day a thick unlighted candle on its altar of yellow granite, by night a pillar of flame. What was worrying Marcy? Was she still upset because he hadn't written her from the hospital? But the tie between them had always been so strong he'd thought she'd understand without words that he had to get hold of himself, be whole again, before he could be any good to her. How could he offer her a man with no legs, no future, a man unsure of his ability even to put a roof over her head? Naturally he loved her; she knew that already. Serena had scolded him for not writing, but he'd insisted: "Marcy can read your letters to Ma. She knows I'm all right." Maybe he had acted like a sullen child, but the last thing he'd wanted from Marcy had been pity. He'd torn up enough letters to stock a post office, but the right words simply would not come.

David sighed, moved uneasily on his hard perch, breathed deeply, gratefully, of the clear air. How often your ambitions were realized in the wrong way! He'd dreamed of living in Bellport again, but not as a cripple, and certainly not with Marcy working to support him. . . . He glanced over at the lighthouse slip where Pa's dory was still drawn up; he and Rye and Useless would be along pretty soon now for the mail. Rye appointed himself godfather to a family of phoebes in

David's back yard, dug worms for them, and came daily to feed the yawning mouths of the clamoring young birds.

"If one of my babies was to fall, a cat might git him," he explained to David. You'd think he'd hatched those eggs himself!

Strange how important little things became in this quiet life, David mused: the sunrise, the murmur of the river against the piles down there, the scream of the hungry gulls, and the delighted laughter of a little boy. These were your rosary of peace. If only Marcy could have been contented, relaxed, too . . . But she was like quicksilver; when he stretched out his hand to grasp her she was there in body but not in spirit. Not in body either, David realized ruefully, remember-their separate bedrooms. It was humiliating, her having to wait on him mornings before she left for work, fixing his leg brace so he could get out of bed, refusing to let him go out into the shed in the early morning chill, seeing his crutches and lunch were handy before she rushed off to catch the eight-thirty bus to Bath. She was as impersonal in her care of him as one of the nurses in the hospital. Maybe he could have changed that, but, David wondered bitterly, how could a man make love, hanging from a couple of crutches?

"Pretty mornin', David!"

"Cap'n Eri! Good morning to you!" David, glad to have his shadowed thoughts interrupted, beamed up at the little brown dried-up pod of an old man, Cap'n Eri Shedd, who'd known David since he could talk. As far as he could see the cap'n wore the same wrinkled shapeless brown pants of his youth, but now over his thick brown sweater a Paisley shawl was fastened over his shoulders with an enormous safety pin, and his sharp black eyes peered out from under a white canvas hat with a slit of green plastic set in the visor. Cap'n Eri undid the safety pin, tossed off the shawl irritably, sat down upon the empty wooden bait barrel beside which David's crutches rested.

The cap'n grumbled, "Them dang boys baby me. I ain't only eighty-five. Pa could saw wood when he was ninety."

"Maybe he hadn't just got out of bed from flu," David suggested.

"Wa'n' nuthin' but the sniffles." Cap'n Eri sounded disgusted, but he was proud of his three bachelor fisherman sons who lived with him, took such finicky care of his health. Dammy—short for Damascus—cooked, Timmy redded up the house after he got in from his traps, and Hezzie didn't do "nuthin' but fish 'n' fuss." To the cap'n, all three were still boys to be bossed, to be watched proudly every Sunday morning when Dammy rang the big church bell, clanging importantly from the steeple, and Tommy and Hezzie in their dark-blue best suits and heavy black shoes tramped down the aisle with the collection plates, a parade to an unheard drumbeat. The old man's eyes slid over David relaxed in the sun, and then to the left where stood the ancient church, white and lovely in its classic simplicity of line.

"Them young whippersnappers, student supplies we have summers, can't give communion," he grumbled. "We ain't had one for four years! 'Bout time we did, seems like, if we ain't gonna go plumb heathen."

"Only an ordained priest can offer the sacraments," David agreed. "I never could figure out, though, does the creed of your church believe in the divinity of Christ?"

"Who says we don't?" the cap'n snapped. He glared about the sun-warmed pier. "Believe in sunshine, don't we? Got to come from Someone. We ain't purely anythin', no set creed. Church was endowed by my great-grandad, left to four trustees fifty years ago to keep open for anyone who wanted to come. I'm the only one of the three trustees left." He turned his sharp black gaze upon David, exploded his verbal bomb.

"I was wondern': why don't you give us communion next Sunday?"

David started, gasped, "But—I couldn't—"

"Pay you ten dollars, if there's that much in the collection plate or not."

In the present state of their finances, ten dollars was not to be refused lightly, as the cap'n well knew. But it wasn't the money; David would be glad to give his services if . . . How could he make a spectacle of himself, stumbling up the aisle on his crutches? How could he pass the bread and wine? David stammered in panic, "I—I'm sorry. I'd like to help you out, Cap'n Eri. But I couldn't, not possibly."

"Folks could cruise up to you; Pete Epps' got a wheelchair in his shed his stepmother used till she passed on." The cap'n had it all planned out. "I read somewheres that the Lord don't pleasure hisself none in the legs of a man." The old man got up, reached for his shawl and safety pin. "Think it over, David, 'n' let me know what you decide."

"There's nothing to decide. It's a physical impossibility. . . ." The old man had stumped off down the pier, disregarding his protests as if they meant no more than the lap of the river around the piers below, or the inarticulate scream of the gulls. At eighty-five you no longer listened to a spate of foolish words, his shawled back said. David thought, shaken, that Cap'n Eri was a spoiled old man.

"Ahoy there, David!"

Rye's eager towhead appeared above the top rung of the ladder, with Useless's rough yellow head peering from under his arm, the pup's long, awkward legs dangling. Rye set the pooch down on the gray floorboards, showed David a tin can crawling with worms. "Breakfast for my phoebes. I'll get your crutches." As he handed them to David, Pa Snow came up the ladder with a brown paper bag in his hand.

"Apple pie Ma sent for your lunch," he explained. "I'll set

it in the kitchen as I go by. She says, couldn't you 'n' Marcy come over for supper tonight? I'll stop by for you about five, when Marcy's bus gets in."

"Thanks." But it was hard to have to hobble along, watching a man over twice your age eat up the ground so easily, with Rye and Useless rushing ahead, impatient to feed his "family."

"David! David, help!" came Rye's frantic scream.

What could so frighten him in the back yard? David, swinging along as fast as he could, arrived in time to see a huge black snake, his body almost as thick as the tree trunk, swarming up the maple sapling. "He's after my babies!" Rye grabbed a hoe from the garden, began whacking desperately at the snake's body while the frantic little phoebe mother screaming, pecked at the snake's head with little rushes; but the snake's beady eyes were fixed inexorably on his breakfast, the five little phoebes shrilling their terror from the nest. David hung there on his crutches, unable to help Rye or to look away. . . . Tears were running down the little boy's cheeks as he whacked and prayed, "Don't let him, God! Please don't let him eat my phoebes—Oh!" For the snake's head had whipped out faster than sight, and the nest was empty.

"I hate You! I hate You!" Riley flung down his useless hoe, dropped himself to the grass, sobbing his heart out, for he'd trusted in David and the Lord, and both of them had failed him. The bottom had dropped clean out of his world.

"Don't cry, Rye. You did all you could," David comforted, hobbling closer.

"God could've stopped him! He let the snake eat my babies!"

How to get through to him in words he could understand? "Rye, what did you have for dinner last Sunday?"

Rye turned his tear-stained face. "Fried chicken. Ma always saves me the gizzard. Why?"

"I expect this was a chicken gizzard for the snake," David explained. "He gets hungry, too."

"You mean, we have to *eat each other?*" Riley asked horrified.

"Something like that," David admitted. "Life is terrible and beautiful, wonderful and cruel. We have to learn to live with it." His voice roughened. "Do you think I haven't prayed for my leg to get well? But I don't hate God because it doesn't."

But when Rye had gone home in the dory with Pa, David told himself bitterly that he'd been just as childish as the little boy, the same savage anger boiling up in him when he was in the hospital at the injustice of being stopped so peremptorily when he'd been about the Lord's business night and day, or at least he'd thought so. And he'd taken out his spleen on Marcy, his little love. He'd married a lovely child. Had he tried too hard to pattern her into what he wanted her to be rather than letting her blossom in her own way? She'd done all right. Supporting him, wasn't she? O God, let me get strong fast. . . .

Marcy was glad enough on that hot summer evening to have Ma's supper offered her, although she knew how hard it was for David to get down the ladder to Pa's dory. Pa went behind him, placing David's feet carefully on each rung, but when they finally reached the lighthouse slip, David was grateful to hobble only as far as Carrie, to sit down beside Pa on the wooden walk to rest while Marcy went on up to the kitchen to help Ma. But David wasn't prepared for Pa's queries.

"Rene ain't been home all summer. You know any reason, David?"

David looked at Pa, startled. "Granny Drexel needs her. And they're short-handed at the hospital."

"You see quite a lot of Rene at the hospital?" Pa pushed on.

"Every day. She said when we drove up she'd be back soon to sell the *Sans Souci*."

"Her'n now," Pa agreed; his hooded eyes regarded David without expression. What was he getting at?

Meanwhile, in the kitchen, Ma was taking a pan of biscuits out of the oven, giving Marcy a plate to put them on the dining-room table. She had her own reasons for asking her and David to supper. She said, suddenly: "Pa's sick. I found him lyin' out at the bottom of them steps, at the Light, this mornin'."

Those narrow, winding, dangerous iron steps that led up and up. But Pa'd climbed them safely for years. Marcy said: "It was an awfully hot day. Maybe he was just dizzy from too much sun."

"When you've been married to a man thirty years, six months, and four days you don't need no doctor to tell you when he's mortal sick," Ma told her grimly. "Pa's due to retire in six months, if he kin hold out till then. Put that plate on the table, Marcy, before you drop them biscuits."

Marcy murmured, "I don't wonder you don't want to leave the Light."

"I can't hardly wait to git ashore." Ma set the biscuit pan in the sink with a tinny bang. "I liked to cried my eyes out, my first six months."

"But I thought you adored it here!"

"Twenty-one years, parked on a lonesome rock?" Ma snapped. "How'd you like never once seein' a movie through at Bath? Have no one to talk to but Carrie, the foghorn? Sure, I got to go to church acrosst there and to the post office, but the Light couldn't never be left alone; worse'n a two-weeks-old baby!"

"Ma! I never dreamed—"

"It was Pa's own fault, some of it. He coulda got a relief keeper if he'd wanted to. But would he? Not him." Marcy still stared, not believing what she heard, as Ma insisted: "I wish Pa'd go ashore tomorrow, but he won't. He won't go outa here till he's carried feet first, most likely. Marcy, put that butter on the table."

Marcy moved automatically to obey. "You never told Pa? How you feel?"

"What was the sense? I married him, didn't I? A man has to do what he wants. If he finds a pair o' pants that fits him, he's got to put 'em on, else he might go naked all his life. No use gettin' in a hassle over it. Pa's mouth ain't jest right; the spit runs down one corner. I figure he's had slight shock. He might have another most any day."

How could Ma talk so calmly? Marcy offered, "If there's any thing I can do . . ."

"You 'n' David can keep watch acrosst here. If Pa gits another spell, I'll ring Carrie. No use the whole shore knowin' yet that Pa's ailin'. If he's real bad, I'll hang a dishtowel out the kitchen window." Ma had it all planned out. "If you or David see that, phone the station at Popham. They'll send a relief keeper for the Light and an ambulance." Ma was thinking first of the Light, as Pa would want her to. "Heave out a yell to the menfolks that supper's on, will you, Marcy?"

Pa Snow carried them back ashore early, so David could see his way. Strangely, he didn't seem to be much upset when Marcy told him about Pa's being sick; his mind was on something else He burst out, "Cap'n Eri wants me to preach at the church next Sunday, to give communion. Of all the idiotic . . ."

"Why, Davey, that'd be wonderful!"

"Make a holy show of myself?" David kicked angrily at his crutch propped on the kitchen table so that it crashed to the floor. "No, thank you!"

"Oh, Davey, please try it! You've got to begin sometime."

He stared at her morosely, bitterly. "Does ten dollars mean so much to you?"

This was sheer panic. "Seeing you do something positive does. Even if they didn't pay you a cent, David Gallant, it'd be worth it, having you doing something besides being sorry for yourself!" There, the words she'd been hoarding, thinking for weeks, were out. David flushed a painful red; his eyes made her feel as if she'd kicked Useless, Riley's pup, but who was to tell him the truth but her? "If you stay forever on a couple of sticks, what's going to become of us?"

David's face was stricken. He grabbed up his crutches, swung himself erect, started for his own room. His door was shut, and when she moved to open it for him he choked, "Leave me alone!" The bedroom door banged to behind him. Had she hurt him beyond need? Sometimes you had to be cruel to be kind. What she'd said was true, and when he thought it over he'd know it was. David was always fair.

All the way to Bath in the bus next morning, in the shop, Marcy worried over speaking to David so bluntly. Why did everything she said to David these days come out differently from the way she meant it? The hot July day seemed endless and the customers complete morons. She snapped at a woman who'd taken home a book on approval, brought it back with a smear of butter on the cover, saying she'd decided not to read it, after all, "You've read it already! On your breakfast tray." When the insulted customer stamped out of the shop, Etta, Marcy's boss, came over to her.

"What's wrong with you today? I don't want you petering out on me before Labor Day. You'd better go home early this afternoon, lie down."

That was how Marcy happened to take the early bus home. As she came up the road, she caught a glimpse of David out back of the house. He was swinging along with only one crutch, with a cane in his other hand! She watched him struggle awkwardly along the mossy path, stumble. . . . He was falling! Marcy started to run, stopped as David picked himself up and, wobbling but triumphant, started out doggedly again. Lord, love him. . . . She couldn't watch his uncertain progress any longer; quietly she turned, tiptoed back down the road to the pier where she sat, hidden behind a smelly empty bait barrel, listening to the soothing murmur of the river for an hour until her regular bus arrived.

When she came into the kitchen, David was lying on the couch, exhausted. He called jubilantly, "Hi, there! Have a good day?"

"Fine. And you?"

"Oh, so-so."

If he wanted to surprise her, let him. Three weeks later David met Marcy at the bus stop, leaning only on two canes while Riley danced about him, yelling, "Lookit, no crutches!"

"David!" she gasped, radiant. "Did you walk clear from the house? How did you manage?"

"He leaned on me when he got tired," Rye boasted.

"Oh, I've been practicing on the sly," David confessed. They walked along home together, very slowly, Marcy chattering casually about the shoppe, while David flung out his stiff leg, balanced himself carefully; she didn't even glance at him when he slipped on the pine needles of their path, caught his balance again. As he lowered himself triumphantly down upon their back steps, he gasped, "I told Cap'n Eri I'd take the communion next Sunday."

"Davey! I'm so glad!" But it'd be easier to learn to walk, yourself.

Word of the long-awaited communion and of David's coming spread about the countryside so that the next Sunday morning the little church was full to the last pew by the time Dammy Shedd had stopped pulling the heavy rope that swung the last bell. David, Marcy, and Riley had waited at the cottage for Cap'n Eri's battered Ford truck, driven by Hezzie, to pick them up. They had to drive up clear to the church door to find parking space, the road and field next door were so cluttered up by cars, buggies, farm wagons, and even bicycles. A group of fishermen, awkward in their stiff Sunday collars, the backs of their necks showing a line of white where they'd had a haircut for the occasion, muttered, "Mornin'" to the parsonage family. Riley, very important, handed David his two canes as he slowly disembarked from the Ford; Marcy, tense, walked beside him. So the little procession made its slow way up the church steps, to the entrance hall to where Mr. Epps' stepmother's wheelchair waited. David flushed, but sat down in the chair which Hezzie pushed. Heads turned to smile at them, but others looked carefully away in order not to let on there was anything unusual about David's progress. In their own way, Marcy realized, the congregation was trying to help David.

When they came to the step up to the red-carpeted space behind the communion railing, the huge-shouldered Hezzie lifted David, wheelchair and all, easily. Riley slipped in beside Marcy in the front pew. Her eyes were glued to the pattern of the red carpet, for she couldn't bear to look at the wobbly David who had climbed so surely in his long black robe to the high pulpit at Silverton! If he wasn't able to carry through the service, he'd be too discouraged to try again.

Cap'n Eri read the lesson as usual, rather like a little black crow hopping along in his dark Sunday suit; his head barely topped the lectern. "The little hills rejoice. . . ." Rejoiced over David's being a pastor again? This was a lovely little church Cap'n Eri's great-granddad had built. Marcy's glance slid out the open clear-glass window to the tall pines, quiet as if listening, too. She could even hear the whisper of the rote, down below on the river shore. Suddenly, up in the top of the tallest pine, a thrush began to sing, pouring out its liquid song. It'd be a lot nicer, Marcy thought, glancing up at Millie Epps in the choir, brave in her bird's-nest

Sunday hat, if they skipped the offertory solo, listened to the thrush.

David was getting out of his chair! He stood there clutching the railing for support, announcing the next hymn, "If you can't sing, at least make a joyous noise unto the Lord like the thrush and the river." You and he were thinking together again, the same thoughts, as you used to when you were first married! Marcy's throat was too choked to sing, but she moved her lips so no one would know:

> "There's a wideness in God's mercy,
> Like the wideness of the sea—"

As the organ music died away, David still stood there, steadying himself by the railing, his voice low but clear, carrying to every packed pew: "Friends, my sermon this morning will be very brief. As you know, this is my first time back in the pulpit and I find myself a bit . . . wobbly. But I should like you to think with me for a few moments about the promise, 'Cast thy bread upon the waters; for thou shalt find it after many days.'" David grinned at the front pew. "When I was talking this over with Riley there, he said, 'But, David, the bread'd get soggy!'" There was a ripple of amusement. David now had his audience with him in the old way, Marcy marveled; bread was a simple thing nearly every country housewife here had made herself.

David went on: "I told Rye about the book I'd been reading recently where the author suggested that the Greek word in the New Testament might mean not 'bread' but 'grain.' In Egypt, the farmers literally cast their bread upon the Nile. Without water, the land there would be desert, so when the great river overflows, watering the thirsty land, the farmers broadcast their grain upon the rich damp soil, where it grows tall and green, giving back a rich harvest.

"Every farmer and fisherman here knows that you have to

give to get. The farmer gives seed, fertilizer, back-breaking toil with a hoe; the fisherman fights wind, water, tide, and fog. A man gives of himself to get back a return. Businessmen know this, too. Take a brush salesman. Going into a new territory, he doesn't expect to sell many brushes at first; he rings your doorbell, gives you a sample maybe, makes friends. If his product is a good one, gradually the goodwill he has scattered upon the water comes back to him in sales. You might call this 'a calculated business risk.' Or you might call it casting your bread with faith upon the waters."

David was getting flushed; was he never going to say "Finally"?

"Love is like bread; it must be cast away to be returned," David explained. "Some people may think it sacrilegious to speak of the love of God and that of a man for his wife in the same breath, but to me these are the two legs upon which a man may walk erect." Marcy's hand holding the hymnbook began to tremble, for it was she with whom he was pleading! David was saying to her publically what he could not say when they were alone; he was trying to break through the glass wall between them, to smash it forever. He ended slowly, "That is why two people who have had a child can never be divorced; the judge may say the words, but the bond remains."

David swayed, sat down abruptly in the wheelchair, but his hand was steady as he reached to the white-covered table for the silver plate of broken bread. "Our Father invites you all to come to His table. If you love Him, intend to lead a new life, in love and charity with your neighbor, come, eat of the bread of life, freely."

He was looking directly at Marcy. A new life. He was telling her they could go on together in a new, better way. But she couldn't possibly go up to that table. She couldn't, not with the black guilt of her lie about being with Dare when he died between them. Even now she often woke up nights, sobbing, seeing Dare's lolling head. Perhaps if she told David, the nightmare would go away. But wouldn't she just be transferring her burden to his shoulders when he was still too weak to bear it? She couldn't possibly go up to God's table with a lie in her heart.

As David sat there, holding out the silver plate of bread, Cap'n Eri and his three sons stumped up the aisle, knelt at the railing, took the bread and then the wine which David offered them. Once shown the way, the congregation crowded after them; young and old flocked up toward David. Marcy, her face burning, sat still in her pew and watched them go. One old lady's hand shook so with palsy she dropped the bread, and a little girl in a short pink dress picked it up and handed it back to her; fishermen, their faces burned with wind and sun, tiptoed in their squeaky shoes to kneel at the Lord's family table; since David could not walk with the bread and wine, they came to him, humbly, gratefully. One young housewife, trailing three small children with her up the aisle, seated two down in the front pew, and knelt with the baby between her knees. The wide-eyed baby saw her mother take the bread, held up her own hand, begged, "Me, too!" David, smiling, put a small fragment unto her small waiting palm. And so they knelt together, whole families, young and old, feeble and strong, proud and humble, saint and termagant, side by side at the table of their Father.

All but Marcy. She wanted to go but she could not. Peter Andrew was dead, but she still had David to hold onto; her faith in him was all she had left. It was better to regret faith in a heaven where the three of them would be together again than to pretend it. You had to go honestly to God's table. She saw David's hurt questioning glance as the last communicant left, and felt the curious eyes of the congregation upon her, but her legs refused to carry her. The hurt in David's eyes deepened; his head fell back against the wheelchair.

"Stay here!" Marcy whispered fiercely to Riley beside her. She got to her feet, but before she could reach David, Hezzie Shedd got there, pushed the wheelchair swiftly down the aisle, amid the murmur of the concerned congregation. As Marcy all but ran up the aisle after the little procession, she heard Cap'n Eri call out behind her, "Don't go yit, friends. We ain't took up the collection. Didn't think you'd git outa here without that, did you?" There was a ripple of relieved laughter; the organ began to play, and Marcy hurried out the front door to find that the husky Shedd boys had already lifted David's wheelchair up onto the truck body. "You steady the chair so it won't roll, Timmy. Miz Gallant, climb up here on the front seat with me. Preacher's a mite tired," Hezzie murmured.

As they drove off, the shrill soprano of Millie Epps unfolding the portals everlasting came after them. Hezzie chuckled, "Millie'd be almost as good in a fog as Carrie!" Looking at David, so white and spent, Marcy's heart beat in heavy frightened thuds. How was she going to explain to him why she couldn't possibly come up to the railing? She watched Cap'n Eri's boys carry David into the Gallant kitchen and ease him onto the waiting cot because he was too exhausted to manage by himself. "You feelin' chipper, Preacher? Want we should stay a while?" Hezzie asked, looking down anxiously at David.

"Stay, please, stay," Marcy urged them silently, but David insisted, "Go back to the church so they won't worry. I'll be all right. My good wife's here."

His good wife . . . Marcy saw the boys to the door, lingered there as long as she dared. She turned blindly toward the stove, offering, "I'll make us some coffee."

"No, sit down here by me," David begged. "I want to ask your forgiveness."

"My forgiveness!" she gasped. She sank down on the kitchen floor beside him, the black despair of being alone, cut off from David forever, swept over her in a dark wave, so that she had to speak. "Davey! I lied to you. . . ."

David's lips were warm on hers, stopping her. There was salt from her tears in her mouth, as he rushed on, "I failed you in the hospital. I left you to carry all the burden alone, without even a word from me—"

"Hey, lookit!" Rye's voice cut between them as he stood in the doorway, his arms laden with a huge market basket and a thermos bottle. As David and Marcy drew apart hastily, he stammered, "Ma sent—she said to hot 'em up." He was scarlet with embarrassment for he'd never seen Pa and Ma Snow kiss. Torn between laughter and tears, Marcy knew that it would always be the same; all their married life the parish would burst in on her and David this way.

She invited, "You'll stay, and help us eat up all this lovely chicken Ma sent, Rye?"

"I'd better git along."

"Before you go, Rye, can you help me move this cot into the bedroom?" David got to his shaky feet, reached for his canes.

"Sit down, Davey." Marcy's face flushed, but her eyes met his steadily. Their moment for complete honesty had passed, but perhaps it would come again, bringing that oneness that Ma Snow knew with her Pa, the final, wonderful peace. Meanwhile it was enough that David wanted her. "Take hold of the other end of the mattress," she ordered Riley briskly. "We'll move my cot into David's room."

Chapter Twenty-two

TOMORROW would be the first day of September, and Marcy, getting supper by lamplight, for already the days were closing in and the kitchen was dark because of the pines, was almost certain she was going to have another baby. When she'd confided her thought to David last night, he had been at once delighted and concerned; she was to go tomorrow to the doctor in Bath, and she must stop work instantly.

"But I won't be sure for a couple of more weeks!" she protested. "I never felt better. I promised Etta I'd stay till after Labor Day. Besides, we need the money for the September rent."

They'd have to decide soon what they were going to do. They could hardly chance the rigors of a Maine winter in an unplastered cottage, exposed to every wind. David's blue eyes were guilty. He'd promised Marcy he'd write the bishop, ask to supply a pulpit near Boston, if possible. Since his leg was not yet strong enough to drive Jehu, the Silverton church was out, but, as Marcy had pointed out, they could rent a small apartment; at least the powers that be would know he was alive, not buried in the Maine woods. He promised, "I'll write tonight." Naturally, if they were going to have a baby . . .

"We'll call him John," David twinkled. "John the Beloved."

"Johnny," Marcy amended. "Or Joanna?" After what had happened to Peter Andrew, she was wary of the disciples; or was that just being superstitious? David would hate leaving this little Bellport church which this summer he'd galvanized into unwonted activity. He'd organized Wednesday night "sings" where both village and summer young people bellowed nautical hymns happily together, "Throw out the life line" and "For those in peril on the deep." He'd backed up the

Ladies' Aid in their famous fish chowder Saturday-night suppers which were to help pay for a new organ with all its keys. He'd even started Scout Troops, though the boys had to tie their knots evenings because most of them worked daytimes on the farms or at hauling traps or digging clams, those indigestible lumps New Englanders cherished. Marcy shuddered: she'd as soon gnaw rubber tires.

"You and Rye going fishing again tomorrow?" she asked David.

"Sure. The *Gallant Lady* runs like a bird now I got to know her engine." She was an ancient powerboat so old and balky her former owner had given her to David's Scouts rather than pay for her storage that coming winter.

"*Old Crow*'d fit her better!" Pa Snow had snorted the first time he laid eyes on David whirling and pulling at her cranky wheel, till he was red in the face, to get her started. He and Rye once the *Gallant Lady* was hauled ashore, had calked her worst leaks (though they still had to bail frantically in rough weather), and had tinkered for long, happy, oil-smudged hours with her temperamental engine till she finally sputtered grudgingly into a roar. Pa had grumbled: "Summer folks git 'em a craft, hop in, start her up 'n' think they's sea cap'ns. Mostly they don't know starboard from port—think it's somethin' to drink."

"But I know, Pa," Rye pointed out eagerly. "I ben out with you so often, I know every snag in the river, almost. I kin run her good."

"Walk her right up on the rocks most likely," Pa had snorted, throwing up his hands. He had glared at David and Rye, warning, "Well, don't come howlin' to me when you're drownded."

Actually Riley's boast was not far from the truth. The Scouts had already cruised downriver to the open sea, to Ocean Point, Christmas Cove, Pemaquid. David and Rye went out in the *Gallant Lady* almost every day, but Marcy always heaved a sigh of relief when she heard her engine come chugging safely back around the bend in the river.

Boats had almost as different sounds as voices, Marcy was thinking as she sat there on the cottage front steps the following afternoon; she'd recognized the *Gallant Lady* before the little craft hove in sight. David and Rye left her out at her mooring, rowed up in the dingy with Useless, the yellow pup, standing barking in her bow. He hated water but refused to be separated from Rye. All three of them were singing as they came up the path, Riley lugging the bucket of fish, the yellow pup leaping ahead, happy to be on land. He must be a lot of help in catching fish, yapping that way:

"Mary Ann McCarty went a-diggin after clams—
Bark! Bark!—
But she didn't get a gosh-darn clam!"

David was so relaxed, so brown and carefree. He'd improved so rapidly these past weeks, he walked without a cane, though he still limped badly, but he no longer minded "making a show of himself"; he thumped gaily up the aisle on Sunday mornings to the pulpit, started each day with a zest that welled up into song as he shaved at the small crooked mirror in the kitchen. David exulted in just being alive, in walking, breathing. He didn't seem to worry about anything, least of all money, Marcy thought, wryly. Sometimes he acted as if he weren't much older than Rye. Look at him, throwing a stick for Useless, rough-housing when he knew she was waiting supper!

David yelled something at Useless, but the truck rattling up the road drowned out his words. It was Cap'n Eri's Ford, Marcy saw, watching Useless dart toward the road.

"Hey, Useless, you come back here!" Rye yelled; Hezzie slammed on the brakes, and Rye screamed as the little dog disappeared under the truck. Marcy jumped to her feet, horrified; Hezzie, too paralyzed to move, still sat there on the front seat; but Cap'n Eri, his shawl flapping, scrambled down to investigate. "You've killed him! You've killed my dog!" Rye howled.

"Only his tail's run over," Cap'n Eri announced shrilly. "Pretty tight squeak though, Riley. Quit makin' like Carrie. You'd ought to teach your dog to heel. Useless ain't hurt bad; he jest can't sit down for a spell."

"They often cut off dogs' tails on purpose to make show dogs of them," David limping up, breathless, soothed.

"Ayuh?" Riley rubbed his hand across his wet eyes, leaving a streak of dirt, stared down at the pup's limp tail, hanging by a narrow strip of flesh. He rushed up to the kitchen, and was back in a few seconds with the First Aid kit which David had bought for the Boy Scouts to learn to bandage wounds. Riley began winding sterile gauze round and round what was left of Useless's tail, while the pup whimpered and shook; he didn't seem enthusiastic about First Aid. "There!" Riley said proudly. Useless sniffed suspiciously at the bandage, gave one frantic wag, and off came both bandage and tail, in one piece. "Oh, oh! He's all bluggy!"

Cap'n Eri allowed: "Can't nobody bandage a snake, Rye. There's some ointment under the seat I bought for our Old Baldy. Cure anythin', includin' warts. Hezzie, take both them howlin' banshees out back 'n' put some ointment on that pup's rear end. I want to talk quiet to David 'n' Miz Gallant."

The Bellport people, like Mrs. Minnie, had adopted "David" but not her, Marcy thought ruefully, but, after all, she hadn't grown up here. That old Eri Shedd was up to something. She gazed apprehensively at the old man wrapped in his ridiculous Paisley shawl, though the thermometer had hovered today in the eighties. Cap'n Eri piped: "How'd you two like to stick around Bellport this winter? Church committee had a meetin' yestiday, me 'n' Rile Snow 'n' Pete Epps. Voted unan—unan— Every dang one of us voted to ask ye to be our pastor—permanent."

"That's a great compliment, Cap'n Eri." David's face lighted with pleasure, but Marcy thought, Oh, no!

"Ain't much cash salary," the cap'n admitted. "Only $25 a week. But we got a real snug parsonage. Got plenty furniture 'n' a wood furnace. Hezzie 'n' the boys'd cut what fuel you needed out 'n our woodlot. Wood's money. We ain't had a preacher livin' in, winters, for twelve years."

"It seems a shame to have to shut up so many of our lovely old churches every fall for lack of a preacher," David admitted. "Most theologues'd rather start in the city—like I did." He glanced over at the slender white tower, tall against the sky. "These were the cradles of liberty in New England. We owe them a lot."

The cap'n nodded. "Built the meetin' house fust off, after they cut down the trees here in Bellport Point. Our'n had a dirt floor. Used it for town meetin', too, 'n' the parsonage was the noonin' house where folks ate their lunch before they went back for more jawin'." He glanced out over the river which had sparkled that way in the afternoon sun for his father, his grandfather, his great-grandfather, and before that for the heathen Indians who'd left their clamshells mounded alongshore. "Some says we ought to put all the little churches together or shut 'em up. But I calculate to go on settin' in the pew my Pa did." His old eyes became almost defiant as he muttered, "Seems like Pa's still there, sometimes. I guess I'm gittin' old." He whirled to ask Marcy flatly, "You fancy stayin' on in Bellport?"

"Why . . ." Marcy hesitated. Bellport was a nice little town, friendly, snug, a heavenly place for David to recuperate this summer, but . . . Oh, dear, David was fairly wagging with eagerness like poor Useless. David wanted to stay! Riley res-

cued her by running back with the pup wrapped in a blanket
in his arms, enjoying the fuss made over him, lapping the
little boy's cheek happily.

"Useless 'n' me are some hungry," Riley complained. "Kin
I give him some milk?"

"I suppose so. Put a newspaper under the dish on the
floor," Marcy called as Rye raced away. Cap'n Eri looked after
him shrewdly, told David, "It don't matter so much about
us old-timers; we kin make out. But them young uns need
someone like you to pattern after." He shot David a sharp
glance. "Riley looks enough like you to be your'n."

Why, it was true! Marcy saw, with a sense of shock. With
David's hair bleached that way by being out most of the
day in the sun, and their eyes the same shade of blue, Rye
and David might have indeed been father and son. Being with
David this summer had done a lot for the little boy. Rye
used to hang his head in an agony of shyness, didn't like to
be touched, but nowadays he stood erect, talked back squarely;
when David flung out an arm around his shoulders, rumpled
his towhead, Rye looked up with something like worship in
his eyes.

"My good wife and I will talk this over," David was telling
the cap'n as he and Hezzie climbed back onto the seat of the
truck. "We'll let you know soon, within a week. And thanks."
As the truck rattled away, David told Marcy eagerly, "That
means more than being offered the cathedral in Washington!
Summer folks can come here for years, not be taken in, really
belong. Cap'n Eri's generation is almost the last of the Simon-
pure Yankees, independent as the Fourth of July. But once
they offer you their friendship, you can count on it for the
rest of your days."

"If," Marcy couldn't help murmuring, "you want to be a
Simon-pure Yankee."

He stared at her, and the light died out of his face. She

went on, "We could go back to Fort Worth for the winter."
Sam and Li'l Emily had both written, inviting, "We have
lots of room. Why don't you come, get acquainted with your
new niece?" Marcy pointed out, "You could supply in Fort
Worth as well as Boston. Living wouldn't cost us a cent. Paw
and Momi'd want us to stay, too." And if she didn't feel well,
Aunt Riah'd bring her her breakfast in bed, on a silver tray,
oh, luxury!

Go home as a failure? Marcy'd hate it, too. David worried:
"If I could only find something to do here, to piece out. . . .
Maybe I could teach in the high school!" He waited for Marcy
to urge him to go see the principal, and when she didn't his
face grew even longer and Ma's words echoed uneasily in
Marcy's mind:

"If a man finds a pair of pants that fits him, he's got to
put 'em on, else he might go naked all his life." But surely
David was fitted for bigger things than Bellport! If he stayed
here away from his friends, he'd be as forgotten as last year's
Christmas card. He begged: "Go see the doctor tomorrow?
They have tests. Make sure, Marcy."

The doctor beamed that both Marcy and her baby were
doing fine but that she ought to stay off her feet for a while.
A pretty prescription for a saleslady in a busy shop, with
tourists still thicker than sandfleas! By the end of the day
when she got off the bus at Bellport, and found that David
and Rye were still out in the *Gallant Lady*, Marcy was too
tired to start supper, and sank down instead upon the front
steps to watch for them to come back upriver. Fortunately
she wasn't sick at her stomach, as she'd been with Peter
Andrew. She wished she hadn't given all Peter Andrew's little
clothes away, because now she'd have to start from scratch.
Well, Ma Snow'd taught her to knit. . . . The river really
was gorgeous flashing that way in the sun, a silver ribbon

gift-wrapping the yellow rocks. You'd miss this loveliness if
you went away—

"Hello, Marcy! How are you?"

"Serena!" Marcy had been so wrapped up in her thoughts,
she hadn't heard the other girl's footsteps on the path, but
she jumped up, holding out both hands. "You look wonderful.
How's Granny?"

"Rarin' to go." Serena dropped down upon the lowest step,
careless of her white silk suit, took off her chic white hat,
dropped her gloves and white bag on the grass, and drew a
deep satisfied breath. "It's grand to be home! I drove down
in the Packard; I left it up at Epps' barn. David home? How
is he?"

"Fine. He walks without a cane, but of course his leg's
still stiff. He and Rye went fishing. I suppose Ma wrote you
about the *Gallant Lady?*"

Serena nodded. "Sounds like a terrible old tub." She glanced
at Marcy uneasily and then away. Did she have something
special on her mind to tell her? Marcy asked eagerly, "Did
you get your black ribbon at the hospital?"

"Yes. But I've left the hospital. I've come down to say
good-by to my folks," Serena announced, not looking at
Marcy, but out across the river to where the windows of the
keeper's house were blazing in the setting sun. There was
something worrying her. "Granny's decided she wants to
join Dandy. In Hong Kong. She can't go alone, so I'm
elected." But it didn't seem like Serena to go off and leave
Rye so long. Her eyes came back to Marcy's face. "I've come
to ask a favor. Will you and David keep Rye this winter?"

Marcy gasped, "But Ma—"

"It'd help Pa," Serena told her. "He wouldn't have to come
ashore only once every day unless he had to meet the school
bus, morning and night. But Rye would be near, if you and
David lived in the Bellport parsonage."

"But we may not be in the Bellport church!" Marcy told her. For this birth, Marcy wanted a city doctor and a private nurse. If Peter Andrew had been more closely watched, he might be here today. A country doctor might not know the newest in medicine, but a Boston hospital would. Suddenly Marcy's face grew hot, her hands clenched, for perhaps the reason Serena was going so far away was easy to guess, after all. It was a terrible thing to ask, yet harder not to. She gasped: "You've found out what I said was true! You were the reason David didn't write to me from the hospital?"

"No! I was just another pair of hands to him, someone to talk to about Maine where you were. Hospitals are a different world; what happens there doesn't seem real, outside." It was Serena's turn to try to explain to Marcy as she had about Dare. Serena lifted her lovely chin. "All right, I was in love with him! But I give you my word I didn't know it until I took care of him. What more can I do but go as far away as I can?" Her lips trembled. "But it'd ease my mind if you took Rye. Ma's wonderful with him, but with Pa sick . . ."

"The chances are, we'll be in Boston. Davey's already written the bishop about supplying there."

"But you can't take him away from Bellport! He isn't well enough to adjust to a lot of new people. He needs peace yet, healing. His roots are here." Serena rushed on desperately, "Why, mornings when I poked my head in the ward door, David would call, 'Hi, Mainiac! Boy, what I'd give for a sniff of good Bellport air, even of Timmy's bait barrel!'"

Marcy held onto herself tightly. Naturally, she wanted what was best for David and for Rye, too, but— Marcy stared down, startled, at the slip of blue paper the other girl had thrust into her hand. It was a check for a thousand dollars!

Serena apologized, "Granny insisted upon my giving you this. She said: 'I guess I can pay for my own great-grandson's

keep. Don't take any nonsense from Marcy or David either.'
You know how Granny is."

The hot red ran up Marcy's cheeks as she tore the paper
to bits which fluttered down onto the grass. There were some
things money couldn't buy, but at least you would pay your
debts. She said slowly: "I reckon I owe Rye a father. We'll
take him wherever we are."

"Forget it! You don't owe him anything!"

The blowing of the silly squealing horn of the *Gallant Lady*
rounding the bend in the river made them both turn to watch.
Marcy promised, ignoring Serena's outburst, "I'll talk to
David tonight." She knew perfectly well what he would say:
"What's home without a boy and his dog?" Being with David
this summer had made a new boy of Rye, given him confidence. He was the son of David's spirit. Serena got to her
feet, reached for her bag, and drew out a strip of linen and
lace. Not every woman could look beautiful blowing her nose,
but Serena managed it.

"I'm driving back tomorrow morning," she promised.
"We're sailing from New York Monday. I probably won't
see you again. Good-by—and thanks."

She began to run down toward the pier, waving and calling.
Marcy watched the *Gallant Lady* chug up to the ladder, saw
Serena climb lightly down the ladder, leap aboard. They were
ferrying her over to the Light. Even five minutes of being with
David were precious to her. Surely you didn't begrudge her so
small a thing? But if you kept Rye with you and David this
winter, Serena would always be there too, watching you out
of Rye's eyes.

As Marcy turned slowly, went back up the path to get
supper, the late afternoon sun reflected from the slender
white church tower reminded her suddenly of David's panic
before his first communion there and of her own terrified re-
fusal to kneel at the altar. Was it possible one had to be

broken like the Bread to achieve peace? The words of the old hymn the river people had sung together echoed again in her taut, puzzled mind:

"There's a wideness in God's mercy,
Like the wideness of the sea...."

Chapter Twenty-three

THAT evening David sat in the big armchair in the kitchen, relaxed, content not to talk, waiting for Marcy to finish getting the stew ready for him to warm up tomorrow just before her bus got in from Bath. The lamplight glinted on the little curls at the nape of her neck; it would be pleasant to touch their softness but he was too lazy to move. Living in Bellport was like taking off too tight shoes, putting on carpet slippers, finding out how satisfying were small daily blessings of quietness.

David murmured, "Poor Rye, with all that cash! It's hard enough to live through adolescence without being able to do every single thing you want—when you don't know exactly what you do want."

Marcy burst into such hysterical laughter that she almost cut her finger on the knife with which she was peeling a potato. It was so like David to pity a boy because he'd inherited half a million dollars! Your new son, Johnny, didn't even have a diaper to his name as yet. Had Serena told David that Marcy'd torn up a thousand dollars?

"You know why I think most people get married?" David mused aloud. "Because they're lonesome." His eyes slid dreamily over the lovely curve of her cheek, down her slenderness. A man met a girl whose glance set him on fire with desire and married her—and found he was lonesome still. Until he realized that his wife was lonely too; no matter how hard they tried to reach each other, they could only call encouragingly across the sea of their loneliness. Maybe he had learned a little these past months; nothing was lost: sorrow, pain, joy, terror. Small everyday things like watching Marcy dip her knife to clean it into the dishpan of bright suds ("poor man's diamonds," Ma Snow called them) wove a strand of affection stronger, more durable than passion. No wonder there was no marriage in heaven. If two people had what he and Marcy had, they didn't need marriage, and if they hadn't achieved a oneness that was more than body, that was of the soul, they were better apart for all eternity.

"If anyone had told me two years ago that I'd get a kick out of watching you peel an onion, I'd have laughed my head off," David murmured contentedly to Marcy. "I'm kind of jealous, even of John the Beloved. Now that we're about to lose it, I discover how nice it is, our being alone."

Happiness rose in her so poignantly she was frightened, afraid it would be snatched from her, as Peter Andrew had been. She didn't want to talk about anything or anyone; she wanted this lovely moment to go on and on.

"You're crying, sweet!" David came to her in one great awkward leap, and she leaned her head for an instant back against his big shoulder.

"It's only this onion I'm peeling."

What more did she want for their new son than David's arms around him? Yet as she gently freed herself to go on making her stew, she knew that she did want more for Johnny than a continual pinching of pennies; she passionately wanted security. Someone in this family had to be practical about money.

David told her hopefully, "When Pa gets him his deer this fall, Ma'll can us some; she'll send over butter, this winter, when she churns. She says it's her tithe for the church."

Ma, Rye, Cap'n Eri and his ridiculous shawl. Just for one night, couldn't they stop talking about them? They might just as well have been right here in the room. Marcy snapped, "We've still got five days to decide, haven't we? I'm tired. Let's go to bed."

"The ladies are having their last supper Saturday night before the holiday," David reminded her, limping behind her into their bedroom. "Rye and I are going out early tomorrow to get cod for the chowder, but you're not to get up, hear?

Hezzie says, if this hot spell of weather holds, the only place we can get good-sized fellers is off Outer Ledge."

Marcy worried, "You sure you ought to go out that far? What if the engine conks out again? The sea's so darn big, it frightens me."

"Don't fret. Popham Coast Guard Station keeps a glass on all that area." He grinned at her. "Remember, she's a *Gallant Lady*, too."

She didn't deceive David, Marcy realized; he knew how upset she was. But the more she thought about it, the more she knew that David would have to make his own decision about staying here or not. Otherwise Bellport might stand, a ghost church, forever between them.

The next morning she overslept: it was almost eight when she woke up with a start, glanced at David's empty bed, jumped up. Could she make the eight-thirty bus? David's breakfast dishes were piled in the sink with a sign DO NOT WASH WILL DO LATER and there was a frantic scrabbling behind the stove as Useless appeared, stretched, came to put his mournful muzzle in her hand.

"Did they leave you behind today, Useless, too?" Marcy soothed. "How about some milk?"

As he lapped noisily she made herself some toast, and went, munching, to the window to look out. The sky was a cloudless hot blue, and a queer breathlessness hung over the too smooth river; there was no wind at all; the leaves on the maple sapling hung limp. It reminded her of that awful night when Pa almost didn't make it home from Bath! She wished David and Rye hadn't gone to Outer Ledge, but surely if it began to blow David would have sense enough to make for home. Pa Snow said the Popham Station knew most of the local powerboats and sailboats by sight, to whom they belonged, and even their mechanical idiosyncrasies. David and Rye would be safe enough; she'd better hurry or she'd miss her bus. Useless followed her to the bus, wagged where his tail should have been, and took off down to the pier to wait for Rye.

The day in the shop was hot, endless; the thermometer hovered around ninety; by the time Marcy started for home the sky had clabbered over and her back stuck to the bus seat with perspiration. Whatever parsonage they moved into would have a bathtub, she promised herself; to get really clean you needed clear oceans of hot water, with a handful of lavender bath salts, not a sponge bath at an iron sink. As Marcy got off the bus, she took a deep breath of the heavy air, glanced over at the lighthouse . . . and her heart stopped beating, then raced. A white towel was hanging out Ma's kitchen window! As Marcy watched, Carrie began to toll mournfully. The sound released her paralysis of apprehension so that she ran into the store.

"Pete!" she gasped. "Ma needs help over at the Light!"

Pete never got excited. He was weighing out sugar for a customer, seemingly balancing the weight with his tongue caught between his teeth; he didn't even look up. "Half a pound on the button. Jest some visitors, likely, tryin' out Carrie."

Marcy could have shaken him. "Ma told me that Pa's had a slight shock. She said if he had another, she'd hang out a towel, and to come over, quick!"

"Rene's over there. She's a nurse." But Pete was already taking off his apron with economical motions which looked maddeningly slow but were actually efficient. He said, "Timmy's just got in from hauling his traps. He can run us over."

"You and Timmy go!" Marcy gasped. "Ma said to call Popham Station, the very first thing." As Pete took off for the river, Marcy ran to the wall telephone, cranked madly.

"Gertie? Get me the Station at Popham, will you? It's an emergency. Pa Snow's awful sick!"

The slow Maine drawl that answered her, quickened at

once as Marcy poured out her news. The officer of the day promised, "I'll send a relief keeper downriver on the picket boat at once. It'd save time, Miz Gallant, if Rile Snow was brought ashore now, so the ambulance can pick him up, soon as it gets there."

"Pete Epps and Timmy Shedd have already gone across for him." The Coast Guard were wonderful; they took care of their own. And those they didn't alert, Gertie would; by now every one of the eight subscribers on the store phone knew there was trouble at the Light. Marcy was about to hang up when the officer spoke again. "Just a minute, Miz Gallant. Have the Reverend and Rye made port yet?"

"Why, no." A cold finger of alarm ran down Marcy's spine. "They went out early this morning to Outer Ledge. Is anything wrong?"

"We ben watching them," the voice reassured her. "But it's breezin' up some out there. Figured it was the *Gallant Lady* but we kinda lost track of her, this last hour. Likely they're makin' for home. Good-by."

Marcy's fingers fumbled as she hung up the receiver. What Maine people called "breezin' up" might mean anything from a few whitecaps to a hurricane. A cool east wind had come up in just the few moments she'd been inside; as she went out the store door it caught at her blue linen skirts. Her eyes sought the river anxiously; it had turned a dirty gray like the sky; was it only her imagination that the dark current was running faster? The *Gallant Lady* was a small, leaky power-boat with a cranky engine. . . . The roar of Timmy's motor coming ashore from the Light brought her back to the present emergency, and she hurried down toward the pier.

Gertie had done her job well, for already Hezzie and a group of fishermen were gathered there, waiting to help lift Pa from the dory, up the ladder onto the pier. He was wrapped in a red blanket, and he looked terrible with his face so white and empty. One corner of his mouth had sagged, and Serena, efficient in a dark-blue dress that might have been a uniform, leaned over to wipe where he'd drooled. Ma stared at Pa, her eyes helpless, agonized, as Serena asked sharply, "Has anyone phoned for the ambulance?"

"Yes." Marcy said, "I did."

At the sound of her voice, Pa's heavy lids lifted. His eyes were empty, and he mumbled so thickly she could hardly make out his meaning. "Them idjits—made port yit?"

She mustn't upset Pa when he was so sick. Marcy soothed: "No, but Popham's got a glass on them. They'll be home any minute now."

"Ebb tide. Whirlpools. Rye'd ought—to know better."

"Don't try to talk, Pa," Serena ordered. Marcy flushed, moved away from Pa.

"The ambulance is here!" a small boy in patched overalls rushed up to announce importantly. "They're gonna back down so's they kin shove him right in. Is he dead yit?"

"Stow it, you!" Hezzie's big hand yanked the boy away, but Ma said gratefully, "They musta tore up the road some, gittin' here."

It was all over in a moment, strong hands lifting Pa onto the stretcher where he lay with closed eyes, his breathing stertorous, frightening to listen to. There wasn't any doctor in a country ambulance, so Serena announced: "I'm going with him. You want to come, too, Ma?"

Ma looked at Pa through the ambulance window, lying there with his eyes closed, and then out toward the gray, restless river. "No," she decided. "Nothing I can do." The ambulance door slammed, and Hezzie offered: "I'll follow them over in the truck. I can bring Rene back when she wants to come."

You'd have thought Ma couldn't be pried loose from Pa! She looked forlorn standing there staring after the ambulance.

Marcy offered, "Let's go up to the house, Ma, have a cup of coffee."

"Ayuh." Ma walked slowly, let herself down carefully, an old woman, into the big armchair, while Marcy lighted the oil stove which heated water quickly. Had Ma waited to be sure the relief keeper came for the Light, as Pa would want her to? Ma drank the hot black coffee, but she couldn't eat any of Marcy's sugar cookies. Her hand trembled as she put down her mug on the kitchen table, worrying, "On an ebb tide like this, with the wind 'n' water fightin' each other, river's apt to give a little powerboat rough passage."

Marcy's mouth had the sudden copper taste of fear. So that was the reason Ma hadn't gone with Pa! If both he and she were worried about the *Gallant Lady* . . . Rye was their only grandson, born at the Light, and had lived there with them seven years now; he was almost more theirs than Serena's. . . . Without a word, Marcy jumped up, started back down toward the pier with Ma close at her heels where they could watch, see the *Gallant Lady* as soon as she rounded the bend in the river. In her haste, Marcy all but ran down Cap'n Eri, his shawl floating out behind him in the wind. "Breezin' up," he admitted.

"Ayuh," Ma agreed.

Both wind and waves had risen, unbelievably: there were whitecaps already out in the river, and those dark holes must be the whirlpools made by tide and wind fighting each other, as Ma had warned. Marcy ran her tongue over her dry lips as Useless rushed up to her, and whined; she patted his rough, yellow head; he was waiting for his master to come home, too.

Quite a few people had collected on the pier, Marcy saw: Hezzie, Timmy, Dammy, and several other fishermen. But this was their suppertime; usually Bellport ate about five. When the men saw Ma and Marcy, they pretended to have something urgent to do, heading up a bait barrel, coiling a rope, peering wisely out over the white-capped river. Were they thinking David was one of them crazy summer people, like Pa'd said, who hopped into boats and thought they were sea captains? What did she care what they thought? All she wanted was to hear the *Gallant Lady's* cranky engine come chugging up the angry river, safe from the sea. . . .

"The Reverend's likely tied her up to someone's wharf, downstream," Pete Epps' voice reassured behind Marcy. "Wait till the tide slacks off."

But David would have phoned her, Marcy knew; he'd never have let her worry unnecessarily. If there wasn't any danger, why had Pete Epps left his store untended? As the Light suddenly flashed on across the dark river, she realized how late it was; sunset. One yellow beam, one red, another yellow, shouting silently, *Danger! Look out!*

"Relief keeper must've come upriver on the picket boat while we was in the kitchen," Ma said, relieved. "I was just figurin', had I ought to take a run over?"

The rattle of a truck coming precariously down the rickety pier behind them and the scream of hard-hit brakes made all heads turn to where Serena sat on the front seat beside Hezzie. Why was she back so soon? Pa couldn't possibly be—gone? "Pa's asleep. They gave him a sedative." Serena jumped down, demanding anxiously, "No signs of Rye and Davo?" As Ma shook her head there was one of those sudden inexplicable lulls in the wind so that Hezzie's voice came to them clearly, excitedly.

"I phoned Popham like you said, Pa, but they can't locate her with the glasses. The picket boat didn't pass her goin' back downriver, neither. They're cruisin' out to the Ledge. She musta capsized before she made the river mouth. . . ."

"Hush up, you idgit!" But it was already too late. Serena's hand had frozen, halfway to her throat, and Marcy stared, horrified, at the old cap'n who'd sailed up and down this coast for nearly a century; if he'd called out the Coast Guard . . .

Ma's face lost every vestige of color as she demanded of Hezzie, who could be depended upon to blurt out the truth, "You think they're overboard?"

Cap'n Eri scowled blackly at his hapless son. "Most likely that rackety engine conked out on them. Breezin' up this way, the craft'd fill faster'n they could bail. But they got lifebelts. They'd keep afloat all right till the picket boat picked 'em up."

"But how could they find them? It's getting dark!" Marcy's voice was shrill with fear. The sea that went on and on, gray till the night swallowed it in blackness. How long could they stand it, overboard in this icy Maine water? She could feel the terrible cold in her own body as she cried, "Rye's only a little boy, and Davey isn't strong yet. If he gets pneumonia . . ."

"Get hold of yourself, Marcy," Serena murmured in her ear. "Ma's had about all she can stand."

Maybe Serena was satisfied to stand there like a rock, to do nothing, but she wasn't! Marcy grabbed desperately at Hezzie's arm, begged: "Couldn't we take your powerboat? Go look for them, too?"

Hezzie shook his big head dumbly. Cap'n Eri explained, "'Twouldn't be no use. Rollers is too high out there. Couldn't spot 'em from a powerboat with the light grayin' out this way. The picket boat's got a searchlight on her mast."

What good was that? Two tiny black specks in the endless waste of the sea, tossing helplessly in the icy trough of the great waves, with night coming on . . . As Marcy shivered convulsively, something soft and warm fell over her shoulders. "Here, Marcy. You frizzled?" Cap'n Eri had called her "Marcy"; he'd given her his shawl and Hezzie'd let him. She tried to smile her thanks but achieved only a grimace, her lips, her whole body stiff with terror. When Useless put back his head and howled, the wharf went round and round Marcy's head in dizzy pinwheels of disaster. Was it true a dog scented death sooner than human beings? They hadn't even found David's folks' bodies.

"Folks is standin' by," Ma murmured. Marcy realized, numbly, that the pier had almost filled with people. They'd come silently, slowly, almost like a funeral procession. She wanted to scream at them, "Go home. There's nothing to see yet!" People were ghouls.

"Miz Gallant? I jest dodged up with some hot gingerbread. . . ."

Marcy stared at the thin stranger in a shapeless dark sweater, the wind blowing wisps of her tan-colored hair about her plain, pleasant face as she stood there, holding out a flat tin pan covered with a red-and-white checked napkin.

"Make you acquainted with Addie Cottle," Ma introduced.

Was Ma mad? This was no time to chatter with perfect strangers.

"The preacher ate two pieces of my gingerbread at the last church supper," Addie Cottle beamed to Marcy. "I thought he might relish some for supper tonight. I'll slide it into your oven to keep warm."

She was trying to tell you that David would surely be home for supper. It was as if a warm hand had grasped Marcy's icy one, rubbing it back to life. *Bless her, oh, bless her. . . .* Marcy gasped, "Thank you! He loves—" She couldn't finish, but as she watched Addie Cottle push her way back through the crowd with her brave pan of gingerbread Marcy realized that she'd been wrong about these Bellport people. *These were David's people come to see him and Rye safely home.* They couldn't swallow their own suppers until their preacher had his. She stared at the farmers with muddy-kneed overalls who'd dropped their hoes to come; several of David's Scouts were here, kicking a piece of wood across the pier as kids do; Pete Epps had left his store untended; Cap'n Eri and his sons, all these lean, close-mouthed fishermen who knew and respected the terrible power of wind and of the river were standing by. They smelled of fish, of manure, of the good earth, and of loyalty. . . .

Impulsively Marcy moved toward Serena standing there staring upriver as if her very longing would bring back Rye and David. Marcy laid her hand almost timidly on Serena's arm, which was stiff with tension; the two of them could wait together.

Serena's face was white in the dusk as she gasped, "If Rye doesn't come back, it's God's punishment to me!"

"No, oh, no!" Marcy protested, shocked. "He isn't like that—"

"*He took Peter Andrew!*"

Marcy drew back as if Serena had slapped her across the face, for it was true. You'd rebelled against this very injustice, the blind cruelty that had snatched Peter Andrew into the nothingness called death. Serena's hands were clenching and unclenching as she cried hysterically: "If Rye comes back to me, I'll never let him go again. He's all I got!"

And David was all you had. All you wanted. If only you hadn't found out too late . . .

"O God, give me another chance!" Tears slid down Marcy's cheeks, and she didn't care who saw them as she prayed silently, desperately. "Send David back, and John the Beloved'll be born right here in Bellport where he belongs. I promise!"

But you didn't bargain with Almighty God. Was it wicked of her to try? Nothing else mattered if only David came back to her; money didn't matter, not even his being bishop. The lost moonlight magic of Texas seemed long ago and far away, unimportant. Being married to David had been so much more than remembered rapture! It had been laughing together over

Useless's sore tail; suffering with Tommy Gandy's and Winnie Mae's folks till you found compassion for all who bore their hurt bravely; it had been dying a little with old Aunt Lottie who'd thought David her long-ago lover. Yes, even losing Peter Andrew had been a part of their great love, had drawn them closer. But now if she lost David too—She begged blindly: *I've got nothing to give! Just give me another chance.* . . .

The Light flashed over her drawn, yearning face like a benediction. Even behind her closed lids she could see the glow, almost as if the Light were trying to tell her something, something bright and wonderful, if only she could understand.

"I hear her! The picket boat's a-comin'!" Cap'n Eri's shrill pipe ringing out made Marcy's eyes flash open, see the blurred white faces of David's people, straining to see the invisible. The old man insisted, "I guess I know her engines!"

Then Marcy heard it too, the rhythmic murmur of powerful engines driving a hull knifing through the turbulent dark river where a smaller boat might have floundered, coming surely home. Were they bringing back David and Rye or—or their bodies? Or had they abandoned the search till daylight? She began to tremble, to shake all over, her heart beating so loudly she could no longer hear anything else, but as the picket boat rounded the bend in the river, her searchlight swept ahead of her, blazed blindingly white on the crowded pier. Then it switched off, and from the dark deck a small bright light began to blink. ". . . After the fire, a still small voice . . ."

"She's signalin'!" Marcy, unable to read code like the fishermen, could only wait, agonized, for Hezzie's delighted roar. "Great jumpin' Jehoshaphat, she's got 'em both, drydocked on deck!"

David was safe; he was home; she had another chance! A great triumphant shout of thankfulness filled Marcy's whole shaken body. "There's a wideness in His mercy . . ." Wide enough for everyone, for saints and for sinners such as she, wide enough to hold in its greatness all hurt, lost people. Even the quick and the dead? And why not? Though she couldn't see unborn little Johnny either, he was none the less real, none the less hers. *This was the miracle of His mercy that Peter Andrew was alive!*

"Oh, Davey, Davey, I didn't understand!"

She began to run toward the top of the ladder where he would climb to her, as the Light clashed shining cymbals over her head, for she knew at last what it meant: "Underneath are the everlasting arms. . . ."